Chronicles of Heroes: Untamed Nature

Copyright © 2021 Poncho Bosque

All rights reserved.

ISBN-13: 979-8-9899034-1-2

Dedication

This is dedicated to everyone who supported me through the years, especially when I started writing. To my family, if not for their insistence in following my dreams I wouldn't be writing and creating stories. To my brothers, Adrian and Andrés, who not only helped me when I needed to brainstorm but had a hand in helping me choose the cover art and design for the book. To my friend, Hazi, who has been there all the time cheering me on and believing in me. And to all of my friends who have endured my insane creative thoughts and ideas over the years as I rambled on and on about my characters, their abilities, and the world they live in. This also goes to everyone in need of a reminder that we might stumble, suffer, and struggle along the way, but that there is hope. That there will be people out there who might get us or even help us. That even if everything seems dark and hopeless, there is light, compassion, kindness, and love for each and every one of us.

A Note to the Reader's

First of all, thank you for believing in this story, I appreciate the support. You don't know how much it means to me for you to read Chronicles of Heroes and be part of Theon's journey.

With that out of the way. This book contains themes and content that might upset some readers. If you aren't concerned about this skip the next paragraph as it will contain spoilers.

This book deals with themes of Depression, Self-Harm, and Suicide that will be part of the narrative. It also contains Violence Toward Animals, and Harm to Teens and Children.

CHAPTER ONE: TRASH PANDA

November 09, 2012

"The topic of today is forgiveness," my teacher says in a deceptively sweet voice. Her cold stare reminds me not to move a muscle.

A shadow grows under me. The ruthless predator has finally caught up. A shiver crawls up my spine in tune with that inescapable stalker. My stomach turns and twists to the imaginary smell of blood. I pull out a notebook filled with unreal events, ways to escape into the wilderness. Ways prey like me could never get caught. My notebook's open and my pencil flows, in a rhythm that could never compete with a beluga's sonata. **Please don't let me go back to that, not to that.**

A paper lands on my desk. The instructions spell my demise: *Write a forgiveness letter to someone who wronged you.* I'm ready to lie. I have to do what other people do, and just roll with it. Pretend I'm fine. As I'm about to place my pen on the page, it trembles. The pen flounders, colliding with the marble floors. I rub my eyes, tempering the tears from falling. My other hand searches in my backpack for anything to hide me from the judgmental eyes of my classmates. **They won't see me like this; it won't be a repeat of my last high school.**

I grab my bag and leave, hoping no one notices. The door betrays me with a creak. It stays open as I flee, and my classmates' voices chase me until I'm finally out of the hallway.

Their laughter and gossip, nothing more than fluttering feathers in the wind. I wish...

My feet move on their own through the school grounds, leaving the artificial walkways, in favor of the natural greenery at the school margins.

The untamed creek and its inhabitants keep me company in my loneliness. It's been almost three years, and I still haven't been able get over what happened to me. No one cares; no one can help me. Everyone pretends like nothing happened. Like it doesn't matter, like I don't matter. They see the scar on my eyebrow and pretend it was there all along. Like I was born with it.

I endure this solitary hibernation. Animals are the only ones who get me. Nightingales land on my shoulders and sing their cheerful songs. Stray dogs sit by my sides, kissing me until my tears die down. Even the frogs and lizards join us, resting on my arms and chest, showing their unconditional support.

It's not until Mom comes to pick me up that I force myself to return to the school grounds and pretend seriousness. Nobody wants the sad me. No one likes to see the part of me that constantly struggles to keep going. Somehow the herd of students I navigate through pick me out from the rest. Creating space around me and filling it with their pity.

I step into the car. My mom, more oblivious than any parent should be, says, "Theon, your past high school classmates are having a Posada tonight. Are you going?"

I press my fists against my jeans. "Why would I want to celebrate the upcoming Christmas and New Year's with the people who almost made me not have another one?" Heat builds inside as my voice takes a militant stand with each word. I look outside, only to notice my reflection, and then avoid it. ***Where do you run when there's nowhere to?***

The car slows. I smile automatically. More lies. More of the same, since my parents are incapable of human decency. Although human decency is an illusion. One invented to make humans look good. Superior. But pretending to be something doesn't make it true. My mom has gotten that attitude to perfection. "Think about how your friends will look at our family name."

"I don't have friends!" I interrupt her. I'm not going back there. To return home like a raccoon that was caught in the trash. With black eyes and blood dripping. Anything but that.

She twists her head. "Should I take that as a yes or a no?" The void-black of her hair—a trait that I unfortunately inherited—matches the obliviousness of her question. An identifiable characteristic that tracks me to her bloodline.

Nails sink in the palm of my hands. "No!"

"If you change your mind, tell us." She doesn't want to get it.

The car stops under the shelter of the garage and before she can add anything, I'm out. I storm into my room and open the windows. Thoughts of the past flood my mind. Bloodied me coming back from school. Names and tags marked for me and me alone. People on the street, at school, and at home looking away. I wanted to escape. Every day a new bruise, a new cut or scar. Some new insult, a name that was meant take me down. There were days when I thought of ending my misery. I'd rather not think about it, not now, not ever.

Back then, my only respite was the garden. Animals never criticized or hurt me. The peace they gave me was more than enough to keep going. Especially that one day. The day they saved me. I swear they spoke, but that was my mind playing tricks on me. Animals can't speak Spanish or English. I wish they could. Things would have never gone so far if they did. If only they did…

CHAPTER TWO: SHARK WOMB

I don't even have time to settle into my bed, before my dad stomps his way in. I knew I forgot something. I glance at the open door. Tranquility would still be a foreign word, but keeping a barrier between them would have made a difference. I share none of his beliefs, a stroke of good luck or bad. "You're going to the party." His voice travels. Multiple species spectate from the bamboos swaying beside my window.

I sigh. I have no moves to survive. "Why?" My voice is dulled by experience, barely giving them the emotions, they desperately want from me. I roll out of bed, keeping it between us.

He moves around the bed until he's right in front of me. "'Cause I said so!" He raises his voice. The alternative is way less pleasurable.

I hold my arms close to me. **Why do they insist on making me suffer?** They saw the blood. The hospital bills. "I'm not going. I don't have to." This will go as expected. Bird species throw their children from the nest if they are too weak, but that's a mercy my parents can't afford.

"It's final." His fists and jaw clench. Sooner than expected.

I brace myself for the impact. I knew it was coming. Nothing new. Claws scurry up and down rocky surfaces. Feathers rustle as winds and branches bounce against my window. A mass of cream—colored fur runs past my father. Thor faces my father. He stands poorly as a guard dog, but I love him all the same. "I won't go to be hurt again." Thor barks alongside me, though his bark sounds friendly.

"Then man up."

What's that supposed to mean? I don't move, "You want me to fight against ninety people?" I swallow the almost solid saliva. "They will kill me." I shake. Only my mind stops itself from feeling everything I've been through. My ankle feels heavier, stiffer. Each breath hurts. I stumble, dizzy with the nauseous smell of blood.

"Deal with it." He crosses his arms. "No son of mine will be a bitch." He gets closer to me.

I stumble back against the window. Nowhere left to hide or run. **Why can't he leave me alone? Just let me forget and get over it!** Keep them away. I jolt as if an electric eel discharged on me. My eyes mountain springs.

"What have I said about crying?" He approaches. I know what's next. I can feel it. Leather or steel.

The pug snarls, an expression I've never seen on him before. He bears his fangs against the massive human. Squawks, squeaks, milliards of hisses concert around me. That's when I notice every single animal on the block has made it into my room. From rats to cats, to owls and ravens. Animals that would usually attack each other glaring at one person. My father. Feathers flurry in the winds. Fur rises as a warning. My father takes a step back. The animals keep alert, warning him of what will happen if he doesn't listen.

He takes a step back "Get ready. We're leaving at six." That creates a ripple of bestial reverberations. All beginning with Thor's snarls. Father's face turns red. "Shut up." He readies his leg.

I untangle from the matted memories of my past. I'm not sure how I end up imitating a tortoise's shell over Thor. A gust of air flushes out of my system.

"Finally did something brave" He walks away.

The animals keep the racket up. Others from afar join them. Wild howling. Snorts and hoots. A message they seem to spread through the neighborhood.

My side throbs with the impact. Air in and out. Nothing feels broken. The city creatures wait a minute until I sit up, before scuttling back outside, leaving me with my little puppy. I glance up. My younger brother, Roy, barely acknowledges my existence.

Roy stands at the room's edge. His long, mangled hair reaches his shoulders. "Stop being a pussy and go. Fucking show them who's boss." He immediately turns his back. His strides are shorter than mine, which makes all the difference in how he reaches his domain: the living room sofa.

Roy walks into a room and everyone accepts him for the lion prince he is. When I walk into a room, the guns are ready for the hunt. His gaze, which only ever holds contempt for me, issues a dare. I'm better than that. I can't fall for something so blatantly provoking. A clear trap to see me fail. Once it was a surprise, now it's just a habit. He doesn't pick up his controller, nor his headphones. He stares and arcs one eyebrow.

I release Thor, who immediately starts licking my face.

I must reply to Roy with something that makes me seem as strong as the saltwater crocodile's bones.

Lucas peeks from his own room. "Go! Maybe things will change." With each syllable, he taps the door's wooden frame. Lucas's voice wears the colorful plumage of the hoatzin and shares the smell of it too. If he wanted, his voice would be as crystalline as the nightingales. It would match his beluga-like skin. His eyes shimmer as in a plead, that I must ignore. His words sing a funerary ballad dedicated to me, his sixteen-year-old brother.

"People don't change." I glance at Thor. "Animals do."

Thor wiggles his tail, by which I mean he wiggles his hips. Thor playfully snorts and runs at Lucas. Both kids run around the house, playing chase for one minute since Thor can only last that long.

This leaves me alone in my room. The animals back outside. They watch with expectation.

I'm not going to that party.

Not going is a statement of survival. And yet, not going is also admitting defeat. An admission of their control over me, and lack of evolution on my behalf. It would mean I'm human.

Anything but that. I'm an animal, I can change. I can break the exhibit they contained me in. Maybe Roy is right; I should show them. They won't break me. I am Theon Untamed; I won't be controlled by anyone. I can't let them win, not after everything they did to me. Not after endless nightmares and countless injuries. I touch the hairless space on my brow.

I'm not a circus elephant. I'm not their class pet waiting for attention. My brain spins out of control, reliving every instance of pain and suffering. In this game of survival, I will triumph. They will see a cornered viper always strikes back. The sinking feeling has turned into a wildfire. Lucas may be wrong about people changing, but I'm an animal. I will adapt and evolve. Roy is right about one thing, and one thing only. I can take a stand. No one else cares enough, so I might as well do it. I won't tell him he's right; I don't need his crown to get bigger. "Fine. I'll go."

Roy glances at me. His smile uneven, one side higher than the other. His eyes, like mine, darker than grizzly brown. Soon after they abandon me. Headphones on and controller in hand. He goes back to his friends, to his pride. I cross Roy's domain and head to my parents' room. Lucas waves at me with Thor in his arms. He giggles as I travel to the other end of the house.

My mom speaks up as I open the door to my parents' room. "It's so lovely you'll go to see your friends."

"Friends?" I pause. I'm done being their toy. My better judgment tells me to stop, but they don't deserve any kindness.

"I've met blind spiders that are more aware of the world. If you want to ignore reality, fine by me, just keep it to yourself." I look her dead in the eyes. Callous as the diamond back rattlesnake looking at a mouse. "I'm going there to take my life back, because I'm better than that."

My dad's disregard is usual, not that I care anymore. "Good. You didn't have a choice. You were going." He sits beside his desk.

"I had one. If you disagreed, what would have happened outside?" I glance at the edge of the city just a couple of blocks away from us. I doubt the bears, deer and jaguars didn't listen to the ruckus created by the more domesticated creatures. Then I look back at him. "I'm not your property and you won't control me either. Your commands are noted, but otherwise disregarded."

Silence overcomes the house as my dad turns visibly red. I return to my room and get ready to go out.

CHAPTER THREE: THE VERGE OF EVOLUTION

I step out of the car and stare at the large two-story house. Music blaring through the windows, and bonfire smoke billowing from behind it. With every step I take, my body wavers. The small voice in the back of my mind gets louder. ***It's a mistake.*** I turn around, and the car is gone.

I master my dread of being here and plaster a sheepish smile on my face. Four girls, including Maria, open the door and greet me like it's been years since we last saw. I reciprocate in this social dance of fakeness and lies. This pretend appreciation. ***I'm here for one thing and one thing only. To get over it, and to prove them all wrong. They won't win. I'm taking control of my life.***

"How's life Theon? We haven't seen you since ninth grade graduation," Maria asks kindly. The other girls lean in.

I step into the house and shrug as maria closes the door behind me. "It's fine. How have you all been?" I push myself back, towards the wall, keeping my distance from them as we traverse the length of the house towards the backyard. They feint interest. Before they can answer, a voice I never wanted to hear again speaks.

"Theon! It's awesome to see you again!" That insidious voice that belongs to the person who caused of so much pain. I shake as Miguel approaches, but my frail body stiffens as he places his hand on my shoulder. "I missed you so much best friend!"

My fear turns into sobering anger. A resting bison you don't want to poke. I force a smile.

The girls "Aww…" in unison. Maria speaks up, "You hung out all the time."

What! How can you say that? You saw me bleeding. Offered to help me get to the nurse. You! I knew it. For an instant, my guard drops. My blood pressure rises. I imagine my eyes to be like a short-horned lizard's, filling with blood and ready to squirt. All these people would be bloodied. Don't show any weakness. I force my timid voice to rise. "Can't say I remember." It's only a few steps to the back door. I take them and am outside again. Hopefully, the departure looked more natural than it felt.

More people fill the backyard. Tacos and bottles are stacked on the table. To the side, a couple of guys prepare burgers. I wander around, keeping to myself. None of them have changed.

A couple of guys and girls trade formalities with me. I shouldn't be here. Just a few more minutes, then I can leave in peace. Give them a busy facade. And my struggle will conclude.

Maria's voice startles me. "I love this song. Let's dance." She pulls me to the dance floor. A couple of people join her. The rest form a circle. All eyes on the center duet. Maria moves freely and smoothly. I barely move. My heart climbs up my throat. They scrutinize my every move. "Doesn't it feel good to be around friends?" Maria asks.

"What friends?" I focus on the circle. Pointing fingers, giggles and rumors flying. ***Not again! Not this.*** My lips quiver. I step back.

"The ones here," she replies, not stopping her fluent movements.

I clench my fists. Bite my tongue, but it's not enough. I'm done playing a part I don't deserve. "I didn't have any." My body feels like a chameleon's, rigid and sluggish. My breath hastens. My hands shake and my chest feels empty. My nails attempt to sink inside my skin. The music is gone. The overwhelming smell of alcohol and cigars usurps my senses. These people laughed at me, ignored me, pretended I was okay. **Liars.**

She steps closer to me.

From behind a hand. "What's up!" Miguel's bitter breath brushes my cheek.

Dormant defense mechanisms awaken. "Don't touch me." I slap his hand and take another step towards the edge of the packed circle.

Miguel leans in, ignoring his spilled drink. "Why not, friend?" he stresses the last word and smiles, though his eyes remain flat.

"We're not friends!" I push him away. He stumbles to the ground. ***I did it?*** With one glance, I know I didn't. He looks at me, and on his lips, a vague trace of a smile. The circle is three people thick. Music stops and the spotlight is on me. People gasp as Miguel stays on the ground. If it was up to me, I would do what he did to me all those years ago. Humiliate him, hurt him, make him wish he was never born. But I won't do that, I am not like him. Animals only attack when necessary.

Maria crouches and shakes the downed bully. He moves. His gaze searches for his drink.

She turns back to me. "Theon, you should apologize. He's your friend."

"He is not my friend." My voice is colder than wood frog during winter. It switches to the heat of the bombardier beetle. "I won't apologize until he does!"

Her lips hide a smile. "He did." She looks at him with care and at me like a foreign object disturbing her space. If she thinks that hurts, she's wrong. I've been treated this way by everyone. I won't let them hurt me anymore.

"He called me a friend. You think that makes things right? All my scars will be gone? My pain and suffering will magically disappear?" Everyone stares. Some have their phones out. "No! It won't. He doesn't get to be forgiven! Friends don't send each other to the hospital." I turn around. With my back facing the two of them I walk away. The circle opens up. "I knew coming here was a mistake, but I did it anyway. I'm an idiot." I don't glance back.

"That hasn't changed," a guy shouts. The group laughs.

I look down. My feet keep dragging me away. The music smothers the laughter. Between breaths I mumble, "It's better than being like all of you." Animals are the ones who have shown me kindness. I wish I could be like them. I wish I was never alone.

I sit on the sidewalk. A starless night under city lights. The sounds of nature forgotten to the city. Instead of animals, cars parked in lines one after the other. The single spark of life isolated from the world belongs to me. I stare at my phone. The screen void of comfort. My shoulders sink.

"Theon!" The guy's voice is vaguely familiar, but I don't turn. "Sorry for what happened back there." He sits beside me.

"Juan?" I ask before my voice turns into a growl. "What do you want? Haven't all of you done enough?"

He scoots away. "No! Not at all. I wanted to apologize." His palms touch the ground. His gaze looks to the obscured sky. "I invited you. I hoped you'd considered hanging out with me." His mouth arcs up, then goes back down.

My thoughts freeze. "What?" My anger retires to the back of my mind. Juan. He doesn't evoke my rage or pain. Only the cold-blooded indifference he showed me before. "Why?"

"Part of me wanted to get to know you in middle school. Another part feels guilty I never stood up for you." His voice is softer than I remember. He always appeared so sure and strong. He used to be like an ox, but now he mirrors me. Is it his reluctance to look at me, or that he's acting like a cheetah surrounded by other big cats?

I breathe slowly, like a cold-blooded animal. "I don't need your pity." I turn to him, and he looks towards the gray asphalt. "And I don't need to be saved. I can handle things as I've always done. Alone." My body keeps on alert. I won't fall for any tricks. The city has silenced just for this.

It takes him a minute to meet my eyes. I, in turn, look away.

He doesn't move an inch. "I am sorry. I hope you can forgive me one day." He scoots away.

I open my mouth again. "I do forgive you." Forgiveness, what a silly word. ***Do I mean it?*** He never did anything to help me, but he wasn't the one doing it either. The snarling dog and the compliant horse struggle inside me. Both of them roam freely, yet I'm shackled.

His lips twitch. "That's gr—"

"I appreciate the intention, but it's way too late. You could have made a difference." That's what hurts the most. He could have changed everything. He didn't care enough to stand up and help me. I wasn't asking for a hero, or a shield, just someone who saw me and told me that I'm worth it. Maybe someday we could be friends, but not now. If we do, I'll always be stuck. A constant reminder of my past, and the pain it brought me. I won't be tied to him or them anymore. And if we became friends, he'd suffer like I did, because he still associates with my tormentors. I'm not worth that pain. "I'm sorry, but I can't. Not right now."

He stands up, takes one final look at me. "I understand. You deserve better friends." It's better this way. They won't target him. They won't make him as miserable as I was.

Friends? Animals love me unconditionally. Human friends sound like an impossibility, but could they be real? My arms rest on my knees. I don't want to be so alone anymore. I turn around and see Juan walking back inside. My mouth curves down. **That was the right survival strategy. He understands, right? I had to protect him from living my fate.**

His silhouette changes to red and yellow with a white core. The house has gone from white to dark blue. The parked cars and grass are purples and blues. I take a look at my hand, white, yellow, and red dye it. Random flickers of light shine all the same. The dark sky dismisses the colors too. Houses fade into the background, while the people inside them burn red and yellow. The people in the party look like a mass of bright white. The circle stays as it was when I left. A passing car burns white in the middle but fades into a marine blue background. For one second, just an instant, the world is different. Then it returns to normal. Grass green and my hand back to tan. *What happened? What was that?* My head stings, but I ignore it. I stand and slowly make my way through the city back home.

CHAPTER FOUR: BELUGA POD

November 10, 2012

The morning sun dazzles me through the blinds. The birds and dogs stopped singing good morning hours ago. As for me, my head bangs with a remnant pain behind my eyes. I stumble groggily out of bed, opening the blinds, letting the late morning sunlight in. The usual nightingales and hummingbirds flutter around the back garden. The green bamboos and vines hide a jade world that shimmers every dawn and dusk. It's a pity I missed it.

My phone is bombarded with notifications about the party. I do what every rational vertebrate would do in my position. Block them all, except for Juan. I can't find it in my heart to hate him. It doesn't sit right. His knife was a dull one, but one I can endure looking at for longer.

I throw my phone on the bed. My feet drag me slowly towards the door. On the other side shouts, giggles, and the snorts of a dog. As I open it, Thor runs in. He snuggles my legs and sniffs the fabric of my pajamas. He jumps with his usual request to be carried. I oblige. He deserves nothing more than my care and love, as the only family member other than my tortoises to notice my presence. With my beloved house companion in my arms, I open the door further.

Roy sits up as he shouts at the TV. The maniacal roars he emits are mostly a warning to anyone approaching. They work I turn back to my bed before he slams his feet on the floor. "You fucking grew some balls!" I turn to glimpse him. He looks at me not with his usual look, but with pure pride and a bit of arrogance.

"What are you talking about?" My voice trails off in the sluggishness of my waking minutes.

He clicks his phone. My voice plays from it, "He is not my friend!" The words continue, building up to phrases that are too real to be a lie. ***Yesterday's party. How did he? Oh no! I'll have to change city now! Can't they leave me alone?*** I shake and tremble. Thor does his best to calm me by licking my face.

"Don't wuss out on me!" Roy stands on the table, looking down on me as he does to everyone. "Never thought you had it in you. Growing a damn backbone and standing up for yourself. Mad respect." He smirks, freckles almost disappearing in the light.

I take one deep breath. "Now everyone will know, about what happened to me." I bite my lip, cutting myself short from saying anything else. This is the worst-case scenario, changing high schools isn't safe anymore. Everyone will know it's online; they will know about me and how I'm easy prey.

"Everyone will fucking know, not to mess with the Untameds!" He stands straight, fist closed as to punch. "Now fuck off! You ruin the mood." Roy jumps back on his throne. He spreads himself over every inch of the sofa and nods his head slowly. Twice. Just as he is about to wear his headphones again, Lucas pops out.

"Show him the next part." Lucas peeks out from my parents' room. The nest in which he spends most of his time. On occasion, he does this. Dangle a worm above the hatchings, only to see the impending fight.

Thor wiggles in my arm. *I get it.* I start scratching. Sand colored hair falls to the marble floors. I turn to Lucas, who has bounced three times toward the center of the living room.

"Show me what?" My stomach swirls. *Why did I ask?*

Roy rolls his eyes. "Show him yourself." He takes one moment to stare down at us. Except for Thor and his goofy face. "Fine! I'll fucking do it myself." He tosses his phone on the table. Lucas smiles and takes his place beside the phone. Three taps invite me closer to the screen.

Thor takes the opportunity to lick Lucas's face. I do my best to watch the hand sized screen while Lucas and Thor play. One tap. Two taps. Three taps. Four taps. The reel forgets about me getting bullied one more time in my life. It jumps to Juan returning to the party. The circle of students surrounds Maria and Miguel. Most of them hold their phones at the center. The others snicker. The music prevents anyone from hearing their mockery, but I know what they're saying. Experience has taught me that.

"Maria! What was that for?" Juan stands in the center. His posture strong and steady. He towers over both Miguel and Maria.

Maria turns around. Her tone friendly, it prospering in deceit, "He acted crazy. We were being nice."

"You mocked him." He turns away from her. "In what world does pretending nothing happened make it right?" As his words leave his mouth, a couple of my ex-classmates go silent. Even here, I can feel the tension. No surprise, it took a popular guy and three years for some of them to realize what they did. As much as I would like to care, I can't. I turn away from the phone.

"You'll miss the best part." Lucas whistles in the wind. That sugary voice of his turning me back to last night's events.

"Chill out. What's to you?" Miguel stands between Maria and Juan, but doesn't wait for a response. He punches Juan in the jaw.

Juan returns the aggression, and soon after guys are fighting for both sides. I turn away as the party becomes a murderous frenzy I should have expected. **Why did he do that? I made it really clear. I gave him an out. He shouldn't have put himself out there!**

I rush back to my room. Lucas's giggles stop. Thor carefully lands on the floor before I close the door and sink into bed. My head palpitates. Lucas knocks on the door five times. Three fast and two slow. "He's fine. I thought you would like having a friend." His voice slows down. "I'm sorry." His voice dwindles. Then he leaves me be.

I glance at my phone. I want nothing to do with any of them, but I can't abandon someone who's hurt. Not like they did me. I cover my face with the pillow and scream. Cursing the people around me and cursing him. With phone in hand, I create a new chat.

Theon: How are you? I saw what happened.

Juan: I'm fine. Bruises. A couple of cuts.

Theon: Great.

Juan: How did you know?

Theon: It's viral.

Juan: Oh. I'll have to change schools next semester.

Theon: You shouldn't have done what you did.

Juan: I couldn't stand it.

Theon: So?

I force my phone to silence the conversation. If he answered, I'll never know. I take two deep breaths. The air has a tinge of human and animal in it. One smell from Thor, the other, lamentably, mine. I get up and open the door to my enclosed sanctuary. Roy has moved on. Instead of looking down on me, he's looking down on his teammates. Nothing motivates teammates more than, "Even my dog could play better than you." In this case, I do believe Thor might be able to play better than him and his team.

I cross his domain without attracting attention. He's satiated with his digital prey. Lucas sits bopping his head inside my parents' room. No one else wanders the house. Once he notices me, he shuffles the tablet. His head bopping swaps to giggles and laughter.

"I'm sorry. Want to go to the park?" Thor jumps aimlessly when I mention that magical word. I'm not sure why. He never walks more than a single minute. Lucas nods. I leave him to put his shoes. Thor chases me downstairs as if I ever thought of leaving him behind. He makes me wrangle festive orange leash around his body.

CHAPTER FIVE: TRUST IN YOUR INSTINCTS

Thor and I sit at the bottom of the stairs. We wait while Lucas picks up the toys he wants to bring. I avoid looking at my messaging apps. I'd hate to see if Juan answered and most importantly what he answered. Thor takes the opportunity to jump on my lap and snore his life away. ***What would I do to have my problems leave as I sleep.*** Seeing him that way brings me peace. But it's my life we are talking about. Peace is fleeting.

A bombardment of noise consumes me. Roy roars. The singing birds put on a concert. Tempestuous leaves rustle. Steps thunder. Plastic bursts. A phone booms an alert. Thor bellows in his sleep. Motors crash. I tense, giving Thor the signal to move. My knees jolt against my chest. My head digs itself between my legs. Thor scratches my side, adding sandpaper to scorch my ears. The sounds ease off, giving me a second to compose myself.

I glance around. Thor scratches my legs. Roy's shouts reach the lower floor, but never extend past the house. In the garden, the fluttering birds sing. Lucas taps me on the shoulder as he takes his final step. Sound rises again and I cover my ears. My breath grows deeper and heavier in a failed endeavor to release the pressure. This time mechanical sounds overwhelm me. The roar of two raging motors. Or are there three? Short fast-paced collisions fly through the air. I look for answers bewildered.

Lucas takes a step back. "Are you okay?" His voice is amplified, as if he is a blue whale singing beside me.

I shake my head. Glass explodes. Panicked screams and painful cries disperse away. The repeating sound gets louder. "Can you hear the screams?"

Lucas looks normal. "Roy's?" He looks above. "Roy! Theon says you're too loud!" Lucas's voice booms inside my head.

I recoil, covering my ears harder than before.

"Shut the fuck up!" Roy shouts back.

His voice crashes against my already sensitive ears. I yelp, trembling as the other noises get louder. I crumble under the pressure. Both my brothers stop. Other voices consume theirs. Metal collisions ring. Tears roll down my face seeking to destroy the lustrous wooden floors. The metal crashing sounds rowdier. Followed by hallowed barks and runaway squawks. The motor rampages through the narrow suburban roads.

My heart races. Deep breaths move the air around me. The mildly annoying clattering of my teeth resonates through my bones. My head heavy. Slowly but surely, the elephant pressure in my head releases its grasp. My ear canals flood with liquid. ***What just happened? What was all that?*** Collisions and crashes can't be good. And they were getting louder, approaching. ***But what exactly did I experience? I must be out of my mind.*** My fingers fidget on my palms. Lucas didn't hear it. That can't be right. It must not be real.

"I'm scared." Lucas points at my ears.

My palms are dressed in red. I touch my ear and my fingers come away coated in gooey liquid. I glance at my red dipped fingers. Then at Lucas, who's shaking.

"What the hell is wrong with you!" Roy shouts, hundreds if not thousands of decibels lower than a moment ago. He smacks the back of my head.

I don't feel it. That pain is nothing compared to what I just endured. My heads still thumps from the cacophony. It takes one minute before my overwhelming sense of disorientation silences. I uncover my ears. I'm ready to listen. Whatever the world throws at me, I'm ready. Thor's fur puffs up. He growls at the door. Strange. "Everything was too loud. Did a window break?"

"The fuck you talking about?" Roy throws his hands in the air. He turns and stomps his way up to the second floor.

They didn't hear anything? Thor continues to growl. Birds and dogs panic. *Something is wrong. What are you sensing?* Animals would only act like this as a collective if something were to happen. A natural disaster or the likes. It can't be. There are no earthquakes and hurricane season passed three months ago. Human made? *Okay, let's assume what I heard was real.* People do have a sixth sense. And my stress could have triggered an adrenaline response to it. Nature's sounds are normal. The broken glass, the screams and the motors are dissonant to me. They were louder by a few decibels, but they were closer too.

It dawns on me. A sound every Mexican would know to distinguish. A trained litter of puppies would know what it means. I've been too slow. "Lucas, get to my room and hide in the closet." My heart thumps against my ribcage. A small trace of chaos approaching. I gulp. "Lucas. Run!" I pick up Thor and take Lucas's hand.

Lucas's small legs struggle to follow me. "I'm scared!" From up the street, echoes of frenzied screams. Destroyed windows fall to the curb.

"Get to my closet. You heard that Thor? Take Lucas to my closet." I put Thor down. He licks Lucas and dashes to my room, waiting for the little cub to follow. Lucas looks at me with tears welling in his eyes, then turns to Thor and runs with him. He drags the small red and blue backpack where all the park toys will reside until this madness is over.

Metal clinks on the walls of distant houses. It's all clear now. Roy continues obliviously, while he does the same thing people threaten to do to us. End our lives in a storm of metal. His ears suffer from a menace, headphones. Their sound reaches me. I shiver at the thought of it, and glance at the TV and the console. ***I'll be dead or both of us will be. He'll kill me. He'll kill me anyway.*** In a swift move, both devices die. He glares at me. The look a shark gives their unborn sibling. He throws his headphones, approaches me, and prepares to punch. The motors rumble through the concave cannon we call the street.

"What the fuck? My console is off." He turns towards it.

"It's real." My words shake in the air, with enough urgency for the prince of the pride to follow Lucas and Thor. I track behind him, slamming the door. Lucas plays with one of his toys in the darkness. Roy grabs a box and sits on it, looking down on the rest of us. I instruct Lucas to lie on the cold marble floor. He does and between the two of us we manage to hold Thor in place. We wait for minutes. Time ticks. Maybe they won't pass near us. ***Maybe we'll get lucky.***

Lucas silently pets Thor at a slow rhythm. Thor relaxes in our hands. Chaos encroaches with a promise of death. My heart sets the beat that will last an eternity. The more we wait, the slower time feels. Time doesn't flow. I'm used to the feeling of being hunted, but this is different. Dread. Deep and all-consuming. A massive void threatening to absorb us, like looking at the depths of the sea.

A loud motor roars close by. Windows crash. Metal and stone pop. Swirling blades cut through the air, deafening communication. The storm of bullets reaches a fleeting climax around us, becoming a tempest. Lucas cries, prompting Thor to bark aggressively at the air. Thor's barks fail to scare the unnatural opponents. He has much to learn, but so do I. I hold both kids close to me. A futile attempt to calm them. I glance at Roy, who covers his ears. He gives a death glare to the known assailant. The sounds go on for what feels like an eternity.

That next minute is replaced by absolute silence. The one after a big hunt in the savanna. Once the prey is caught, everything crashes down, leaving only those alive to find one small moment of tranquility. A moment where they aren't hunters or prey, they are survivors for another day. Same here. Oddly quiet. I stand and lean toward the door. Only the wind and the far gone sound of disaster. "It's over."

Thor decides Lucas requires face licks, which work wonders to calm the crying five-year-old.

Roy rolls his eyes. "How the fuck did you know it was coming?"

"I heard it." I shrug.

"Sounds like BS." He opens the door.

I gawk. Why do I even try? Lucas stands up and pulls on my shirt. "He didn't lie."

"I fucking know. Theon is a shit liar." He takes a step back. "But you better fess up bro. Thor and you heard it, but not Lucas."

I shrug again. This time I scratch my palms to relief the stress. I glance at my pockets, the phone lays still tempting me to search for answers. I'll do it later when I know what went on with my ears. I had to warn them, but why trust them? Roy's never done anything for me. Why should I think either of them will keep it a secret? Still, they did talk to me in the morning, and they are kids. Maybe they can change. I want to believe they don't see me as a carcass on the road. "I'm not sure. It was weird. Can you keep it a secret until I figure it out?"

"I'm not a snitch." With arms crossed he nods at Lucas.

Lucas pouts before saying, "I promise." He doesn't have the devious smile or the puppy eyes he usually wears as a mask. The real him stands with us, more serious and more connected to anyone than he has ever been.

I hold his hand and guide him out of the closet. "I'll keep you updated." Roy nods at my statement without saying anything else. He reclaims his domain and continues his virtual massacre. Lucas stays in my room until he's ready to explore the glass wasteland on the opposite end of the house.

CHAPTER SIX: WILDERNESS CALLS

November 12, 2012

School is, as per usual, the habitat of gossip and remarks about whoever made it viral. This week I'm the circus's main act. Whenever I go in or out of a room, people clear the area. They maintain distance as if I was some dangerous, wild creature roaming the courtyard. They aren't silent. It's off putting to have everyone say things to me in Spanish. Back in the other school, English dominated, and it felt right. Direct and straight to the point, there was no playfulness to it. The message rings loud and clear. **Yes, I know you're talking about me. Don't feel. Don't react. Keep walking. Pretend they can never hurt you.** Not the giggles of the preppy girls. Not the bumps from the jocks passing me. And 'specially not those who stare at Mika and Larry rubbing their fur against my neck, they act as if this was a new occurrence, but every time I step out animals accompany me. Those are the worst. Both Allen's squirrels are innocent.

I feed them two more nuts. The way to class is like walking through the forest and knowing a pack of wolves is hunting you. The glares put unneeded pressure into my every step. Unlike carnivores, teens hunt for satisfaction. I continue my planned migration toward the next class as the sun is midway to its peak. I rub my eyes, staving off the tiredness of staying up all night two days in a row trying to figure out what happened. The only logical conclusion is hallucinations cause by stress. I don't believe that. For a moment, my hearing was better than a canine's. It was equivalent to an African elephant's.

"Theon!" A guy shouts energetically. Intercepting me next to the plaza. He pats my back, causing both of my squirrel friends to abandon ship. "Bro! I need to talk to you."

I turn back and see Jayson's booming smile. If he was an animal, he would be a chocolate labrador dog. Everything but his eyelashes reflect that. "If it's about that video. I'm not in the mood." I keep trekking forward to the class we share. Ever since day one, Jayson has been on my case. Asking me to present my work to class, or constantly talking to me about parties.

"It's something else." He stands beside me and suddenly everyone in the plaza takes a step toward us. The air changes. The other students wave as he walks with me, the lone fox. Their gazes focus on the jock beside me. They must be planning something. He has to be on it. He isn't innocent. No one ever is.

I roll my eyes and before he can react, I'm already moving. "Sure, I can help you with biology studying." My voice drags as much as my feet. I inhale and everything livens up. The scent of burgers and hot-dogs fills my nose. Human stench conquers the environment. Idyllic hints of nature struggle against the toxic gases of the gray city. Last, but not least, one nauseous smell cuts the corner in front of us. It's acrid and acidic. It burns through my nose. I cover my nose and mouth with a hand and turn around.

"Class is that way," Jayson says.

"You wanted to talk to me. We can take the long way." I huff and puff and hope he says no. I don't even take two steps, before he's beside me, brimming with joy. ***Alright Theon, keep your guard up. He might be looking for an in. A way to make me the focus of the pack.*** We take two more steps.

The doors to one of the classroom buildings swing open and a girl screams her lungs out as what sounds like a burp erupts. We turn back. The girl attempts to clean off the chunky vomit that covers her, while another girl stands beside her, stunned as the vomit drips from her mouth. ***It could have been us.*** A crowd forms around them. People call lawyers sharks, but I disagree. Teens are more like sharks, except even more savage and ruthless. Flashes of light dazzle them. Whispers vary. "So disgusting, like her wardrobe." "You got it on video?" Their comments irk me. If the girls are lucky, everyone will forget about it by tomorrow.

Jay frowns and turns back to the scene. He gulps. His body leans toward them but is equally pulled my way. ***If he leaves to help them fine, but…*** I twiddle my thumbs near my nose, no liquid running down. I glance at him. His long eyelashes make his gaze more dramatic than it should be. I take a step. He follows. "What did you want to talk about?"

He shakes my shoulders gripping me with the same intensity as an octopus has with its prey. I hunch in response, trying to avoid the soft yet strong grip. "Want to hangout Friday after school?" The same question he has asked every single day of the semester. At first, I thought it was a prank, now I believe this has to be a strange compulsion popular kids have when someone says no. The more you say it, the more they want it. Once they experience it, they can move on.

Where would that leave me? The shiny new ball a puppy gets, uses a bit, and forgets about. That would be the least hurtful thing anyone my age has ever done to me. I bite my lip. His body can't contain his excitement, it trembles, waiting for my answer. We turn the corner around the library. The stragglers of Jayson's specie run past us. They search for whatever source will give them a sense of belonging among their peers. "Why do you keep inviting me?"

He jumps in front of me, blocking my path to liberation. "Cause you're cool!"

I raise my parted brow. "You don't even know me." I shrug him off and continue on my way.

He smiles, putting his hand softly on my shoulder. In a sad tone, he says, "We could be friends." That word. It reminds me of Juan, and I don't want to think about him. It's so foreign. Like an Andean condor befriending a dumbo octopus.

My stomach churns, revolting against the thought. This could be the last time he asks. *Animals are my friends; people only mean to hurt me*. My leg moves forward, but I can't take the step. No one sees me in this school unless there's bad news, and yet Jayson tries to make me part of his pack. Even though I'm just a stray. *What if he's different? I can't trust him, I know 'cause if I do, I'll be alone again. I… I… I don't know.* I'll twist it to my favor, 'cause his proposition can't be real.

"Fine. On one condition. If it doesn't work out, you won't bother me again."

His eyes open wide, "Yes! We have to tell the others!" He grabs my arm, dragging me to a pair. Arvo with a black cap and one eye covered by hair. And Katherine with scarlet hair. As Jayson talks, he moves around almost crashing into other students leaving the library. I stand back, trying to hide myself behind his energy. If people see me, they'll ask about the video or worse, judge me about it.

I stand still on the walkway, but my legs wobble. The world trembles. When I look at Jayson and the others, they are stable. The constant trembling reminds me of a rattlesnake. Quick and light. Fast and unequal. "Let's move."

"Right, we'll be late to class." Arvo says.

What is happening to me?

Arvo packs his laptop, and he and Katherine follow us toward class. "I'm so glad you are joining for game night!" She opens her arms for a hug, but I stumble back.

As my feet hover above the ground, the marching drums beating against them stop. But then I hit the ground.

She offers her hand. "Not a hugger. Got it." Her smile and energy are more contained than Jayson's. Maybe resembling a bird of some type. People stare at us, at me. "Are you okay? Everyone is being mean to you."

I stand up on my own. ***I can take care of myself. I've have survived on my own, I'll keep on surviving.*** "It's okay.

Nothing new." I shrug the dirt off my back. Her lips twist as the words leave my mouth. **Not her too.** Good humans can't exist. It has to be impossible.

Arvo chimes in, "I'm sorry for what I asked in your first day. I didn't know…"

I scowl. "It's fine." **How could he know I was running away? That my life was horrible. Or about the other thing. I can't blame him, no matter how much the questions bothered me.** Why did I transfer and where did I come from? Those questions are simple for others. For me, they're the source of my nightmares. A revivification of my scars. My fingers run through the broken area of my brow, the line without hair cutting through the middle. I start walking, but before we turn the corner, the sprinklers burst. It rains over the area Kat and Arvo had been sitting. I stagger, but continue to follow them.

"Are you sure?" Arvo presses. "What do you think happened to the other guy in the video? Is he a friend of yours?"

I stomp the ground. "I'm fine. I don't want to talk about it. I want people to forget about it. I want everyone to leave me and what happened alone." My body shakes against my will. "He's fine. And no, he isn't my friend." Arvo just had to remind me. I hope Juan doesn't transfer here. That's the last thing I need. I take a step back, away from them. **Are they predators? Or are the something else?** A lonely tear falls.

Katherine takes my hand. "We won't ask anymore. You're safe." There's a wave of relief. My body stills, and the lonely tear remains lonely. She glances at the two guys. Arvo nods hauling her black and neon backpack with him. Jayson reaches out for me, but she catches his hand before it grasps my clothing. For a second, his face does the same thing it did when he saw the girls in trouble. He walks ahead and leans on Arvo.

We turn to the left of the library. On this side, there are no windows because the soccer field is so close. Most students avoid this route for the same reason. Our group is mostly silent, except for Jayson. I can't find the energy to talk. My head spirals with the experiences of the past few days and that party. The gun fight, vomit, colorful night, and the tremors. All those experiences are unnatural for a human. If I've somehow developed animal-like senses, it would be the greatest news I've had! I could be officially considered an animal. I'd belong with those who have been kind to me all along. My lips arc upward, then they go back to rest.

Our group joins up with two girls. Lucy is small with a red beanie and glasses. The only reason I remember her is because she saw the drawing I made the first day of class. And her friend Haruka, who also saw that drawing. A rat about to get squished by a tennis shoe. It's the same drawing Jayson almost made me present to the class.

I clean my eyes. A drop of water hits my upper lips. The world feels different. There is a sense of static, like when a body part goes numb. Or like when you charge with electricity after rubbing your socks against the carpet and touching something. It's volatile but doesn't hurt. It never reaches electric eel magnitude. A massive burst pulls me to the right. A flare of sparks. I let go of Katherine. My body acts on its own. I pass both guys and reach Lucy and Haruka in time to pull them back. A ball darts past where Lucy's head was. It hits the wall and flies through where Haruka had been with enough force to have knocked her out.

"Sorry!" a guy in the field shouts, as he catches the instrument of death.

Jayson pats my shoulder. "Nice reflexes. You should join the tennis team."

"No." I muster the word. The pull vanishes like every other time it has happened. This one is stranger. Pulls and pushes. The only sense I've read about that fits is electro-reception. That should be outside my ability field, unless… It makes no sense.

"Thanks," Haruka says. She types on her phone, then turns to me. "Do you mind if I write about you?"

"Stop." Lucy snaps at her friend. She turns to me, fixing her red beanie, "Sorry about her. And thank you for saving us." Lucy swirls a gray pen. In her other hand is a tablet with a drawing of a boy and a dinosaur.

I stare at it. He seems familiar.

Jayson says, "Game night. Friday. My house." Then he drags me and Lucy to class as the others follow behind us.

CHAPTER SEVEN: LEARNING THE LANGUAGE

As we walk to class, I avoid the shy and nervous gazes of Lucy and Haruka. Arvo's cold, reptilian walk is reminiscent of a chameleon. Every once in a while, he turns toward me, raises his hand but stops himself. Slowly but surely advancing. Katherine and Jayson are as energetic as always, carrying what the rest of us lack.

Why? Such a mismatch wouldn't happen in nature and yet here we are. I slow my steps. My mind swirls with thoughts of the morning. I glance at the science department building. Unlike the other gray buildings, this one is blue. The stinky scene in front of the language building blocks the flow of students. The world's center of gravity pulls me away from humanity. The green forest near the creek buzzes to me. Home. A place I can be alone and think. I drift further and further away from my group.

Jayson turns my way. "Class isn't leg day, don't skip it." He smiles, reaching out for my arm. I flinch. It makes him stop. His mood change unnerves me. Unnaturally frozen. He stares at me like he stared at those girls. The silent discomfort creates an ocean between us. If only I had wings or fins. I am but a mouse, not ready to scurry into the light of day. I'm not ready for anything.

My breath quickens. "Sorry. I'm not feeling well." I hunch while taking a backward step.

Katherine steps between us. "It's okay. We'll tell the teacher." She smiles softly. I waver on my decisions, a moment of weakness. Maybe I should go with them. She takes Jayson away from me, his gaze never faltering. Haruka and Lucy wave as they head inside. Arvo shakes his head, mutters something, but it's too low to hear. He turns his back swiftly, too human-like.

It stops me from going with them. I turn into the green lunch area. Unlike the central plaza, this one is mostly filled with animals. My pack. Humans are unlikely visitors. It makes it the perfect place to be alone with my thoughts. I take a seat at my usual picnic table. Surrounded by shrubs and trees. Glazed by the breeze from the nearby creek.

I crumple. My hands act as a clam's shell over my face. My brain has been swirling with deprecatory thoughts. "This can't be real. Why are people being nice to me? If they knew me, they would leave me. I'm not worth it." I claw at my arms and hands, as I usually do when I feel like this.

Multiple birds sing. Nightingales, a peacock, mockingbirds, ducks, parrots, magpies, doves, and many more species. "Why would someone ever think that?" A nasal voice cuts through the greenery. It's elegant and poised, it carries some weight.

My body jolts. **Who said that?** I can't change schools again because someone saw me talking to myself. I look up. No humans around, only the birds, the trees and me. The wall of green camouflages me from members of my own species. I keep looking around and nothing.

"He stinks." The raspy voice says being barely understandable. I take a sniff at the air. I do stink. The jittery smell of cheap perfume made of onions emanates from my body. *I don't even use perfume! They'll think I'm a freak. And even in animal societies, outcasts die. But in my case, it's worse. That can't happen again.* My arms act as barriers against the breeze flowing from the stream. I let myself fall onto the picnic table.

"Your stress scent is too much. No wonder the ladies avoid you," a condescending voice adds to the fire burning in my skin.

Another voice? My neck does as the owl's. It spins and spins. *There's too many. They will never leave me alone! Am I destined to be in the spotlight?* If the video wasn't enough, this will be. It's only a matter of time before rumors spread. *What am I supposed to do? I'm going extinct any way I slice it.*

"It's rude to ignore others," says the condescending voice.

"What is going on?" I grab my stuff and stand as fast as I can.

A sweeter voice joins the discussion. "They're just teasing. No need to leave…" It pauses.

"Stop," the nasal voice reprimands them.

"Have you figured out who we are?" the voice that attempts to imitate mine asks.

Before I say anything, I look around once more. No humans. And an absence of mechanical noises too. I've eliminated the possible. They must have seen me here for the last hour or so, ranting about my problems. That isn't human behavior. Humans would get bored. The voices must know my current state, so the only other logical answer is… I give it a second, but no, I have no other clues, so I guess the weirdness continues today. "You're birds. To be specific a nightingale, a great egret, a mallard, an Indian peacock, and a mockingbird." My voice sounds more like a lion when I mention each species. It's different than talking about myself. I know animals.

"See, it wasn't that hard." The russet nightingale-thursh flutters and lands on the table. He whistles sweetly and the other birds get closer.

The mallard bites my leg from behind. The northern mockingbird lands beside the nightingale and imitates my voice once more as a joke. The condescending peacock doesn't stop trying to impress the female. She tries her best to continue with her life as he obstructs her search for food. Lastly, the egret lands on a seat beside me.

On the one hand, this is awesome. On the other hand, this is weirder than before. I have to be dreaming or hallucinating, or going insane. I take a seat, defeated. Overwhelmed. Mixed feelings surfacing. I feel my face twist as the emotions fight. I hide my hands in my hair as I attempt to make sense of the world. I can't control it. I'm laughing. "I can understand you! I knew animals were intelligent!" I pause and look around. "This is the best thing that has ever happened to me!" *I'm not alone. They can hear me. I can hear them clearly. I'm an animal. As I have always been, but this time I have company. I have someone!*

"We broke him." The mockingbird copies my voice.

I don't care! This is great. This shouldn't be possible. Does this mean that the last three days I have been sensing like them? If that's the case, then my brain had to go through changes, not only my brain my whole body. I'd need the receptors in my eyes and nose, and changes in my brain cortex distribution. The implications are massive. "Do you know what's happening to me?"

"Yes, we can explain." The nightingale gets closer. He speaks softly, harmonizing with my chaotic voice. It climbs and chimes between the gaps in my breath.

"No. He must figure it out on his own," the egret scolds. There is something regal about her. She takes a step and beats her wings once.

The mockingbird imitates my voice, but makes it sound way cooler. Deeper and determined. "But we could help him gain control. Shouldn't be a problem."

"He needs all the help he can get." The contemptuous peacock belittles before getting belittled himself.

"You need the help too." The raspy voice gets more incomprehensible by the minute. Is he spitting?

I shrink, but ask for more. "Wait. Please tell me. I need to know." **That's me. Always in-debt to them. Never being able to pay back.**

The birds look at each other. A series of yeses and noes. Glances. Those I can't understand; their body language is different, similar in that everyone has a body language, but too different for each specie. The egret scoffs and turns her back. "Tell him what he must know."

The mocking-bird flutters to my shoulder. "You are growing. It's natural." He pauses glances at the others, receiving a nod. "Your abilities are unique. We want to help you control them."

Animals have given me so much. I shouldn't ask for more, shouldn't make them help if they're not all willing. The birds discuss among themselves, but I speak up, give them an out in a quiet voice. "I understand, but you don't need to help me anymore. I'll be fine."

"Pathetic." The peacock roams after the fowl, who has yet to bat an eye.

The egret moves closer, her head lowers. Her eyes try to connect with mine, then she turns to the mallard. She clears her throat, commanding the attention of the other birds.

"We want to help," the nightingale sings. "You start training singing tomorrow." That seems to be the sign every bird was waiting for. Lessons about singing, dancing, sight, and flight. I don't even have wings. Some comment on vocals and displays. While the egret mentions equilibrium and balance. The topics are mostly addressed with grace and lightness. They have a sense of beauty to them.

I raise my head, watching the birds discussing my future. Thinking about how beauty isn't how I would describe myself. *I don't fit this mold the birds have so easily landed on. How can't they see that? It would be rude to say no after they considered this for my wellbeing. But still, why bother? I'm just going to disappoint them. They'll see how hopeless I am.* "But." My eyes avert from them.

"Is everything alright?" The mockingbird turns to me.

With a sigh, I reply, "Yes." I force a smile, as I always do. *'Cause I'm fine. I'm strong. I can handle it. And I'm never not okay.*

"Perfect. Time to spread the news. We birds can't do all of it on our own." The nightingale flutters around.

"Dibs on telling mammals!" they all shout at the same time.

The egret is clearly unamused by the display. "I'll tell the other birds." She takes off, her flight not as elegant as her speech.

The peacock returns to dance for the peafowl. The extremely bored and busy bird ignores my presence even when I feed him. He doesn't have to be that rude.

"I'll tell the amphibians and tell them to deal with the fish. No one wants to deal with the fish." Is it me or is the mallard easier to understand?

Curiosity wins me over and, I interrupt, leaning closer to the smaller avians on the table. "Why does no one like fish?"

"They're forgetful," the nightingale says.

"I'll get the reptiles," the mockingbird says, but instead of flying off, he takes into the shelter of the trees. Thunder crackles. The gray sky turns closer to black. Wind strikes, turning the cool air frigid. I take the jacket from inside the bag. The mallard walks away and groups up with the other ducks. They line up, following each other to the small pen, where they huddle and fall asleep.

The nightingale stays with me. "Lessons start tomorrow. See you!" The thought makes me sick. The nightingale flies away from the looming storm. Shortly after, water drops crash upon the earth, soaking both my skin and clothing.

CHAPTER EIGHT: LONE

November 17, 2012

My week hasn't been easy. Dealing with school, the whispers and rumor floating everywhere I go make it hard to celebrate. They only stop when Jayson or Katherine are around. She insists I call her Kat. I don't know if I can. It seems like that would be allowing them close to me. Jayson has banned me from using Jayson. It's Jay and Jay only. People turn my way because I'm with someone popular, they don't care about me. At home, things are a bit better with my siblings. They don't care, but they're avoiding making things harder for me. Lucas even asked me to translate what Thor is saying. It's good to see him smiling. My parents are another topic, but I don't want to talk about it, some things will never change.

This doesn't include extracurriculars, upcoming finals and Jay's party. He only invited the six of us. He kept asking about how I felt and if I liked it. I couldn't answer. I wanted to say something, but my mind has been distancing me from the present. **What about the future? If you say yes, you'll open yourself to pain.** I'm not sure about any of them. Good humans don't exist, yet they are nice. It shouldn't happen in my life. I probably did something to deserve all the pain. They'll figure me out.

"Greetings. I'm Serena, your instructor for today." A gray crane awaits on the middle, of the creek, standing on unstable. The rocks never move, even when Serena looks my way. She doesn't seem like she could ever get wet. I stand at the edge of the creek. Water sculpts the rocks little by little. Another cool morning, another lesson I have to learn. Each time there is a different location. A cliff side to use my sight. A valley's edge to sing. The yoga room in school to dance. I don't know how the birds got keys. Serena speaks again, "My sincerest apologies, my cousins, the Japanese cranes can't teach you. I'll do my upmost to teach you about balance and equilibrium."

I can't be this important. They're calling on creatures from around the world to help me. I know I'm not worth it. ***Why are they making it such a big deal? Why aren't they treating me like an outsider or someone not worth their time? It's just a matter of time. They'll get bored. They'll mock me and forget me. They'll do what everyone does. So don't get your hopes up.*** "It's not a problem. I just hope to be the student both you and your cousins are looking for."

The crane moves her head. She looks confused, but even then, her regal demeanor outshines her other emotions. "You already are. Shall we begin?" Her wings point toward the smaller round rocks. She then points at my feet. "Please take off your shoes and socks."

The comment makes me pause for an instant. I shake my head. She is only being nice. I do as she says and barefoot, I step on the cold rocks. The small slippery rocks prove more of a challenge than I expected. They tumble and roll. None of the falls are bad. My butt is looking similar to a mandrill's. Other than that, no new bruises. I can't find my footing. At most, I can stand still for one minute on the flopping stones.

Each time my feet touch the water, a thousand red-bellied piranhas bite me, leaving no mark of their existence. The crane's rock hasn't moved. Her poise is elegant and refined. Showing off the talents of her species with grace and precision. Water numbs my sense of touch, and the wind shoves my body down once more. I take my position again and do as the garden eels, moving myself with the flow of the wind.

My clothing is soaked. My flattened hair drips. I rise from the water. **Trash. Useless. You can't even do a simple task. Disappointing. Hahahaha and you wonder why people don't like you. They never will. No one will want you.** "I'm not worth the time." I don't have the strength to look at Serena.

"You are worth. You are the only human that looks at others and treats them right—" her voice is interrupted. I can hear the squawks clearly. She gets closer moving out of her pose and rubbing her beak against my cheek. I stand, take my place and balance. "Balance starts in the mind. In order to achieve physical balance, you need psychological balance."

"I don't get it." I sigh. My feet stop feeling the cold water constantly biting at my toes. I turn away from her. It makes it easier.

She beats her wings once, but there's no change in the water or the rocks, or even the air. Everlasting stillness in this moment. "What I mean is that your mind has to be calm and balanced for your body to be. Is something bothering you?"

I sigh. Roy is right, I'm too easy to read. "What would you do if a group wanted you, but you still don't know their intentions?" I splash water onto the tree line, away from Serena.

"Hmm. I would try with caution. There are always opportunities and surprises. Why do you ask?"

I keep walking through the chilled waters. Careful not to slip on the smooth rocks. "Because people at school are asking me to hang out with them. And I don't know what to do."

"Do what is right for you. And what you want." She walks gracefully beside me. Interrupting the flow of the water ever so slightly. She brushes my hair with her feathers.

"I want to believe them, but they might leave me." I sit back down in the creek. The weight of my clothing threatens to drag me into the weak current. I embrace my knees under the fleeting sunlight hiding behind the foliage.

Serena's head matches my height. "I think you should try."

"What if it hurts?" I clam up. Speaking my fears aloud is worse.

"Would you stop walking just because you could trip?" She takes a couple of steps away from me.

I shake my head.

"Then why would you stop now? Hurting is part of life. You must accept it and live with it."

I glance at her. The wind might blow, and the pebbles slip with the current, but she remains. "I guess so."

"We shall postpone the rest of your training. I believe it will be more fruitful if you come to see me the weekend after your finals." She bows. "I bid you farewell." She spreads her wings and takes flight. The wind picks her up, the current pushes her down, then she turns and flies against it.

"Sorry," I muster. "I'll see you then." I head back to the shore and pick up my phone from my bag beside the creek. Still dry. I scroll through the messages and waver when I see Jay's. I pace like an animal in a small cage desperately looking for a way out. I should stay hidden, away from the dangers. I know Serena means well and that she wouldn't say something to hurt me.

Jay: So, what did you think?

My free hand scratches itself. Nails run through the barren palms. ***Why is it so difficult to say no? I shouldn't think about a yes. Humans only hurt me. Why would these ones be different? I'm a pest they hate. I… can see his face looking at me. His expression haunts me. Why did he look at me with kindness and concern? That never happens to me!*** I'm about to throw my phone against the rocks.

I do the opposite as Serena said. We brave through the pain. That's the only thing we can do.

Theon: I had fun.

Jay: Yas! Yas! Let's hangout more!

I stay there considering what might be my biggest mistake, and what Serena considered my greatest opportunity. My chest inflates and deflates slowly. I take a look at the bigger rock in the center of the creek. Serena left, but I can still practice. I can do it. I step on the smooth rock. For one minute, I stand still, and I then fall. Little by little, I can stand longer. This is the only way I can get my head away from the pain.

CHAPTER NINE: WILD TAKEOVER

January 5, 2013

    The parking to the movie theater is filling up quickly. Half an hour before the movie starts. Perfect timing, or it would be if they were here. My mind tells me to go in and save some seats, with the money I don't have. My stomach grumbles. I pace anxiously before the entrance. It had to be horror.

    Close to the entrance, a feast attracts my eyes. A sapphire racing motorcycle. My gaze sticks to the target. An eagle marking its prey. I feel fluid dropping from my mouth. The owner takes their helmet off. I swipe my mouth, striving to look like a normal person. The blond girl causes the same reaction as the motorcycle. Her blue eyes have a red tone in them. She reminds me of a giant Pacific octopus with those cold and analytic. Unattainable. She's too human, and I'm too much of an animal. eye

    Within ten minutes, the group arrives. Lucy and Haruka insist on waiting for the next horror film. I abstain from commenting, who knows when they'll get tired of me. The only words I want to say are thank you Jay and Katherine for intervening. An action-adventure movie. I can handle that. If you've listened to a vixen scream then you would understand, why I don't watch horror movies. The movie goes without a hitch. I'd like to say the rest of the night goes accordingly, but I know it won't last.

Jay parked his car far from the entrance.

Maureen, the black cat joins us. She drops gracefully from the blue motorcycle. I divert my gaze. No more drooling tonight. The girl is nowhere to be seen. I'm in luck. She won't see me as a starved lion looking at a zebra.

My senses go awry. The external cinema lights turn off. There's only one vehicle in sight, a black van. The fading light of the moon darkens the night. My body tells me to keep my guard up. Maybe it's the prey in me. Or maybe the predator knows the hunt is about to start. A crackle and a giggle. That's the beginning. Some steps in water.

"Boo-hind you!" Jay jumps from behind me as we approach an alley.

"Ahhh!" I flinch. "Not funny." My soles rub noisily against the walkway. Why does it have to be bat hearing? More splashes. A normally inaudible beep attracting my attention. One voice grows louder than I prefer. The sounds bounce out of the alley. The heavy breaths coming from there are concerning. I know animals can do this in seconds, but I have to slow down and take it all in. "Did you hear that?"

"Obviously." She purrs at my feet.

Arvo looks at me with his cold, disapproving stare. "Why are you meowing?"

"Sorry." I shrink, slowing my pace as he walks further away.

The herd gets ahead of me. I have to focus. I need feline eyes tonight. I blink and the world looks brighter, a bit more yellowish. A massive grin decorates my face. At least this works, even if my hearing has returned to normal. The dark alley is black to the human eye. To me it's bright as day. Garbage bins are lined up on opposite sides of the alley. A set of emergency stairs hangs above the right-side garbage bin. Up above, cables crisscross the buildings, they almost fuse with the black empty sky.

The most important part is in the far back. A burly man corners a teenage girl. Her face is cold and serious. The owner of the motorcycle. I see her lips moving. An odd blue light shines inside her jeans. The girl scowls, and her right arm tenses as she clutches the blue light. The guy looks at her. He shakes her and pushes her against the wall. The man reaches under her belt. My throat tenses and I growl.

"Theon, there's nothing there." Arvo points to the alley. He keeps his distance after witnessing my animalistic side.

I can't let this happen. I can't let others suffer. Satisfaction from suffering, a sickening look for a member of the animal kingdom. Human don't even deserve to be part of the kingdom. "A guy is harassing a girl," I say, bearing my teeth. ***She won't be a victim. I'll be there for her, just like how animals were there for me.*** I turn to Maureen. She shrugs and leads the way into the alley.

Lucy moves further away. She doesn't look directly at me. Jay catches my shoulder.

The light of a phone illuminates Arvo as he speaks. "You don't have to go there. Let the authorities handle it."

Shadows hide my disgruntled face. "It'll be too late."

Haruka jumps in, "Let's help. We could be like an anime hero team!" She poses.

"Call the police, maybe the ambulance." I look at them. "Arvo, the police. Jay, if things go badly get everyone away. I'll distract him." I glance at the girls. Pause to regain my focus. "Kat." It's odd calling her that when she doesn't feel like a cat at all. "Can you keep them quiet?" I take another step and shadows engulf me.

She nods and takes Lucy's hand, pulling her away from the scene. Haruka follows them as the air grows silent. The darkness weights on me.

"Good luck!" Jay salutes me with his goofy smile. Kat pulls him away before he alerts the enemy.

Arvo mumbles, but words are lost in the cold, humid air. He looks at me curiously with a singe of disappointment before hiding around the corner.

My feet move on their own, leading to the right side of the alley. I walk on pure instinct. My feet gracefully avoid the water. I won't sell my advantage to this guy. I go past the first dumpster, the one on the left. I pass the second. I trip over a small object. *Clank.* A can bounces to the side. That's the equivalent of a leopard roaring before the hunt.

"Meow," Maureen improvises from the rooftop.

He looks back. I freeze. "Stupid cat! Get out!" He unzips his pants.

I take a good look at his face. He makes the squishy, slimy blobfish look like beauty queen. He's taller than me. It would require a bull to match him, not a frail cheetah. ***I can't win this.*** Not in a straight fight. Speed is useless when his prey is under his grasp. I can't use trickery or venom, and I don't have spikes or armor.

I turn back, and my friends' heads pop around the corners of the wall. They remind me of birds. The killdeer is famous for using auditory and visual distractions to protect their nests. I don't have to lie or pretend I have a broken wing. I have to anger him. What a better way to distract a Mexican than to attack his ego? My voice rips its leash. "No wonder you have to force yourself on a minor. People like you make everything look pretty in contrast." ***This has to be the dumbest thing I've done in a while.*** I'll do whatever it takes to prevent someone else from being subjugated.

He cracks his knuckles and reaches toward his belt. "What did you say?" He points a shimmering triangle shaped object points at my chest.

"I didn't think any vertebrate was naturally deaf." I pause. He frowns. The pause lasts a long time.

She pulls the device from her jeans. Sparks fly from the two proves. She shrugs at me.

I sigh. "I meant you are dumb."

That gives him the push to charge my way. I blink, focusing on the shark's senses. Once my eyes open, my vision fades to darkness. This new feeling, muffled vibrations traveling through leather. Small ripples pulsate from the ugly giant. My back presses against the cold metal container. From it, pulsations, miniature scratches digging through the garbage. My hairs rises. My right arm collides with the alley wall. **Worst time for this sense! I can make it work.** One more vibration comes from the floor. More powerful, earth trembles with it. My eyes widen, my gazelle instincts kick in. I jump to my left, avoiding the impact. My right arm explodes in pain.

Metal collides with a body. The human grunts. *Clink.* An iron shard bounces over the asphalt and water. I take the opportunity to run to the opposite wall. to run to the opposite wall.

I relax. **This time, I'll get the right. I can get my electroreceptors.** Raw onion smelling sweat emanates from my skin. The bitter smell in the air gets more pungent. A rotten scent comes from every corner of the alley. The stale water and the empty containers reek of it. From outside the alley, another type of smell overflows my senses. A musky odor from the five hiding people. Signs of smoke infiltrate my nostrils.

Blood falls. Right ahead there's a splash of water followed by an explosion of the rotten smell. I push me toward the alley's exit. His fists miss me. He stops before hitting the wall. **Smell is not what I need! Give me electroreception.** Halfway to the alley's exit the smells diminish. Small tugs pull in every direction. Keep him focused, so he ignores my friends and the girl. With a twinge of satisfaction, I say, "Finally! Get ready ugly, you are going down."

He roars. My skin feels a pull. The tense muscles send their signals. The path to his right arm lights up. I crouch. His fist flies above me. I take a step closer. Static fills the air around him; it gets stronger closer to him. I might be blind, but the world has never been clearer or slower. Behind me, there are five weak signals. At the end of the alley, sparks fly. The massive surge catches me by surprise. She didn't even need me… I sigh.

Another surge. His hand sweeps right beside my injured arm. I jump back. His body moves closer. He prepares another punch. Before he can act, my right leg begins its course. His fist hits my face. The electrical stimulation overloads my sense. My foot hits the mark, sinking into his center. His body tenses and withdraws into a more stable position. Electricity runs to his center and toward his legs.

My usually dry lips are moist. I can handle a punch or two. *I won't fall. I'm not easy prey.* The electricity stabilizes, no sudden surges in his extremities. I ready my fist and pay back what was given to me. The punch bounces off him. He stays silent. I do too. I hold my weak hand close to me. "Are you made of steel or something?"

His electricity starts flowing faster. His arms electrify. My eyes widen. I back off. In the scramble, I end up on the ground. I sense one last growing spark before my sense shuts down. He looks at me, his face hidden in shadow. I'm dead, but least I helped her. The giant closes up the space between us. I close my eyes and shield my face.

He blabbers. The giant collapses toward on me, but I roll out of the way. Where he stood now stands the girl. She holds a device that flickers with electricity.

"Thank you for the help," I say, as I stand up from the filthy ground.

"I had it handled, but thank you for giving me extra time." She pauses and looks at her phone. "Contact me when you're better. Can you exchange contacts with Theon Untamed?" She glances around before moving into the artificial lights of the city.

I pull out my phone. The moment it's unlocked, the contact info of *Corinna Blackpaint* pops up. I stand there peering into the darkness. **What just happened? And how did she know my name and last name or my phone number?** Her coughs reaching me even when she has turned the corner. **Did she do something to the phone when I wasn't looking? And who did she ask about trading my info?** The wind guides my body out of the alley and my pupils are dazzled by the sudden lights. Her motorcycle purrs, a blue flash crosses my line of sight.

"Theon! You're hurt!" Lucy shouts. The five humans stare at me. That's when it hits me. A tearing pain swallowing my arm. Another scar. I can wear this one proudly. I earned it by helping someone. My cheek numbs and my lip purses.

Keeping his distance, Arvo asks, "How did you know she was there?" He stares at his phone, avoiding my damaged body.

Kat pulls him away shaking her head in the process. In the night sky, her hair looks as black as Roy's or mine. It hides her true colors.

"Theon has a girlfriend!" Jay carries me around.

Haruka shouts, "You're a hero! Is it okay if I write about you in my fanfics?" She stares at me eagerly before Lucy pulls her away. Haruka and Lucy mumble something. *I wish I had my sense of hearing.* Their faces tell a sad story, a worried one.

"I don't! And no!" I reply.

The ride home is the group's recollection of what happened in the alley. All extremely inaccurate. For some reason they think I'm able to fight like a Siberian tiger, when I can barely defend myself as a mouse. Whenever I tried to correct the stories, Kat would glance back and tell me to enjoy it. She would smile, and immediately after I would too.

When I get home, I take out the bandages and wrap my arm. I look in the mirror. Bruised cheek, broken lips, dried river of blood from my nose and mouth, same scar as always, a pair of oryx horns. Normal. Wait, oryx horns. "What!"

"Shut the fuck up!" Roy shouts from next door.

CHAPTER TEN: REDISCOVERING THE EXTINCT

January 7, 2013

As usual Jay and Kat lead the conversations. We sit at our usual spot alone. They followed me to beside the creek, and made it to our spot. Trees and animals surround us. The nearby creek provides a much-needed breeze. The peacock, nightingale, egret, mocking bird and mallard keep an eye on me. After Saturday's disaster, I appreciate their concern and company.

"Thanks for the save!" Haruka shouts. She scribbles in her notebook. It has to be the fanfiction. Even when she's beside me, I'm scared to look at which fantastical way I'm getting hunted.

Jay thumbs up her. "No worries sis." He says it so casually. They are a Labrador puppy and a baby seal, a nice contrast to the rest of us.

I keep my mouth closed. **Whatever, avoid paying attention to me.** Even when I'm wearing a hoodie, sunglasses, two scarves, and per Lucas's request gloves, Arvo's brown eyes have been staring for the last five hours. Lucy has done it too. For resembling mostly, a flying fox and a fawn, they haven't been shy about the hunter's gaze.

Kat sits in the opposite corner beside Arvo. All of her being screams macaw, from her dyed red hair to her small, curved nose resembling a beak, she even has the energy of a vibrant rainbow feathered bird ready to make things better for everyone. Her fingers dance to the rhythm of Arvo's keyboarding.

Arvo's black hair covers one eye, but even so, his gaze intensifies. I'm in his sights. "What happened after the movies?" That cues everyone else to stare at me.

Haruka holds her notebook and pen close to her. More material of my barely functioning life. Jay leans over the table. He stares at me with anticipation. Kat glances at the table, she looks worried.

I shrink. "Nothing happened." The hoodie is a full-grown parasite devouring me from view. My gaze aims at the birds, who have disappeared from view. *If they see me as the animal I am, they will abandon me.*

Arvo's lips part slightly. "We all saw it." His gaze doesn't leave me. His usually emotionless eyes scrutinize my words. I wish I had mastered the art of camouflage. My feet shift, pointing away from the table. What they don't know won't hurt them or me.

Kat moves between Arvo and Jay. One seat closer. Yet, the sniper's aim still follows me. "He saved that girl." She slowly turns toward the others, protecting me from Arvo's gaze. *An opening! I can run! I can walk away. It would end the same way. Alone. Outcast. An animal to their mostly human world.* They would never accept me if they knew what's been happening to me.

Jay climbs up the table. "My hero!" He poses like superman. His smiling face turns toward me, his finger points at the only visible area of my body, my nose. Everyone, except me, moves their lunch away from his feet.

I half turn away. "She didn't need saving. She had it under control." I waver on the words. They may not see my hands, but my nails scratch my palms. They try to dig past the wool gloves.

Haruka tugs Jay's light blue jeans. In an instant, he's back in his seat, right in front of me. Her lips purse. "You did the right thing! You helped her!" Her pen quivers with anticipation, inching closer to the page.

It awaits my move. The situation has shifted. There are three hunters at the table. Two starve and the other avoids the sickly soon to be corpse.

Kat glows a little. "You did great! If you don't want, we don't have to talk about it." She backs away. The air around the table relaxes.

Haruka drops her pen and notebook. Stretch her hands, giving them a required break from tense writing. Lucy perks up. I can still sense her hunting eyes. Jay and Kat act as normal. Arvo keeps observing me. Studying my every move. I hunch, maybe if he sees less of me, he will forget.

"How did you know she was there?" Arvo's voice breaks through the silence. He clears the hair off his face. No more flying fox. He's a vampire bat. His intense gaze, has me on edge. *I wish, I was flying away.* It would be better.

Lucy has shrunk to a small forest shadow. Her presence concealed.

I bet the eagles don't have to face this. They dance dangerously, but never suffer complete oblivion. I squeak, "I saw them." The patch under my eyes, dry and scaly. Scaly? With my free hand, I pull on the hoodie as if it was a second skin. My sunglasses bounce off my hand and drop to the table. Arvo and the world around him are in blue and violet tones. A couple of trees in the distance are red.

"It was pitch black." He raises his weirdly brown and purple eyebrow.

Which bird's eyes did I get? I keep scratching my hands. "She had a phone. I heard them too." My voice becomes higher pitched. If they were a wolf pack, they would not keep asking. Inside the hoodie, a furry feeling tickles my long ears. I pull harder on the hoodie. Cotton strains to the maximum. ***They will see me as a freak. A freak of nature! I can't go back to before. Just stop, Arvo. Please.***

"You heard them, but no one else did?" His voice isn't flat, there are sharp tones like when the felines taught me to hunt.

Haruka scribbles faster. I want to make an effort to look at the others, but I have to hide my face. The bench shakes with their movements. Mostly adding weight to my side.

"That can happen," Lucy adds, her voice is quieter. The longer the conversation goes, the more she shrinks. A stonefish, that's what she has become.

He crosses his arms. "Are you going to tell us you smelled them too." His tone rises.

"Stop." Kat sits on the table, blocking our view of each other. She's more of a bird than a mammal. Defending others as birds defend their nests.

Arvo stands up. "Why? He is hiding something!" He points at me coiled on the opposite end of the table.

Kat remains unmoving. "You're making everyone feel awkward."

Haruka hugs a trembling Lucy. Her notebook and pen on the grass. Lucy has completely turned away from the situation. Her back is to Arvo and Haruka blocks me from her. Jay shrugs, then pats my shoulder.

I lean away. If he touches my head, it's over. I'll have five hunters after me. Under my many layers of clothing, sweat forms and drops down. The subtle scent rises, the stench reminds me of the alley. I pull both scarfs to cover my face. The whiskers on my lips ask me to sneeze. They're almost begging. I contain it for now. Hiding my covered face from everyone. I'm attempting to be stoic, but it feels like I'm a mantis shrimp inching closer to burst a bubble.

Arvo's smell is provocative, it smells like blood, burns through every cell. Worst of all, it triggers something in me. "Look at him! He hides his face."

I flinch and look behind me. No other people getting closer? In the distance, the nightingales and mockingbirds sing together. Once in a while, the peacock boasts. A territorial dispute. People gawk. Cameras shoot for internet fame.

The bench trembles. Haruka intervenes this time. "Does it matter?" Lucy and I are shaking for entirely different reasons.

Arvo raises his voice. It's almost a growl. "Why are you wearing two scarves?"

I rest easy. My gaze turns from side to side. The world is still blue and purple. The smells powerful enough to negate each other's effects. One on the edge of tears, another a starving fox, the last three neutral the petrichor of a rainy day. My voice becomes a mouse's pitch. "To hide the bruise."

He points at my covered arm. "It's just a bruise! You came in with bandages."

"It's big, red and bulgy like a frog's air sac." My throat fills with air. I breath rapidly hoping the new pouch doesn't connect to my vocal cords.

Jay leans closer. "Battle scars are cool! Let me see!" The weight of the table concentrates on my side. Only Kat has restrained herself from leaning closer.

I shake my head. The only thing that could make this worse, would be purple feathers and a tail. Weak claws hold on to the tearing hoodie. My arms swell, not because I became an apex predator but because light decorations work as an enthralling display to females. On my back they expand pushing me up and forward closer to Jay's face. I jump away from the table and run toward the creek. My tennis shoes crash against the moist grass blades.

Kat shouts behind me, "You forgot your bag!"

I don't turn back. I keep on running. My backpack will be fine there. I can't turn back. The creek and its breeze get closer. I'm free, and yet when have animals attempting to use camouflage been faster than their hunters? A faster creature shadows my footsteps. It touches my shoulder. Jay runs beside me with ease. He smiles, and it's not even a run. He jogs casually. I accelerate, sliding out of his reach.

The thickening trees overshadow the clear skies. The slope is mild and yet I find it harder to keep stable. Behind us are the flat school grounds and who people that used to call me their friend. I'm not convinced about friends, but we were a herd. My feet sink in the undergrowth. Birds and mammals all turn my way. They say nothing about my visage. I like to think they see me as normal, when in reality I'm something different.

A pair of light steps follow behind. One of them stomps the mud harder than before. What feels like a pouncing tiger hits me from behind, taking me under his claws. My assailant and I roll down the hill. My pants are the first to succumb to nature, revealing the purple feathers. A couple of them float above us, thrashed by the game, by my indistinguishable fight for self-preservation. My scarf unravels, revealing the scarlet air sac. As much as I want to hate Jay, I can't allow him to get hurt. I'm his shield against the rocks, roots, and cold, hard dirt. Roots slam into my back. Branches slap my legs. Mud invades my hoodie and leaves my hair heavier.

I take the hit against the rocks in the creek. I'm bruised, but I can still make it. Except, I can't. The cotton strands of my clothing absorb the frigid water. It cleanses my hair at the cost of displacing my hoodie. Two massive golden fennec fox ears pop from my head. I look up and there is Jay. Staring at me. Holding my arms from flailing. Using his strength to keep me here. **He has to be judging me.** The moment they all waited for. My downfall. I feel so stupid. Me having something nice has to be the greatest prank life has pulled on me. I'm a nobody and life will never favor me. Tears well in my eyes. They unite with the water below me.

Jay's smile disappears. He's on his knees. For a brief second, he glances at his hands and lets go, raising them up in the sky. Before he says a word, I scurry back, covering my face. My drenched feathers. My ears. I quiver in place as Jay tries to reach for me. He hesitates, as he looks at my teary eyes.

A lighter pair of footsteps splashes beside me. Hands touch my back. "Theon, are you okay?" I shake my head in response, still scared that my air sac will be more than decoration. Kat sits next to me. She leans in closer. "It's going to be okay." She slowly pats my back. My heartbeat slows in response. I tremble from cold, not fear. I don't get how she does it. **How can she make human emotions feel so easy?** They are too complicated, too erratic. Yet they feel the same way animals feel them.

Jay takes this as a sign to jump in. "Woah! Bro, you are so cool! You gotta teach me that trick." He leans in, head-locking me and messing up my muddied hair. He laughs. That smile of his returns as if it had never left.

I open my mouth. The mass of air is still in my throat. "I'm not sure how to." The air deflates fast. Not so smooth skin, but no bulge. Five fingers per hand? No purple feathers? I turn around and my body absorbs the tail. I touch my ears they feel normal. "I'm back."

"You never left." Jay says. Kat and he have those warm, short smiles that can make you feel fine.

Kat's smile is magical. So much peace and tranquility. **Why was I worried? They aren't hunters.** Jay, on the other hand, makes my heart race and flutter. Much like the girl on the blue bike, being too close feels like a cat bit my tongue off.

I look at the edge of the woods, Haruka stands there. She glances at her notebook, scribbles something and shrugs. I grimace. She replies with a finger on her lips and a nod. She turns and heads away. I wish I could say the same about Arvo. He became monochrome like an artic hare in winter, losing the deepness of the brown it used to have. He stares at me. Eyes unfocused. His mouth moves but never loud enough for someone to hear.

"Can you keep it a secret?" I mutter, still hugging my knees.

Jay nods aggressively. "Keep what?"

Kat nods with him. "Don't worry, they will too. I pinky promise."

I push him out of my radius and giggle a bit. "Thanks."

"One question," Jay adds.

"What is it?"

Jay sits in front of me. He leans in, not respecting my personal space. I avoid his eyes and push a bit back. His hazel eyes keep track of me. They shine just like his smile. "Tell us! Radioactive waste? Magic? Genetically modified lizard? Alien technology? Alien? And can I get it too?"

My shoulders relax. "None. I don't really know." I look down, not because I'm embarrassed. The emotion is close enough though, as Jay leans closer and closer with each of my words.

CHAPTER ELEVEN: MUDSKIPPER

My phone vibrates. Jay's relentless attempts to get me to teach him debilitate me. Not as much as Haruka's attempts to get me to cooperate in her fan fiction. I shiver at the thought of it. Kat sends me another music album, soothing and calming. Lucy and Arvo have been absent. I can't blame them, but my brain will never stop swirling on the possibility that they'll sell me out.

The door slowly opens. Lucas walks at the tempo of the racetrack noise coming from Roy's video game. He stops bopping his head and twists it to the side. He stares at me. The rest of his body keeps moving in sync. "Are you okay?" He places a food tray on my bed.

"I'm… fine." I throw my phone under the sheets, pretending it isn't causing misery. Lucy and Arvo must hate me. I throw myself onto my pillows. I have to hide my face from him, or he will tell me…

Lucas taps my bed, then my arm. "You're lying." No whimsy. His warm hand rests on my arm. "What happened?"

I raise my head to not muffle my voice. "My friends figured things out. They saw purple feathers." I resist the urge to pile more pillows on my head by grunting. I feel like an ostrich, too heavy to fly with the other birds. "They hate me!"

Lucas pats my head in a calm, slow rhythm. At least getting treated like a puppy is nice. My ears shift and fold.

"Pretty! The horns last week were scary." One of his hands spirals from his head upward.

I shift my body to face him. "Maybe…" The phone calls me. I know I have to reply someday. It won't find me, not in this state.

Lucas takes the phone and smiles almost as big as Jay's. "See!" He does a tiny hop. In a few clicks, he plays Kat's recommended album. As the music flows so does he.

"What?" I cock my head as I figure out the words.

He hums. "They still like you." He turns the phone. Kat has sent another play list, this one named jungle life and the picture of a macaw. Haruka's message is unnerving. She asks about the details of how it feels and how do I feel. And if I could use my tongue like a chameleon's. To which my answer would be, maybe. Lastly, Jay again asks to hang out. Out of the three, he is the weirdest.

I cover the screen with my bare hands. "They are pretending."

"They're nice." He scrolls up, looking at past conversations. He smiles, has to be the one with Jay.

I sigh. Turn to the gray outside. "They're human. It's in their nature." The flora outside as green as ever, greener than any summer would let it be.

He does a small pause, arrhythmical to the video game's music. "I'm human too." He returns to rhythm. "What about me?"

"It's different." I slouch. I know he makes sense. ***Why would it be different? They could have left me alone. What about the long game? They could play it. And if they are, would I survive a next one? But they could also...*** "Ahhh! I don't know what to think."

Lucas sits beside me. "They're your friends. Trust them!" His legs swing to the drums. He looks up at the fan. For the next minute he opens his mouth, but sound never comes out. Until it does. "Did it hurt saying the truth?" His Amazonian brown eyes stare at me. They remind me of a sugar glider's. They are bittersweet in a way I can't explain. Maybe I'm reading too much into them.

A couple of my chilaquiles make their way into my mouth. At this point, they're soggy. The tortilla chips have been soaked in salsa for a few minutes, but they are food my body has been begging for since the morning. I shrug. "It did, but..." I pause. My phone vibrates again. Lucas might be right. They might be looking out for me. "Maybe it was worth it."

He twiddles his thumbs at the same speed as the words coming out of his mouth. "But it hurt you." He looks down. One of his legs moves faster than the other.

"It did." I place the fork back on the tray. The soothing music lowers my heart rate. My breaths are deeper and slower. On cue, my phone rings again. Jay. Never giving up on transformation lessons. If only I knew how to control them. "Why do you ask?"

"Because…" He mutters under his breath, going completely silent.

I hide my phone back under the pillows and pat beside me. "You can tell me anything." *I can repay the favor. So far, the one acting mature has been the five-year-old. I should be doing more for him. The last thing I want if for my little brother to suffer as much as I have.*

He takes a moment. "Do you think I can stop lying?" Lucas looks up at me. His eyes do the puppy look, the one he uses to get what he wants. This is the first time it feels like they beg me to give him answers he doesn't want to hear.

I look out the window. A small nightingale sits on my windowsill. Birds have wings to fly, fish have fins to swim, and my brother has his truth, and that's his to use if he wants to. "If that's what you want. Yes." I glance at him. He doesn't do it back. I take a scoop of chilaquiles and consume it.

He lets out a deep, smooth sigh. It almost fits the tone of Kat's songs. He takes his knees and does a bad impression of an armadillo. A blue mockingbird's wings aren't meant to pretend to be shields. They are meant to spread different songs. "I want to. But people will get mad at me."

"It's your life, not theirs." I keep staring outside. Different bird species fly past the window Passeriformes, pigeons, woodpeckers, magpies, and hummingbirds. They all rest in the trees of the backyard. None of them say anything, but I know they are waiting for something.

He hesitates. "What if they don't like me? What if Mom and Dad get mad at me?" He doesn't break form. Lucas and I aren't so different after all. He struggles with what others think of him too.

The birds outside talk among themselves mostly ignoring us. "Does that matter? Will you do something bad?" *Look at me giving advice, and struggling with my own choices. What do I want? What will I be? Who will I become? I'm in high school. I should have the answers soon. But I don't. I love animals, but I'm no scientist. How can I tell my brother to do something so hard when he is barely five?*

He shakes his head. Those brown Amazonian eyes meet mine. "No! Music." They sparkle. I have never seen his eyes shine toward lively green before.

"If it makes you happy." I eat from my dish. Ugh, soggy.

He smiles. A smile so big it might match Jay's. "I like music. I like songs." My brother leaves the bed. He hops and taps his fingers to Kat's playlist. "I don't like Roy's music." He turns to me, frowning. "I like hers."

"Then be who you want to be." I can't match his smile. Mine is forced. *Did I do the right thing? What if this hurts him? What if they treat him like me? It would be my fault. My fault alone.*

He hugs me. "Thank you!" He elongates the phrase, giving a smooth, high melody. "Don't tell Mom and Dad. Please…"

Now they'll have a reason to treat me as they have. It all fits into place. "They will never know."

He whistles, flowing with the music from my phone. He so perfectly synchronizes with it. A lyrebird singing a tune that wasn't made for it, but doing it perfectly. Lucas moves his body to the rhythm. It's not a dance, but he bounces slowly and lightly. The music is mild, never going too high or too low.

Blop The sound's on repeat. Lucas leads the sound with a hop. The humid sound adds nicely to the song. The sound continues through the musical experience my brother is taking me on. It never comes from the phone. In fact, it comes from my nightstand. The glass of water shakes. It amplifies the noise. I glimpse the jumping droplets in the middle. Ripples and waves that chase after the rhythm.

I turn toward Lucas. The air around him shimmers. ***Should I tell him? No, it would ruin the moment. What if he's doing this by accident? Then it's my fault if he gets discovered by anyone. What do I do?*** I stare at him, then back at the water. "Are you doing this?" I point to my cup.

He stops and tilts his head. I show him the still water. "Doing what?"

"The water was moving while you whistled."

"Let me see!" He whistles, eyes open. Entranced on the subject of study. As soon as he goes high and low, water waves in the same motion. He stops and the water stills. "Can I do that to a river?"

"Don't try."

"Okay." His little hands swipe a dessert, the last of the brownies. He turns around. His hand slams into his face.

"Did you take my last brownie?" I grab his shoulder.

He turns around. Lips covered in chocolate. "No," he mumbles, showing dark brown teeth.

I take a sip at my water. As it touches my tongue, an acrid taste invades my senses. My stomach revolts. I spit the sewer tasting water in the cup. I take a look at my glass. Murky petrol sticks to the sides. I poke at it, the substance glues to my finger. It creates a web like bridge between my finger and the cup.

"Did you do this?" I pause and stare at the chocolate. I fake swipe at my face to let Lucas know how to clean his.

He sticks his tongue out. "No." He shakes his head. "I won't lie anymore. I promise." He keeps munching. "Sorry about the brownie." He cleans his lips.

The black ooze dissolves, revealing clear water. I place the cup on the night stand and push it away. My stomach churns when I look at it. Nothing to think about other than throwing the water out. The smell has already invaded my nostrils. Food looks unappetizing.

Lucas walks out. His eyes and body shinning more than usual. He returns to my room and sings. The water rains upon me. The small storm cloud has an infinite supply. Outside rain pours. The gray sky has turned dark. Once Lucas stops whistling, the sky clears, and my bed stays wet.

CHAPTER TWELVE: JAYSON AND THE FAUNAUTS

January 12, 2013

Jay parks in front of my house.

This day can't get any worse.

"Theon! Get the fuck out!" Roy shouts.

I cover the brightly colored feathers on my head with a gray hoodie. The feathers fold under the cotton encasing me. I hide my phone in my pocket and leave the house. "What are you doing here?" I keep my distance from the golden oriole car, which matches the color of my feathers. If I show them, he'll make a fuss about it. I stand awkwardly under the thirty-degree sunlit walkway. Sweat pours out of my pores.

He leans toward the copilot seat and waves at me. "Come over! We're going out!" He has that goofy smile. That Labrador smile. It bothers me, no one can be that happy.

"I can't." I point to my head without releasing my grip on the hoodie. I hide my eyes under the shadow of the hoodie. He waves, calling me closer. I'm stuck to the ground. He insists and I trust him. "What is it?" I lean on the door. Big mistake. He pulls me inside the car. The hoodie makes space for the line of yellow feathers to rise. One of them hangs between my eyes.

Jay grins. He steps on the accelerator. The motor runs. My legs occupy the seats headrest. My head hangs from the seat. I glare at my so-called friend. He keeps his smile. "You dyed your hair? And you didn't invite me? You gotta tell me next time. How would my hair look in green?" He tilts his head, signaling me to join him.

Green? What? When both my head and feet are on the designated area, I reply, "It's a yellow crested cockatoo feather." With a simple move, the feather is hidden under the hoodie. I cross my arms and turn away from him. I'm not even staring outside. I'm only looking to avoid him. Him and his goofy smile that says everything is fine, but it isn't.

His brown eyes, with eyelashes everyone at school envies, seek me. They veer away from the road. With his free hand, he pokes me. "We'll have fun! I promise." His gaze never abandons me.

For a couple minutes, I can't look at him. I can't be angry at him. I take a deep breath, then look at my feet.

After a while without sound, he stops. I look out. T green leafy ceiling opens up to the blue sky. A thin waterfall creates a small pond and a small creek that seeps deeper into the woods. A cool breeze invites me to take off my hoodie. Smooth gray pebbles bar the trees from entering the clear space.

Jay leaves the car. He slides over the hood, landing on my side. He opens the door. Still smiling because nothing gets him down. I glance around. Animals and plants. The scent of water and Jay. No figures following in the dark.

Jay pats me on the back, "Relax! We're alone."

The animals talking and Jay's smile help me relax. My shoulders drop. I take off my hoodie.

"Cool! Teach me how to get a mohawk. I've been thinking about a thin spiky mohawk."

I stare at his stubby hair. No way. My feathery mohawk rises. The front feather flops between my eyes. Pristine wilderness, absent of metallic grays. And although far away, cars scream for attention, but the waterfall and the creatures of the forest muffle those sounds. The yellow feather shrinks. My hand passes through hopefully black hair. "Why?" I mutter.

"Why what?" He pulls me closer.

"Why me? You could have asked Arvo, Haruka, or Kat. Or anyone in school. You're popular." I turn my back to him. I'd rather see the green forest. **Doesn't he get that being seen with me might get him in trouble? What if I lose control?** He actively puts his life in danger for me. **I'm not worth it.** He wouldn't lose anything by staying away from me.

He grips my wrist, pulling me closer to the pond. "'Cause you're fun!" He smiles at me. His eyes don't look fully happy. He doesn't believe what he's saying. He pities me. His scent dampens. I don't know how to describe this smell. The closest thing is those candles they use at church. They smell fine, but there is something somber. Something that makes me feel more tired, even bleak.

"That isn't true. Don't lie, Jay." I resist his pull, but I'm a chihuahua pleading with the German shepherd to stop. I dig my heels into the rocky surface. "I can smell it." My arm slips through his grip.

"What's cooler than my best friend transforming into animals, talking to animals, smelling how people feel?" He shrugs my doubts away as easily as the air shrugs pollen off a pine tree.

How and when did I become his best friend? I don't deserve that honor. I'm a disappointment as a friend and as a human being. Even as an animal, I fail. "I don't get it." My opossum instincts kick in. My paralyzed body stands statically.

He turns with his usual smile. Naturally casual and happy. "What? You're cool."

I wriggle free of his hold. "I'm not. Without those things, I'm not worth it. Everyone knows it…" I glance down. My shoulders hunch, feeling slightly heavier. Dragging my weight down.

"Bro! Who else could destroy us when playing video games? Or teach us what kind of rare bird flies around?" He chuckles. "No one else could keep up with me. You can. You're never tired. Always up for some fun!"

I stumble over rebuttals. He takes the opportunity, and picks me up. I struggle, but no matter what I do, he doesn't budge. Water splashes under him.

"Jay don't!"

He keeps walking effortlessly with me in tow. On the edge of the water, he stands. On the edge of the water, he continues to stand as I'm flung through the air. The cold water is a nice change from the heat. **Wait, my phone!** I rush out toward the surface. "My phone!"

"You left it in the car." He shrugs. He extends his hand to help me up.

I take his offer. Instead of getting out of the water, I attempt to drag him with me. Given that my mind is barely telling my body to pull him, he holds out, no bothered by the nuisance I am. My grip softens. "Ahh! Ahh!" He stumbles above me. We both submerge.

As soon as I take a gasp of air, he splashes water on me. He has his goofy smile. His hair barely looks wet. The swimming team forces them to keep it short. I splash him back. For a while we keep at it. My stomach grumbles. "Let's get out." He splashes me once more as I step out.

He helps me out of the water. "Before we get food show me how to become a dino. Are you bready for this?" He superhero poses, blocking my escape from the water.

I turn back. "I don't know how." I hide my hands in the damp pockets of my jeans.

He shakes me. "Just do it!" With his free hand, he messes up my hair.

I push him away. "What if I hurt you? What if I lose control?" I sit at the edge of the pond, pretending to be a curled armadillo.

He places his hand on my back. "I know you won't. You'd never do something like that." He punches my shoulder with less force than the wind and makes me topple. He keeps the smile, it's filled with warmth and honesty, before once again helping me up. It's like he's always helping me, and I can't do anything for him.

I slowly remove my swamped clothing and pass it to Jay, so it doesn't get ruined when I change. If I change. He pretends to throw money at me. He whistles. I cover what I assume is my pink face. I take glimpses of him. Jay takes his shirt off. I stare, more than I should, then shake my head and return to my situation. "Stand far away."

Jay takes a step back. I keep signaling him to do so until he's beside the car. He lays the clothing on the hood. ***I'm naked in front of my friend! What am I doing?*** "Gray Wolf." I stare at my hands. No claws, no fur, not even feathers or scales. I repeat it five more times. With each repetition my voice becomes more agitated. A fawn cry. I stare down. "I can't do it."

He slumps on his car. "Relax." His arm motions a wave in the sea.

I inhale and let it go, then look at my friend. He gives me a thumbs up. It doesn't help me feel safer, but it does give me the push I need. I thumb up him too.

Focus on the animal. It's the same as the senses. You can do it. You'll have gray fur and a snout. Jay gets shorter. I look at my gray hands. Thick skin covers me. I feel heavy. Rough. His silhouette becomes blurry. He becomes a grainy figure. ***Where is everything?*** A click ruptures the air. My body shakes.

"That's so cool!"

I shake my head and snort. Walking backward, I hit the water. I snort and gurgle. Deep bellows surge from my bigger frame. I stare at the blurry figures. ***No! It's only Jay.*** Jay and his car. His sea salt scent keeps me on track. I feel like running away and hiding. For an animal this big, the world looks so scary and fuzzed out. I get why they would run over anything. I snort.

My body shifts. Jay grows taller. There are more colors in the world, similar to what birds showed me, but even more. The world is a luminous rainbow it shines. The yellow car looks vibrant, a polished emerald with tones of orange and blue. My stance is lighter and upright. I flap my arms. They reveal feathered wings. I skip and flap wildly. My claws bounce from pebble to pebble. Jay runs up to me. My body reacts by flailing its lighter frame. He slows down, stopping before getting closer. He places his hand in front of me. I climb his arm. A couple of feathers float on the water. Jay stands easily, as if my presence wasn't there. He turns and tickles my neck. I rub my beak against his neck. He doesn't use force and is gentle with my delicate body.

"It isn't bad." He smiles and pats my head.

It's not so bad. I squawk. ***Maybe there is a bit of hope for me.***

His phone flashes. On the screen, a pretty bird with a long beak.

Jay stumbles. He stares at my body. It's heavier. Sluggish. I can't feel my arms or legs. He tilts his body. I slide back to the ground. Before, Jay was tall. Now he's a giant. His scent is more detailed. Sea salt with sugar. My neck retracts along with my long body.

"Bro, it's okay. I won't hurt you." He takes a step back. As he does, he takes a picture.

My muscles relax, breaking the *S* shape my body had taken. I coil, waiting to return to my form. Everything is so high and far away. ***What would happen if someone stepped on me?*** I can't run away. I get why snakes feel like they have to attack. They don't have many options.

The air gets heavy. It's too thin. My body grows. ***No! Don't!*** I flap on the ground. I get to Jay's knee size. I wrangle the air. The lack of oxygen is killing me. I see him clearly. His movements and his phone pull and tug at my skin. Sparks like the ones in the alley. My insides burn. My head beats as if a car were constantly ramming into it. My tail splashes the water erratically. My gray fins move as I struggle against an invisible foe.

Jay runs past me. He splashes water on my side. A bit of oxygen. He does it again. "Theon, calm down." He places his hand on my gills.

I keep struggling. More liquid drops inside my gills. I calm down. Sunlight bounces off him, creating a crown of light. My body stops thrashing. I can't breathe, but I'm at peace.

Air! Sweet relief. *Am I returning to normal?* My size beats Jay. He goes back to his car. I grow taller than some of the trees. "No!" I say as my body shifts. Green scales and razor-sharp claws hang from my forearms. A mall tail and a giant sail deform my body. I step under the waterfall. This feels more like home. Water washes over my body.

"You are so cool!" Jay shouts, as he takes multiple pictures.

I walk his way. My claws covering my jaws. The trees become taller. Jay is his normal size, a bit taller than me, as always.

"Did I do that?" I point at his bleeding hands.

"Just a scratch." He smiles, then shows me his phone. "Check the pics!" He keeps smiling even thought his hands and phone are tainted red.

"Do you have bandages?" My breakfast wants to escape my body. I gulp, keeping it where it should be.

"Yeah. Chill." His voice remains calm, calmer than the wind right now.

Is he trying to keep me from panicking? No, he's keeping me from randomly shifting. Another creature could be the death of him. I would be to blame. I avoid looking at him and struggle to keep upright. I sway from left to right. Taking a couple of steps to each side. Until I reach the hood of the car with my drying clothes. I put on my pants and underwear. I pass Jay and get his gym bag.

"Bro, you, okay?"

"I'm fine… Let's fix your hands." I move past him. My legs give in. Jay catches me. I can't look at him. "I'm a failure. You are injured because of me, and I still need your help. It should be the other way around."

"It was an accident." He pats my back, pushing me close to the water's edge.

We take a seat. I open the gym bag. Instead of gym clothing, there are desserts, food, drinks and a first aid kit. My jaw unclenches. "You brought all of these?" I take a moment. "Will they taste like sweat?"

"Swimmers don't sweat." He smiles. "You ain't seen nothing sweat." He takes a moment before talking once more. "Lucy made the food. Haruka brought a first aid kit. Kat added a playlist. She said you liked it." He leans back, showing that camaraderie through his eyes.

My throat lets go of the toucan croak. I take the alcohol and bandages. "Want to hold on to something?" I ask as I take his bloody hands and the alcohol.

"I can handle a little bit of alcohol." He does as Jay does.

"What did this to you?" I pour the alcohol.

"A Sharrrrk!" He shrieks as the alcohol touches his skin. I stop pouring. "You couldn't breathe. I had to help you." I wrap his hands in bandages too light for his skin. I narrow my focus to cover the wound without leaving gaps.

A shark. I hug him. "I appreciate it, but never touch a shark. Their scales are like sharp sandpaper." He tries to take stuff from the bag, but I don't let him. I place the picnic blanket, get the food out, plates and even spare shirts for both of us. He thought of everything. **He knew I was gonna mess up.** I turn to him. "You could hang with anyone you wanted. Yet you choose to be stuck with me. Look at me. What a friend I am, always—"

"Making life more interesting. Normal is boring. You are and always will be the coolest guy at school." He interrupts me, then punches my shoulder. This time I'm ready. Jay can't help it, he grins. I smile back. It feels so alien, so unnatural, but then I look at the peaceful and colorful scenery. At the guy in front of me.

He and I know that isn't true. I'm not cool. I'm an outsider. I'm an animal stuck in the human world. It's a matter of time before he realizes it. For just one second, I allow my mind to go to the best parts of the day. Then my gaze land on footprints and black feathers left behind. I waver. "You have pictures?"

He sits beside me, and shows me the first picture. "You went big. How did it feel? Would you give me a ride? Could you chase me as if it was JP? It would be dope. One more thing off the bucket list."

I scoot closer to him. "A white rhinoceros. For an animal that large, the world is filled with anxiety. Everything looks blurry. I knew you were there, but I couldn't really see you. I can't imagine living all the time, not being able to see far or well. You can have other senses, but it isn't the same."

"For real? Next time show me how it looks!" He jumps a bit in place. "Next one is easy. A toucan." He jumps the gun before I get to say anything. He radiates a contagious joy.

"Not any toucan. It's a keel billed toucan, also known as a rainbow-billed toucan and sulfur-breasted toucan. Very colorful and social creatures. Thank you for handling with care." I turn to him, not bothered by the closeness. Not anymore.

He hugs me. "No problem! That goes for the toucan you and the you you." He swipes to the next picture. "What is that snake?"

I freeze. That's bad. It's a brownish snake. I act without thinking, searching his ankles and legs, for two small red dots. "Did it bite you?"

"No." He places his hand on my shoulder. It gently brings me back up, and his jeans down.

I lighten up, "Good. That's the inland taipan. The world's most venomous snake. One bite can kill a hundred men. You'd have forty-five minutes. I wouldn't be able to get you to a hospital that has an anti-venom." I shake at the thought and grab his arm.

"You didn't." He keeps his warm smile. He swipes once more revealing a tiger shark. "You know that shark?"

"A tiger shark named for the stripes on its back." I point at the slightly darker lines on its back. "Fun fact, tiger sharks are also known for eating stuff like metal. They have found medieval helmets and cans, among other objects, in their stomachs."

He nods. Follows every word I say. His eyes sparkle with some intriguing passion. As if he was always this passionate about what I like. "What do you know about this one? It was big and cool and colorful." He shows me the picture of a dinosaur. It has a crocodile-like head. A tail that mimics sea snakes. And a sail with different colors. Emerald green, sapphire blue and scarlet red. It feels like an ancient peacock. *I wonder would they be as arrogant as peacocks?*

"I think that's a Spinosaurus. Based on the look, I'd say they were piscivores. And if we can base it on birds, then I'd say that's a male. Vibrant colors to attract a female." I take a sip of water. He swipes again and the sail goes from mainly red to blue. "Blood regulated, that could change our knowledge of dinosaurs as we know it!"

"Bro, you can be any creature. You could be immortal as a roach. Or as strong as an elephant! You could even be a pet and live the life, the good life!" He shakes me around.

"I haven't transformed into any amphibians, but I can speak with them. I can't understand insects or any invertebrate. I think those are out of my reach." He tries taking my sandwich.

I swipe it from his reach, faster than I've ever done before and I munch on it.

"Teach me!" He shakes me more. "What cool stuff could you do with your superpower?"

I gulp and stare up at the sky. "Fly, breath underwater, have bones that could endure bullets, see in the dark, electrocute others, regenerate, be more specific."

"The fastest, strongest, all the bests! Everything! I want to know every single animal you can tell me about! So, I can figure out how to become one!"

"With a diving speed of three-hundred and eighty-nine kilometers per hour, the fastest animal registered to date is the peregrine falcon. My strongest creature has to be the Dreadnoughtus. It could easily destroy small building by accident, but if we're talking about a predator then the Tyrannosaurus Rex or the Giganotosaurus. Most venomous, you've seen it. Most poisonous I'd give to the golden poison frog. It can kill a man in ten minutes and has no cure." Jay follows my words as if I was an albatross leading a flight.

Even without the photos, he sits close. "You're helping me study for bio."

"Was already going to do it." I punch him back. "Thanks Jay, you're a great friend." My smile forces my eyes to squint.

"The greatestestest!" He sticks out his tongue. For the first time since I know him, I push him. I play along with his jokes. For the first time in a long time, I feel alive. I feel like I am fine. And it's all thanks to him.

CHAPTER THIRTEEN: THE ONE IN THE SWARM

January 13, 2013

A week has passed since Jay and the others saw me transform. Lucas has had fewer incidents with water turning black. Not sure if he's constantly lying or if he's telling the truth all the time. I hope for the latter. I want him to do what he wants. The news and internet have reported sightings of bigfoot. Since that moment, I changed my training location. The accidental transformation into a Gigantopithecus instead of a Komodo dragon did bring too much attention. Although in retrospective, switching into a black bear would have been better. But now people have started to hunt a mythical creature.

Roy sits in front of the couch his loud forgotten. His vibrant intensity dimmed. Music fills the void left by Roy's routine. The screen flashes on his face and his fingers click on the controller. A lack of action compels me to look. No headset, no mic, and no other players. Roy's character is alone in the midst of opponents. "Weird," I mutter.

"All your fucking fault." He scoffs, not taking his eyes off the screen. Then his character dies.

"What? Why?" Avoid him. His face is filled with disgust as he covers his ears. As Roy pumps up the music, Lucas shakes his head more violently.

Lucas sticks his tongue out and points at the insides of his mouth.

Roy shoves a controller at my chest. "They all went to look for bigfoot!"

"You know I was practicing so I can control over it." I signal Lucas to come over. He sighs. Roy, the lion prince, allows me to take a seat beside him.

Lucas peeks. "Did you tell them not to search?"

"Yeah, but they're idiots! Whatever!" He passes a controller to Lucas, who looks uncomfortable and attempting to cover his ears. Lucas places the controller aside. As he passes me, there's a trail of chill air left behind.

Roy starts the game. He is a honey badger calling for everyone's attention. Bullets rain all around him. I hate these games. I unequip my character's guns. One knife, that's all I need. I imitate the leopards and go into the shadows. Lucas ignores the game. He picks up Roy's phone and turns the music off.

Roy's freckled face wrinkles. "That was a recommendation from my friends!" He pulls his long, wild hair backward.

Lucas shakes his head, humming a slower calmer tune. "It's bad." There's a cold tone in his voice. His hands leave his ears and grab a controller. He clicks twice and randomly throws a dancing grenade in the middle of a group. He keeps doing that.

He giggles as he keeps everyone stuck in an endless dancing frenzy.

I take my knife and kill everyone dancing while they're distracted. I'm cold, emotionless, closer to a crocodile than a human. "They have terrible taste." My eyes don't leave the screen.

"Yeah, I fucking know. They have a shit taste. Idiots…" He smashes his buttons faster. "But I have to like it." He lingers, then refocuses on the game fight.

I shrug. "You don't have to follow them."

"You don't get it." His voice rougher, sharper.

"There's a difference between blindly following and being friends." I purse my lips.

"Fucking ending up like you? Not a chance."

My character stops moving. "It's my last level." I sigh. It stings, but it's true. My tension is released when Lucas changes to the calmer smooth melody from Kat's album.

Lucas stops laughing. He glances around. "That was mean."

"Pussy, I didn't mean it that way."

"It's alright." My eyes focus on the screen.

Lucas's gaze pierces me; the chill in the air has returned. He knows I'm lying. So much for the leopard. It was as obvious as the kookaburra's laughs.

"Anyway, you guys got it fucking easy." He throws his hands up. As the top scores in kill participation are Lucas and me.

I roll my eyes harder than a barreleye fish. "Yes, I was beaten, bruised, bullied, publicly humiliated, and attacked. Easy." I emphasize on the last word and leave the controller on the table.

"Being Dad's favorite sounds hard." Lucas giggles. His controller slips but lands uneventfully on the couch.

Roy shakes his head. He avoids looking at us directly. "No, your fucking abilities. Easy as fuck to get." There goes the attitude Yash, the peacock, gave me. If he only knew he had competition.

"If they are that easy, why don't you have one?" Lucas asks innocently, not noticing that his question feels more like a sea urchin's spike than a swan's feather.

"'Cause mine is hard." Another excuse from the prince. Expected.

"Ease is relative. They were hard to obtain for us too." I stand and head to the stairs.

Roy grunts. "Fucking excuses. Fucking smart-ass."

I put my hand on Lucas's head and mess up his hair. He smiles and laughs.

"Look. I'm not sure how we got them, but we did. Given the odds, you'll get them too. This isn't a competition, Roy. It doesn't matter when you get them."

"It's bull." He occupies the whole sofa. Making it impossible for us to claim his throne, not that we wanted to.

Lucas raises his arms, asking me to carry him. Under normal circumstances, I wouldn't be able, but since November I feel stronger and lift him with ease. He returns me the favor of messing my hair. I smile. Since last week, he has been cheerier. I can't feel anything less than happiness for him.

"Why is it that important? It's not like you would want our abilities." I shrug before tickling Lucas.

"'Cause that's awesome!" He doesn't look at us. Once a lion, he seems more like the black sheep painted white.

Lucas flails in my arms under the tickle wars. He does what a baby chimp would do to an older one. He tries his best to beat them in their own game, but ends up laughing more than he tickles. I tilt my head as I glance at Roy. I guess even a lion can doubt. **I won't leave him behind. I helped Lucas. I can help him. I can.** "You are telling us. Roy Untamed isn't awesome?"

Roy's brow arcs upward. "Which moron said I wasn't? I'm Roy fucking Untamed. I'm fucking awesome." Lucas and I share a smile toward our brother. "The fuck you looking at?"

I drop Lucas to the ground. He points at the prince. "You! Silly!" He jumps around, picks his stuff up and makes a run toward my room. That child is like a flea, but larger. And I can't be mad at him.

"Nothing." I shrug. "Glad to see you in a good mood. Anyway, I'll head out to the woods." I wave at both.

"Can I use your room?" Lucas yells from my room.

I make my way down the stairs. Out to where I've always belonged, the wilderness. "Yes."

"Thank you!"

CHAPTER FOURTEEN: HIVE MIND

Once again, I find myself under the canopies of the evergreen mountains in Monterrey. The sun blazes above, threatening heat during the winter. Brown sheds of the mild winter weather decorate the floor. It crunches where soil should be. From time to time, large roots or the rocky face of the mountain pop out of the leafy carpet. The animals promised no one would be looking for bigfoot in this area. So far, it has been true. I'm the only human. Animal life has also been scarce. Hibernation and migration have cut populations by more than by half. Few species roam about, but one of them my instructor.

The owl looks around. "Rumor says you are promising. Let's get this new trick under control. Name's Cal," the great horned owl says. Wise and methodical, every word had its purpose.

"Hi. I'm Theon. It's nice to meet you." I wave at him as I place my backpack on the roots of the tree.

He lightly waves the tip of his left wing. "Take off your clothing and start."

I glance awkwardly at my surroundings. As I take off my shirt, I ask, "Am I normal?" My nails dig into my palm. Once the shirt leaves my hands, my fingers relax. The backpack devours the first piece.

The owl tilts his head. He takes one moment to reply, "More normal than you think."

I untie my boots. "How am I normal? I grow horns, feathers, and gills. I understand animals. My brother makes it rain!" I'm tired of the non-answers. My voice grows raspier. I bite my lips, keeping myself under control. My boots act as containers for my socks, which smell as bad as my armpits.

Cal flutters to a lower branch. As all birds, he does it elegantly and gracefully, but uniquely silently as owls do. "I can't tell you much, but this is the norm." He turns his head almost a hundred and eighty degrees, observing for other creatures. "It's been quite some time since anyone has gotten this far. Much less two under the same roof."

I take off the rest of my clothing, dumping it in the backpack. I have to trust Cal on this. "One last question. If it's normal why isn't there more of us?"

Cal lands in front of me. His wooden colors make him nearly invisible while on the forest floor. "Because your kind is hunted. Humans are so fearful of what you can do, they are blind to the fact that everyone has this potential." He glances at my eyes. I want to ask another question, but he raises his left wing. "Before you ask how to tap that potential, know that each human has a unique ability." Cal flies back to the upper branches. He stares at me in expectation.

The bitter wind pretends to be from the tundra. "Thank you for answering. So, what do I do?" I shake and tremble. My lack of fat is proving a disadvantage today.

Cal turns to survey the area. He stares at the forest and at me with his big yellow eyes. "Transform into a gray wolf."

I gulp, remembering what happened with Jay. I ended up as a white rhinoceros. This is not what I expected to do today. Not much I can do except for to disappoint him with my lack of control. "I'll try."

He glares.

I gulp again. "Okay, okay. I'll do it." I close my eyes. "Gray Wolf." My body shifts and shrinks. My weight is lighter than it should. Small feathers extend from my arms.

"A woodpecker. It starts with a *W*. It's a start." The owl looks at me with hungry eyes. He keeps to the branches, waiting for me to do something.

I chirp, repeating the same words in my head. **Gray Wolf.** I'm heavier, much heavier. The cool breeze becomes as hot as summer. Hooves rasp against the roots beneath. "Beeehhh" My lower jaw moves in a circular manner, even though there is nothing in my mouth.

Cal glides to my head and pecks me between the horns. "No! Not a sheep. You are a gray mammal covered in wool, but not a wolf." He flies back up to his branch. "Again."

Once more, I attempt to change into a wolf. My body is smaller than that of a woodpecker. The icy air bites at me. I feel sleepy. Sluggish. My body contracts. It huddles converting to an oval.

"Not a frog! Change fast!" The owl screeches.

I panic. My thoughts swirl and mix up. ***Gray. I need something gray!*** My body gets bigger and bigger. It reaches the branches. It's thicker than the trunks of the trees. My own trunk reaches the canopies. The two tusks are hard to maneuver through the thick foliage. In order to move, I'd have to plow everything down. I trumpet once by accident as the adrenaline hits and the cold resides.

"No, no. Focus!" The owl scolds in disapproval. "Stop pretending you're an animal, and be the animal." He looks at my ivory tusks and stump like legs.

The goal was a gray wolf, not an African elephant. My body shrinks back to normal. My breaths are shorter, faster. Erratic and dismayed. My arms rest on my knees. My eyes divert to the owl. He hasn't stopped lecturing me. "Try again. Remember, you are the animal. What makes the gray wolf special in your mind?"

A loyal member of a pack surrounded by others who love and protect him. "Gray wolf." Fur covers my skin. Bone reshapes my snout and canines adjust to their new home. The wagging tail gives me some balance. The undergrowth supports my paws. Ears poke out of head. I look directly at Cal. I expected it to be shorter.

"A dire wolf. You're getting close. Try once more."

I do as he says. My body becomes smaller. The tail wags faster. My howl is a higher pitch. I glance up, the angle higher. Cal is further away. "Good. A healthy gray wolf." He says with some pride. "Let us finish this training."

I jump. My claws dance around the undergrowth. I can't stop wagging my tail. I tilt my head and pretend to pounce. Other creatures watch me carefully from a safe distance above the forest floor. I arc my body just like small puppies do when interacting with their peers. My tongue hangs from the side of my mouth. I may look dorky, but I'm free! I'm in control of my changes! Other creatures climb down. We roll over the leaves and chase each other. Bird swoop and I jump after them. Squirrels race me from tree to tree. An hour might have passed, but I don't care. I could stay like this forever!

I start panting. That's the signal to end my short-lived dream. My body shifts back. My stomach rumbles. Sweat trickles down my skin. I stumble back to the tree. Leaves scatter away. Squirrels gather around me with nuts and berries. My body stiffens. Every bite regains a portion of something lost. "Why am I feeling this way?" I mumble loudly enough for my teacher to hear.

"So, you pay with energy." He flutters to my level, seeing as I can barely raise my head.

"What do you mean by pay? I didn't feel like this as a wolf." I take another of the berries to my mouth.

"Abilities don't just appear. They require something in exchange. In your case, energy." He pauses. "Consider this: what would be more taxing staying in one form for a week or changing forms every day?" He moves his wings as if they were arms, flailing them and pointing at me.

"Changing. Everything in my body would change instead of staying like normal." I shift, straightening my back against the tree.

"Correct. Seeing your performance today, I calculate a maximum of seven changes before you are drained."

Just enough color returns to my skin, a tiny bit of life.

"Go home and rest. We will resume training next week." He flies away, occasionally looking back at me.

The trek home is uneventful. The waning moon has risen. Roy isn't shouting. The opposite, complete silence. From time to time, I hear him give orders under his breath. He keeps me awake through the night. My ears twitch with every sound. There's some buzzing. The noise is too loud for my bat hearing.

I sneak out of my room and place my ears on his door. "Steal this from the sports store in the mall close to the office buildings," he whispers. Bellow me, a black mass tickles my bare feet. ***It moves? Wait, it does.*** Tiny soldiers march, covering my feet. I panic and stumble back.

The noise is enough for Roy to storm out of his room. A cell-phone lights his face, his eye-bags denoting a will to stay awake. "What are you doing?"

"You were making a lot of noise," I whisper back.

He waves me. "Go away." The black mass of ants retreats clearing the white floor.

"You got your ability." I slap at my body. It tingles as if the ants are walking on me. "Do you know why?"

He looks down on me, leaning on the door frame. "Obviously."

I sit there waiting for the explanation that never comes. He scornfully looks at me waiting for me to go away. So much for brotherly love. "That's great. Don't overdo it."

His smile disappears. "Bro, I'm not an idiot! Go back to bed." With that, he closes the door and continues to murmur. Whatever Roy is planning. I'll trust him. It's not every day you see the metamorphosis of two different species.

CHAPTER FIFTEEN: THE TYRANT KING

January 18, 2013

The week hasn't been easy. My body is out of control more than before. Senses are easy to hide but cat ears aren't. Those are the simple ones. Haruka miraculously invented a story about using me to try some cosplay. On Tuesday feathers grew on my arms. And then on Wednesday, I got markhor horns after I arrived home. Roy started commanding his kingdom and got Lucas to make our parents focus on him. The horns are something, but suddenly growing a green iguana tail mid class was an experience. One of my legs was visibly thicker than the other. I doubt it went unnoticed. That brings us to today, up until now, nothing. It's strange, nothing usually ends with catastrophe.

"Mr. Untamed! Wearing hoodies in class is against the rules!" The teacher screeches.

"I'm sorry, teacher. I'm just not feeling too well. I rather not attract attention to how sick I look," I lie. The entire class is looking at me. They all contrast perfectly against the white walls. Haruka sits beside me, acting as a wall between Lucy and me. Every couple of seconds, she glances over. She knows another accident is bound to happen.

"I guess I can let it go this time, since you hold the highest grade in the class." She glares at me and returns to her lesson about how animal classifications are given. This is way too easy. I'm only here 'cause attendance counts for the grades.

"Thank you very much…" I cough, and hide my relief. My body relaxes, but my shoulders are stiff from hunching. My neck hurts from looking over my shoulder, my body smells from the sweat simmering under my layered clothing.

"Class, work on your assignments. I'll be in my office if you need assistance." She takes her leave glaring at all of us again.

One of my classmates asks, "Hey, Theon. Can you help me studying for exams?" This catches me off guard. My hands keep moving from the desk into my bag.

"Is it urgent? I'm not feeling really well." I feign a cough.

Lucy passes me, rushing to secure a seat in an isolated area. She's avoiding me. Haruka stays with me, observing any changes in my body.

"No, but when you can, can you help us?" He grabs his phone and starts swiping.

"Yes, I'd have no problem with that. Send me the topics you want to study, and I'll organize myself." I place the bag on my shoulder. Haruka leads the way.

"Do you have time for one question?"

I don't pay attention to who says it, thinking it's one of the study group members. "Sure."

"How does a no one from that fancy English school, becomes the center of attention here?" A girl says in Spanish. Her voice is like nails on a chalkboard.

There is a brief pause. "What?" Something swirls within me. Hot magma rising and cool ice pushing it down. They dance inside me. I take a step back and stare at the floor.

"You know. How does the reject of that school brings so much attention? The black sheep was too ugly he got left behind." Dia takes center stage in front of the classroom. "Should I ask that Juan guy?"

Why is this happening to me? Why do I have to face this over and over? I did nothing wrong. Why can't I be left alone? My lips tremble, my throat is parched. *And she wants to involve Juan? Why did he have to follow me here!* I never mentioned anything to anyone at this school. My ex-classmates don't know the people I know now. Damn it. I should have erased my social media accounts. It's hard to come up with a reply. *She's right. I'm a reject.* I am a sardine in a South African feeding frenzy. Sharks, sea lions, dolphins, whales, seagulls, and pelicans all approaching for a bite.

"See! Maybe that teach you your place." She giggles.

The skin on my neck has become jagged and dry. The air flows between the scales' crevasses.

"Let's go, Theon." Haruka pulls my sleeves. I avoid looking at anyone. Haruka emits humid metallic smells. Her fingers shake as they touch my shoulder. Her pulse accelerates, as well as her breathing.

"You nobodies should stick together."

Red. The only color I see. A deep growl comes from my throat. Haruka jumps away.

The bully keeps taunting me. "What a freak? What are you an animal?"

"Calm down." Haruka covers her mouth, so the others don't hear. She gives up on pulling me away from the impending fight.

I tense up. Sharp dagger like teeth grow inside my re-forming jaw. Most of my classmates have stepped back.

Haruka picks up her phone. She runs out, disappearing from class. "Arvo! We need your help!" The others follow her example. I stand in the center of the class. My blood boils. My hair is gone.

"Better than being you! Someone so empty she finds pleasure in putting others down." My voice it deeper than usual. The letter *G* and *R* prolong inside my throat.

"You think I care about what a reject thinks?"

Finally. Someone gets to taste their own medicine. "Yes, crawl back to the into woodwork." A smile appears, hidden in the shadows of my hoodie. My hands seek shelter from the light. Hiding their nature from others. Six of my fingers are lost, and the skin that once covered me is replaced by dark scales. The remaining classmates watch as she leaves. Fists clenched. Feet stomping the floor. My newly grown claws are hidden inside my sleeves. Everything is still red, there's blood in the air.

I force my feet into the floor. Instinct drives my nose toward my prey, but she left. She ran away humiliated, but that's not enough. I have to make sure she pays. My body asks for that, and in the back of my mind I feel that push. My feet move, they drag me closer to the door. Boots barely contain my expanding feet. I lower my head, covering my monstrous expression.

The fire alarm resonates through the hallways. It slaps my ears, temporarily deafening me. Most of my classmates already left. The rest walk out now. Some run as a joke. I drop to the floor. The bell is inside my head. My claws touch the white floors. My boots clash against each other, a vain attempt to release the pressure of my growing feet. A crowd of voices reaches the classroom.

"Bro, let me help you." Jay runs to my side. He wastes no time in picking up my bag, then he hunches down and says, with concern in his voice, "Haruka told me you needed help." He tries to grab my arm, but the sleeve is empty. He tries with the other, the sleeve flaps as his arm passes it.

"Take my stuff… And run." I keep the growls controlled for the moment. My lower back arches.

"I can't leave you like this." Jay has the goofiest smile. "Looking snazzy. You had a makeover?"

Light connects with my scales. "No… I'll explain later. Just take my stuff and…clothing." My teeth start piercing my gums. The thick flavor of blood embeds on my tongue.

"Bruh, I don't swing that way." He laughs and pulls my boots off. He pokes at my three claws. "This is so cool!"

"Just…" I growl. "Hurry up." My breathing gets harder and deeper. I stand at the edge of a feeding frenzy. For once, I feel powerful enough to fight back, but I'm losing control. Control I've never had on these abilities of mine.

My legs look less human. Talons half the size of my legs extend on the floor. My knees are closer to my torso. Jay takes more of my clothing. Each piece leaves him more amazed than the last. He rushes. No ears, yet my hearing has improved. Human fear stains the air. Animals in the area release a mix of excitement and concern. Jay yanks my t-shirt. He packs all the stuff, then looks at my claws. He pokes at them again. They sprout longer and cut Jay's arm.

"Are you okay?" I ask.

He keeps the smile, as if his dark skin was intact. "Yeah, it's nothing." I know he lies. Blood's scent is strong. A viscous, dangerous smell. It repulses me, but a part of me resonates with it. It calls the deeper part of me to take action.

"I'm sorry. I don't know how to stop this." Every word is a fight with my receding vocal cords.

"It's cool dude! This is so cool!" He picks up the stuff and runs out. The door closes behind him. That detail won't matter in a couple of seconds. I sense it. I know ancient creatures, even if I can't see them. My tail extends out of my body. Desks open a path for an ancient ruler. My head becoming faster than my body. Hand sized teeth find their required space. Gravity fights me. On any other occasion, I would resent this force of nature. Not today. My legs concede to the extreme change.

More desks are thrown across the room. Primal feathers sprout from my back. Lightly brushing the dusty ceiling. The ceiling only contains me, for now. *Crack.* It comes from above. My head pushes against the whiteboard. I will not be caged any longer! Concrete breaks. From every direction, the structure gives in to the pressure. My curled-up tail finds a cavity in the wall. Glass bounces off my scales, falling to its demise.

The floor continues to sustain my new weight. Another crack. I shift. The ground grumbles in mutiny, the walls too. The alarm keeps ringing. The floor breaks, shaking the foundations of the wall and the building. The rectangular white walls cave in. Different sizes and pieces of concrete fall alongside me. Shards of glass and twisted metal decor the wasteland under my feet. Plastic desks act as shrubs in the plains. Cables slither in and out of their burrows.

The floor trembles for the last time. The outer wall is gone. **Freedom! I am what I always should have been!** By instinct or some other force, with my body moving into the open, I roar. An ancient roar. One that hasn't been heard in sixty-six million years. The deep, low roar travels through the school, announcing one thing only. That the tyrant king is back, ready to take his domain. A part of me can't contain my excitement. Echoes of my roar bounce back. This is a warning.

The students shout back at me. The stampeding frenzy that consumes them only serves to pull on my hunter instinct. The dust clouds protect them. And I, in my mind restrain my body. Although it's difficult. Not every single part of my mind wants restraint. This leaves me vulnerable to my thoughts. They claim me as a mark to be hunted.

I see the canopies of the trees. The smell of fear makes me nostalgic. It hasn't changed. The canopies leave me behind. They stay near the birds in the sky, and I get closer to the mammals on the land. Dust hardens my hair. The rubble soils my feet. A building fragment falls onto the mound, adding to my destruction.

The ground scratches my soles. Disorienting dust causes me to walk aimlessly. My feet dance with the grace of bank of Komodo dragons eating a water buffalo. My senses help me avoid the electrical veins of the broken building. The dust cloud prevents smells from piercing through. If anything, the T-Rex's smell would have been useful. In the grass, I catch glimpses of sharp shards that wouldn't have been able to pierce my scales but could easily open my skin.

Magpies converse in the distance. They shout loud enough to silence the humans shouting. Those ladies in black call to me. The forest area, the usual hangout. The residue tickles my nose and waters my eyes. The cloud begins to disperse. Something inside me pushes through the staggering. Animals would say live, my mind says hide and survive. Right in the margin, where the sky meets the grass, blue and green feathers wait for me.

The cocky Indian peacock provides a wall of feathers.

The female says, "I'm not interested but, for this to work we need to act." She sighs at the end of the phrase. I can't see her face, but by how he walks, I know she dances with him. A small show, where the audience isn't her.

"Thanks—" I cough. Dust has made it inside my throat. "I appreciate it a lot." I move along behind them stumbling many times during my crouched escape. They guide me toward the fence and the creek.

Another of the peafowls joins. "Yash, you shouldn't have. Shyla doesn't deserve you." She giggles at her own snide remark.

He dances faster. One wouldn't think he has some semblance to an ostrich. He runs fast even with his tail open. I run with him, partly because I'm naked, but also, I feel for him. That new peafowl's personality isn't pleasant.

"Darsha we are busy." Shyla, the first more reasonable, peafowl adds, "He isn't even interested in you." She keeps running with him, with none of his ostrich characteristics.

Their discussion continues as I slam into a bush. My abrupt stop did nothing for Yash. He closes his fan and runs as fast as he can. Darsha, not weighed down by a massive tail keeps up fairly easily.

Shyla sits with me. She turns away from the fleeing disaster, while also avoiding the naked teen inside the bush. "Are you okay?"

"I think so. Did anyone get hurt?" I keep myself hidden inside the flora.

She shakes her head. "Cuts and bruises."

"I'm sorry."

"It's not your fault. It was an accident" After Yash leaves, her voice is calmer, the initial shock gone. She glances my way. "We're here to help you. Everything will be fine." After she finishes the sentence, birds and smaller mammals call to me. My heart slows. This is the void after the hunt. No frenzy, no panic, only the quiet stillness of nature.

Grass crunches under the rubber of tennis shoes. Shyla runs away. I'm not sure if that is a signal or a warning. Her gray feathers still contrast with the greenery. The footfalls get louder. **What I would do for my cat ears.** Whispers fly among the dusts, settling on the near plant life. The birds silence themselves, and the small area filled with life is voided. I curl, imitating the armadillo. The shrubbery opens to the light of day.

"Here we find Theon Untamed in his natural habitat. He prowls, naked searching for the elusive clothing," Jay says playfully.

"Have some clothes?" I wince a smile, clearing the leaves and twigs in my hair. Branches poke at my bare skin.

"Suit yourself." He wears a paper mustache. The black paper flaps with his lips. He kisses the air and makes a French accent.

As I get dressed, the intercoms send the last message of the day. "We are going to investigate this incident. We ask all students to cooperate with the investigation and to not share any videos online."

My head pops out of the bush. Haruka turns to the distance, one of her hands blocking the sunlight from her eyes. She oscillates keeping her back to me. I don't blame her. I might still be naked. I did start with my underwear and pants, just in case. Arvo is nowhere to be seen, but Kat stands behind the others, glancing at me from time to time.

Jay holds his hand out. He helps me get up. "Are you ready for another Faunaut hangout?" He keeps smiling. That's the name he insists on giving the two of us. I never agreed with it, but that's how we are getting known. I shake my head. I'm more afraid than ever of what could happen to Jay.

Kat joins the conversation, "What's a Faunaut?"

"Our group. Theon and I." He blinks twice before going on. "Want to join?"

She hops with excitement. "Yes! I love the name!"

I'm never going to escape that name, am I?

CHAPTER SIXTEEN: THE SECRET OF ANIMALS

January 21, 2013

With a collapsed building, classes are an afterthought. Other schools followed the pack leader and closed for inspection. My phone vibrates, more news about what they call "The Monterrey Monster" **Monster. That's not what I am. At least I hope I'm not.** Thoughts of each creature that lives or has lived cross my mind. **Which one is the original one, is it me or is it another specie?** The Monterrey Monster news is followed talk of the "Insect Thief" Roy has kept himself busy stealing for himself and from time to time for his siblings.

My brothers have continued with their natural course. For them it's life as usual, not the panicked preview of the hunt. Roy commands his friends into frenzies, and the insects are his butlers and maids. Things at home find a different kind of peace when my parents aren't around. Multitudes of animals roam the house. Some days we get snow, others we get water and rarely we get vapor.

Lucas comes by my room. "Want to watch a movie?" He almost sounds concerned, almost. His voice has a tone of sadness. My brother stays at the door. The glass of black soda he holds bubbles. This soda smells fetid. I know a movie would help me get out of this anxious state of mind, but I don't think it's helpful. I have to be on maximum alert.

"No, I'm fine." My gaze is lost outside the window. "But you can use my room."

Lucas jumps on my bed as I leave it. Thor runs around, playing on his own. The puppy barks, "Come outside! Let's play!"

I traverse the house. Passing beside my shouting brother, down the stairs and the forgotten Christmas tree. The garden door is nothing special, a glass sliding door. Outside, the four tortoises form a semi-circle, waiting for my arrival. Thor chases a butterfly, that tries to mind her own business. I mindlessly throw the ball as I stare at the tortoises. I can't help it. "Am I going to be hunted?"

The four of them lay under the shade of our green garden. Under the bamboo sprouts and above the fickle grass blades. The three small coniferous trees sway in front of the ivy, and yet my tortoises are immovable. The female tortoise, with her slow, elderly voice, says, "Yes." Her tongue sticks to the top of her mouth and lingers. "But we will help you."

My body moves on its own. It circles around. Every couple of seconds, Thor returns and asks me to throw the ball. I do so. It echoes inside the house. That isn't good enough. **What about my brothers? What about my friends? We're dead. We're so, so dead.** My fur frizzles. I stop. I stare at the tortoises. "Why is this happening to me?" My voice breaks and chirps in different parts. My heartbeat accelerates, leaving behind any semblance of not being prey.

"We can't answer that. You have done this stuff before.

Thor licks one of their shells.

"What a sweet little puppy," the female tortoise says.

A male tortoise turns to look at her. "He was eating his feces a minute ago."

"Run!" The four tortoises scatter at tortoise speed, with Thor jumping around, licking their shells. The puppy laughs. He runs in a circle, continuously licking.

Great trick. The animals avoid answering. The sun continues to rise, and I take that as a signal to get back inside. Any peace is disturbed by the doorbell, followed by Thor's cries.

A honey badger possesses Thor. The unusual growls and rabid barks translate to, "Get away! Evil!" which is more than enough to put me on edge. My hair feels like that of a porcupine and my skin like an octopus camouflaging as stone.

Lucas joins me downstairs with a glass of clear water in hand. He takes a peek outside. "A weird person is bothering Thor." It's the same glass that had the bubbly black ichor. He doesn't notice my stare, but considering the scene outside, it isn't important. The small bird ring tone lures me to my phone.

Kat: Anyone else get interrogated?

Haruka: He was scary. Take care.

Theon: What about Arvo and Lucy?

Haruka: Lucy is fine.

Jay sends an image of a TV and its controller, with the controller saying, "Don't worry, everything is under control." He manages to pull a smile out of me.

On the road is a black car like they use at funerals. The bald man takes out his glasses. I notice the emptiness in his eyes. A black void. One glance at Thor is all it takes to make him whimper. Thor's whimpering becomes a full out cry. The tortoises do their best to calm him, but our puppy's voice shrieks through the neighborhood.

"The fuck is going on!" Roy marches down the stairs. Not sure if he is pissed, the dog is crying or that Thor's howling interrupted his game. He looks outside, then turns toward me. "You better not destroy the house." Roy pushes me toward the door, forcing me to open it.

Lucas passes me. "Why are you bothering our dog?" He crosses his arms, with the cup of water between his arms.

"I might have scared him." Penumbra stands motionless. There is a creeping smile on his face.

Lucas leans away, seeking to flee through the window or the front door. He quivers behind me and asks, "Can you stop?"

Before the man gets the chance to reply I ask, "Do you need something?" I hide one hand behind my back and crossing my fingers. Something tells me to avoid his eyes.

He looks at me. His eyes suck the soul out of my body. I get why Thor is acting the way he is. "I'm agent Penumbra. I'm looking for Theon, Lucas and Roy Untamed." **Why would he be looking for my brothers?** They weren't at my school. **This isn't right.**

I tense. Lucas pulls my shirt. He stands on the tip of his feet, and points at the glass of pristine water. It looks as if it was taken from a spring. The water ripples as my little brother avoids the man outside.

"Tell Roy."

Lucas lets go. His relatively tiny feet cross the house faster than expected.

I turn toward Penumbra, who still tries to suck out my soul. "That's us." I force a smile. No way I'm letting him see me falter.

"I come to get your testimonies." He smiles. There's nothing comforting about it, it's sinister. A human poisoning a house cat and enjoying it.

I gulp. "I'll call my parents to make sure. Wait here." I close the door. It creaks behind me. I follow Lucas to the kitchen, where he's getting shouted at by the prince.

He glares at me. "The fuck did you do?" He corners me against the wall. "I messaged dad, and he says it's fine. Fucking idiot!"

My palms wide open, sticking to the wall avoiding the furious display my nails would do otherwise. Words fill my throat and delay the way out like wildebeests delay jumping into the Maasai Mara river scared of the crocodiles lurking under the murky waters until one brave demonstration incites stampede. And in this case Thor, has the last word by crying out.

Thor reminds me of the tortoises warning. "Animals said we're going to be hunted. I think he's a hunter."

"Fucking Hell!" Roy stomps toward Lucas. "Lie like you have never done before."

Lucas trembles. "I can't." His voice strums the wrong chord. Lucas points at the glass. "I'm the oldest." The water darkens and putrefies. The stench emanates from the sinks, the fridge, the bathroom, even the garden. "I'm the youngest." Water clears out. It's as if the event never happened.

"Fuck off. I'll talk. Don't fucking say anything." He pauses after each word, emphasizing the last syllable, then leads the way out of the kitchen.

Lucas taps the counter fast enough to create a song. "But what if he asks?"

"Shut your trap!"

I glance at our little brother. "Tap the table in tempo. When you lie, break it. I'll try to help you."

Lucas nods. The two of us follow Roy to the entrance. The man stands there with the unnerving smile.

I grunt. "Our parents said it was fine."

With one click, the gate opens for him. All my instincts tell me to run and hide. Thor keeps whimpering in the backyard. ***What did he do to him?*** Agent Penumbra walks behind me. He stalks my every move. I can't use my senses to track him. He might notice them.

Inside the house, my brothers sit in the living room. Roy's on a chair near the kitchen entrance. He frowns at me and then at Lucas. Trading the blame for whose fault it is. Lucas is on the bench opposite to Roy. The glass of water is missing. He slowly taps his finger on the table. He deafens himself in the trance of the lyrebird's show. I sit down next to Roy; it gives me the clearest view of Lucas.

The man sits in the middle of the couch. His dark eyes scan the panorama. The three kids are within his grasp. He pulls out a black thermos. The thermos swings, revealing liquid inside. ***Please don't be water.*** He takes a sip. No smell, only ours, the pets and his. He looks like a walking grim reaper.

Roy says nothing, but is frowning. My debt to him is stacking. It worries me more than getting discovered. ***What malevolent intentions does Roy have planned?*** My hands crush each other behind my back. My jaws hold my tongue in place, saying less is safer.

"Let's get this over with." Roy scoffs. He puts his feet on the coffee table.

"Where were you the day of the incident?" Penumbra holds a notebook, then scans the room.

"Stupid question! School! Next!" Roy looks directly at the agent. The rebellious prince of the house has had it. In his domain the only stupidity allowed is his own.

"Right. I need everyone to answer on their own." He pauses and raises his eyebrows while glaring at the prince. He continues to scribble in his notebook. "Have any of you noticed anything out of the ordinary?"

"Other than the creeper interviewing kids without any other adults around? No! Fucking useless!" Roy swats the air around him.

Penumbras eyes finally get some color, which makes them less creepy. Or that's what I want to say, but reddish and black is creepier. They feel like the scope on a rifle, choosing the target. His gaze aims at me. Sweat beads roll down my body.

The man swirls the container, "Please let them answer. Or I'll have to question you separately." He catches our eyes darting at Lucas and smirks at us.

Roy glares at me. The agent starts turning to Lucas. "No. Nothing out of the norm." I focus on what Cal said. I'm normal. My gaze drifts toward the ceiling, toward the luminous chandelier. I can't scratch my hands without looking suspicious. I do the second-best thing and bite my inner lip.

Penumbra turns to Lucas. "Sorry, but no…" My brother shakes his head, his body sways with him. The taps completely stop.

I intervene. "Nothing other than the news. A monster? Insects stealing electronics. What's next a robot uprising?"

Roy slaps the back of my head. *I wish my ears were more sensitive.* Maybe that way I could tell what Penumbra really thinks.

Lucas looks at me. The table vibrates as he returns to rhythm. "What he said." Lucas' eyes widen. "Theon is weird!" The taps remain in tune. His gaze avoids mine. He just placed me in front of a firing squadron. **Lucas!** The smell dissipates.

Penumbra takes a sip. "He is?" He's about to turn on me.

A force pushes me down and turns the view dark. Cloth drapes over my black hair. Roy leans close. "Don't take it off." He keeps pushing me down, then punches me in the stomach.

I comb my hair, finding two furrier than usual ears. If I have to guess, grasshopper mouse ears. I pull the hoodie even lower. Flattening the otherwise abnormal ears.

"Hell yeah. He doesn't party. He's lame…" Roy adds. His smile leans toward the side. He laughs right after, not in the funny way.

Lucas does his best to keep quiet. After all, lies can't be told when you aren't talking. That's a lie since deception in the animal world occurs through all means. The eastern-hog nosed snake pretends to be dead, while releasing a rotting smell.

The man dismisses the comment. Penumbra chuckles under his breath. "Is something the matter?"

Roy intervenes. "He annoyed me." He shrugs. "He's chronically stupid."

Lucas nods with Roy. The putrid smell permeates the room.

Penumbra opens his thermos. Slowly, he leans the container to his lips. The stench doesn't hit him, but the flavor and texture will. I have to do something. I glance at Roy, he shrugs. Lucas panics and takes shelter behind Roy.

"He means I'm a scatterbrain."

Lucas nods. The scent disappears. The agent takes a sip. He grins, an even more sinister expression than his serious or hateful face. Lucas trembles.

"Next questions are only for Theon."

I sense his glare, and look up at him. I keep pulling the hoodie down, blocking any view of my ears.

"You were in the room that was destroyed before the incident?"

Roy grips his chair harder. I shift awkwardly on my seat. "Yeah, I had class. But it finished early." My ears perk up, they try to force my hands away. The fur on my back rises colliding with the chair's fabric.

"Did something happen?"

"Nothing of importance." I bite harder.

"Classmates say you got into an argument." He digs deeper. Screw them all. They aimed the gun.

My gaze avoids his, every cell in my body tells me the only course of action is to flee. "Yeah. I didn't think that was relevant." I desperately scramble for logic, but that evolutionary path has left me behind. *Why would that be important to them? I know it triggered me, but they wouldn't know that. They shouldn't.* Unless Arvo didn't hack the cameras. In that case, I would be trapped already.

"We just want to know all the events that took place."

Who are "we"? Why would that matter? It doesn't matter, he's not onto me. It's not a coincidence. I gotta turn this hunter prey game. "Yeah, I guess it did matter. Jay and I planned revenge. He pulled the fire alarm, and I was supposed to keep her busy, so she got drenched." My nails sink into my sleeves and scratch my scalp.

"I see. Usually that would mean consequences for both of you, but we can overlook that, since those actions saved a lot of people." His gaze aims for Roy. *Does he know something I don't?* "What do you think about the reports of a monster?"

"Morons speaking out of their asses."

Penumbra rolls his eyes and returns to me.

He's ignored Lucas. And that's fine. If he dares lay a finger on him. I'll. I'll stop myself before it triggers more changes. "I think my schoolmates were too scared to make sense of the world." Time to turn it around. I refuse to be prey.

"You were found covered in dust. Why?" Penumbra leans toward me again, ignoring my brothers.

My throat rumbles. "I ran to check if anyone was injured. Wouldn't you do the same?"

"Of course. An upstanding member of society. Did you see anything?" Is there contempt in his voice, no it's more sinister. It's like he laid a bear trap, and I the oblivious woodland creature stepped on it.

Roy stands up. "He asked a question fucker."

"I'm the one asking questions here."

"You're pretty shit at it." He looks down on the tall man. "Here, let me help you, dumbass. Why don't you fucking leave?" Roy points at the door. His body covers Lucas from the horrifying visage that the rest of us have to see.

The man stands and glares intensely at Roy. "I'm not done yet. I can show you why I have this job."

Roy, being who he is, glares back. Roy's fists clench, his whole-body tenses. The grind of his teeth resounds inside my head. I turn to him. His body a nautilus needing a shell. Thor cries in the background. The prince's stare is empty, purposeless.

Lucas stands beside him. "Roy, are you okay?" He repeats the questions. His voice breaks a little more each time. He shakes our brother as hard as he can. His teary eyes look at the man. "What did you do to him?"

"Nothing." Penumbra looks at Lucas.

Lucas crumples. A tweeting bird hiding from the oncoming tempest. He shakes and quivers violently. In a snap, tears drop from his eyes. His fingers stop moving. He high tails it under the chair. Sobs causing disharmony in my brother. Between sobs his distraught voice goes on. "No Dad… Please… I want… Music." He overshadows Thor's cries.

The man looks at me.

All I know is not to look.

He sits down right beside me. "How did Jayson Orion get that injury in his arm?" His hand hovers above my head. "Now answer."

Lucas cries. Roy's frozen in place. The animals outside are trying to help Thor. *I'm alone. I'm alone with this monster. What can I do? He's going to figure me out. He's going to kill us all!*

He looks at me, but I avoid his empty eyes. My teeth pierce through my lip. Blood. Its disgusting taste invades my system. Four of my teeth are longer. Sharper. *I'm not going to become what he wants me to be. He'll pay for what he did to Thor, to my brothers. My friends!*

"Describe what you saw in the dust?" Penumbra leans in. Those devoid of life eyes try to get me. "Tell me about the monster." He keeps trying to make eye contact, more of a reason not to look. If it was me last Friday, he wouldn't be standing. But I'm not the thing he makes me out to be.

I am not a monster. Jay said so. It was an accident. I'm an animal. As usual, humans try to dehumanize others. Lucas and Roy did nothing. They weren't part of what happened, and Penumbra targeted them. "I'm seeing it right now." My gaze is glued to my brothers. That's what monsters do. They cage us when we don't act how they want. They drive us to the edge, expecting our hopes to die. They distort our perspective, making us the bad guys. He is the monster. My sight turns red. "The only monster I've seen is you. What did you do to them?" An imperceptive rumble resonates down the street. It comes from me.

"You are mistaken. I didn't do anything." He withdraws. His lips twitch. He can't fool me. I sniff the air. A strong, unpleasant smell takes over. It collides with the one coming from behind me. Penumbra oozes excess of perfume, trying to mask something revolting. The same smell comes from my brothers. Theirs is familiar. Provoking. Contagious. It smells almost as a disease, except the disease wants to make you move. Fight it or run from it. Fear. My teeth, my fangs and my lips are red.

I catch his sly smile as he drinks from the thermos.

I want to tear it apart! Thick fur encapsulates my legs. *I can't lose control. Not now!* I take a deep breath. "Leave." I stand between him and my brothers.

His voice keeps calm, but his sweat betrays him. "In the middle of the investigation? Are you hiding something?"

What would Roy do? What would Lucas say? Insults, more insults, another spark of insults. That won't work. Lucas would lie, make puppy eyes, or call for our parents. Our parents! For once, they can help me. I never really called them. I use my hoodie as a shield. "I'm calling the police. I wonder if making a five-year-old cry is part of your work." He doesn't answer. Not so brave when I turn the tables.

He looks around, trying to find a way to peek into my eyes. "No need. I'll leave." He stands, then takes a step toward us.

Fine, he made me do this. Barn owls don't deceive. This will make me the first one to do so. I close my eyes, open my mouth and a nightmarish scream leaves my lungs. I cup hands around my mouth, and I scream again, making sure every animal and human hears me. My arms and chest are covered with thick fur. He puts his weight on the balls of his feet. One vibration gets too close for comfort. My voice drops low. There is uncontrollable rage, ready to burst out.

His hand hovers over my hoodie. He laughs. "Threatening a military officer?"

"Yes, for physically and psychologically attacking minors." I stop moving. I don't know if any other body part has changed. My fingers are slowly disappearing. It's not like during school or training.

"I never…" He walks back to his place. The realization of my actions hits him. I might be a horrible human liar, but as an animal I can excel. An owl's screech is disturbing enough in the woods. In the city, that's an invitation to see who's getting murdered. He picks up his things. Without saying a word, he walks out the door.

As soon as he's out the gates. I run to my brothers. The red hues dissipate from my vision. I grab Lucas and carry him with his head on my shoulder. "It's okay! Everything is fine." I cradle him as if he was a baby chimpanzee. "He's gone."

"It was so scary." He sobs. Tears slowly becoming morning dew.

I walk toward the other victim. "Roy, are you okay?" I shake him. Harder. I pinch him.

"What the fuck was that for?" Roy stands up. "Get off me!" he shouts. He doesn't push us away.

I sit close to him. "What happened to you?"

His fists clench. His face twists into a frown. "Next time I see him, he is fucking dead…"

CHAPTER SEVENTEEN: PREDATORY DISASTER

January 26, 2013

The sun peeks through the window, illuminating not only my math classwork but also my survival rations. A couple of brownies, chocolate milk and a cinnamon roll, along with some cookies I brought for Minos. He squeaks from my shirt pocket. The cookie crumbles in my hand and falls upon little Minos. He nibbles the newly created landscape. The constant sugar rush is the only thing keeping me awake while the teacher talks about triangles and how they are useful.

Jay is drowsing off on the side; Saturday morning is no one's good day. We fell a bit behind due to my T-Rex accident. The other twenty people or so are like Jay. Lucy looks like an opossum, but she still gives more signs of life than the rest. Even Haruka is barely holding on to the light of day. Arvo probably got some lucky rabbit, 'cause he got sick. It's better for him. He doesn't want anything to do with me. The only one with some degree of energy is the teacher, but she doesn't count.

I zone out and look toward the main gate. The Atacama Desert has more life that the wasteland we call our parking lot. I hear multiple conversations from the flocks passing by. The loud argument between two, maybe three dogs, and the classy group of four cats shouting at them to shut up. They suppress my instincts to go to bed. Minos pops his head out. "It's only one more hour." He then wiggles his tiny paws, asking for more.

More cookies fall upon him. "I know, but this is so boring and useless." My mouth barely moves, squeaking back at him. I cover it with one hand, so it looks as if I'm yawning. A wave of yawns propagates through the classroom, making me yawn for real this time. I search for anything else to distract myself.

A black van parks in our parking lot. I wait and watch to see which unfortunate individuals have been dragged to school on a Saturday morning. Men dressed in black with helmets and thick vests get out. One is a giant who smells even from this distance. The second holds a long gun; Roy would know what type. The remaining three aren't that remarkable. Radio static intervenes. "Understood, Agent Penumbra."

The hairs on my back stand. I imitate the pigeons call, it translates to, "I need help!" I scribble in my notebook, rushing through the page. Each letter a step closer, each breath I take inside this room brings me closer to death. *We are in trouble. Stay calm. I'll get us out of it.* I glance outside. The men have disappeared. Sweat gathers on my forehead. Jay, Haruka, or Lucy? I hate myself for forcing this on her. She won't talk, at least they won't think about her. The crumpled note leaves my hand, landing on Lucy's desk. With Minos and my phone in tow, I sneak out.

Outside, strolling footsteps echo through campus. Some overconfident poachers thinking the animal kingdom is easy prey. My instincts want me to hide, but I want to beat the poachers in their own game. I feel my body leaning toward the stairs, awaiting the men. Small tugs on my shirt bring me back to reality. "Go to the bathroom upstairs." Minos's little squeaks barely make it to my ear.

With some effort the bathroom door opens and closes silently. The four stalls are closed. I'd like to say the sparkling white floor is pristine, but it has more of an ochre tone to it. Creased papers fill the trash can. A skunk's smell is more floral than whatever is in one of those stalls. I pull out my phone and message my only hope.

Theon: Hack the school cameras.

My eyes dart up and down the barren room. I pace. **He's going to see me as a reptile in it for himself. A dangerous, venomous snake ready to strike.**

Arvo: No! Not covering the dinosaur thing again.

I knew it. He sees me as an unwanted reptile, dangerous to everything around him. My pupils disappear. My hair recedes, showcasing a black scaled scalp. Noticing my changes, Minos flees toward the floor grates, with horrified squeaks.

Theon: Everyone will die if we don't.

Shouts and screams rush from the classroom. The sickening smell of blood and terror permeates the building. The herd of students falls prey to hunters. They nervously bargain for their lives. Footsteps fill the air, approaching to an inevitable encounter with the real target.

Hopefully, Arvo will cover me, but if he doesn't, this might be my life until I die. With one click, the phone shuts down. My thoughts spiral, and my body replies in kind. My arms and legs vanish. I collapse into the ochre tiles. My body is a black rope. My jaws hold on to the phone. With massive effort, I slither under the sink. I keep slithering until the darkness, and I are one and the same. The rusty pipes above might hide me, but the phone would be out in the open, it's more than I can do for clothes. I straighten up and stay immobile in the corner. Hoping my camouflage is more than enough.

Slam! The door crashes into the wall. I wait for the creak of the door closing, but it never happens. Black military boots traverse the room. He stops in front of my clothing, searches the jeans' pockets. **I forgot about my wallet!** He opens it. "I know you're here. Come out." His potent voice shakes me. It overflows with confidence.

He stops in front of a bathroom stall. His foot crashes into the door, leaving it hanging. He takes another step, and repeats the move. "Don't make this hard." He bounces from side to side. He rips the stall's door and throws it against the mirror. Shards rain upon my clothing. Try as it may, gravity never brings the door back down. His footsteps get closer, slower. They stalk, gracing the sink area. His foot slams into the trashcan.

My heart can't race faster, my tears can never fall. He bends. His head scours the under-dark. I freeze in my own camouflage. His gaze passes my darkened body. He grunts. The sink vibrates once more. "Stupid kid…" There are metallic clicks and beeps before he continues. "He isn't here. He's naked and took his phone. I'll kill them all."

A distorted voice replies, "Keep searching. Bring him here, then you can do whatever."

The footsteps move further away. "Looking forward to beating you." He savors the moment. "Don't make me wait."

I stay unmoving. Once he leaves, I return to human. Dangerous mirror shards cling to my clothes. I take my time cleaning them off as I listen to ensure he's really gone.

Arvo: What?

Arvo: I see.

Arvo: Fine.

Arvo: You owe me an explanation.

Miniature claws scratch the floor. "It's safe. We have to move." Minos positions himself beside me.

My limbs shake frantically. My breaths are short and rapid. "What am I going to do? I'm screwed." I look in the mirror. My scales are completely gone. Behind me, all the metal doors are broken, bent, or folded. The ceramic toilets are cracked and spilling water. The hollowed garbage bin a thin sheet of metal. And the wall holding it is fractured. The main door was thrown all the way to the first stall. It destroyed the three urinals. "And if that guy finds me, I'd be a butterfly and he'd be a fly swatter."

Minos climbs up my jeans and into my shirt pocket. "It's up to you. We will all support you." As if on cue dogs bark, cats meow, pigeons coo and the other birds chatter. More and more animal noises join. Frogs and toads croak. From up above, screeches as raptors come to help. The grates rumble with the squeaks of the rodents moving through them.

"I can't leave Lucy, Jay, and Haruka behind. They're my friends." My body like a crocodile ready to hunt. There will be no ripples, no trace of me. I touch the scar on my eyebrow, feeling primal. "I will win this. I won't let them hurt the people I care about. I'll need help." The animal inside me won't let me die. Survival is the goal and the priority.

Minos jumps on my hand. This time he avoids my pocket, asking me to put him higher. He scrambles in my hair, forming a comfortable nest. I pick up my phone, "You said it was safe."

The small mouse nods. I go through the message list. The call starts, *beep*. I recoil, it's like turning on the TV and everyone is asleep, and the TV makes the loudest sound ever.

"Explain," Arvo finally answers. His voice hitting high notes.

I pet Minos. We both head toward the classroom. The two of us slowly crawl down the stairs. No echoes. They aren't in this building. "Some people are trying to capture me or worse, kill everyone who knows about me."

"What!" Arvo shouts. "I'm calling the police."

My neck twists like an owl's. *Shhh* I freeze. "I don't think that will work." The classroom looks like a Tasmanian Devil feast. Papers crushed. Blood splattered. Desks and chairs flung around. Chaos and disaster. My stomach turns. What did they do to my friends? Lucy's and Haruka's places are undisturbed. On the top of the pile, Lucy's notebook lays closed.

"Why? What did you do?"

I hide under a desk, as if it would muffle the sound. "Right. It's my fault, as everything is. Call them Arvo, get rid of me. You'd be happier that way." I growl. **Focus, ignore him.**

"I wouldn't. I didn't mean to blame you. I'm serious. I don't know. Kat and Jay haven't told me much." His fingers slow on the keyboard. He crunches some of his chips.

I roll my eyes. "I wonder." Before I can continue, I take a deep breath. I have to focus. Lives are on the line. "They mentioned Penumbra." My body gags at the thought of him. Roy has been relentless all week. And Lucas often wakes up crying. I've had him sleep in my room with Thor.

He squeaks. His voice quivers, "Him." He pauses for a minute. "Jay and Haruka said stuff about him." He threads carefully, avoiding telling me something.

"What happened with him?"

"He's the one who interrogated us."

"Did something happen with him? He made Lucas and Thor cry." Arvo hums back at me. "Why didn't they tell me? Did anything happen to you and Kat?"

He stops typing. His voice monotone. "You would blame yourself. No, nothing happened to her."

I let my breath out. "Good." I put my hand over my chest. "Do you think they are like me?"

He's typing again, "Can't be sure." His throat gets stuck when he mentions the abilities.

"It's up to me to save them." I get out from under the desk. Jay's desk calls to me. I scavenge for anything useful. Ear buds, perfect.

Arvo viciously clicks at his mouse and keyboard. More viciously than hyenas attacking prey. "Us. I'll help. What's your plan?"

"We have to avoid the guy from the bathroom." Every tick of the clock makes my heart pound harder. I scavenge other desks, finding rubber bands, papers, and phones. "Do you know where everyone is?" Rubber bands could come in handy. I stockpile them in my pockets.

"The top floor of the science building."

Ironic, they chose the building that started this. It puts me at a disadvantage.

"He's in the language building." Right next door. I can't move with him around.

"Tell me when he moves. What about the other agents?" I stand by the door, one ear on the conversation, the other on the lookout.

"Two agents with the students in the science building, one walking the perimeter and the last on the library rooftop."

I have to eliminate their eye in the sky first. This trick might rid me of two at most before the others figure out what happened. "They think my abilities are controlling insects and transforming into monsters. We can use that against them." I walk to the window and slowly open it.

"What are you—" I can imagine him leaning into his monitor trying to figure out my plan.

"Cover your ears." I clear my throat. A loud screech announcing the hunt resounds. All the birds reply. Not one species in the area misses their chance. The screeches of raptors and the tweets of smaller birds resonate within me. A gun fires. I feel no joy or sadness. I don't crave for more, but I'm ready for what's to come. That's nature, the eternal struggle for survival. And our survival takes priority. Those humans can pay the price for all I care.

Wing-beats collide against each other. A human screams in agony. The eagles found their mark. Something metal bounces of concrete. Boots frantically stomp toward the sounds. The screams continue. The stomping stops with a dry thud. I hear cracking sounds, and as quickly as it started, the hunt ends. I screech again. Silently, the birds retreat into the mountains.

Arvo's voice is unusually brittle. "What did you do?"

I step away from the window and head out the door. "I asked eagles to throw him off the building." My voice is cold. The only thing that matters right now is my pack.

"You killed him! That's murder!" I hear him pacing, then a brief moment of silence followed by a click and more footsteps. "That's—"

"Survival. You wouldn't say murder if I were to kill an animal." I block the hypocrisy from my mind. It will always come down to our species is special. **They're distracted. We can reposition and plan the next ambush.**

Arvo types. He clicks multiple times. Static interferes with the call, but returns to normal. "That's no it." His voice becomes faster and higher pitched.

I take my first silent step down the stairs avoiding erratic movements.

Minos jumps out of my pocket and takes the lead. "I'll scout." The tiny mouse slides down the handrail. Part of me believes he's checking on his family, the other part believes he's scouting for me.

I nod, taking slower steps than usual. "So if I killed a lion to save you, would you call me a murderer?" I'm agitated. I want to rush down the stairs, forget this conversation. I take a deep breath and slow down. Every step measured. A door slamming echoes through the halls. I stop. They aren't close. I'm safe for now.

"No." He doesn't raise his voice, but I can feel that hint of contempt. "You wouldn't kill the lion to save me. You'd try something else. Save us both."

I stop. With Minos scouting, ahead I can afford a minute or two. **He's annoyingly right.** I could easily handle a lion, speak to it, and negotiate. Simple. Animals would have never reached the point of attacking me or my friends. Animals, in a sense, are easy. Or at least traditional thinking says they are. They would never turn on me. People are another thing. "Fine... What do you propose this murderer do?" I lean on the wall, waiting for my signal to move.

"You aren't that." His keyboard composes a monotone vibration. "You have an alternative. Knock them out. Use paralyzing venoms." The infuriating sound of the fan on his end makes the air as monotone as his voice.

"I don't have that much control. You would know if you wanted to be around me." I raise my voice. Red tones cloud my vision. I take a deep breath. Say what you want to say. *I'm immature. A kid. But it stings. He called himself my friend, and dropped ship immediately.*

"I'm sorry." He pauses again. At moments, I feel like he became a hippo, but I know he's forever a bat. "I needed time to adjust. You were a chimera and then a dinosaur. How am I suppose to react?"

I hunch with telephone in hand. "Like I'm not a monster. Like I'm your friend." We sit in silence. Humans are complicated. Animals are simple. *I'm not sure why. I'll never get them.*

Arvo breaks the silence, "I…"

"Forget it. You clearly think we aren't friends and I'm a monster." I stomp down the stairs. My body is stiff. I was a fool to believe people would think positively about me. Jay, Haruka, and Kat probably already think the same as Arvo or will soon.

"Wait!" Arvo's voice invades my ear canals. "We are friends. You aren't a monster. I had to process that the world may not be as I thought. Can't I do that?" He pleads. It's the first time I've hear this. A baby bat asking their mom for milk. Chirping the night away.

My nails turn into reptilian claws. "Sure. It's more than I deserve." My hands stiffen.

"You could trust me to return." The coldness is still in his voice and it in no way comforts me.

My throat rumbles. "Why would you expect me to do that? People leave me. Hurt me. You saw that video. It was mild compared to what I lived through." I descend the stairs, ignoring the need for Minos to return. My long natural weapons are ready. Not to tear through the enemies, but to target myself.

"You don't get to put that on me." He puffs. "You never open up. How should we know?"

I knew it. They all me. That's why they stuck around. Pity doesn't last, it becomes hatred and abandonment. *Why would I tell them? How do I bring that up? What if I don't want to remember the pain? What if it makes them think the same as my bullies? No, I can't let him see my weakness and pain.*

My claws retract. "You're right, I don't say anything." I cut myself short. Don't let it be a predatory relationship. I can't have two predators hunting me. It would spell disaster even for the mighty elephants. "I'm sorry." For now, we should leave this. We should focus on the others, they have it worse. ***If it comes to it, I can take the blow for everyone else.***

"I'm sorry too." We both keep silent. There's nothing to say, not now. Not while the others depend on us.

Minos runs at me. I pick him up and place him in my hair. He sits down calmly. "It's clear." I gently pet him. My mind might be elsewhere, but I must move if I want to save the others.

Arvo hesitates. "What's the plan?"

"I'll do what every specie does. Fight back. Survive." I reach the ground floor.

He taps his fingers against the keyboard. "You could choose something different," his voice dwindles.

I won't budge. I meant it, whatever it takes. Surrendering will be a last resort. Much how like venom is for snakes. "I'm not letting Jay and the others die 'cause of me." Silence. I can't think of anything else. It's my fault they're stuck in this mess. It's my fault they're targeted. Words stumble out almost as a whisper, "I'd rather be a human murderer, than let my friends die."

"You don't have to be a killer."

"You don't get it. It's survival. I can't let them die. It's Kat and the others, or the people endangering everyone" My feline instincts cause me to stay still.

"I understand that." He clicks the keys, as if pretending to be busy. "But I don't understand why you force yourself into that mentality." I don't have an answer. I know it's what I need to do. Don't have to like it. "Can we talk about it later?"

I stand on the last stair. "Yes."

His end is silent, except for the fan swirling the air in his room.

I walk down the hallway. Glass doors reveal the outside. Nothing is normal anymore. Not the plaza empty of people, or the dull fan whooshing on the background. I stand next to the door. With one deep gulp, I swallow my anger. "What's our status?"

He clicks faster. After a minute of typing and clicking, he replies, "Clear outside. One of them is in the neighboring building, be careful. Your success rate is at a forty-five percent."

"I'll take anything above zero." I feel empty. A starving blue whale swimming to rescue a pod of dolphins from hunters, while having a harpoon aimed at my back.

CHAPTER EIGHTEEN: MUTUALISM

I take a peek through the glass door. Nothing outside. "Anyone heading to check the body?" I slide out. The door sluggishly returns to place, creaking as it does. I attempt the prowlers walk, but my boots are too rigid for flexible movement. In my ears, everything sounds as loud as fireworks. With each step, an airplane motor ignites. I walk away from the brick path and try to camouflage myself under the green shrubs.

"Yes. Are you?" he asks.

I interrupt him with a howl that makes my body rumble with anticipation. The pack howls back with squeaky barks and bone chilling full howls. Some are feral, most are domestic. The air swirls with a tense, agitated smell. It's like a spark of electricity being unleashed. There's something intoxicating about it, but I can't falter. I have to wait for now. "Wolf hearing."

Leaves rustle in the wind. Wild plants silence themselves. Fragments of plastic and metal crash against concrete from the neighboring building. I still. Heavy boots fall. A spring clicks. "I found Mike. He's dead, covered in scratches." Static ends the message.

Arched backs in every corner, they stalk the unsuspecting man. It's time. "*Aaauuuw!*" It riles up a chorus, haunting the unfortunate wannabe predator. One after the other, they all join. Many breeds run toward the target. The target growls a curse, and the dogs howl their answer. The canines go silent as they maul their prey. The man screams.

"Hide!" Arvo's voice shakes. His end goes quiet. Even the fan stops.

Minos stills. His fur conceals him in the entangled mess that is my hair. I throw myself inside the bush. The leaves do nothing to soften the branches. They poke my clothing and scratch my skin. I cover my mouth and wait silently.

The door swings violently open, shattering the glass. Heavy footsteps crush the glass. Each makes me to run away. The big guy, from the bathroom, takes in the air, the wailing, the pure scent of a recent hunt. His pupils shine a crimson red. He steps closer to the shrubbery. Minos can't stop shaking. My blood has gone so cold it barely flows. He stands above the bush. Minos and I have relinquished oxygen.

His radio beeps distracting him from us. "Check on Trevor."

He clicks on the radio. "Weakling is dying. You shouldn't have brought him."

"Those were the orders." The voice is young but rough. It could be my age, but there's more to it. An unnerving quality that it shares with the giant towering over us.

He breaks a picnic table in two, then throws it through the doors of the building. Inside the hallway, a hailstorm of glass and wood obliterates the lockers. I cover Minos from the few the shrapnel. A couple of shards lacerate me. Bubbles of liquid form on my face, neck, and arms.

This triggers him. He turns around, eyes glowing embers even under the clear sun. It's as if they're fire. He bends a parasol, and throws it our way. It collides with the shrub, cleanly tearing up the section to my right. Only soft dirt remains. He grabs another parasol, like a javelin. It flies right above us. Some branches fly off the shrub. The parasol impales the concrete wall. ***I'm going to die. He's going to kill all of us.*** He aims a metal trashcan. His eyes stare at my spot.

The sprinklers rain on us. The bells deafen me. Nearby, bright lights and phones flash. Even their van's alarm goes off. My wolf ears sting, they disappear. He turns away as he throws the trash can. It lands to our left. The bush nearly explodes from the force. Garbage decorates the plants behind us. The trashcan bounces as far as the fence.

His eyes turn a calm gray blue. He leaves a wake of destruction as he walks away.

For the next five minutes, neither Minos, Arvo, nor I dare to move. The plaza is trashed.

The fan starts up again, interrupted by intense typing. Once in a while the alarm, and the bell synchronize, temporarily deafening me. They're erratic and I find myself wincing even when they aren't ringing.

Arvo says, "That is a monster. Do what you need."

That kicks me out of the bush. "What are my chances?" I ask as I check my cuts and let the sprinkler water clean me off. I step onto the brick path.

He pauses before saying, "Ten percent. The police have one percent."

Ten percent. *I've killed us all.* I'm in a daze. I kneel on the hard, wet ground. This is illegal poachers versus the black rhino. The rhino eventually goes extinct. I am the rhino. "Ouch!"

Minos nibbles on my hair. "Stop! That won't help." He nibbles again when I slouch.

"Please stop," my voice lowers.

Arvo stops typing. "What did I do?"

"Not you. Minos is nibbling my hair."

"Get up. You can save them." Minos and Arvo say in sync despite sounding differently. The squeak language is shorter.

"But—"

"I was complicit in murder. You aren't giving up." He keeps this cold voice. I can't answer. Not with all the blame I have in this. "Remember last term. When I said you had a ninety-nine percent of winning that contest?"

"Yes."

He clears his throat, "I lied. You had fifty percent or less, but you showed everyone. You got one hundred percent right."

His voice is still very bat-like, monotone, with the occasional erratic spike. "So how are you planning to save everyone?"

I'm shocked. My brain stops spiraling. ***Arvo doesn't hate me? He believes in me.*** It feels like a ray of sun after months of dark winter in Antarctica. Maybe he is lying, but it warms me up. "Sorry about this and my outburst earlier. I'll try to get us out of this."

My heart slows down. A straight up fight will kill me. Then I have to do like the animals and adapt. Circumvent the rules. I have to eliminate his raw strength, speed, and agility.

I scratch Minos head. I need something small and silent that creates its own rules. Animal attack and defense tactics. Vomit, pee, blood, quills, armor, claws, fangs, poison, electricity. Venom. Venom is the easiest and most viable. "I got it. What are my chances with venom?"

"Woah, Woah. You're poisoning them? I'd say back to seventy."

"I need to inject it. Need a knife and the venom." I tap my lip and walk away from all the shattered glass. "Minos, can you get me a cup and thin cloth or plastic?" I dig into my pockets. Rubber bands wiggle between my fingers.

He squeaks, leaving me with Arvo. Arvo's footsteps are loud, almost stomps. He starts clicking at the computer, "I'll get native—"

"No need." I look back at the creek. "There are around sixty species of snakes in our region plus the Gila monster. Our best option is coral snakes." I pace back to where Minos scampered off. "Our best venom is Coral Snakes. Most species aren't commonly found in the region and the anti-venoms are only obtainable in the States."

"You could apply a non-lethal dose." He sparks up, the same way that he did in November. His chair collides with the ground.

I tap my feet. A bit faster cause I know he will hate me. "I can't do that. Too exact. Coral snake venom is a neurotoxin, so they have time. People rarely die from it, and it gives us a way to win." I shake my head. I know where to find knives. I have to follow the scent of blood and the path of destruction.

My stomach churns as I slowly approach the corner. My feet instinctively follow the lessons the felines taught me. They tip toe around the glass and wood splinters. They stick to dry land, avoiding the puddles formed by Arvo's trick. My rigid boots are perfect for this. Never making a squawk. Same could be said about the animals. They've all have gone unnaturally silent.

I lean on the wall and take a glance around the corner. A nightmare stands over mangled, bloodied bodies. The monster's eyes glow as bright as the sun. He turns in my direction. The carnage churns my insides. I hold my breath. My body stills. Nails strike against my palm.

"They're dead weight." He laughs at his own joke.

My ears pick up more than just him. "Come back. He'll come to us." That younger voice again. It infects my brain with dread. He orders this thing around! **Who does that?**

Any animals that were in the vicinity ran away.

"He better find us. The more he makes me wait, the more I want to kill him." The air is tighter, and the silence is broken by the piercing sound of a gunshot. The scent he expels triggers something. My sight turns an intense red. It smells like freshly drawn blood. No, it's more intense, think of fire burning meat.

"What was that?" Arvo's voice trembles. This is Kitti's Hog-Nosed Bat if it were a person.

I move back. My feline flexibility is gone. All that's left is a stump, one that missteps. Wood snaps under my weight. "I think they shot someone." My voice is broken, short-lived. My nails dig deeper into my skin. It doesn't help, this is too much. I need the knife.

When the guy has left, I approach the two mangled bodies. Both dressed in crimson, one more so than the other. The contorted one features a few swipes and feathers. His neck is twisted in a way it shouldn't be. His long gun on the ground, still in one piece. The other body is missing chunks, mostly from his neck and legs.

I turn around, spewing my snacks. I take one slow, deep breath. Ignoring the smell of blood. Avoiding looking at the horrible scene in front of me. I turn toward the bodies. The sooner I get the weapon, the faster I can forget about them.

I crouch and lean toward the feathered body. My hand slithers inside the vest pocket. The dagger is surprisingly dry. Perfectly clean, perfectly sharp. I walk away. Run back through the wasted plaza. Hide behind the shredded bush. Minos sits inside a cup with a dirty piece of cloth. He squeaks, "Brownies next time."

"Peanut butter filled," I promise, slowing me down.

Before he can reply. "Ah…" Arvo is hyperventilating. "Why are they killing each other?" He snivels loudly. The typing stops.

"I don't know. I'm glad they didn't shoot our friends." I pause to think clearly. "Do me a favor. Get Kat and call my siblings. If in thirty minutes you don't hear from me run." He keeps sniveling. This must be rough for him, and I forced him to help. I say the most reasonable thing since this started, "You can stop. I can handle it." The phone goes silent. He needs time.

Minos scurries to my hair.

"Are there any snakes around?" With the cup already standing, I place the cloth on top of it. The rubber band holds the makeshift cloth lid.

"No," Minos squeaks.

I sigh. "I'll have to try myself." I just need the fangs and the venom glands. Eastern coral snake. I picture it. The red, yellow, and black pattern. The powerful venom and the lack of limbs. "Eastern coral snake fangs." My body replies, my canines curve. Their fine tips tickle my palate. I open my mouth, both fangs stretch out, a cool drop falls onto my lip. My fangs sink into the cloth.

I chew the cloth; it tastes like dirt. I hope it's dirt. My pinched nose still receives some of the smell. My fangs return to human teeth, without control or will. The saliva covered cup is filled with an acrid scent and a light-yellow fluid. One knife. "This will get one shot. Let's go. I have to rescue everyone." Slowly and steadily, we move toward the half-broken science building. Another reflection of me. Of my eyebrow.

Yellow tape clings to the building's southern wall. The rubble has been cleared. No more glass shards refracting the green tones of the grass. I gaze upward at the fourth floor. Walking into a bear's den would be safer, even without my abilities. I howl, "Non rodents, leave. Thank you for your help." I take the first step. It's quieter than my pounding heart. "Minos, could you scout ahead?" The tiny mouse uses my body as a bridge to the handrails. It doesn't take long for him to reach the next floor.

I take slow steps, crouching beside the handrails. The poisoned cup is in my jacket's left pocket. The knife in my hand is ready to be dipped in either flesh or venom. I catch thousands of small steps crawling within the building. Two pairs of footsteps and many sobs come from the fourth floor. I hate how the scent of fear makes me feel. Always on edge.

This flight of stairs keeps spiraling, with no signs of life. Minos is coming back down from the top. I make it to the third floor, still nothing. Empty. In the distance, a chorus of wildlife evacuates the scene. As long as they don't get found, they'll be fine.

Minos gets to me, keeping himself on the handrail. "They are locked inside the show hall. No one is outside." He then climbs back up.

The stench of blood thickens with every step I take. On the fourth floor, a stain of red covers the otherwise white floor. A body clad in black, just like the others. It breaths no more; the bullet wound springs blood slowly. His body keeps the automatic doors open. A trap made for me.

The white hall ends with three pairs of doors. All closed. No way I can get in through there. Not without a bullet to the head. There's weeping and traces of blood inside that room. My friends' unique scents slip through the rest. They're still alive. I move toward the girls' bathroom. It's a safer bet than the boys' side. It looks exactly the same as the previous bathroom, although cleaner. The grates on the top give me an idea. "Minos, get all the rodents."

"They're already here." Thousands of squeaks reach my ears. Black matter flows into the bathroom, through the grates and air vents.

"Make sure no light comes in from the windows." With that, I place my cup on the floor and explain the details of the plan.

The rats and mice leave, except for hundred still in the bathroom. A couple inside the grates. I look at my phone. Arvo hasn't messaged. I want to check on him one last time before I get killed.

Theon: Are you okay?

Arvo: Not great. Kat is picking your brothers up.

Theon: That's great news. Are you up for one last thing?

Arvo: Is someone dying?

Theon: No. I need a blackout and fire sprinklers. Can you make it happen?

Arvo: I can do it. Why?

Theon: It gives me a fighting chance. Blackout to stab them, sprinklers to dissolve the venom. If things go wrong call the police.

Arvo: I will. The dots on the phone wave at me. *Good luck.*

I leave a message for him before leaving the phone inside my jeans. My jacket hangs from the door. I place my shoes under the sinks, with my phone stored inside them. Both the knife and the cup find their places in the grates, with currents of mice pushing them to their destination. I climb last, to the all-consuming darkness.

I prepare myself. Only one animal will do it for me, a black rat. Smart, adaptable, and inconspicuous. **Collaborate with me body.** As I pull myself up, I shift into a black rat.

Slowly but surely, I creep into the never-ending darkness. The bathroom light becomes a memory. The stagnant air prevents any other smells from reaching me. No blood, no fear. My eyes distinguish only what is right in front of me.

When the smell of blood and fear finally reaches me again, I know I am close. ***This has to work. It will work.*** The rodents stop in front of an open grate, with cup and knife ready. Time to wait for the signal.

My heart beats faster than a hummingbird's. The stagnant heat in no way helps. Many of my rodent friends have left the ducts. Only a few stand with me, holding the knife and cup. The others have crept up the edges of the room. I can turn the hunt around, or at least stall it for a while. My heart beats fast, but there's no point in calming myself. It's all or nothing.

"What's going on?" A handful of gasps follow the leader's words. "Check the lights."

The rodents dip the knife in the venom, leaving the cup on the edge. I sprint and jump into the darkness. As I jump between the knife and cup, the rats push them over the edge. My body grows back to human as I fall.

The hard stone fails to mask my entry. I manage to catch the knife before it crashed onto the floor. The cup on the other hand splashes my ankles with venom. Hopefully, the knife has enough. I slip into darkness away from the cup.

"Flashlights!" the leader from the radio commands. "Check what's there." I try to ignore how he order the monster, but I can't.

I gulp. I'm not ready for this.

The big guy from the bathroom runs toward the landing spot. I've scurried away, but he follows my movement. The leader stands near my classmates sobbing. I move further away from the big guy, trying to get close to the center of the room. My muffled movements allow me to get closer to my classmates, without being noticed. Or so I thought.

There's a strong vibration beside me. The big guy! A slight grace pushes me way from my classmates. My arm pulses. I keep my course, and crawl toward the students. His vibrations come at me again. I hold my breath and don't move. If I could hide my scent, I would too.

The monster stops in its tracks. "Kid, I know you're there." The bloodlust is clear in his voice. Some of my classmates whimper and recoil.

I hear my friends. Now to wait for the leader to get closer. ***Slow down, just as the reptiles taught you.*** With a knife in hand, I crawl toward the one who seems to be in charge. He takes his position beside the group. He's one step away from me. Now or never! I jump and stab his leg. The blade sticks to him.

"Argh!" he jerks away from me with the knife still embedded in his leg.

Heavy stomps come my way. Red flashes of light dash from the other end of the room. I try to stand, but he connects. I'm sent flying and crash against the wall. Everything goes dark. The giant drags me by the shirt, then slams my back against the wall. A dull, swollen pain bursts from my chest. I think he broke my ribs.

I gasp for air, more like beg for it, but the airflow is constricted. My limbs flail wildly. With little force, they strike the big guy. Nails scratching, feet missing the mark. Life flees from me. My gasps become desperate growls. Light creeps into the room as the rodents abandon their places at the windows and swarm the floor. Lights turn back on right after. My body acting on instinct. I feel a tail growing. **No! Don't! I can't show them that.**

The big guy's hand wraps around my throat. He's taking his time, smiling, enjoying every second of it. Behind him, my classmates watching in horror. None of them move. The leader is on his knees. **Yes. If I die, you'll die with me.**

"Stop!" Jay leaves the group. His cut has reopened! It drips blood. Burning red. It douses the pain in my chest. I feel heat in my upper body.

The big guy strangling me laughs. "Once I finish with him, I'll get to you."

Water falls upon us. An alarm! **Arvo or Minos? It doesn't matter. Thank you! That will bring attention to us.** The part that I missed.

"Theon, what did you do?" The leader struggles to stand. His one of his legs drags behind him. It doesn't support his weight. He points a gun at Jay.

I flail, trying release the big guy's grasp of my neck.

"Release him." The leader forces his will on the big guy.

The big guy listens. I slide down, hitting the floor. My teary eyes seeing more clearly. ***Leaving the wallet behind was a mistake. Not that it mattered. I was the target all along.*** I cough and grasp my throbbing throat. Desperate currents of air fill me. "You miscalculated." A pause. "Let us go, alive, and I'll tell you what I did."

He closes in on Jay. Gun to his head. "You're in no position to bargain."

Lucy and Haruka are frozen. My mind wanders to Arvo. I'm sure he's panicking too. Jay smiles at me, like nothing frazzles him.

I can save us. "You're wrong. You were going to kill all of us anyway. If I'm going to die, so will you."

Everyone's faces twist in horror at my words. Except Jay. His hopeful eyes stay on me. They never leave me. I fluster. I won't let your trust be misplaced.

The leader grunts. His black hair matches mine; his pierced ears contrast us. His face covered by a mask. He has a similar build to Jay. His skin is darker than mine. "Tell us." He pushes the gun to Jay's temple.

My face radiates heat. "If he dies, I'll kill you." I'm tired, but a lion within me demands what's his. His pride. His scorching lava red pride. *I will kill him.*

The big guy shadows me. "You have to fight me first." His eyes are two bloody diamonds on display.

My focus is on Jay and the leader. "He dies anyway." I point at the leader.

He pulls the gun away, then turns it on me. I feel nothing. I'd rather he kills me than my friends. He lowers the gun after failing to get a reaction. "What are the terms?"

"I knew you were smart." I stand tall. I feel like a brachiosaurus. "You leave all of us alone. No one dies. I'll tell you why you'll die. If you try anything else, you're dead." I slow on the final words. I wheeze. My chest hurts.

"We have a deal." He staggers, but continues to walk away from the group. "What did you do?"

Weird, the venom shouldn't affect him this fast. Not even with rushing blood. Could he be allergic? This is better than I planned. I lean on the wall. The pain in my chest and back beg me to lie down. **I can't show weakness. That's the first rule of survival.** I wince. "Once you get to your van, I'll tell you" I have a dead stare, mostly 'cause my energy is running low. My body pushes me to stay straight.

He points the gun at Jay. "You can't change the deal." The students gasp. They're shaking like a group of lemmings waiting for winter to end. Jay's face is somber. His joyful smile gone. I can't tell what he reminds me of. **Could it be that snake I failed to protect at the farm? Or that run over dog I had to take to the vet to euthanize?** He looks so calm, and it scares me. That Jay isn't the one I have gotten to know.

"I'm not changing it. Just making sure you can complete your side of the bargain." I avoid looking at Jay. **This is my fault.**

He's in danger cause of me. He's my best friend. He doesn't deserve to die because of it.

"Not good enough." The gun touches Jay's temple. I see red. ***I'll murder them. How would they deal with a dinosaur?*** The big guy might, but not his leader.

I smirk. "I guess you'll die with the rest of us." I lean against the wall. My chest burns. In another world, I would have been the one with venom in his veins.

The captain lowers the gun again and leads the way out. The giant follows. His red eyes stare at me. "You're lucky. Next time, I'll kill you."

"You are more than welcome to try…" I stagger, don't know his name.

"Berserker." He smiles, savoring his victory. Berserk takes his stumbling leader out.

I look at the camera in the corner. "Arvo, can you make the speakers play a message for me?"

"Yes." The speakers make a low-pitched sound that makes me want to tear my ears off.

The recording has my voice, pretending to be like Roy's. Grand and sure. "Eastern coral snake venom. That's what I injected you. You have around two hours, maybe a bit more. The anti-venom is exclusive to certain regions of the USA." At that moment, I fall to my knees. The pressure of the world finally falling off my shoulders. I can feel my heart again and my breath deepens.

Minos crawls inside the room, climbs to my hair, and says, "It's okay. It's all over now." His tiny paws scratch my scalp.

"You did it!" Arvo and Kat shout at the same time from the speakers. His voice trembles. Not as much as earlier. Hers, as usual, is a macaw bringing a party to life. "Police are on their way." Arvo adds, his voice regaining his cold logic.

My body continues to withdraw to the floor, using my legs to cover my nakedness from my classmates. *We made it. We survived. Somehow, I did it.*

Jay stands beside me. He extends his hand to me. "Holding out for a hero?"

I take it with a smile on my face and embrace him. "Yeah, I am." He squiggles his injured arm out. Right, I forgot he is sensitive. "I thought we were all going to die because of me."

He hugs me back. "I knew you had it. You wouldn't let us die." I wince to the pressure. He immediately backs away. His calm attitude feels forced. Not sure, he doesn't smell like fear. But his pale face and lost eyes worry me. I want to know what's on his mind, but it's best I don't get to close to anyone. Not if this will become my life.

In the back many of my class makes hug and cry. Most of them barely move. They huddle like emperor penguins in the Antarctic. A couple of them spread out. And two of the jocks leave slowly and cautiously. Their tennis shoes squeak against the floor and splash in the puddles.

"What was that?" A classmate walks toward us. "They knew your name. They were going to kill us for you? And why are you naked?"

Jay puts his hand on my shoulder. Haruka rushes to our side. Her teary eyes don't hide her feelings. "Hostage situation went wrong! I saw it in an anime. They panicked because was Theon missing." Lucy walks behind her, face in shock. I scratch my head. What do I say?

"That's fantasy." Our classmate throws his hands in the air.

"Theon called the police." Haruka winks at the camera.

"I did." I flow with her, anything to get us out of this situation and make things right. Haruka turns her back on our classmate and hugs the three of us, crying. She lets go when I start complaining about my chest and neck.

Lucy looks at me. The reflection of her glasses blocks the tears flowing down her face. "We thought they shot you. That you died." Her face sinks into Haruka's shoulder. She sobs. I try to respond, but the words won't come out. They can't. My throat swells in agony, leaving little space for air flow. I reach my neck. It's stiff. Jay takes me by the shoulder and slowly helps me down.

CHAPTER NINETEEN: THREE MAKES A PACK

January 29, 2013

My parents' TV roars, "Multiple robberies have been committed by insects." The TV continues without much reaction from my parents, "Authorities have opened an investigation regarding both the Insect Thief and Monterrey's Monster." A couple of grunts come from their room. A rant is about to start.

On my phone, I scroll the news about both weird circumstances. They're received with doubt. "In other news, a high school was attacked by an extortion ring. Most of the victims were uninjured. Some had minor injuries but required no hospitalization."

I slowly travel to my brothers' room. The bandages on my chest make me itch. Each time I inhale, it pains me. I open the door. Lucas sits on his bed. He hides the tablet and ear buds. His innocent smile disappears when he sees me. He pulls his gadgets out, but hesitates to complete the action. Roy stares me down like I violated lion pride territory rules.

I close the door behind me. "We're in trouble." I hold the doorknob just in case.

"Chillax. No one will figure it out." He looks down on me, even though he's shorter. "I know what I'm doing."

"Not talking about that." A pause, while my feet tap anxiously. My phone vibrates. Ugh, not right now. I hide it in my pocket again. "We need to lay low. The people hunting me will try again soon."

"Those fuckers? You kicked their asses. If you could anyone can." He stands on his bed, and looks down on me, as usual. His red freckles are less noticeable in this light. Each day, his presence gets more and more similar to a lion's commanding aura.

"I almost died!" I raise my arms way too fast. My chest begs against it. I hold my stomach and slump against the door. Lucas comes and helps me sit on the floor.

Roy rolls his eyes. "Pussy." He jumps down, leans his elbow on the foosball table.

I grind my teeth against the pain. "They broke my ribs. If he kicked me any harder my back bones would have broken. I can barely speak." My strained voice begs me to stop, but I can't. I raise my still purple neck. The harder tissue is shaped like a hand. I haven't dared leave out the house since the fight.

Lucas stands. "Did you take your pain medicine?" I nod. He goes back to his bed and sits. His tablet plays the sound of a forest filled with life. His fingers mimic the wind. They rise with the chirp of the birds and lower with the sound of a cascade.

He crosses his arms. "Not doing shit if you don't have a plan." His brown eyes try to break me apart. I've seen worse than that, felt worse than anything he can throw at me.

I look at Lucas and feel his soothing rhythm. To the distant birds, like those who supported me. "We need to recruit others like us." The taste is bitter. More people, I hate the thought but risking animals isn't an option, not after everything they've done for me. We can risk other people. Spread the word. Get the attention away from us. They won't be able to deal with a rabbit-like plague.

"Why?" Lucas inquires. His hair bounces with the flow of the river.

"To defeat an army, you need one of your own."

Roy flicks a foosball my way. "We can fucking take them." He smirks, giving me a look, he doesn't give anyone else. It's warmer and kinder than usual. It has that defiance that so represents him.

I ready myself. I wince as my lungs push a bit too much. "Think about it. They sent Penumbra, Berserker, and other four people for me, how many others are there? They even pretended to be part of the military. They could be affiliated with people in power."

"Who cares? You dunked them." More condescension.

I raise my voice. "I got lucky!" My hands turn a scaly red. Deep breaths, deep breaths. It shifts back.

Roy turns his back on me. He slowly gets up from his bed, shakes his head in disapproval, like a lion telling their cubs to not bother him.

Lucas switches to a faster song. One that has extremely high notes. He stands up, whistling almost as high and fast as the music. "You said they done it before. And you lived. It doesn't sound like luck…" His voice trembles but manages to hold the last syllable.

"I—"

"You fucking beat them. Own it." Roy crosses his arms, barely looks at me. That's never a good sign.

Oddly enough, I don't shake or move. "I barely did it." Life abandons my voice. "Penumbra took you two out. And Berserker squashed me."

Lucas sits next to me. "We can do better next time!"

I… Can keep it together. I'll figure things out. Their bathroom sounds like a water park. There is too much splashing for it to be only the toilet or a rat swimming in it. I point in its direction. Roy fervently shakes his head. My phone rings again. I pick it up, ready to turn it off before reading the notification.

Lucy: I need to show you something.

I turn back at them. "Give me a minute."

Lucas peeks. "Your friends are calling you!" Roy takes Lucas's tablet and changes the music to louder, spikier tones. It's edgy, dark, and rough like a black panther. Lucas runs. He tries to wrestle the tablet away from the prince.

Theon: What is it?

Lucy: I've been drawing weird things.

She sends three pictures. An image of a guy with short messy hair. He's fit, and looks at the horizon. His eyes are filled with rage and desperation to protect. His eyebrow is broken like mine. He looks like me. At some point, I was like this. An out of reach dream. In the background, a dinosaur rising. A T-Rex roars as it destroys a building. The rubble falls and I stand, ready to attack again.

Second, is Lucas playing the piano. A golden guitar hangs from his back. His outfit contrasts with the landscape. The ice white surface is mismatched by his beach wear and scuba-diving goggles. He happily sings the piano's tune. Or at least that's how it looks like. My gaze darts to him, then returns.

Roy sits on an obsidian throne. His eyes are covered by sunglasses. Metal bracelets and necklaces hang from him. The torn jeans and sleeves jacket fit him like spots on a jaguar. A golden crown sits over his hair. Each hand holds a gun, one pointing straight at me, the other resting on the armrest. The throne doesn't look made out of metal or wood. It looks much more alive.

Lucy: Your brothers have abilities?

Theon: Yes. How did you know?

Lucy: I'm scared. There are four more. What's happening to me?

Theon: I think you have an ability. Everything is going to be fine. I'll protect us.

Lucy: Am I a freak?

Theon: No, not at all. Could you wait until I'm at school so I can explain what I know?

Lucy: Yes. But will those people target me?

Theon: I don't think they would know you have one. Unless they caught anyone in your drawings.

Lucy: Okay. I'll see you on Friday?

Theon: Yes. Don't tell anyone other than our friends. And please bring all the drawings. If there is someone in there we don't know, we have to get to them before they get caught.

Lucy: I will. Thank you.

I scroll back to the image of me. A grin shows canine fangs. "I found a solution to one problem." From Lucas's toybox, I pick out the chessboard and some plushies and toys. I place the board on the foosball table. Place a king, a wolf, and a guitar on one side and the pawns and minions opposite.

"Hell yeah! Let's kick some ass!" Roy shouts before I start my plan.

I lean on the foosball table. "First, we convince my friends to help us. We use Lucy's abilities to identify others with abilities, have Arvo track them down, and we recruit them. We take two birds with one stone." I pick up pieces of Lucas's chessboard and I place them on the table. "As we recruit others, we thin out the hunters' numbers and learn about them. Key members, locations, goals, and weaknesses." I topple the pieces one by one, leaving the king, the wolf and the guitar standing. "Then we strike."

"Fuck yeah! That's more like it." Roy jumps off his bed.

"I knew you could do it." Lucas runs and hugs me. "We will save others! Are we heroes?"

"No!" Roy shouts.

I can't tell him the truth. I only care about my brothers and friends. Everyone else, I don't know. "Not sure. The plan will get more detailed as we go, but I'll handle that." So, we begin training to be more than survivors. We will play prey for now, an innocent group of African buffaloes wanting peace, but don't test us or underestimate us because we can kill any predator.

CHAPTER TWENTY: ADAPTATION

February 1, 2013

The room is tense as Haruka scribbles in her notebook. The other four people at the table aren't making it better. Jay and Kat are acting like okapis. Lucy hides her face from us, maybe she connected with her inner tortoise. Arvo or how Jay has named him, DJ, hides behind his laptop, but out of everyone he seems the least affected by last week.

None of the animals come close to us, and since last week's disaster we are the most avoided teens in school. Our seat pattern rarely changes.

I pop one of the pills they gave me for my broken ribs. The pain lowers significantly as long as I take one every eight hours.

Haruka slams her pen against the thick notebook. "This is weird."

Kat plays her music, choosing something less natural and more festive. A group of friends having a small celebration. Glasses clink, a bonfire burns, it's filled with laugher and giggles. "Let's talk about what happened." She puts her hand on DJ's back and softly pats him.

DJ digs deeper into his laptop. "There's nothing to talk about." His voice is cold, like when we argued. I'm afraid to turn his way. He lowers his cap to make sure we can't see his face.

Beside him, Jay is silent. He stares out into the distance. He barely moves, and from time to time he inexplicably shakes.

I hesitate, but then say, "We should talk about it." Our survival depends on it. After Saturday, I'm not taking any chances. It's the only way we can protect each other. I lean in closer, but I can't keep from staring at Jay. He doesn't notice, but neither the others.

DJ slams his laptop closed. Jay flinches and slowly shrinks, avoiding the ruckus. Haruka looks up. She gets two more notebooks and juggles writing in each of them. Her head as low as Lucy's, who once again seems on the verge of running away.

"You want to talk about how I witnessed three murders at the hands of a friend? Or about how you four almost died?" DJ stands. His eyes are red, and the purple hagfish hang from then do little to hide the contrast. "Dude! I saw you getting overpowered. What will happen next time?" He tries to keep calm, but his voice cracks and breaks in the worst ways possible. It's like wildfire scarred forest. The patches of green consumed by gray and black. Although new life will spring, it's never pretty while it happens. Kat holds his hands, keeping him tied to the table.

"I'm sorry. If there was another way, I would have taken it." I look down at the table. At the few nuts and cashews left by wandering birds and playful squirrels. I close my hands to prevent the urge to scratch my palms. "I'll protect us."

He stares directly into my eyes. "Don't use your powers. Forget about them. It's not worth it."

"Don't ask that of me." I look at the creek. The swaying trees. The fresh breeze. The wildest scenery in school. I sigh. I shouldn't have said anything. Now they'll ask. I don't want that. "How would you feel if you had to give up something so essential to yourself? It's much greater than the air we breathe. It's like taking the spines of the porcupine or the smell of the skunks. I don't know how to explain it. I wouldn't be me without it."

Jay glances at me. "I get it." His lips twitch, then he goes somber again.

I'm not sure how to make people feel better. Kat nods toward Jay as if she knew what I was thinking. I stand beside him and hug him, despite the pain. I don't say anything, 'cause I know that doesn't help. Words are meaningless without the right thoughts and actions. His body slackens.

Kat steps aside. Her dazzling colors do their magic. I see Jay smile.

"Don't worry, we aren't doing that." She twirls. "But you are more than your abilities." She winks at me. She just knows what to say to make the air flow freely between us.

"It would be a waste not to use it. The adventures! The stories! The mischief!" Haruka trembles with excitement, shaking the table with her.

"We made the right decisions, but they don't feel right." With his hands, DJ covers his face. His hair flows between his fingers. "I don't know if I can do that again."

Kat returns to him. "You don't have to." She brushes his black bat hair. Even today, she manages to be that crimson macaw. It's like she isn't affected. Her red hair helps, but it's the way she smiles and says it's okay that makes everything feel like it really will be. Like there is sunlight after the meteor dust clears.

"You did nothing wrong. I made the decision. You tried to stop me. You got Kat and my brothers to safety. Without you, only Kat would be at this table today. You were the true hero." I try to get close, but Kat shakes her head. Maybe she's right he needs time. No teenager should ever see what we saw.

Kat sits between Jay and DJ. She touches Jay's shoulder. He flinches and jumps, hitting me in the ribs in the process. I take a step back. My breaths get heavier, rougher. My chest asks for mercy and forgiveness. Jay lands on the edge of his seat. He glances at me. In his eyes is something I've never seen before. A deer looking at the puma as it pounces. They strain as he realizes what happened. Why I'm crumpling to the ground. And why Kat has taken a step back. She shudders, while her hands are steady on DJ. Haruka closes her notebook. DJ clears his hair from his eyes.

Kat tries to reach Jay, but he moves away. "Are you okay?"

"Sorry." His gaze stares past me. I turn back, but there's only the verdant expanse of plants that protect us from other people. His hazel eyes are teary. Eye-bags larger than DJ's hang from his face. He shakes his head. "I'm fine." He forms a smile that never reaches his eyes. It feels familiar.

Kat attempts to hold his hand. He dodges her. Kat's eyes are teary and she's shaking. DJ barely responds to her movements. Her voice trembles as she pronounces one letter. "O." She hugs herself. It does little to change how much she quakes.

"You can talk to us." I get closer to him. She turns to me and nods. Her body trembles slightly less.

He sits static. This is more like a hognose snake's act than my friend. "Don't worry, I'm fine."

"Don't lie. Please don't force me to figure it out."

He jumps out of his seat and raises his arms. Jay's smile continues to be way smaller than usual. He lands on his feet, but there's something off about how he does it. "Bro, I'm gucchilicious." He never moves forward, or invades my personal space. I step toward him, and he steps back.

Haruka moves to the other side of the table. She stands behind Kat, and hugs to keep her from shaking. Jay quivers when he notices them.

"I warned you. Gray Wolf sense of smell." Different stenches hit me. Nature's smells disintegrate the moment they drift near our table. Six different scents cloud the others. DJ's is bitter and sickening. I want to throw up to it. Kat's is light and flowery. A relaxing lavender. Haruka and Lucy share one; it's agitated. My heart pumps faster when focusing on it. Mine is the third strongest, rotten onions and garlic. I know it's guilt.

Jay's is a storm cloud of skunk pee. It's too strong. So strong I abandon the sense of smell with the first sniff. I've smelled it before. I want to run from it. The closest human version I can think of is gasoline burning, but that doesn't do it justice. Jay reeks it.

"It's okay to be afraid." I take a step toward him, and this time he doesn't move. His hands shake. I take one. The tremors travel through me.

His eyes refocus on us. "I… I'm fine. Donut worry, be happy." He strains his smile to uncomfortable levels. It fills me with pain and regret.

I shouldn't have told any of them. They would have been better off without me. Jay's joy wouldn't have disappeared. DJ wouldn't be juggling this fight of survival. Lucy would have a normal life, powerless. "Stop pretending. You don't have to." Acting as a crutch is the bare minimum I can do. I approach, but my friends point at my chest. Right, I can't help Jay when it matters, again.

He starts crying. "I don't know what to do. What if—" Sobs make a break for it, just like the tears he had been holding.

"You died?" DJ replies. Their eyes lock. It mirrors the way Lucy and Haruka look at each other. There is that deep, unspoken understanding. *I envy them. I hate myself. When I experience that, it's undeserved.*

"But—"

I take his arm and put it over my shoulder. "What about you?" Haruka takes his other arm and helps me get him to his seat. Even with her help, the pressure on my ribs threatens to do more damage. I don't care if break my ribs again. I sit beside him. My arms do the rest as they embrace him. "I'm so sorry." I slowly pat his back. My hands invite him to rest his head on my shoulder. The throbbing pain in my chest screams, but I can handle it. He's helped me multiple times. This is the least I can do for him. Soon after Haruka and Kat join the hug. DJ drags his dazed body to us.

Lucy scoots away. She isn't able to make eye contact. Haruka waves her over. She shakes her head in response. Her shadow darkens her glasses, and she keeps quiet.

Kat, DJ, and Haruka take seats opposite ours. Haruka hides her notebooks inside her backpack before sitting down. I keep holding Jay, I won't let him fall into whatever fear he's holding. I'm staying here, until he's free of it.

Jay leans on me. It takes effort to keep him straight and the pain in my ribs flares. I wince, almost bending to his weight. DJ helps him off me. We slowly rest his hands and head on the table.

I nod to DJ. Pain, regret, and guilt are all mixed up inside me. I'm not sure I know how happiness feels anymore. I feel empty. I feel like parasitic worms are eating from my supply.

DJ nods back. His eyes less strained. Flying fox like, curious and hopeful. Especially when he looks at everyone else. He sits in front of Jay.

DJ looks at me. "How long do you think he hasn't slept?"

"I'd say since Saturday. Maybe only naps."

Kat takes DJ's hand. Her smile is back. She tilts her head. "Let's get him help." She closes her eyes. Her warm smile gives me hope that my best friend will be fine.

Haruka chimes in with her phone in hand, "I'm on it!"

Lucy takes out her tablet. She looks like she wants to pull her beanie over her fawn eyes. "I have something to show you." She opens the drawing of me. Or the wannabe me. He looks out of control. Enraged. Frightened. It can't be me. "I have abilities like Theon."

Their faces don't change much. Haruka has to know. Kat is busy calming DJ.

DJ stares at the drawing, not believing what she said, though it took him a while to come to terms with mine. "That's the T-Rex." DJ points at the tablet. "It happened two weeks ago." DJ says, though his tone is inquisitive. I guess he still believes it is fake.

Lucy squeaks, "I drew it the day you confronted Theon. When we found about his ability." Haruka hugs her. She stays with her best friend just like I stay with mine.

Kat stands looking at the not-me. She leans over, taking in the details. "He looks unlike you." I'm glad she didn't use my name. She points at my not-face and accidentally flicks. It reveals the second picture. A picture of Lucy sitting in a white room surrounded by six different objects. To her left, a picture of a fox and a cockatoo guiding a stampede of animals. To her right, a knight holding a shining shield and black sword. Above her musical notes, hearts, and a glass figurine hanging from the ceiling. Lastly, a sword broken to pieces. Each fragment reflects one of the other artifacts in the room. The sword sometimes looks like it's complete and sometimes fragmented.

"How did you make the sword shift?" My gaze is stuck to that image.

"I had to use different techniques and programs. It took me a week to get it right." She fixes her glasses. Light finally hits them and refracts from the glass.

"Has that happened?" DJ's wheels are spinning. If anyone can figure this out, it's him. Lucy warily shakes her head, still acting like a fawn, but less skittish. He mutters, "A type of future sight." He puts his cap on and takes out his laptop. As it boots up, he asks, "Do you have others? Could you send them to me?"

"Yes. Why do you want the pictures?" Lucy asks, while sending the drawing. She looks back at DJ.

"Theon and I can find a pattern." I get up. He turns the laptop to halfway face me. "Tomorrow, we have Jay too."

Both Kat and Haruka stop on the third image. Kat looks similar, her red hair almost fades to the pink hearts behind her. She wears a pink leather jacket and headphones. Other than that, the image looks normal. Except for the hearts filling the background. "I love it!" She takes Lucy's hands and jumps. "Can I get a copy?"

Lucy sends her images before Haruka takes control of the tablet. She swipes again "The girl from the movies." She keeps swiping. "Who are those three?" She shows us the two images of my brothers.

"My brothers." I look toward Jay.

His chest rises and falls. It takes my hand on a slow and soothing ride. He reminds me to bear cubs hibernating. The same intensity and the same will to sleep.

The last image is a girl. Her black hair flows along the air current. Two braids form a crown on her head and then descend along with the rest. Her simple brown eyes don't pop as much in contrast with her fair skin. Her dress flows with the wind as if it's made of wind. The most impressive part is the swirling storm around her. The rotating tornado dances in harmony with her.

This drawing is the best one. A swan dancing. It makes me feel like she's dancing in front of us. Kat and I lean into her magnificent display. I take care not to leave Jay; he deserves the sleep. More than anything, he shouldn't have nightmares. That's on me.

DJ stares at his computer, "Have your brothers got their abilities yet?"

"Yes." I zone out, admiring Lucy's creations. Haruka keeps swiping reeling Kat in, but pushing me away. The drawings are pretty, but there's something else eating at me.

DJ glances above the laptop, ignoring the girls and their interest on the unrelated drawings. "I have a theory, but I need more samples."

I hold my chest as I lean in. "Can you find the last one?"

He turns his cap back. "I think so. Why?"

I glance at the girls. "There's safety in numbers. Easier to protect each other."

He sighs and gives me an eye roll. "Easier to get caught." He types. "I'll do it, though. We need it." He glances at Kat and at the sleeping Jay. The rest will be up to me. In animal terms, we are facing extinction.

CHAPTER TWENTY-ONE: WINGS OF CHANGE

February 27, 2013

"Don't fucking waste our time," Roy barks as we leave the car.

I step away from the parking lot. The gray grounds covered in metallic machines to replace stamina. "We'll find her."

"Are you sure?" Lucas chimes in. He holds my hand tightly. It shakes a little as we approach the melodies on the opposite end of the door to the music and dance academy. Lucas tugs, as the songs of humanity call to him.

"DJ wouldn't send us here if he wasn't sure." I trust him, but there's something that makes me doubt him. **_Human morality? We're so different, and the way he looks at me. I'm not sure he thinks of me as a person anymore. He sees something worse._** I snap myself out of the thought before it drags me back to the darkness of my mind.

Roy pushes us aside. Without a reply, he leaves us behind. I'm sure he expects us to follow. We enter an open courtyard, flowers and fountains refresh the space. Nature, this something I need. The second floor has balconies to observe the sun and the nature below. Some of the windowed rooms resonate with musical instruments, others with singers. I hold on to Lucas, once the stream of music becomes a sea, he disappears. Belugas are meant to swim free in the oceans if they so desire. And Lucas has found the sea he wants to swim in. I stand back, keeping an eye on him. Roy is lost, prowling, but Lucas has found a nice cove of like-minded individuals.

The crowd fluctuates in front of a studio. We can admire the inside of the clear glass cage. Although for a cage, it looks so free. The girls inside dance. Gracefully taking to the wind, before coming back down. The crowd is hypnotized. Have they never seen the beauty of a coral reef or the elegance of the crane? They probably haven't heard the song of a blue whale or the deadly dance of the eagles. The lead dancer changes my mind. There is something about her. She flows but isn't a jellyfish to the currents. There is a strength to her moves, determination, but above all, cat-like grace. Her black hair hovers behind her. It's ethereal. The crowd gawks as she spins in the air, before landing perfectly, continuing the motion.

Since Lucas is fixated, I stay to keep an eye on him. Roy will find us after realizing he's on his own. He'll complain about something, so I might as well enjoy this quiet moment. The trip is worth it, even if it's only for Lucas's enjoyment. Back on the edge of the walkway, a bench stands empty. I sit. Observing. Vigilant to my little brother. Whenever the dancer comes to view, my gaze can't help but follow her.

The bench shudders. I glance to see to see who's joined me and if I need to make space, but it's just a guy in a sports jacket. He's older than me, what everyone else hopes to look like when they're older. I turn away, staring at the dancer. He takes up space beyond the physical, tries to crowd me off the bench. I've dealt with people like him, and I won't shrink to someone like that again. I clear my throat, so everyone hears me by using the lion's vocal chords. He doesn't even turn. Seeing the call wasn't for them, everyone else returns to their business.

"Do you mind?" My fists close, I tense.

He glances at me. He has that condescending look Roy is famous for. There's a key difference Roy is a lion at heart. He looks down on everyone. No one is that special in his eyes. This guy has the energy of a chimpanzee. He looks down on certain people, just because he can. "No." He returns to watching the lead dancer. Now he looks different. There's a softness. I still think he is an asshole.

I stand. He isn't worth the time. I start walking toward Lucas and can feel the glare on my back. Looking at something acknowledges it, and he is acknowledging me in the worst way.

He speaks again, "Haven't seen you around before. What are you doing here?"

I continue toward Lucas. There is nothing important about this guy. If anything hurts his type, it's being ignored.

He grabs my arm. "I asked you a question."

I wriggle and pull. He keeps a steady grip. "I don't owe you answers. Let go of me." I glare at his emerald eyes.

"No." This guy is used to commanding humans, but I'm no human.

"Fine," I say. He raises his other arm. Of course, he wants to assert his dominance physically, but that was never my intention. I smile. Under my breath, a whisper, "Fire salamander slime." My arm slips through his grasp, and I continue away from him.

This isn't enough. He pulls me back by my shirt. "Then answer this. Why are you staring at Helena?" I assume that's the lead dancer, but I don't have to answer that either. And I won't.

Slipping out of the shirt isn't an option. I push back at him, but he locks my neck. Not the chest. I shouldn't even be in this situation. Fine. Quills, claws, and scales are all fair game now. I take a deep breath. I won't lose control, no matter what shade of red I see. "Let me go." The frosty cool of my blood makes me feel sleepy under the shadows. I messed up, one down. So, reptile, amphibian, or fish blood. No matter, it won't be visible.

"Not until you answer."

I roll my eyes. We know he won't. His ego is bruised, so the only way to get back at me is to hurt me. "Whatever." What animal defense should I use? I can't go overboard. Shark scales won't do much. Porcupine quills are too extreme. The middle ground is the hedgehog. The price to pay is my shirt. "Hedgehog quills." I make sure my head never bumps into him. The face is a terrible place to get quilled, that's what a bunch of canines said, and who am I to not listen?

He puffs back as my body tenses. "What the hell?" he doesn't let me go, but his lock on me releases for a second.

The crowd Lucas is part of disperses. It leaves my brother alone, gushing over the girls. The lead dancer talks to my brother. The girl inside the whirlwind. The braid that crowns her hair fixed in place. I clear my mind. No more animals. Just me. Normal black hair. Normal skin. And no slime oozing from my pores. I take a deep breath. The bully tightens the headlock.

That's fine. None of the girls are coming toward us, which means the lead is Helena. Lucas does as the elf owl and searches for me. We lock eyes and he waves and jumps. I awkwardly wave at him while not fighting this brute. "So, when are you letting me go? I have stuff to do." My voice like my blood, slowly losing its vibrancy. I let out a yawn. I glance at Lucas. He and the girl walk toward us. Their hands intertwined.

"Until you answer." He's more stable than I. The cold-blood making my body more rigid. I have to practice using cold-blood to get better at it, adding it to electro-reception, echolocation, infrared vision and using fins. Believe it or not that's harder than flying. Mostly because large bodies of water are very limiting, and well, the sky is limitless and everywhere.

"Everyone here likes arts." Lucas jumps closer to me. "I like it a lot."

The bully's anaconda grip tightens after each exhale. No. That's wrong. It's a hangman's rope ready to snap me. When they arrive Helena's airy demeanor sulks. She glances at me, similar to a butterfly. And just like her eyes sink. A blue morpho butterfly caught under a net. Her wings battering desperately against the fibers.

Then there's Lucas. He's an innocent victim, one never meant to be caught. A vaquita tangled in a web of fishing nets, binding him to a slow death. "You made… a new—" He pauses, looking for someone, something to save us, "friend?" The fountain water slows down and the dew emits the acrid smell we have both learned to hate.

Three of us victims and the guy behind me standing as if the world worked just right. Three different nets and three different creatures searching for the freedom they so desire. He pretends to not see it. To be more blind than a mole. Even they have eyes for what's going on.

My vision turns red. It's all because of him. Next time, there won't be a warning. He'll learn that a Utahraptor is more dangerous than paleontologists think. For a minute, we stand quietly. No one moves. My voice rumbles, "Yes, like cats and dogs." My nails grow sharper and thicker.

Before anyone moves, Roy throws a sand skinned boy to the ground. He smirks, "Fucking creep."

This guy's grip slips. I take my chance and move toward Lucas. I'm the barrier between this bully and my little brother.

The girl stands between us. "Ardal, You brought Daemon! What were you doing to Lucas's brother?" Her body trembles as her fists close. Her voice, equally shaky, forces a step back. She turns our way quickly, her hair slapping Ardal, is what she called him, in the face. "I'm sorry."

Lucas smiles. The fountain's water is transparent, "You don't have to apologize." He skips beside me. "We need to talk to you." With a skip and a hop, he pokes at Daemon.

"I knew it!" Ardal points at me.

Roy takes over the bench, his temporary domain. "Fucking pathetic. Jealous of that?" He points at me, ending the remark with an eye roll.

Ardal turns to Roy. Helena seems to know what will happen next and stands between Roy, Ardal, and Daemon. Her dress floats at her sides. It mimics wings. The thin barrier divides them.

"Why?" She keeps her eyes on the conflict, but asks us for more information.

Lucas glances at me. This isn't his job, it's mine.

"To warn you. You're in danger." I glance back. "We're forming a pack. To protect each other." I stumble upon the words. If she could only be a swan, it would be easier. Roy shakes his head as he looks at me judgmentally. I pull Lucas by the arm toward me. We both take a step back. Without the swan beside us, we have no cover.

Ardal stands between her and us. "I'd like to see you try protecting anything."

"Proving anything to your kind would be pointless." I bite my lip. I won't let the beast take over, but I won't let him treat me like this. It's not like I can do anything, my ribs are still sensitive. I take a deep breath and return my attention to Helena.

"This is serious. You're in danger. We're trying to help you." My throat gurgles. It creates an ominous ripple to my voice.

Lucas takes my jeans, poking his head out for a little bit. Then hiding again. "It's true. Bad people will come for you." The fountain's water regain momentum.

She looks at us, deciding. I glance at my little brother and give him a thumbs up. My blood settles. Ardal steps forward. The moment slows. His hands touch my chest. A surge of pain overruns my nervous system. My body distracted by the pain loses balance. I trip backward colliding with Lucas. I hit the ground with a thud. The bully looks down on us. "You can't protect anyone." He crosses his arms.

I clench my fists, inhale. The air behind me smells like the moments before a storm. Lucas is sobbing. Red. I don't care what I'm becoming, this bully is going to hurt. He will feel what it is to be thrown around like a rag doll. My hand feels heavier. Nails are sharper than usual. I rise up. My ribs sting as the melding into another creature begins. Fur divides skin from cotton. I take one step closer to him, as my paws grow to the size of a human head. My arm coils back, ready to strike.

The sand-skinned boy stands between us, quivering but pretending to be a mountain anyway. "Stop." Daemon, as Helena called him, glances back and gives me a slight nod.

I wheeze, holding my chest. Roy maintains his smile; he knows something we don't. Helena helps Lucas. She brushes his hair and hugs him, lightly singing an off-tune melody, a slow lullaby. Lucas snivels in her arms.

She clears the hair from her face. She glares at Ardal but says nothing, before turning her attention to me, "Sorry. are you okay?"

"Nah. That fucking idiot pushed the other idiot's injured ribs." Roy glances at the insect filled garden, then back at me. I roll my eyes and nod.

Ardal's face contorts. Between Lucas sobbing on the ground, Helena's condemning glares, and my wincing, he can't decide where to look at. Most of the time, he stares at Helena, his eyes devoid of anything but longing. Once in a while he looks at me, but I don't even try to look back.

"Helena, I'm trying to protect you," Ardal says.

"You hit a guy and hurt a kid!" she says. People turn our way. It's like hearing the kookaburra laugh. So distinctive that you must see it with your own eyes.

He glances at us, tries to reach out for me. Damon pushes Ardal's arm away. "Enough Ardal. Leave them alone." Daemon acts as the ceratopsians are thought to have acted, as a wall between the weak and the predators.

I take a step away from him, closer to her. "I don't care about him. You're the one in danger, you can choose to trust us or not." I glance at my brother, who's smirking. He smiles not at us, but at the bug filled garden. The attention of those in the courtyard shifts back to their own business.

Roy lives for these moments, like a humpback whale breaching for the skies. It's a spectacle. "I command you." He shows the white combs before saying it, "Write my message." He snaps his fingers. A swirl of iridescent butterflies descends on a nearby bush. The blue ones gather in lines of three. The yellow ones cover the entire bush. They open their wings and spell, "Fuck you!" Roy snaps his finger. "Point at the idiot." Orange butterflies become an arrow pointing at Ardal.

Daemon snorts. Roy nods in agreement. Does Roy tolerate him? Well, he isn't insulting him, so I guess he does.

Ardal grinds his teeth. "So? Butterflies arranged themselves, big deal."

Roy picks up his phone. "Dismissed." He glances at the device and dials. "Bro, I'm sitting beside the greatest moron to walk this earth." His chat continues on the other end.

I glance at Helena "It doesn't matter. You get it." I point at the residing grizzly fur on my hands. "Don't you?" She blinks twice, before my hand is normal. She slowly nods, looks at Lucas, and shrugs.

Lucas's eyes shine. "Can I?" He does his famous puppy eyes.

"Another day if she joins us. There are too many people for you."

She lets him go. Lucas takes my hand and rubs my stomach. He sings, "Sana, sana. Colita de Rana. Si no sana hoy, sanara mañana." Hoping that if it doesn't heal today, it will heal tomorrow. His melodic voice attracts attention. If only briefly, strangers acknowledge him.

She stands beside Daemon and Ardal. "Yes, but they have to come too."

"Him?" I point at Ardal.

She nods. "He isn't a bad guy once you get to know him."

Daemon yes. Bully? I'll take my chances on my own. Why would she want him there? He's a menace. A danger. No way. Over my dead body. Lucas does the face. His goddamned face. He imitates the baby seals from the Arctic. Puffy cheeks, deep dark eyes, and a face that would melt the ice caps. She awaits and answer, turning Daemon toward us. He shakes like a dik-dik, but inside him there is a Sinoceratops. The one time I look at the bully, his hands are on the other two's shoulders.

"Fine. I make the rules." *He won't win. I can protect these two from him.* "Lucas, Helena. Daemon, you're with Roy." I defiantly stare at him. "Jock. I'll train you."

Roy drops his phone. Lucas tugs on my shirt with a smile on his face. The jock looks at me. "I have a name. Ardal."

Like I care, like your kind cared about my name. That's how I sealed my fate as an Adélie penguin, and him as the leopard seal, ready to sink me into the depths of my own nightmares. This is my bullet to bite if we're to survive.

CHAPTER TWENTY-TWO: CORNERED ANIMAL

March 2, 2013

My natural habitat opens up a path toward the clearing. Harsh sunlight draws out sweat, even though of the area has shade. A couple of rocks and logs lay dead on the ground. It's silent, lonely, as I requested. There will be no distracting me. I turn around. Ardal avoids my gaze. No matter how much distance he keeps between us, I can catch him. He can't outrun a puma. Ardal has barely talked to me; I'm fine with it. I didn't want this task, but if Helena and Daemon are to join us, I must keep him around.

"What are we doing here?" Ardal asks in voice that doesn't match the powerful being he pretended to be.

"Nothing." My eyes drift back into the woods, focusing on any misplaced sound or smell. After the bigfoot fiasco, I can't be too relaxed. Specially if I'm stuck with this character. I'm only here for the sake of our survival.

"You said we were going to train and figure out my ability." Just for a second, his face lightens. "If we aren't doing anything, I'll go back to Helena." He turns around. His back to me, but he doesn't walk away.

"That's exactly why you're here." I stare at him. I am the poacher, and he is the game. "You'll distract her." I stomp my foot. My body is rigid. I won't be the weak mouse he thinks I am.

"I'm not here to fight you." He stands there. Hands in the air. He increases his distance. Every second glancing at me, checking for my next move.

I turn my back. "Do whatever you want. You and I don't want to be here." I move. My hands find their den inside my pockets. He follows. Thankfully, never closing in the distance.

We arrive at a small clearing not far from the others. I take a seat on the outer edge, back against the oaks. The smell of guano stings lightly on the water filled breeze. A low rhythm and buzz converge in my ears. I can't smile, I don't have it in me today. Solstice, the peregrine falcon, screeches with pleasure. Rejoicing at the fresh meat my brother gave her for guiding them.

"I'm sorry. I want to protect her…" He stands in front of me. Eyes locked in, not quite like last time. He quietly exhales. That doesn't change anything. I hate him, his sports team getup, his attitude, and his kind. They're all monsters. They snuffle life when they get the chance, but I need Helena, so I'm stuck with this guy.

"By forcing it on her? Is hurting five-year-olds how you protect?" I close my fist, claws pierce into my skin. As much as I want to let go, I won't. *I'm better than him. I'm better than all of them. I won't actively try to ruin his happiness or his life. I'm not like them.*

Ardal sits on the rock in the middle of the clearing. Hunching and looking down, trying to convince me of his excuses. "You don't know her situation at home."

I know there has to be something else. It doesn't matter, people like him thrive on stepping over those like me. Blood trickles from my hand, feeding the tree an unrequired sacrifice. "Always an excuse. I don't expect anything from your type. You take everything for granted and do whatever you want. If you don't get your way, others suffer." I hide my hand behind me. I can't show him weakness. I'm losing my grip.

"My type?" He leans forward. "What do you mean?" His emerald eyes seem to fuse with the forest's calming background.

I look away from him. "You know what I mean." My words carry infrasonic bellows. He won't be able to hear them. The creatures of the forest are on edge. There's a mix of flight and fight responses. All of them because of my pheromones.

"I don't know what you mean." He stays put. None of that itching smell releases. Fearless, like the poison arrow frogs.

He has to be pretending. He should know well enough. "Forget it." This isn't a conversation I'll have with anyone like them. I was fine, and then he had to come into my life. He brought back those chains, those nightmares.

He sighs. "No." He hasn't stopped looking at me. "You have issues with me. Come out and say them." He sits across from me, keeping his distance, and rests his elbows on his knees as if he has no intention of going anywhere.

I match him. Body equally tense and unmovable. Blood sustains the plants behind me. I keep silent. *He won't get inside my brain. If I show any weakness, it'll be over.* I am moth looking like an owl to dissuade predators from hunting me. If it works for them, it'll work for me.

"We're a team. We have to get along or at least work together." His body softens. "We have to communicate."

Other people would call him perfect. Ivory smile, perfect good looks, black hair combed to complement his attributes, his defined physique. A complete contrast to me and my broken features. My broken eyebrow, my scars, my hair and clothing that distract others from the rest of me. We couldn't be more opposite. He embodies the peacock or the bird of paradise; everything exactly where it should be to attract others. I'm more like the lionfish, the weird display warning everyone to keep their distance. That one touch will mean a poisonous barb or a nasty bite.

Ardal frowns. For the first time today, he shows what he's really like. "I'm not perfect." He leans back, crossing his arms.

I shake my head. "I know you aren't." The carving in my hand finally does its job. It stings less than the alternative. A little self-consciousness doesn't change thing. He and I are from different worlds. *People will see us only as the feral cat and the perfect guy. I'm fine being called untamed. Nothing much has changed.*

He tilts his head. Of course, when I call him imperfect, he takes it as a compliment. He ignores my response. "You don't seem okay with being called feral."

How does he know that? My lungs violently release the air inside.

He holds the sides of his head. "You don't have to shout." He winces, then returns to normal.

"I didn't say anything." I grow increasingly irritated. Those ultrasonic bellows are slowly becoming growls. They rumble underneath the tissue of my throat. His jacket brings me back. Same type of clothing they used to wear. I tire of outrunning the shadowy predatory. Although rare, even the blue-ringed octopus has predators. It doesn't matter how much we display our venomous nature; we are always in danger. One bite could kill twenty-six people and they still pick us up. Curious. Poking and disturbing our peaceful nature.

Ardal goes limp. He falls back on a patch of grass. My sight cross-wires. I slouch. As the world turns black, I feel the bark of the tree holding me up.

CHAPTER TWENTY-THREE: PHANTOM ELEPHANT

Once again, I find myself engulfed in shadows despite the harsh sunlight. Ardal is gone. The verdant forest has withered. A few trees provide protection from the desert heat. Squirrels and sparrows comfort me. They squeak and squawk, but I can't understand them. **What's going on? Where am I? Where has the forest gone?**

I turn around. Concrete walkways cut through plastic evergreens. A sole low building stands in front of me. Farther away, basketball and soccer fields are being used by some kids. I glance at the building. It dawns on me. My heart stops. **Ardal!** Anyone else would see a normal school. To me, it has always been a gladiator's arena, with me wondering when I'll get broken. When will they be entertained enough to leave me alone? How many times will they force me to fight for my life?

I glance at my lap. A sandwich. On its own, it would mean nothing. I had many of them before. Most of them shared with woodland creatures who safeguarded me from endless solitude. It never lasted long. The animals run away, leaving me with my specie. I belong to neither. Too much of both, to be considered part of any.

A pair of guys pass by, snickering, "Fagot." The word still stings, and yet, it's not the worst they have said to me, or will say to me. Before it would have crushed me, today it resembles the one fly who can't seem to fly anywhere other than my face. Strangely, those two guys, I saw them at November's Posada. They look younger. *Did he wind back time? If so, I have a chance to save myself. To prevent this horrible day from happening.*

I stop when the shadows above darken. "Disney princess give me your lunch!" Misery, or at least the beginning of it.

This is my chance! I won't be terrorized by him any longer. My sight turns burning red. "Majungasaurus!" Nothing. My body remains human. "Sarcosuchus." Another pause. "Acrocanthosaurus." I stand up. "Smilodon?" *Come on at least give me fangs! Fine. I'm older. I can handle him and his followers. I don't need my abilities.* I lean forward to push Miguel away. My hands go through him. I stumble, fazing through my bullies.

"You realize I'm a guy." It's my voice, but it comes from behind me.

I glance back. And there I am. No scars. Both eyebrows complete. That version of me only sees the harrowing image of his tormentors. Of everyone who made his life hell. I pause, paralyzed. *Do I have to watch? I have the strength of a T-Rex, the speed of a cheetah and the best senses in the world, and yet I can't do anything. Always destined to be prey.*

"Whatever you say fag, Lunch now!" Miguel looms over the younger me.

"I'm sure you're rich enough to not want a dirty half-eaten sandwich." Younger me points toward the one in the dirt, covered in fur and feathers.

"You're right, for once. You aren't worth anyone's time." Miguel picks up a rock and throws it at a flock of pigeons waiting to consume the sandwich.

Am I destined to be tormented to this pain every day of my life? I stop watching. I can't. I'm a hostage and I can't do anything to save myself. I crumple imitating the defensive stance of a porcupine. It's not enough. I can hear myself shouting for help. The drag of my body through the dirt. The frenetic kicks. "Help me!" I know those cries are meant for the teacher walking by me. The same teacher who will shrug it off when Miguel claims it's just a game. The same teacher who will later witness them mocking me in class and asking if I'm fine. It breaks what little armor I had.

A hand touches my shoulder. "Theon, are you okay?" Ardal finally shows up.

I hate when people ask that question. ***If you see I'm on the ground trembling, do you think I'm fine?*** "What did you do to me?" I won't look at him. He did something. He probably knew already and wanted to laugh.

His voice is stricken with surprise. "I...didn't do anything. I've been looking for you." His hand doesn't leave my shoulder.

"Then why are we seeing the worst day of my life?!" I scurry away from him. Tears well in my eyes, a monsoon awaiting to happen. I stand and take a step back, keeping my distance from him. It's all fear. Fear of what I can do to him, but also what he can do to me.

He stands slowly, puts hands where I can see them and sluggishly steps forward. When he sees I take a step back, he stops. "We can work it out." He glances past me, at the younger me. "What happened this day?"

My throat swells. Words won't come out. He stares at where my body was dragged that day. In one quick motion, he's gone past me. I sit on the ground as alone as ever. For the first time, I see something different in him.

Ardal has the unmistakable air of a pack leader. "Fine, I'll stop it." He runs.

Whatever he is trying to do won't work. The events are set in stone. We are spectators on to the show featuring younger me. I don't have the time to catch his arm. "It won't work. I tried." My gaze is far away from them. My eyes have given up on the scene. Much like my voice is doing. Whatever he tried failed.

Younger me's lungs puff violently. He gasps for air. The smell of blood conquers the air. It invades my memories. Something cracks. I've learned that's the sound bones make when they break. Once. Twice. Three times. And it continues. A tinge of saltiness. One would think it's the desert soil, but I know tears when I smell them. The beating stops when a couple of dogs chase the bullies. Once they're gone, three cats curl up with that carcass.

I shrink. "Let me leave. I don't want to be here." My body shields me from younger me. Ardal will do what everyone does when they know what happened to me. Take me as a pet, then throw me to the trash. Ignoring the damage it will do to the world. That's how they create an invasive species. That's what the thoughts have become.

"I'm not sure how." Ardal approaches. He looks sad or disappointed, but that can't be. His type isn't genuine.

I shake my head. "I can't do whatever this is!"

Ardal stands. I don't want to watch, but younger me stands too. We follow without putting in the effort, dragging in his wake as younger me waddles along. He limps, one ankle thicker than the other. His scalp and face red. Little does he knew that his eyebrow is broken forever. A constant reminder of the pain. Drops of blood mark his trail. The gray ground becomes white, and the contrast is even greater.

"Where's he going?" Ardal asks, keeping his distance. I can't tell how far he is. My electroreception is acting up. Everything is charged, even the ground beneath us.

I shrug. "To class." My words are cold. I wonder if the goats brought to Galapagos felt alone when they first arrived before becoming a plague. I hold myself tight, hide my expressions from Ardal. I don't need him knowing what I felt or feel.

He pauses, never reaching for me. I appreciate that. The space is needed. "But you were injured."

"Don't play coy. Humans like every animal smell weakness. Why would I show them it hurts?" Animals use that skill for survival, but people, I'm not so sure it's a skill they should have.

"We aren't like that." He raises his voice.

"I don't know why I bothered." He doesn't answer. I didn't expect him to. He lives in his glass penthouse. How far away he is from the crude reality of nature. "When will you let me free?"

"I'm trying." He glances at me.

I shrug without looking at him. My world is bright red. Even if I looked at him, I would barely recognize his face. I'm more afraid of the faces I'm making. He already sees what makes me tick. It's a matter of time before he uses it. "Hurry." Teeth capture my inner lip.

He speeds past me. "Could you tell me what happened?" There's an attempt to connect with me, but he only drives us from this place.

Somehow, we appear in the hallway. My feet haven't moved. My tears leave no trails, they disappear after leaving my face. I don't have the energy to think of what's going on. I only know that he did this. He wants to see me fall. "No. Not that I can stop you from finding out since we're stuck here." My vocal cords somehow have kept their growl. Another thing this place keeps.

Before he can answer younger me says, "I'm fine." He shrugs Juan off with the same coldness the others give him. He continues to a door as Juan and Maria disappear behind us. I made a mistake. He did try. I pushed people away. I'm partly to blame for my torment. He was nice enough. Maybe someday I can reach out and apologize.

I stand outside of the classroom. Ardal has been peeking in, listening. I pretend to not listen; the words carved in my scars. They reopen them, never allowing them to fully heal. My fingers grace my broken brow. He returns to the hallway with me. "The jokes are cruel. Are you, you know?" He attempts to place his hand on my shoulder.

I flinch. "No. Would it matter if I was?"

"No, it wouldn't." We wait. He leans on the wall. Another thing that doesn't make sense. We were able to go through them, but not right now. My tears have stopped. The shock is gone. I close my fists, prevent them from trembling. They are clean stainless. Strange I remember the blood dripping in the forest. ***I have to get out of here. I can't keep living this, not again.*** I can't handle seeing the rest of the day. Time is weird, and there is fogginess in my head.

The bell announces the end of the day, and the beginning of my misery. There's a flood of kids, and then there's me. The last of the dodos watching over the destroyed nest only made possible by invasive species. Younger me's ankle isn't better. In fact, it looks worse. I've never noticed that day, my ankle was broken along with some of my ribs. I turn away. A million spiders could crawl under my skin, and it would be nothing compared to the trembling inside me. My arms do their best to embrace me as younger me's conversation with the teacher starts. "Is everything alright?" ***I wasn't it obvious? Can't you see my blood drenched body? My bruises? My watery eyes about to give up? Can't you hear the mocks and slurs my classmates throw at me?***

"I'm fine." Younger me fakes a smile. "I fell out of a tree when I returned a hatchling to its nest." He hunches his body. I don't have to look. I know the steps he takes here. He leans on the wall, avoiding putting too much pressure on his limbs.

The teacher touches his younger me's arm. "Let me take you to the nurse's office. Check your injuries."

"No… It's nothing." He limps away. I don't move, but somehow, I'm forced to follow him back to the burning heat. This will be one of two moments of tranquility he'll get. A small nightingale flies down, and sings in his ear. I can't understand it but, in my experience, they only sing sweet happiness or boundless love.

Ardal grabs my shoulder. "Why didn't you tell her? She could have helped. Things could have gotten better."

Younger me is lost on the streets.

I slap Ardal's hand. Now he's going to lecture me on how I should have acted? ***I knew this would happen.*** "It didn't start with broken bones and pouring blood." I sigh. I sense his hand trying to take hold of me, but this time I stop it completely. I grab his wrist. "Don't touch me, again." My voice has completely switched, it got deeper and more tense. I let go of his wrist.

"I can't believe things got worse after you tried." Up until now, his voice has always had an annoying element to it. This is the first time he softens it, and I hate him even more for it. It makes me feel further away. Something to be pitied. Maybe it's the lack of understanding, another common issue when people know about my past. **Everything is my fault. If everyone did stuff to me, maybe I have deserved it. Yeah, that has to be it. I'm to blame. That's how that day came to happen.**

I didn't expect the goose with the golden eggs to understand the mouse trying to survive under the rafters. But I also didn't expect the goose to be so perfect that he missed everything under his feet. My vision is clouded. "Ardal take me back to the forest. Now!" My breathing is erratic. "I'm done watching this. Living it again! Hearing it! And I'm 'specially done with you!" My voice cracks like how a dog's growl cracks when it's cornered.

"Why me? I'm not sure how to control this." He takes a step back, or many. Sound works weird. All of my senses have begun to warp. There are cracks on the walls and floors.

"Since you're so high and mighty, I thought you had all the answers!" I turn to him. The only color visible is red. Even the shaved lines on the sides of his hair fuse with the bloody red in the world. I take one step and the floor cracks under my feet. I might have no powers, but I will get myself out one way or another. Even if it kills me.

Ardal takes a couple of steps back. Very stable ones, even with the ground breaking and the ceiling falling down. He maintains composure. His breath is slow and constant. His eyes don't abandon me as if that meant anything. "Calm down. Take deep breaths. We can get out."

"Stop telling me what to do!" I take another step. The building collapses around us. The ceiling becomes feathers falling to the cracking floors that become scales. "You and everyone else seem to know my life so perfectly that you have all the answers." I wave my arms, emphasizing every word. "Instead of listening to what's going on, you give the perfect solution to something you haven't lived." I punch the wall, turning it to a pile of bones beside me. "So, tell me, did you know they only received a warning after I told a teacher? Did you know they weren't the only ones? Did you know girls and little kids bullied me in the bus? Did you know my parents dismissed the torment as children playing? Or that those who didn't actively participate, watched, and pretended I was fine! What should have I done against all of them?" I'm holding in my tears. I won't cry in front of him. I won't give him an edge. "And now you want me to relive it! Tell me! Since you know everything."

"I..." He stops moving. He bides his time like a reticulated python hunting a raccoon. "I'm sorry. I didn't mean to bring it all back."

"Then get me out of here!" Lightning crackles. The earth quakes. Howling winds create a storm around us.

"I'm not sure how. Please calm down," he shouts, in a tone that begs for his life. I'm not sure what's going on myself. I can finally breath. My throat opens. The tears ride the winds away from me. Ardal slowly approaches me. **What is he doing? Why is he getting close to me?** "You're right, I was telling you how to do stuff, and I shouldn't have." He slows, shows the palms of his hands. His jacket goes through metal and rock, water, and thunder. The airborne debris ignores us. "It's okay to not be okay. What happened to you wasn't right!"

It's been three years, and this is the first time someone says those words. Someone acknowledges it. My chest is able to expand. My breath is small against the hurricane around us. Slower, deeper. My heart matches that feeling. My hair and clothes ignore the receding winds. I stumble to the pile of bones. They become an outer wall holding me in place. I swipe the water flowing down my irritated eyes. As my body becomes slower, the world reconstructs around us. Younger me waddles inside our house. Ardal glances at younger me, the dead animal walking.

He tries to help me up. I just want to slide down, so he sits beside me. "Are you okay?"

"Better."

He scoots away slightly. "Why do you hate me?"

We've both been holding on to the question since the day we met. **Why Ardal?** Jay is in a sports team, and I never hated him. We had friction, but never hated each other. Ardal infuriated me. "You remind me of them. The nightmares! The pain. This memory." My voice struggles to keep up. He doesn't answer. It gives me a chance to catch my breath. The world seems more normal. The colors are fine, the distance a strange fog cloud.

He takes off his jacket and covers me with it. Not all invasive species have to be bad, and Ardal, unfortunately, is one of them. He's the Aldabra tortoise to my ebony tree. After an island off Mauritius lost its mayor herbivore species, this tortoise was introduced. All on its own, the species stabilized the island, preventing the flora from going extinct. He waits a second before asking, "Will you let me see how it ends?"

With the little energy I have, I muster an answer. "You would think less of me." Multiple animals have gathered outside. They knew. And I knew what's coming. "I can't stop you. If you want to see, go ahead." I point at the house. My seemingly normal house. Nothing eerie, nothing special about it. Two floors, a garage, and a garden.

He gives me a smile for the first time. I hate to admit it, it's perfect. I hate him for that, not the way I hate my parents or my bullies or my teachers. The way a pigeon hates the feral parrots. Because try as they might a pigeon is gray, and the parrot is colorful. "I won't go if you don't want me to."

"Fine, but I know you'll think badly."

"Test me." He supports my weight, keeping me up as we slowly walk inside my house, toward the kitchen.

After he feeds the dogs, younger me stands in the middle of the kitchen. His eyes lost in a daze. He barely moves. Slowly showing us the maw of an artificial beast. One that tempted him for a long time, but never quite lured him like it did that day. He toys with the serrated knife. The cold embrace calls to him pricking his finger. Painless. The red fluid flows.

One bite, that's all it would take. His hand blindly follows the command of the knife, of the young kid's frail state of mind. The serrated teeth drawing closer to skin. Two of his free fingers search for the slight pulse in his neck. Now beating faster with an intensity that wouldn't be matched until he was able to transform into a tiny harvest mouse.

In the back, the dogs growl. They jump against the glass door, cracking its surface. The voices of the wild join my pets. Birds passing by screech from a distance. Wandering cats scratch the window, seeking a way in. "Stop!" a woman's voice, what he though was a trick of his mind. A delusional attempt to make sense of the world.

His hand suddenly trembles. The steel pierces his neck. Skin opens and creates a spring of blood. Before the knife gets deeper, the glass crashes. Two large masses of fur crash into the young me, pushing him away from the silver predator. The knife flies through the air, falling away from his grasp. He lies on the floor crying in despair. Both dogs trying to comfort him.

"We would miss you. Please stay," a playful boy's voice says. Leaving younger me wondering who spoke. And now I know, that was the first time I could understand animals.

I open my eyes. Again, the forest. I glance forward. Ardal holds his head. He groans, but once he looks at me, that changes. "You tried to…" His voice hitches, avoiding the complete thought. Maybe for my sake, but probably for his own. He abandons his position in the middle of the clearing.

"End it. Yes, I tried." I look away. Seeing him judge me will hurt. It wouldn't surprise me if he thought I was insane. Or not worth it. He'll would think less of me and leave me to my own devices. He probably hates me after what I did.

He sits beside me. Careful to not invade my space too soon. "I don't understand why you would do it, but I won't judge you for it." He wraps me in his arm and gets me to lean on his shoulder. "It's okay."

"But." **Why isn't he judging me? Scolding me for doing something so lamentable. Horrible. Why is he being nice to me? I don't deserve it.** "I almost killed myself. I almost suicided." Tears flow down my cheeks. My mind is twisting and wandering through so many thoughts. So many screams to do it.

"But you didn't." His voice is calm. More than before. There nothing of the arrogance or mightiness he portrayed. "You're here."

My hands cover my face. I sob uncontrollably continues under Ardal's care until the others come to have lunch with us. He doesn't mention the event or his power. Whenever there's a free moment, he glances at me, tilts his head, and waits for a response. From time to time, I give him a thumbs up or an incidental nod. Maybe I should give him a chance. Maybe, he is different from the others.

CHAPTER TWENTY-FOUR: ZEBRAS AMONG WOLVES

Once again, I climb into Ardal's roofless red car. I don't slam the door like before. I also don't glare when he confidently smiles. He has called the car a she, but for me it's lifeless. Some metal pretending to be a wild creature. Ardal and the car bother me, too human with semblances of wilderness. Maybe a cold reflection of me. I'm an animal desperately clinging to that animalistic world.

I glance quickly at my hands. He doesn't know about my gloves and the bandages underneath. *I'm still not sure about him. I have to only endure the ride.* After that, Jay can shield me from DJ's judgment, Ardal's insight and Daemon's complaints. Being alone with Roy isn't easy. I know that all too well.

Once my seatbelt clicks, he accelerates. The speed slower than before. This ride will be my death. He turns off the music. And with another click, changes the car from roofless to roofed. The air is silent and constrained. I take a big gulp, simmering in my own need to hide from him. I hope he doesn't expect a cicada's welcoming song. What rests inside my throat is the bare-faced go-away-bird alarm signaling against predators.

"What's a bared-faced go-away-bird?" His smile is lustrous.

Of course, he read my mind! "An African bird species…" I pause as he nods to what I'm about to say. I'm not falling for a distraction. I tense, then stop myself by looking at the orange and purple skies. At the shadowy mountains that hide the sun. At the lack of nature in this momentous time. The human settlements stay the same.

My left hand hides inside my jacket pocket. My right one holds my head as I lean away from him. He shouldn't act so casual after what he saw. I know the play: use that information, take over and sell me out to keep his girlfriend safe. In that regard, he reminds me of Yash and Shyla, with the minor exception that Shyla made it clear she didn't like what she saw. **Why do I have to be stuck in this prison with him?** Jay could have picked me up. I'd take DJ's judgments over this.

"We have to talk." The car slows as if in response to him. In this time of transitions birds can't save me as they usually do.

"No, we don't. Forget what you saw, it never happened." *I know I shouldn't have tried it, but I was hopeless. I had nothing. I had no one.* Loneliness and desperation drove me into this corner. I sigh, looking at the sunset. My teeth let go of my lip. I do my best to ignore him. It won't be enough. Bicycles are passing our car leaving us behind. What I'd do to hear the wind deafening me. Or the music blasting thought the roof. Anything other than this. *Whatever he wants to talk about, I've heard it before. I don't need more of it. I don't need more of my past here.*

His hand hovers over my shoulder. It has to be a jock thing. They always want physicality. "Please let me help you."

I swat his hand away. "I don't need help. I'm fine." My voice shifts and twists with every syllable.

"You do." The car stops. "You haven't let anyone in." I glance at him, arms crossed. His sunglasses hang from the t-shirt.

I grunt. Try the door. Locked. "I don't need anyone. I can handle it." ***Ugh! Why is he like this?*** "Why do you care so much? And don't lie, I can tell if you do." This question has been killing me since he saw what happened. I close my fists, pressing my injured palms together, braving through the pain. I can only hope my mind is as blinded as my eyes in this moment. I know it's not. His look at the sight of the suicide attempt is instilled in my head. We both know, and it doesn't make it easier. If anything, I feel suffocated.

There's a pause. He calculates his words much like he did with his movements after the memory was breaking apart. "'Cause we're a team. We help each other." No drastic changes in his heartbeat. A lack of sweat and electricity in the air around him confirm my suspicion. He's being honest. ***Why? If he was lying, I could stick to the brown hyena behavior.*** Mark my territory and keep everyone else at a distance. Another reason he annoys me.

I growl, "We aren't friends."

He sighs. "That doesn't mean I shouldn't care. You don't have to face it all alone." The car starts moving again, but bicycles are still faster than us. We would be dead in the race for survival. I would be better off on my own. "I know I messed up." His voice lowers. The car accelerates past the park, past my salvation, then it slows again. **He has to be reading my mind. He's still inside, never letting me rest.** "Let me make it up to you. Let me help you."

His voice gives out after that ask. Not that I care. I want to leave. Jump out of the car. This dreadful silence. Infinite. A deep as the ocean. As vast as stratosphere. My nails can't reach my skin, as it's covered by leather and cloth. **There has to be something I can do.** The radio. **What tasteless music options does he have?** I switch the dial. **He likes the same music as I do?** Rock. Time to find new music, I can't be related to him. The music dies with hand on the console. The car slows again, settles. It's him and me. He takes my arm. "What happened to your hands?"

He was snooping around. "Nothing." I pull my arm back. It doesn't move. His grip tightens taking off my glove. "Stop!"

"What did you do?" His emerald eyes stare at me.

I keep tugging away. I could destroy the car and leave, but I don't want to do that. "You read minds. You know." I could get rid of the problem, but it isn't like before. Just like how I won't turn into a lion to make Roy stop.

"Say it." His eyebrows straighten. The line they make aligns with the shave design in his hair. If he does that often, I might have to call him a cuttlefish. It fits. Hypnosis, changing attitude and a want for control. It fits him.

I look away. "They're claw marks."

He lets go.

"Happy?"

He shakes his head. "No, why would I be happy about self-harm?" I stay quiet. He doesn't have to listen to what I'm about to say. "And yes, even non-lethal self-harm." Damn him, but not thinking is impossible. I should have never helped him. He'd softened his tone again, taking one he used earlier when apologizing to Lucas. Lucas, clearly more naive and a better person than I'll ever be; forgave Ardal instantly. I can't. He'll turn his back on me.

"Because you could get rid of me."

"When we met, I thought about it. Today, I see that you were right. You can help us. Let us repay the favor." He presses his hand against my shoulder. "There's no shame in needing help. The things you've done weren't right. You didn't feel like there was another way and the world was crushing you, but there is another way. Let your brothers, friends and I help. You don't have to hold the world on your shoulders. We can alleviate the pressure in our own ways." He presses his lip with one finger. "The striker might score all the goals, but he still needs a goalkeeper to prevent the same from happening."

I tilt my head. My broken eyebrow arcs upward. "What?"

He chuckles. "Right. Everyone in a team plays a part. Everyone is good at something, but we have to rely on each other."

"You're calling us an ant colony. Each ant on their own is good at their job, but they work together to cover for what the others can't do."

He nods, putting the sunglasses back on. "Yes."

"I get it." I glance at the purple horizon. ***What would my friends do if they knew about all of it? What would my brothers think? They would leave me.*** I've given them more than enough reasons to flee. They'll take it this time. ***They can't know. Above everyone else, Lucas and Jay shouldn't know.*** My heart thumps faster at the thought of Jay. I stick my hands together preventing any more damage. "But please don't tell anyone else."

"I won't tell them." He keeps his eyes on the road. "Your brothers love you. They think of you. I know your friends will too. Why are you worried about Jay?"

I blush. "I'm not."

He pauses and smiles. "Want me to see how he feels about you?" I don't answer. I abstain from saying what I want to say. ***It's wrong to do that to them. It's a mistake and an invasion of privacy, but maybe I should take it. No one will know, only us.*** Ardal smiles at me. His human standard of perfection bothers me just a little less. The car purrs to Ardal's command. He accelerates, leaving the medium-sized houses behind. He turns up the mountain where mansions cut through the greenery. Another reason to hate him. He spins the dial on the console. The song pumps up deafening my thoughts in the process. Ardal opens his mouth and sings dishonoring whatever the artist might have meant. He pokes my shoulder and waves toward him. I decline the invitation.

He continues to poke. "I know you love this song." *Of course, he knows I do. What would Jay say? You got Theon to sing with you? I thought we were best buds!* And that's how he'll rope me into singing with him in karaoke later tonight.

"Fine." I open my mouth and sing almost decently. The birds would be proud of my improvement, but horrified by the monster they created. Sing as if you were a nightingale, but have the voice of a great frigate bird.

CHAPTER TWENTY-FIVE: PRIMAL

April 12, 2013

Our pack of six leaves the shopping mall. We would have been eleven strong if the others hadn't left early to finish a school project. One that I haven't finished yet, but I will. We head across the open plaza to reach the parking lot. Ardal, who has been massaging the sides of his head, insisted on leaving. He's been delegated to the back of the group, allowing Roy to be in front of everyone. Roy assured all of us that tonight's shopping spree is on the house, which means he will be stealing tonight. I'll keep an eye on Ardal in case he needs me. **When did I start caring about him? Never mind.** As he would say, it's what a team would do.

The cobblestones under my shoes vibrate with the cars passing on the street to our left. To my right, a fountain, a frivolous waste of a precious resource in the desert. Leaves and ivy are carved on the sides, but real plants would have been better. At the fountain's center is a small spire with three basins, each one smaller than the one below. At least birds get a bird bath out of this. Beyond the fountain, a small playground with shouting children. This time is as good as any to bring back my senses. They get overloaded when I'm in crowds.

The orange mountains at the edge of the city are blocked by the office buildings across the street. The city's natural beauty has been ruined by towers and towers of gray and glass.

It would have been a beautiful sunset to witness, and the scant clouds would have allowed it.

With the mall at our back, I continue walking as every sense returns; starting with sight. Eagle eyes are extremely useful on a day-to-day basis. Bear smell. From the apartment building beside the parking lot comes the scent of freshly baked cookies. Finally, I feel like myself again! No shouting crowds reverberating my ears. The million vibrations making me feel like on an earthquake. Just some open space and peace. I sigh in relief.

Daemon collides with me. "Sorry." He scurries after the others, leaving me with Ardal.

Ardal moves slowly toward the pack, so slowly the gap innocuously increases. I wait for him beside the fountain, playing with my senses as he takes heavy steps. His hair is in disarray, not the absolute perfection I expect of him.

"Are you okay?" I offer him my hand or shoulder if he wants to lean.

He glances at me. His forehead profusely sweating. "Yeah. Let's get out." He continues past me, ignoring my offer. So much for teamwork. Only when it's convenient for him, but not for me.

I allow him to walk ahead of me, so I can watch over everyone. Helena and Lucas half-dance, half-walk. Roy takes notes on his phone, surely this time he's planning the heist properly. And Daemon runs behind them, seemingly never able to stop for even a second.

A distant man's voice, "In position. Mission start."

My ears pick up the weirdest things. I glance at the playground, maybe a parent playing with his kids. No males. Back at the entrance of the shopping mall, there are mostly teens. Cars honk as more of them get stuck on the main street, unable to continue their path. It has to be further away. It's concerning. My back fur spikes. **What mission is starting? Could it be a radio show or the movies?**

"Targets in position." A second voice is cut short by static from approximately the same location.

I spin around. It's impossible they know about Helena, much less about Ardal and Daemon. Not even I know what Daemon can do. If it was only me, then it would make sense, but it's plural. There's more than one target. I glance at the offices and apartments. I close my eyes, searching for the sound of sirens. People there are too many of them making noise! **Breathe, maybe this is a series or a movie.** One deep breath fills me with gasoline, people, different foods and… gunpowder. We are surrounded by it, far too much for the guards and police patrols in the area.

Ardal has barely moved. He glances at me. The emerald of his eyes is barely visible as he squints. Helena and Lucas are making their way back to us.

Lucas, lets go of her and waves at me. He skips and hops every two stones. "Are you okay?" His eyes gleam in the purple refractions of the sky.

I strain my voice, containing the severity of the tone inside. The last thing we need is panic. "Something's going on." I take his hand. "We need to leave now." I pull Lucas back to Helena.

She takes his hand. They make their way toward the others, but she stops and glances at Ardal. He puts his weight on the fountain, shaking his head. I run back to him and whisper, "Eastern gorilla arms." My arms feel heavier, pushing my jacket sleeves outward. I slide my arms under his legs and back. I catch up to Lucas and Helena who match my speed. I turn to her. "Give Lucas earphones and prepare a ballad, just in case."

She nods, her free hand rummaging the purse. Lucas pulls her to walk faster. They easily overtake me, with Lucas taking the lead. I follow their pace. Ardal keeps quiet during all of this, not even a peep into my brain.

I focus my hearing as we head for Daemon and Roy. More radio static cuts through the crowd. "Secondary target in a group of six. He's carrying someone. Orders ma'am." It comes from across the street, one of the office buildings on the higher floors. It's too far for me to tell exactly where. If only I could be an owl.

A distorted voice replies, "Capture them. If they resist aim to kill."

"Slow down," Helena says from behind me.

When did I pass her? Roy collides with my shoulder. "The hell is wrong with you!"

How did they know? Nothing strange has happened in the past few days. Jay and DJ would have said so. *It doesn't matter. I can figure it out later. Now's not the time.* "I'm being hunted along with someone else. Take everyone to the car and leave." I place Ardal carefully on the ground.

Roy stomps. "Crap!" He turns around, grinding his teeth. The muscles in his neck tense, welcoming the challenge. He takes the lead and points at Daemon. "Get him to the car!"

Daemon picks Ardal up and rushes to Roy. I take a step back. If I get past the apartment buildings, I can change and fly away with my belongings. There will be no traces of me.

Synchronized vibrations travel from inside the buildings. They're attempting to hide numbers by orchestrating their march, but I can sense them. One, two, three. Three groups, each with more than five members. One comes from the parking lot, the second from the apartments and the third is back at the mall. None from the office building, that's where they're spying from, and they don't want to bring attention to it. We're in trouble, so I walk away from the group. I accelerate. If I could, I'd run faster than a cheetah, but that's a death sentence.

"Where are you going?" Lucas calls for me; he fixes the earphones inside his milky white ears.

I turn, scratching my palms. "I'll distract the bad people. I need you to get out."

No! We aren't leaving you! Ardal's voice resonates in my head.

I hold my temples. His voice creates pressure inside my skull. Everyone except Roy flinches. Holding the same area of their heads. The vibrations are clearer and more powerful. Their source draws nearer from all three sides. They're more distinguishable by the waves scatter. No matter if they walk at the same pace, their distance is different and easier to find once I know what I'm looking for. They're too close. "Roy." I pause. "I need a fly storm. Can you get it here in two minutes?"

Roy smirks at me. "Even better." He comes my way, standing as if he was taller than me. "Swarm me." He crosses his arms and nods, showing his white teeth.

Small hums in the air join together in the distance, echoing between the buildings, traveling like the water of a broken dam. Under my feet, marching rustles against the stone, clanks against cold metals and drags over the dry fibers. There's crawling, and dragging; things flies don't usually do. My brother has gone overboard as usual. Show off. He sounded so certain about the precision, maybe he has to say the name of the creature.

"Now leave." I glance at Roy.

He frowns at me, as if I killed the most basic need he has. I feel a tingling in the back of my head. Ardal is going to shout again. Helena and Daemon drag the others toward the parking lot. If they get to cover, it should be easier for me to handle the rest. Roy shakes his head. He punches my arm and leaves taking.

I sense tremor spikes from behind me. The organized march has become a stampede. They stomp and run; some are dragged. They won't let anyone go. "Stop!" I turn to the apartments, but it's the same thing. The parking lot echoes with complaints. We're out in the open until Roy's army gets here. I spin. The cars could work, but once they see us there we'll be corralled. Inside the parking lot, we have no chances. That leaves the playground or the fountain. Not ideal, but if we sit on the opposite end of the fountain, we can use Lucas's abilities to protect ourselves. I point at the fountain. "It's too late. Get to the fountain fast."

Roy is the first one to act. He turns on his heel. Anyone in his way is pushed aside. Lucas is quick to follow, pulling Helena with him. As soon as she understands what's going on, she carries him. Her longer legs allow her to catch up to Roy quickly. Last is Daemon, who looks to be struggling with Ardal. He throws Ardal over his shoulder and trails in front of me. With the pack moving, I run to take the lead.

I tap Roy's shoulder. "Sit behind the fountain. The side furthest from the business offices."

He nods, pushing a woman in heels out of the way. "Sorry." Lucas says as he and Helena pass her. Daemon catches up to me. He trembles as he passes.

I stay away from them for a second, letting the environment speak to me. The buzzing has grown in power, it's impossible to pinpoint the origin. I only know that no other sounds make it past the swarm. The vibrations get harder to read, as many other creatures include themselves in the mix. **Great, more people.** Men in black hold guns and weapons. Panicked people rush our way. A wave a of mass hysteria spreads between them, becoming the worst possible outcome: a human stampede. Humans collide with each other from all directions. Mothers and kids struggle to reunite. Those who were in groups are scattered and alone.

I slide between people. A flailing arm slaps me in the face. Space becomes a luxury I don't have as I squish through another group of adults, who don't even look at their feet to see kids struggling to keep their footing. I ignore the people stepping on my feet. Except the woman with the high heels. The heel stabs me through my shoe. I push her away, creating a wave of collapsing people. **They don't matter. Where's my pack?** I sniff the air. It's too saturated to find their individual scents. As I'm getting crushed, I smell sooth. **Daemon!** The scent mixes with the lighter breeze of the fountain. The space between people diminishes, and I find it harder to squiggle through them. It would be easier to be a snake or a bear, but I can't do that without outing myself. I stumble to the fountain.

"Fucking finally." Roy rolls his eyes.

Lucas tugs on my jeans. "We were worried." He does the big eyes tactic to make me succumb. **This is not the moment.**

Helena clears the hair from her face. "What's going on?"

The crowd pushes me closer to them, "They're hunting other people and me." I pause, and push back the heavy mass of bodies. "They're rounding us up to catch us." I fiddle with my fingers, and they fiddle with the idea of scratching my palms. I take a deep breath. "Once the swarm is here. I need, you, Lucas to create fog." I point at him. "Helena are the ballads ready?"

They both nod. She fixes hear earphones too, synchronizing what they'll listen to.

Lucas looks up at me the same way a sugar glider looks at a person for fruits. "We should help them." He points around.

"The swarm should be enough. We need to leave." I glance at the sky. Clear.

"He can't drive." Daemon pokes Ardal. Daemon acts the best he can as an armadillo and shields Ardal from the people snuffing the space out of us.

My arms stretch over Helena and Lucas. With my gorilla strength, I keep the rest of the crowd at bay from those two. "I can drive."

"Hell no!" Roy climbs the railing of the fountain.

Sweat accumulates under my arms and beads down my chest, reaching my jeans staining them with my own smell. "You want to stay? We can't win like this."

"Think of something, genius." He crosses his arms, barely looking at me.

I have until Roy's swarm gets here. ***What do I do? We're all going to die because we stayed. If they listened to me at the start, we would have been fine.*** I glare at Ardal. If only he let me go alone. The buzzing gets stronger, along with the stomping vibrations. My skin prickles at the feeling of it. Up above, the orange sky is obscured by thick clouds. The clouds buzz and collide with each other.

"Music."

Helena nods. She clicks on her phone. She sways Lucas with her. Lucas slowly moves his hands.

Black pellets descend and crash against the nearest objects. One hits my ear, another the back of Daemon's head. Soon after, the bugs collide with everyone. Some land on me and crawl all over. A woman screams, possibly after discovering that the black objects are flies, beetles, moths and other flying invertebrates. That's not counting the ones that rush from the ground creating a living black carpet over the gray cobblestones. I close my eyes and mouth, scared that they'll crawl inside.

Roy's commanded chaos spreads. The people flee, trampling those not fast enough to move out of the way. Roy is safe over the fountain rail, but a couple individuals collide with me. They're heavier than expected, and at times, multiple stumble above me. I'll endure the pummeling if it means that Lucas and Helena have the space to get us out. I glance at them as a man's elbow lands on my back. That's nothing I've been through worse.

Helena covers Lucas's mouth. She denies access to the black storm pelleting the rest of the plaza. Lucas sways his head, a slow melody that would captivate a lovers' heart. My brother doesn't realize it but he's a bird at heart. As he sways so does Helena. They imitate the waves at the sea. The water in the fountain forms a cloud. First Roy and the fountain are swallowed in a dirty gray fog. My arms disappear before me.

From inside the cloudy walls, I hear Roy's command. "Avoid the mist."

The fog cloud eats Lucas and Helena. My eagle sight becomes useless as the fog consumes me. It spreads out the from fountain. Roy created chaos, but inside the fountain, only harmony resides. Lucas and Helena ensure we are safe. Their song reflects on the cloud, a silent melody to those who love without bounds. I don't believe in that. Love has to have limits, or in some cases, absences.

"Lucas. Helena. Can you keep it up?" My hands slide down the stony surface, searching for both. Being blind is something I'll never get used to after seeing everything.

Helena's hand touches my arm. "We'll try." She stands, pushing me away and keeping Lucas with her.

"Let's get out of here." I turn around. **Where's the parking lot again?**

Lucas chimes in, "We should stay and help." The mist dwindles as the words leave his mouth.

"Listen to your brother." Helena lifts him up. She dances with her tiny partner. I was mistaken, both of them are birds at heart. Lucas a songbird, Helena a dancing one. Once she resumes her dance, the mist moves swallowing whatever is in the distance.

"Hell nah! We kick their asses." Roy's voice booms from above the railing. He's too far away to see.

I could use my viper sight, but that leaves me with fewer transformations left available. "Roy. We need to leave. We don't have time for this."

"Bruh, we can take them." Roy stomps the ground. "Ardal can't drive. And you aren't fucking driving. Last time you almost killed us."

I cross my arms, blocking the memory. "That's not true."

"We jumped over a fucking bridge, and we were in a police chase."

"Fine. I'm not the best, but better than them." I point that the edge of the mist. Don't know how far they made it.

Lucas tugs on my jeans. "But what about the others?" The mist thins out. Remaining rays of light pierce through, time is running out.

Lucas is right. If the other targets are here, that would be great, but I can't risk everyone just on this. If I can find them on my own, then we have nothing to lose. The vibrations on the ground have almost disappeared. The buzzing has died down too. ***Roy! He's forcing us to stay.*** They won't get to the parking lot. Even with my animal forms we'll be shot immediately. I glare at my brothers. "The swarm isn't here anymore, we can't run."

Ardal and Daemon haven't moved. Ardal winces, his head between his knees. Daemon is there, a statue, frozen. His hands cover his sternum. He glances at the rest, but nothing as meaningful as the stare he gives to whatever he holds in his hands. Helena holds Lucas close. Her pale figure has gone swan white. She matches Lucas. He keeps his focus on the song, but the fog thins with each passing beat.

On the fog's edges, black figures line up. They herd us toward the fountain. Most of the stampeding people have run away.

The opportunity is gone. I need time. There is no way we can escape without scopes aiming at our heads. "Helena, play blues for Lucas." I turn to Roy and shake my head. "You've killed us."

Helena complies. She leaves Lucas on the ground and reaches for her phone. The slow melancholic tune takes over Lucas. He opens his mouth, imitating the first words of the song. As if called upon, the fountain behind us bursts. The flood becomes a trail of water. It surrounds the ground, reaching up to our knees. Lucas sings and the water listens, crawling up to the sky. The coil shares its shape with the shell of a sea snail. The sounds outside of it muffled.

Helena moves elegantly around Lucas. She moves her hips slowly from side to side. The wind pushes the edges of the upside whirlpool, threatening to swallow those who approach. Every once in a while, a tap of her foot and a swing of her leg pushes the edged further and further away as Lucas pulls more water out of the broken fountain.

I glance at Ardal. *What would he do? He's a leader, not me.* Our lives are in my hands. *This is wrong. No one should rely on me.* I'm not sure if sweat or fountain water flows down my body. *This is all my fault. I should have rushed them to the car. I'm expendable. No one would miss me. They're worth more than me.*

A fiery feeling shakes my cheek. Roy stands in front of me, his hand red. My cheek probably brighter. "Snap out of it! Fix your fucking shit!" He drags me closer to the source of Lucas's abilities. Not the water flowing, the phone blasting music. Neither Helena nor Lucas can keep track of the music, so Roy must have taken it.

"What do we do?" Helena takes two steps closer to us, then back to my little brother. Her hair hovering in the wind. She looks at Ardal, then at me.

"I need a minute." I stumble word upon word.

"Pathetic." Roy turns his back on me as I stand overwhelmed by my own mind. "Let's give 'em hell! We go all out!" He crosses his arms and stares down at me. **We shouldn't be here. It's my fault we're all going to die.**

"Theon, you can do it. Remember Kat's music." Lucas says, which temporarily stops the vortex. His focus returns to the song and restores the aquatic barrier between us and the enemies.

One deep breath. I can take us out, just need the perfect survival strategy. "That won't work," I murmur. "It will kill us." I clear the way for Helena, who is now living the song.

She once again taps her foot, and the wall of water grows in diameter. The men surrounding us take a step back. Their guns aimed at us. Once again, the water surges outward and they take a step back carefully. Lucas sings louder and the sprinklers beside the playground blow up. From the apartment building, a river of water converges with skyward river.

Around fifty soldiers on the ground aiming at us. The position is compromised as the fountain is broken. If any one of us lets go, there's a clean shot to someone's head. I take another step toward the broken stone piece, looking that my reflection in the water. I gulp. We have animals, water, and wind. I'm useless, the area of effect from the others will prevent me from fighting in close quarters, and even then, a bullet will kill me. If Helena goes on the offensive, Lucas has to defend. I don't like my odds with that. Lucas's defensive styles include this spiral or a water sphere that pulsates, it's too limiting considering the mix of abilities. I glance at Helena. We need wind as our defense.

"Helena, you're defense. Dance like our lives depend on it."

She sighs touching her heart lightly as the air leaves her, then returns as the breeze under the wings of a bird. Her next step hovers above the ground. She steps higher and higher. The winds spiral faster dust and broken stones swirl in both tornadoes. The men on the ground point at us. *Click* They fire. Water slows the bullets, the wind diverts them, and the debris stops them in their tracks. The metal caskets join the inner storm.

"Lucas, take them for a swim." I point at the ground soldiers.

He continues to sing, eyes closed. The water expands swallowing two of the soldiers into the spiral. They attempt to shoot, but the gunpowder can't ignite. The two men struggle against the current, but it's futile. Their only hope is swimming with it, and even then, that would be deadly. I glance up at the growing spiral, on its way to match the apartment building's height.

I look at Roy. "Take those in the buildings. I'll tell you where." Only one family of animals can help me now, owls.

"Hell yeah!" He grins. He keeps his place, standing looking at the enemies, who ruined his day.

I shake him, "Pay attention." I raise one finger. "Soft Hoot." I raise five. "Scream." Both hands open. "Screech." I turn back to the buildings. Those calls won't cover everything. "If they're on the top five floors and roof, there will be a nightmarish scream. I'll use my wings to point at the buildings." I step toward the broken fountain. One wall still stands. "Barn Owl" My clothing falls off, and creates a trail to the white and orange owl perched on what's left of the fountain.

Click A bullet fires, from the apartment building, but is stopped by the forces of nature. The voracious appetite of the song consumes more debris and soldiers. My wing points at the sixth floor. I scream and hoot. The hoot sounds more like a chirp and the scream is more like a hiss.

Roy stares at me. He shakes his head. "Fuck." He glances over at the building, his gaze fixes on a position, attempting follow my wing. "Ants attack the sixth floor." He turns to me. "That's not a hoot or a scream. Get it fucking right."

I had to give simple instructions or we get shot down. I do my best to ignore the ground bullets swallowed with their shooters. The men struggle in the current. The way Lucas keeps singing calmly with his eyes closed. And the elegant dance Helena does as she flies above the fountain. Above all, I ignore Ardal and Daemon, who cowers in the corner behind Lucas.

Click Second shot. This one is lower, from the mall. A small glint on the rooftop reveals him. I point with my wing and inhale. In one instant, I capture everyone's attention, this nightmarish shriek. Everyone momentarily pauses.

Roy's eyes narrow on me. He disturbs this makeshift peace. "Never fucking do that again!" He swats the air above me. "Bees destroy the one on the mall's rooftop." He swipes the screen of Helena's phone. He smiles and clicks, then places the phone on the fountain side.

Helena's dance changes immediately. The air forms some sort of trampoline, pushing her up and down. Her hands swipe an air guitar. With each movement, balls of air explode around her. When she moves her head, wild wind-slashes cut through the air, leaving their mark on metal, stone, and ice. Another wind explosion cracks the ice sculpture that replaced the water spiral. Lucas suddenly raises his voice. We lost the sweet melody of the nightingale. In return we get the concert of a cicada.

Bullets collide against the cold wall. Wind and metal break chunks of the ice shell. Those trapped inside the current are now entombed in their frozen graves. The ice shatters, forming icicles aimed at our surroundings. And those inside the ice break into uneven pieces.

Shards of ice refract the purple sundown. My brother and Helena combined create a hailstorm of icicles. One wind bubble pushes frozen fractals, skewering a man. Some are fortunate to find cover, but ten of them fall to when ice pierces them. Those civilians left behind from the stampede look for shelter, attempting to avoid the icy death. A wind-slash sends a car flying through the first floor of a business building. The icicles pop a car's wheel. It loses control and crashes into another. A wet thud follows a window shattering. The sniper from the apartment building falls. He becomes the new carpet in front of the entrance.

The wind pushes me dangerously up and down. My lighter body floats above the fountain, mostly avoiding the ice spikes. *Click I know where you are.* Middle office building, fifteenth floor, more or less. A screech and a scream. I ready my lungs as my body is pushed up. Frigid air collects behind my right wing. Once the dull pain cuts me I know it's too late. The red and pink ice shard goes through the door of the apartment building. I screech and scream. The blood taints my white feathers. Roy's face distorts to a frown. It changes as my small body travels to the ground.

Lucas takes steps to catch me, but is stopped by Roy's arms. Helena's fevered performance stops when Lucas does. Wind and ice stop their barrage. The men come out, pointing guns at us.

"Fuck! Keep going!" Roy picks up the phone and changes the music. He carries me in his arms.

"But—" Lucas pleads with his eyes.

"We all die if you two stop," Roy barks. It's not a roar. I might be drowning in pain, but it doesn't feel right. ***It's not right.***

I look up. There's Helena resuming her dance. A different style sharp stops and flowing movements. You only get that kind of movements from a honeybee. Each move stops slightly before transitioning to the next. Lucas turns to her. He begrudgingly follows her leads. Ice melts. Twin rivers rise from the ground, band become sea serpents. Blood bubbles up, forming red orbs above the maws of the dancing dragons. Gales shove two men inside the artificial creatures.

"Bro! Find the last one!" He shakes me, sprinkling blood on his dark green shirt. He places me back on the edge.

My uninjured left wing points at the office building across the street.

Past Roy, a firing squad aims at us. I force my wings to flutter against the pain. Feathers fall from my body. I scream and shout, but he doesn't seem to get it.

Roy looks at me confused, counting fingers. "Fifteen."

No! That's not it, behind you! I jump on his arms. Roy finally turns with me in his arms. He stands strong as five guns point at him. He tenses. I know him, he must be smirking. Ready to insult them. Roy would never show them weakness. I'm about to change in his arms when Daemon takes a stand in front of us. His body trembles like that of a small chihuahua. The three of us stand in front of a hunter's mark. By all means dead.

After the first shot, I expected Daemon to fall. For his blood to cover the ground. The second and third would be for Roy and me, but the fourth one comes and I'm still here. Roy still holds my small body. I glance at Daemon; he keeps shaking. There's nothing other than this unmovable guy. Four bullets land on the ground. More and more bounce off Daemon. He never falters, the bullets give up on him, except for one last stray. It ricochets of his arm.

"Lucas!" Helena shouts. Her wind dissipates. She descends from her flight, catching the stumbling Lucas before he hits the ground. She checks his body, looking for the reason he's down. "He's injured!" She carefully lays him down. Her hands act faster than usual, pausing with each breath.

"Fuck!" Roy's about to move as the sound of metal grinding stops him.

Ardal suddenly shouts, "Stop!" His body lies there.

Daemon falls over face first to the ground. Helena quietly lies beside my little brother. Her arm wrapping his small chest. Each and every person in the plaza falls. The men in black fall like dominoes.

Lastly, Roy sits down. "That stings." He falls asleep on the ground.

Only I remain awake. I hop until I reach Lucas. Blood emanates from his shoulder. They shot him. ***I'll kill them all for hurting him!*** Radio static disturbs the silence. I glance at the office building, my gaze on the fifteenth floor. Red. Bloody red. That's all I see. I transform back to human for one reason only.

My harrowing howl calls upon all animals. They respond with howls, squeaks, snarls, and screeches.

The pain in my arm disappears. There isn't time for pain. My voice sounds like the guttural grunts and savage snarls of a wild predator. "Emerald hummingbird." I want to see him try to shoot me out of the sky. I zig-zag to the building. My green body refracting the sunset's last light. As I get closer, I see the man radioing orders. Even with my blue and purple sight, he stays black. I perch on the scope of his gun. He looks at me surprised. He raises his hand to swat me. As it descends, my body changes. Green turns black, black brings white. The gun and I topple. His hand is impaled by the quills on my back. Trying to squish an African porcupine. I glance at him. He jumps back shouting. He holds his hand. I step forward, and he takes another step back.

Since no one else is conscious here, he gets all my ancient fury. They targeted us for nothing. They hurt my little brother, but he is the unlucky one still standing. My claws grow longer, my neck does too. Feathers cover my body as I crawl. My tail and hind legs force me upwards. My body bulks up. The cracks on the floor concern me, but the job will be done soon. A Therizinosaurus. In any other moment, this would be a scientific discovery. Therizinosaurus having feathers, claws, a plump body and a long, thin neck with a small head. Not today.

He screams in vain. Begs for mercy. Survival calls and I must answer, kill, or be killed. I step forward. He stumbles, tries to crawl toward the safety of the door. I swipe at his stomach. Blood splatters the walls. He screams as I do it again shredding his stomach. And again, piercing his heart. And again, and again, and again. Until I lose count and regain my senses. My stomach stings, but I have to get out of here.

I change again. Claws recede, becoming feathers. My body is sharper, made for speed and sky diving. A peregrine falcon. I extend my wings and take flight. The trip back to my pack. I return to a mournful field of corpses and corpses to be. Whoever isn't dead will be in a couple of minutes thanks to all the canines, felines, rodents, corvids, owls, and other animal families destroying the bodies.

My tired wings land me in front of the pack. Lucas's blood taints the water around the others. Roy's face is smug, even when unconscious. A sigh of relief leaves my lungs. Helena looks fine. I return to human form. I'm drenched in blood. Mine? I'm not sure. My vision gets blurrier. Daemon's body lays close to Roy, but he looks well too.

Ardal welcomes me with, "What—" He looks at my chest. "Lay down!" He forces me to the ground.

"I'll be fine… It's just a scratch. Help Lucas. He got shot." I fumble over the words.

"That's not a scratch." He turns toward Helena and shakes her. "Wake up! Theon's badly hurt."

I look down. My belly looks like a volcano erupting.

She starts moving. Her voice is a lazy wind struggling to pass a mountain range. She wakes. Her brown eyes connect with Ardal.

"Lucas and Theon are injured," Ardal says.

She pushes Ardal back. "Get the first aid kit." She calms herself before looking at Lucas. She sighs. A good sign. "It didn't hit the artery. He'll need a sling."

"It's in the car." Ardal helps her up.

She turns my way and notices the nightmarish scene. Blood pouring from bodies. Hundreds of animals listened to my call and acted my intentions. I'd feel guilty about it, but they shot my little brother. They attacked us first. Fully armed adults against a couple of kids. I can't find a better definition of preying on the weak.

I see sadness in her eyes. She points at Daemon and Roy. "Wake them up."

Ardal moves away. He crouches near Roy shaking him.

Helena closes in, looking at my stomach. Three large gashes cross my chest diagonally. She glances at me, and I nod in return, accepting it's not going to be pleasant. She feels around. "Who did this?" As she closes in on my injury, I hiss in pain.

There's a cold numbness, as if I'm frozen. I look at the bodies. "I did." My uninjured arm touches my chest. Viscous fluid dresses my chest. "I think I did that too." My chest is heavy. Everything is blurry. The sirens are muffled. The smell of blood is eternal.

Her gaze delays on the massacre. One after the other she takes uneven breaths, deeper than before but still on the light side.

Roy stands over us. "Woah, dumbass." His pursed lip fine compared to the redness on the side of his head.

Ardal grabs his shoulder. "Hurry! Take his clothes." He turns away. His eyes avoiding mine. "Daemon get Lucas! Fast!" Ardal acts like a stallion. **You took your time Ardal, but I can't hate you, just like Jay, just like Roy.** He takes one big, long breath with his eyes closed before kneeling beside me. He digs one arm under my knees and the other under my neck. I groan in response.

Helena walks away, taking time to check on Lucas before Daemon picks him up. I glance at Ardal, and he looks away. Everything was fine until he lifts me up. I roar in agony. The throbbing intensifies. My arm remains numb and bleeding.

"Sorry."

"Take him fast!" Helena shouts as she runs with Daemon, who has an easier time with Lucas.

The way to the car is blurry and disorienting. I occasionally notice Ardal glancing at me, or Helena's voice ordering the others around. Ardal's lips move. He places me on the backseat. Helena throws every bit of gauze she can find on my injuries. Daemon holds Lucas in the front with a towel on the shoulder, pressing harder every time Roy looked his way.

Helena holds a bottle of liquid above me. "Hang in there." She pours it on my stomach.

"Ahh!" The alcohol feels as if they poured a bombardier beetles acid on me.

Daemon turns back. "We should take them to the hospital." ***They will find us!***

Ardal places his hand on Daemon's shoulder. "Theon thinks that would make it easier to find us. They could track suspicious injuries and investigate Lucas's bullet wound."

"We need a safe stable space for him." Helena turns to Roy. "Do we have needle and thread?"

"Crap!" He throws the supplies inside the car. "No dice." He shakes his head, looking again. He searches inside his pocket. In his hand is a small device. It pops open. A small dancing flame grows on his fingers. "What if we burn it?"

She opens her palm. "Give me the scissors." She turns to Ardal. "Are your parents home?"

"No." Ardal nods at Helena. That's the last I see before the world goes black.

CHAPTER TWENTY-SIX: WOUNDED PRIDE

April 14, 2013

Our tension seems to permeate the forest impeding the dew from forming and the wind from reaching us. Even the animals keep their distance. Only Roy's servants approach this minefield. The six of us, well seven if you count the person on the phone, sit there in silence. Our typical Sunday has become an extinction level nightmare. Specially with Corinna's cold, calculative deal looming over us.

Corinna: Will you, do it?

Theon: We're talking about it. We really aren't. There's no way I can start this conversation with how they're all acting. And no way I can pull off what she asks without putting someone in danger.

Corinna: Clock's ticking.

Helena sits with the waterfall behind her back. "I told you don't move around." Helena is the first and only one to speak. She glances at Lucas, who's doing better thanks to the sling.

"Sorry." I sigh. "Being in my room is unbearable." This is the only way to get out of my head and the whirling thoughts dragging me under. I never stop looking at my chest. Cotton rubs against cotton. The fibers make me itch. I resist the compulsion to scratch. In fact, my hands have avoided the areas since the accident. It's one of the few times I don't feel the need to scratch my palms. Maybe I should have another pain killer. I lean toward the backpack. Roy, Ardal, Helena, Daemon and Lucas barely look at each other or at me. "Thank you for saving Lucas. I didn't know you knew about medicine."

Her eyes graze over my chest and arm. She smiles as she returns to combing Lucas's jellyfish-styled hair. "My parents wanted me to know it," she says it while looking at the waterfall behind her. "Ardal's parents and the doctor did everything."

Lucas intervenes. "The doctor said you saved Theon." He shifts uncomfortably and his phone plays a gloomy piano song that makes it feel like we're back in the city surrounded by people instead of pristine nature. A sphere of water forms behind Lucas. It turns white and then solidifies, and compacts into the smallest piano I've ever seen.

Ardal stares at the sky. "My parents only called the doctor. They promised to keep our secret."

"More than mine would do," I muster.

We fall back to silence. Peaceful silence. My ears don't ring with anyone's voices or cars or even technology. They had enough at the plaza. Gunshots messed up my ears. I still haven't figured out why everyone fell unconscious, but I'm grateful I didn't. If not, the consequences could have been catastrophic. I glance at the others before looking at my chest.

My phone vibrates again. Corinna. I ignore it. She wants to know if we'll do it. Save the two kids being hunted. It would make us four stronger, but I can't risk everyone else for this.

There are no guarantees. Just like in nature, it's a gamble. One I think we can't take right now, but I'm not telling anyone that. *Just like how I have to keep hidden my lack of abilities.*

Ardal shoots me a glance. It's quick and almost glosses over me, as if I was an octopus mimicking the oak behind me. He knows, but he doesn't speak to me about anything.

What a pack. He doesn't even trust me. I'm only a burden they all carry. Maybe even worse, they see an uncontrollable monster, a savage beast. At least he doesn't know about Corinna.

That's not true, Ardal speaks to my mind, out of pity. It's the logical explanation. *Stop. You aren't a monster.* He finally looks me in the eyes. *I know about Corinna. You should tell them.*

No! Have you seen them? We can't do it. Not like this. I look at Roy sitting in a hammock made by spiders. Bees serve him chips, and flies protect his soda from anyone's grasp. To the right, Daemon's toys with a pendant. His body is purplely bruised from the bullets that bounced off him. He grabs a stick and quickly lets go. A drop of blood falls upon the pebbled grounds. Interesting. Bullets didn't hurt him, but a stick did.

You should try. Ardal's telepathy is annoying! It sounds like those computer programs that read for you. He grabs a few rocks and juggles them in his fingers before opening his mouth, "If you don't, I will."

Roy sits up. His hammock sways with his weight. "The fuck are you blabbering about?" His gaze aims at Ardal, but focuses on me, as if he knew I was the one getting us in trouble.

"They already hate me. This won't change a thing." I glance at Ardal. He seems unimpressed by my response. With the help of the tree behind me, I stand fighting the pain in my chest and the stings on my arm. Bark splinters fall where I used to sit. "Corinna is asking me to save two kids. If I can do that, we can get them and two others into our pack." I glare at Ardal. *If only I was more like Roy, I wouldn't be in this position.*

Ardal purposely avoids my gaze. The reactions are numerous. Roy, our little lion tyrant masquerading as a child smirks. When he bites into his chips, he makes sure they sound as loud as a kakapo's mating call. Lucas's eyes sparkle. I know what he will say, but we both know he won't do it if I'm involved. Killing people changes someone's perspective like that. I don't blame him. Helena nervously glances away. She holds Lucas closer to her as if I the big bad monster would devour him. And last, Daemon, glares at me with an intensity that surpasses my own glare at Ardal.

I turn my back on them. The forest calls me; it wants the animal back. I'm not sure how to get it. "I can do it on my own." If this was last week, my eyes would shine yellow under the trees' shadows, but it's not last week and my eyes won't glow.

"We can all do it." If Ardal did something, it's only noticeable by the pebbles shifting places. "We're a team."

Daemon shouts, "No!" He takes a breath. "It was his fault we almost died!"

"Fucking idiot." Roy crosses his arms. "If Theon kept his cool, we would have been fucking fine."

Daemon continues to blame us, "You changed the music. It's your fault too." He stomps the ground, cracking the pebbles under him. If he continues, he might make the area a beach, which would ruin it as a hideout.

I turn around. "Roy, did you call off the swarm when I wasn't paying attention?" I focus solely on the buzzing black cloud behind him. The swarm is still around even when the orders he gave were pass me the chips.

He turns around and flips the finger. "Fuck off!" In doing so, the flies fly away. The bag of chips falls. "If Lucas had better control of his powers, shit would have worked."

Helena hugs Lucas. "That's not fair. He's a kid." She does her best to cover him from the blow, but it's in vain as Lucas sees how we all turn on each other. She isn't ethereal or light, not the swan swaying with the wind she once was. She feels more like a giant Galapagos tortoise weighed down to earth by the gravity of it all. When she looks at me, she pauses, her gaze aimed at my chest and stomach. At the wounds under the bandages. The marks cross diagonally, starting under my left shoulder and ending over the hip.

"We all are!" I shout. The pain courses from my chest to my words, breaking them apart.

Lucas struggles against Helena's embrace. "Please stop." But his voice is drowned by the rest of us.

Daemon stands between me and Helena. "So, it's all our faults?"

So now you decide to act like a brave bison, not when we were in danger, and just barely when our lives depended on it.

"You hid behind Lucas!" I point at my little brother. "You hid behind a child. I messed up. I counted on you!" I look back at Ardal. I really thought he had my back. "Just get rid of me. I'm the problem. You think so. I think so too. So, blame it on me and we can be done with this." I wince with every word. It feels as if I drank king cobra venom or a jellyfish grabbed my chest and injected me with toxins, as everything turns into what I feared the most.

"Fucking coward."

"Hey…"

"Please."

Ardal stands up. He pushes Daemon away from the center of our circle. "Stop! All of you!" He tries to remain calm, but I can see the vein popping out of his hands. "This isn't helping. We all screwed up." He half turns to Roy. Only the number one on the back of his jacket is visible. "Choosing for us was a mistake."

Roy's fingers rake his longish black hair. "Whatever. You agreed with me about Theon driving." He stomps off the fallen bag of chips and walks away. He lays down in the hammock. I can still hear the snap of his fingers and new command, "Pass me the chips." The buzzing begins again.

Ardal turns his back to me displaying the numbers zero and one with his name on top. "Lucas needs to have more control. And Helena, you could speak up more."

She looks at Lucas. "They wanted to fight. I didn't want to." Her hair becomes a mess as it tangles and loses its weightless properties.

"Theon didn't. He wanted to leave and keep us safe. But no one spoke up." Ardal puts his hands behind him. He turns counter-clockwise, facing the bruised Daemon. Two fingers pinch the bridge of his nose. "Theon is right. You hid, not a word, not a movement until it was almost too late." Daemon stays quiet, nodding at Ardal's scolding, acknowledging his mistake while he holds his pendant close and murmurs to himself. "You aren't being fair to him. He counted on us to help, and I failed him. It's as much our fault as it is his."

Finally, Ardal turns to me. He takes slow steps, not that I would be able to outrun him. He is the cheetah; I am the injured tortoise. Once he's in front of me, he levels with me and puts his hands on my shoulder. "I'm sorry. I wasn't there to help, and that I put you in a position that you weren't ready for. You did the best you could."

I force myself to look away, pause and take one deep breath, inhaling the waterfall's breeze and the forest's spring-pollen-filled air. "It doesn't feel that way. I almost got us killed."

It's because of me they're in danger. The sniper mentioned a single target among six. I was the target. That reason alone should make them to hate me.

"You made a mistake. To err is human."

I squirm away from his grasp. "I'm not human." *I'm not an animal.* It's as if nature rejected me. I stare at the darkness of the forest. At the deep green canopies formed by deciduous trees. Focusing on glimpsing the echoes of nature, but only getting nothingness, I sigh, knowing I don't belong anywhere. *I'm a monster, a freak of nature.* I know they think so. The way DJ keeps his distance. Or how Lucy takes a step away when I mention an animal. Lucas and Ardal avoid me unless completely necessary. Haruka sees me as a freakshow. Only Roy doesn't care, but he wouldn't care in any other circumstance either. *Their lives would be better if I wasn't in them.*

Ardal calmly looks at them. "He says everyone thinks he's a monster." He sighs, then turns to me with his emerald eyes and purple eye-bags. "He thinks we would be better off without him."

The group falls into silence. Daemon whispers to his pendant as if he were a magpie collecting metals. Helena is unmoving and Lucas whistles to a sad, calming tune. He looks at Helena and Daemon. I remember DJ's expressions of disgust when I spoke about keeping my abilities. And Lucy's disappointment when I asked her to keep using her.

"It's better that way." I glance at the others, then at my lap. I bite my lip, hiding everything else. The loneliness and rejection. I was never meant to be part of something. It was all a humane illusion, not the harsh reality of nature. I turn back to the deep green woods.

Ardal makes his move, standing between the forest and myself, but still gives me space, not touching my aching body. "I don't think you are a monster or a burden. You have to fight for you. We can't do that."

I purposely ignore the second part, not because he's wrong, but because it doesn't feel right. "They don't agree with you. They think I'm a monster. Just ask them." I gesture towards Daemon, Helena, and Lucas.

"I don't think that." Lucas looks up at me. The ice piano's keys scratch against each other interrupting the melody before it crumbles. The fragments melt in the waters.

"Lucas you don't have to lie. I can handle the truth." My eyes are fixed on the body of water behind him.

With Helena's help, he stands. "It's the truth." The breeze becomes acrid. Fauna at the source of the river flee.

"Are you scared of me or what I did?" My brows arc.

Roy passionately eats his new chips, brought by a group of honeybees.

Lucas takes a step. "No." The waterfall turns black. The liquid turns into that horrid black slime. Fish and amphibians desperately try to jump out of the water in vain, trapped by the goo. Ooze spills from the fish as they stop drawing breath in their desecrated home. The group stares in horror as the waterfall's flow staggers. Clumps of ooze falls, sending it flying to the shore. The black ooze splatter collides with Daemon and Helena. Her hair stuck in a black mass, the blobs on his face sticking to his fingers as he tries to pick it away. My jaw drops. Lucas looks at Roy, who for once doesn't smirk or smile. "Bu…bu…bu…" Lucas's tears are panther black. "I was saying the truth." He sobs and the sobs echo through the forest.

Helena forgets her hair and hugs him. "It's okay."

"I don't think he's a monster." The black water flows sluggishly. The density of it allows the small animals to free themselves and run away from the ecological disaster I caused. "I'm sorry." It slowly regains its flow. Lucas's wails get louder as loud as blue whales singing.

I move past Ardal and trek down the forest, leaving my brother and the waterfall behind. The further I get, the darker the path. Sunlight is only a memory to those who are worth its light. I'm not worth the light shining upon those at the waterfall. And certainly not worth the artificial light cast by the city at night. The roots slow my pace. The branches swat at me.

Ardal keeps pace. It shouldn't be a surprise, just as people shouldn't be surprised a cheetah can keep up with a tortoise. "Where are you going?"

"Far from you. Life is better without me." I duck under the branches, past the fork in the trail. My foot catches on a root. I'm helpless as the ground approaches. *It only lasted two minutes before I needed to go back to Helena because I injured*

myself. I'm useless. I stop midair, the detritus far from my stomach. I glance back. Ardal holds me by my shirt.

His emerald eyes look serious. The warm, confident smile he uses to inspire his soccer team is gone. "We need you. Our lives depend on it." With only one arm, he pulls me back up. "Let's talk somewhere private." He says it as an option, but it's meant as an order. I can't escape. He drags me for ten minutes through the forest until we arrive at our clearing. The clearing he saw my memories.

"What do you want?" I look away. Arms crossed and legs aiming at anything but him. The clearing isn't bright and sunny. Dead describes it perfectly. The animals that used it are far away. The shadows encroach upon us. Gray clouds obscure the sun. The wind bellows snuffing Lucas's cries from the mountains. The world is getting ready for a tempest.

He takes my shoulders. "Talk to me. What's going on with you?" His voice pleads for an answer he already has. He can read my mind, so what's the point of talking?

"I was clear enough. I'm the reason we're being hunted. You're better without me." My feeble arms push him back. Without the strength of the animal world, he must have let me do it, to make me feel capable. I turn and walk to the edge of the clearing.

He clasps his hands. "We need you!" He takes two steps before stopping. He keeps the distance comfortable. "They may not like it, but we need you. I want you here."

I turn back to him. My nails scratch against my palms. "You wouldn't if you knew what I knew." *That I don't have any abilities anymore.* I sigh, then bite my lips with more force than I should have.

He takes a deep breath. He walks until he's right in front of me. With one finger, he pokes my forehead. "You don't need to be an animal to be capable. We need this, you." He looks me straight in the eyes. "Are you happy about leaving?"

"Do I look happy?"

"Have you…?"

"Tried to end my life again? No." I pause. "You saw my chest." His emerald eyes widen staring at the object of pain and disdain, myself. *If I was worth anything, I wouldn't have done this. It may as well have been a suicide attempt.* Any closer and my claws would have slashed through everything. "It's the same thing, isn't it?"

He's treating me like a delicate sea dragon, but I'm more durable and adaptable. I don't need pity. "Did you do it on purpose?" He's taller than Helena, which is a lot compared to me.

I shrug. I don't want to talk about it, but he won't leave me alone until I do. "Does it matter? I lost control again. Maybe I really wanted to do it, maybe I didn't. I don't know, 'cause I can't remember!" The world wouldn't change without me. Why *does he care? No one ever has and now suddenly everyone does. It's a mistake. I have been a mistake and my lack of abilities proves it. No one would want me without them.*

Ardal's hands go through his hair, unmaking his photogenic look. "It doesn't. We are a team. We protect each other."

Team, that's empty. *I don't deserve that.*

"You don't deserve a pack and friends?" His voice sounds rougher. "I think you do."

Why did he get an ability that gets to know me instantly? Why couldn't it be something like changing gravity or doing magic? He had to read minds. Without shapeshifting I can't escape him either. I'm stuck with him living here all the time. Why did I lose the only thing that made me valuable and worth it? What's so wrong with me that my own body betrays me, leaving me for dead? If I was better, I wouldn't struggle. I'll never be a wolf; I'm stuck being a rat. Everyone hates them. They live short lives in the shadows or are hunted as pests. My abilities are the only reason good things happened to me. My brothers acknowledge me because I have abilities. I have friends because I can become a T-Rex. I have people around me because whatever the problem, I could fix it with my animal abilities. "It doesn't feel that way." My nails try to dig through the palms of my hands.

He keeps me grounded, using none of his strength or size. *Why isn't he pinning me down like the mouse I am?* "If it wasn't for you, Helena might have died. You're doing what you can."

But they fear me. Is he blind? He can read minds, he can hear them, unless he can't. I've been thinking about his abilities in the wrong way. He doesn't read minds, at least not completely. A smile creeps up my face. He's ignorant not by choice, but by the limitations of his own abilities. "They fear me. You just can't read emotions and feelings; you can only read thoughts." It explains the monotone dialogue when we speak through thoughts.

He takes a step back. "Why does that matter?"

"'Cause you can't tell how they feel unless they say it directly." I pause. "Just like how you can't affect animals." I glance at my feet at the plants and the rocks mixing with each other. "It's like with Daemon bullets can't pierce him, but wood splinters can make him bleed."

Ardal pats me on the shoulder. "You figured it out without an ability." His shining smile sparkles in the otherwise darkened void that has become the clearing. I hate it when he's right, 'cause he's not right. There's no way. "Let's head back Lucas will be worried." He glances at the opposite end of the clearing. "Roy, I know you're there. Cursing in your mind is not silent."

"Fuck off!" He storms into the open. "Had to make sure someone kicked his ass." He looks at Ardal. "If it wasn't you. I would have done it." He leaves us behind, trekking back to the waterfall. A small swarm with a bag of chips follows him.

"Are you going to do it?" Corinna forces my phone to receive her call. A call that was never made and would have never been answered. "Save those two, and you get me and another on your team." She ignored everything we talked about.

"We will. I'll make the plan." I tug on Ardal's arm. He helps me walk through the pain. There's only one logical conclusion to this plan. Since I have no abilities, there's less risk of me getting captured. I take a deep breath; this plan will be hard to make it past the others. "I'll go and get them. I have no abilities, so I can do it without risks."

Ardal presses my hand. "What? No, I'm going with you."

"You said I was capable. Let me do it." The wind carries moisture. In the distance booming thunder and a constant collision of water and solids reverberate. Under us, the vibrations continue. **Strange, my abilities came back. At least part of them. I can do it. My brains and my senses should be more than enough, just like when it all started.**

He shakes his head. "We're a team, rely on us." He stands beside me, making sure I don't injure myself again, smiling as he knows what I'm experiencing. "You can hear them?" He stares in the direction of the waterfall. "Helena also lost her abilities. The three of us can go."

So, Helena lost them too? And Lucas is always teetering between having and not having them. Strange. Maybe it's not a me problem. I don't have enough information about our abilities to reach a valid hypothesis. I'll leave it for now, but will revisit it after we save those kids.

Their voices sound like whispers in the background of a crowded room. All of them consoling Lucas, but also confirming what I already knew. They do think I'm a monster.

"Yes, I can." My stomach churns. I hate to ask for his help or accept it, but I'm in no condition to fight. My hand brushes over my ribs. "You two are back-up. I already risked you enough. We get to them before they're targeted again."

He nods, accepting this meager compromise.

CHAPTER TWENTY-SEVEN: SOARING

April 15, 2013

Corina: Are you ready?

Ardal: I don't like this plan.

DJ: Agreed.

Theon: We don't have to like it. It's our best chance. I'm ready.

I put the phone back in my jean pockets. It buzzes a couple more times, but my focus is on the sky. The sun transforms the asphalt into a cooking grill. Cats and dogs hide in the lackluster vegetation's shadows. There are only one or two smaller trees per block. The school grounds hide behind the neighborhood's houses, the gray buildings and verdant areas covered by multicolored homes. My path takes me through the rest of the neighborhood. The pets look my way when I walk by, "H..lo." Their words and phrases cut out. It happens to birds too. I have my senses back, but everything else is fuzzy at best.

I glance at the phone again.

Kat: Good luck Theon!

Theon: Thanks for holding on to my stuff.

Jay: No problemo, mi amigo.

A gust of air abandons my lungs. I look at the skies again. She's taking too long. Something must be wrong. I my chest with my hands. I shouldn't run. Helena warned me against exercise and physical exertion, but I do anyway. The airflow presses my stomach and chest harder than it should. My arm bites in pain. *I'll handle it.* This is nothing compared to previous pain. *I can endure a couple of cuts.* My teeth grit against my desire to complain. My other arm holds a mouse sized basket filled with worms nuts and some other snacks. **Hurry up!** Something is definitively wrong. I take one deep breath. The air is stuffy with the nauseous pheromones and the disorienting skittish scent of an anxious mass of individuals four blocks away.

Theon: Corinna, how far did you say they were from school?

Corinna: Eight or nine blocks.

I dial a number. It beeps. **Come on, answer!** I glance around. Where is she? I stop. I can't go in there without information. If I only have one ability at my disposal, then I need a better plan and knowledge. I pace, never crossing the street, but not going back either. The few normal pedestrians avoid the direction I'm about to take. My unprecedented anxiety works like a stripped skunk's, my glands are excreting smells that everyone would find distasteful. A small common magpie lands on my shoulder. "Lorena. How are things going?"

She tilts her head and pecks my neck as she finds balance over my loose leather jacket. I'm sweating, but survival demands sacrifice. If they notice my injuries, I might draw more attention. ".u.ry the. a.e in tr…le." Between the letters squawks. Take a deep breath, slow down. She tilts her head again. I can't risk animals. Gather the information. Fear and anxiety pheromones travel from the location of the kids we're trying to save. Lorena looks worried, and she was late. This will be terrible.

I raise the basket to her level. "Thank you for the help. Go to your family. Spread the word that we need animals away from that location."

Her dark eyes stare at me. "Okay." She bats her wings, taking flight back to my school, where her nest is. From time to time, she looks back with the basket dangling from her claws. The other animals respond the same way. They stare at me. Static, waiting for my move.

Please listen to me this time, I can do it. I don't have to risk anyone's life. The animal world prowls as I make a painful run to the location. My phone tweets, calling for my attention. "Ardal!"

Helena's voice interrupts my panic. "He's driving. Are you okay?" This is not going to work. They all look at me like I'll unstable. *My friends think I'm insane. Roy keeps saying how much of an idiot I am.* My stomach twists. I should call this off. *If they're around, they'll get hurt. I'll just do it myself.*

"Never mind, it's fine." I pull the phone away from my ear.

Wind howls through the speaker. "Theon," Ardal speaks up. "Tell us what's going on, we have your back." Cars blast their horns, and people throw insults in the backdrop on Ardal's end.

With the burning sensation on my arm. I forget about my palms. Sweats scents the air even more than before. "Plan is ruined. They're in trouble. I'll get to them, don't come near the location. It's dangerous." I wheeze at the end of the sentence. ***What am I going to do? How?*** Corinna said we had two days. ***If they die, it's my fault. That's the only thing I can do right, kill people.***

"Hey!"

"Kat?"

Slow classic music rings from the speakers. "I intercepted the call," Corinna says. Her voice colder than a two-striped garter snake during hibernation. "You're all linked."

"Fuck off! It's my freaking free day!" Roy leaves the call. Most follow him, except Kat.

She hums slowly. "Theon, what can you see?" Her song imitates the slower tempo of Corinna's music.

"I see the asphalt, a desolate park, a blue sky with white clouds, a bunch of colorful houses with different dogs." I can feel my heart letting up. My breath slows. My uninjured arm supports the rest of my body as a pillar between me and my knees.

She adds slowly, "Tell me more about the dogs." Her voice is as comforting as always. She truly is a crimson macaw. All birds have that kindness to them even if they are arrogant like the eagle and peacock.

I glance at the green gates next to me and follow them down the street. "A golden retriever, boxer, Belgian shepherd, Maltese, Doberman, French bulldog." I glance around, I settle into itself. My chest rises evenly up and down. My heart thumps, not aching anymore. I don't feel the tingle. The one I normally feel when Kat's around. She can somehow make everything feel completely fine. Right now, I'm in survival mode. I can do it. "Thank you. I feel better."

"Don't worry. You got it." She goes silent, allowing me to collect my thoughts.

"Ardal. There's a park nearby. Go there and wait. I'll check the school and the kids and then decided our course of action." I walk toward the primary school. Animals keep track of my steps, but hopefully they listened.

"Coordinates sent," Corinna adds, then disconnects. Kat stays her comforting presence reaches me even though she is just here digitally.

Ardal clears his throat. "We'll be there in five minutes. Take care."

"I'll try." I hang up. I move against the throbbing pain. It's not a run. That might damage my stomach permanently, but it's close enough to a trot. I can't fight directly today. I have to think outside the box. I have two more blocks. The closer I get, the more the animals raise their concerns. Howls and meows follow me. Overhead squawks and chirps guide my path through the valley of houses as large black feathers fall on the sidewalk.

The school's colors are overshadowed by an overabundance of black. Trees spouting black feathers, as crows settle on the site. The chaotic herd of adult humans wearing their dull colors shout and scream as they open a path to the black SUVs and military personnel pointing their guns at the crowd. Even the German shepherds who tilt their head sideways when I walk in are wearing black. I stand out like a clown fish in an aviary. My light green tee and khaki shorts do me no favors. Even the strange lady with a black feather pendant fits better in the grim reality and she is further away from the crowd.

In the middle of the path, the military personnel escorts two kids. They can't be much older than Lucas. One is shorter than Lucas, with golden hair and celestial eyes. The other has the eyes of a black panther. The golden eye child kicks the soldier's legs, resisting all attempts to put him in the van. He pulls something from his pocket. The object flies, soaking the soldier in egg yolk. The soldier picks up the kid, taking him over his shoulders.

Naturally, the kid has a tantrum. "Put me down, big idiot!"

The shorter kid murmurs, "I'm sorry. We didn't mean to prank you." Everyone ignores him in favor of the louder one, who has an escort of three armed men instead of the one the short kid has.

How do I save them? I can't transform or fight. I can't even outrun them. I hold my stomach, glancing around. The crows and the dogs could help, but what I really need is a stampede. A true one with chaos and disarray. That gives us the opportunity to escape. The German shepherds have yellow puddles under them. This is not going to be easy. They and the crows alone will end up with too many dead. I shouldn't have said I'd handle it. Roy and Ardal are way better options for this. Kat could have helped too. "Stop!" My voice carries over to the animals. Once everyone looks my way, I freeze. Speed and strength are unavailable, so we use numbers and strategy. "Why are you kidnapping children?" If I learned anything from nature and my past, it's that you don't give the opponent even an inch. Corner them and force them to make a wrong move.

They were already on the edge. The guns pointed at them are frightening, but their instincts should kick in. "He's right. It's a kidnap. We have to do something."

The man with the closest German shepherd closes in, invading my space. "National security matters." There's nothing behind the mask except a heartless human. The dog, on the other hand, wags her tail energetically as she gets close to me. She believes I'll free them all. No more will they be slaves to these… Calm down, think.

I blurt the first thing I think of, "National security? They can't be older than ten. Are they terrorists? They have nuclear codes? Surely, they committed war crimes." I shrug. Hopefully, this works. "Are you arresting yourself too? I see signs of animal abuse." I point at the puddles of pee under the dogs. It's a guess but if people care about any animal, it's pets. Murmurs become open talk. The adults glower, moving to the sides, spreading. They just needed a push.

"Shut up, kid." He points his weapon at my head. I bite my lips standing my ground against his push. The adults freeze. There's fear everywhere. *I didn't count on them being this ruthless.* They're willing to kill everyone here.

Each of the four dogs curve their back. Their tails stiffen, hair pointing upwards. They bare their fangs, but not at the crowd, at the soldiers. The crows cackle and take flight. Their wingspans are unnaturally big, the equivalent of Haast's eagles. While everyone is in a standstill, the two kids continue to be dragged closer to the vehicles.

The lady with the black feathers smiles my way. She waves her hand and stares. The massive shadows of the crows cover the sky, Now everything is truly black. Everyone except the woman looks up. The shadows get bigger and darker, landing on one soldier. They pick him up and fly him away. The other soldiers point up, shooting upon the giant birds. I shudder. The gun hasn't moved from my head, but every shot echoes inside my ears.

He glances upward along with the others. This is our moment. I speak up, "Now." The four dogs jump on their leashes. Maws and claws tearing into whichever weak spot they find. It prompts the adults to rush toward the kids to save them. The stampede I needed. *Did that woman do this? And where did gigantic crows come from?* I glance back at her location. And an ethereal figure remains; she smirks at the carnage of men taking involuntary flight.

The soldier in front of me drops to the ground and rolls with the dog. He hits her snout with the back of the long gun. She staggers, blood falling from her nose. It gives him a moment to reach into his vest pocket. My sight fills with red. Hurting an animal, not on my watch. I stomp his free hand. He rolls toward the dog, taking me down with them. My chest trembles; my nerves overstimulate with pain. I roll onto my back, holding my chest. He gets on top of me with knife in hand. His hand swings down, aiming at my heart. Blood stains my tee, but the soldier's arm is stuck in the dog's maw. He lets go of the knife while his other hand searches for a new weapon.

No time to hesitate. I try to shove him up. The grueling pain halts me as both creatures fight above me. Claws accidentally scratch my chest. The man turns, bruising my damaged torso. Heavy grunts abandon my throat as they continue their struggle on top of me. The weight of them lightens. A small crevasse of air alleviates the burden as they lift into the skies. The dog lets go. Her jaws red, but otherwise unharmed. Drops of blood cover my face as the man screams and shouts, reaching for my hands. I ignore him. whatever happens to him is not my fault.

The giant crow flies him toward the ozone layer. With that the last of the crows fly away with the faint screams of those men. The black feathers fall onto the ground, most gather beside the SUV. In the middle of the feathers, the blond one trembles, the golden-eyed kid shakes his head. "Get destroyed losers!" The adults go to check on them.

I look around. The woman is gone, all my questions will be saved for another day. With a grunt and a push from my good arm, I sit up. The scorching asphalt demands I stand, but I'd rather be with the four dogs. They circle around me, their tails wagging energetically. I pet them all in turn. "Corinna, can you disable their tracking chips?" It's the right thing to do. They didn't want to be here. They don't deserve a life of fear, of being forced into situations they never asked for. I can at least repay that much.

The phone replies from the front pocket of my jeans. "There's no point."

She's wrong. There is a point to freeing them. "They would attack anyone who isn't me. Free them." My tone sharpens, a deep rumbling in my voice. It causes the dogs to react and growl.

A minute passes. "Chips deactivated." The five of us have no time to celebrate. "Three black SUVs incoming."

My heart rate increases. There's six to eight people in each. We need to leave now. Four bloodied dogs stand guard, snarling. Against the pain, I rush toward the kids. The canines are more than enough to open a path among the panicked adults. They bare their fangs, sticking to me.

The two kids couldn't be more different. The blond boy still trembles, holding a slingshot. He's on the verge of tears. Whatever he mumbles scatters in the wind. The other one is vainglorious. He smiles at the attention. The crowd pauses when they see me and my pack. The smaller kid looks up and waves.

The other one does a pale imitation of Roy. As soon as the attention isn't on him, he shrinks.

I shake my head. "You need to leave. There's more coming."

The crowd gasps, a couple of the parents disband. Well, I wasn't counting on their bravery, given that it took giant crows, four dogs and a teen to make them move. Human cowardice knows no bounds. It's no wonder we spread through the world, seeing a lion once traumatized all of them enough to run to other continents, only to be traumatized, by the giant predator variants on those continents.

Golden-eyed boy sticks his tongue out. "We can take them." He stands defiantly before me. Whatever bravado he has is nothing compared to the lions. To them, it comes naturally, as if written in their genes.

The smaller one still on the ground, "Percy, we should—"

"Shut it!" Percy runs past the dogs, who aren't trying to stop them. "They'll never find us." With the adults also doing their absolute best to be useless, Percy runs past them.

The blond boy stops beside me. "I'm sorry." He doesn't look my way and runs past us. His tears draw a path behind him.

I walk faster than the adults, chasing after the kids. My stomach flares up in pain. I take a second to regain my nerves. "Follow them, but don't put yourselves in danger." Three of the dogs chase after them, leaving me with my companion. "I never asked your name." I scratch her behind the ears.

"Qui..ra" She leads both of us, following the trail of salty scented water drops.

CHAPTER TWENTY-EIGHT: SACRED CREATURES

Kyra's vest rubs against my legs. I'm calling her Kyra until I can understand animals again. If I can ever do that completely. Kyra and I leave the kids' school behind. The mass of parents scattering or collecting their children as the rumor of the armed men coming spreads like a deadly virus. If she wanted, she could leave me behind, yet she walks with old useless me. We turn the corner twice. She follows the kids' scent and I follow the dogs.

My phone buzzes, shaking my shorts. I groan as the sound invades my fragile ears. "What's going on? We saw giant birds lifting people." Ardal's voice creates a new headache.

"I think someone summoned them. They were unnaturally big crows." Kyra and I head, toward a wild green park. My free hand checks on my wrapped stomach. Still fine. "Are you at the park?"

He turns his car off under this desert-like heat. "We're here."

"I'm on my way. And make sure no one sees you." I glance at Kyra nodding to accelerate her pace. She trots ahead of me, checking for trouble and barking at the other animals. They reply and spread the word. It's hard to understand as words cut and overlap, and the sound bangs my head.

"On it." He hangs up.

I put my phone away and keep walking, dragging the soles of my shoes, which sound like clattering hooves. I'm careful about the movements as my stomach begs me to stop, and my arm stings. Kyra is back, she takes her place beside me, but doesn't say anything. Not that I can understand her anyway.

We cross another block, another street until we're close to the park. The colorful houses keep going. Behind me, the school is barely visible, only the giant library building is in sight. Since it's beside the main avenue, I can't discern if the armed men got their reinforcements. What I can tell are the two distinctive pheromones of rage and fear. Both provocative, but I won't be their prey. I drag my shoes faster, then stop on the corner before the park. I turn left, then right. Clear.

Kyra runs inside the shrubbery. I follow her. The park is wilder than any park normally is. The grass and shrubs entangle on the metal bars and cover the grainy rocks of the playground. Trees interlock arms, shadowing us from the unforgiving sunlight. Benches smell like pigeon, sparrow, magpie, and cat. The rusted playground's losing its color. And on the other side, a red convertible.

Kyra and I walk through the small jungle. Ardal's car is on the empty street. The park smells abandoned by humans. I slowly make it to the car and lean on it. "Nice to see you." I wheeze, holding my chest. "The kids are being chased."

Ardal looks at my red face. "Woah!" He jumps out of the car. With one hand, he stabilizes me. "Take it easy." He has me lean on the car. My back against the machine.

Helena slowly stands up. Her delicate hands lift my shirt, revealing my chest. "We have to change them and clean them. They're all torn." She looks under her seat, pulling out the first aid kit.

I pull the shirt down. "We can do it after we save those kids. They're in trouble."

"You aren't in condition to fight." Ardal blocks my movement, preventing me from standing straight. His eyes are sad. **Please let me help.**

I look at Kyra. "I'm not risking anyone else. Trust me, I'll make it work." I bite my tongue, careful not to spill more of what's on my mind.

"Dying won't solve anything." Ardal snaps, storming away, to the shade of the artificial forest. He picks up his sunglasses and covers his eyes. With his back resting on a tree, he stares at me. "If you go on your own, we could all die."

I stare back. "If you come with me, we could all die. If you stay at least, you have a chance." I glance at Helena. "I want you to be safe."

Ardal shakes his head. "I wanted you to be okay with it. I'm going. I'm not asking you." He crosses his arms. He moves to take the lead.

Kyra chases after him, standing on his side as a show of support. He stands as pack leader as he was always meant to be. I'm a reject who was never meant to be surrounded by people or animals. I was meant to be solitary, like the skunks.

He glances back at Helena. "In and out. We aren't fighting."

She nods. Instead of walking toward him, she drops the first aid kit and picks up two objects. The first a veil that she wears to cover her face. The second is a small can that she hands over. I open it. Inside is black liquid. It smells similar to paint, but lacks the pungency. Everyone stares at me, expecting something. I dip my fingers in the substance. Without looking, I draw two massive panda bear circles over my eyes and eyebrows. My scar is hidden under the paint. Ardal thought of everything. This is for the best.

His back faces me as if looking at me would be insulting to him. "Where to?"

I glance at Kyra. "Can you take us to them?"

She barks and strides in front of us. Ardal behind her, and Helena by his side. I keep my distance. From time to time, I glance back, making sure no one follows. My senses are active, but my hearing still unreliable. **This is not what I wanted.**

Then what did you want? Ardal quickly glances back.

I sigh as we leave the park behind. **I don't know. Not this. Not to fight for my life every day or put others at risk. It's not worth it.** I toy with my phone inside my pocket. Please help me escape. I glance at the group chat. That woman we need to find her. I message Haruka directly.

Theon: I saw this woman with black feathers. She was strange, I think she made giant ravens. Could you search for her? She had black hair, an angular shaped face, and black eyes, with a little red in them.

Haruka: I'll look for her.

Corinna: Sending you the feeds.

Corinna attaches video files from earlier. Having a digital Ardal is terrible, nowhere is safe. I put my phone away and my senses return to where they should be, alerting us if someone or something is happening around.

Are our lives not worth it? Ardal keeps walking as if nothing was said. He doesn't falter or stumble. He follows without an issue, and Helena follows him.

No. I'm not worth the effort. I know you volunteered because of me. And I'm not worth that. Your life is worth much more than mine.

That makes him stop. He turns to me with the speed of a reticulated python, but the enormity of silverback gorilla. He takes off his sunglasses. The look of horror in his eyes haunts me. His pupils are wide and he's breathing fast. His brows furrow and his fists close. He takes a step forward. I'm shaking.

Kyra looks back but stays still. Helena turns. "Ardal…" She touches his back. That makes him stop, but once he looks at me, all that calm is gone.

"You're wrong. I don't know how many times I have to say it. Or what I need to do to show you I believe it." He stands right in front of me, his voice restrains itself from shouting. It's as if I hit a dog or killed a doe in front of her fawn. "I'm not sure what to do with you or how to help you. It hurts to see you speak of yourself in that way." He turns back. "Let's go." He goes off with Helena near him. She takes his hand as they talk.

We walk two blocks before Kyra stops and stares at a warehouse the size of a whole block. Three black SUVs are parked in front of it. The warehouse is nothing special, metal doors and a dull brown facade. Inside it, there's a constant ringing. It's irritating and hurtful to my senses. Nothing else, except for the smell of dogs and gunpowder. I'll never be free of that smell.

"We need to get rid of their vehicles." I point at the SUVs.

Ardal glances first at Kyra, then at Helena and finally at me. "You do it." He points at me. Whatever kindness he had is gone. He's cold. **Something I deserve.**

"I can't transform." I cross my arms and tap my feet against the sidewalk.

Ardal takes Helena's hand and Kyra's collar. He moves in front of the door. "Disable them, that's an order." He steps inside, forgetting about me. Kyra and Helena also disappear inside the building.

I remain alone under the sun. ***What am I going to do? I can't do it. I don't have any animal abilities for this.*** I glance at the wheels. If only I had stegosaurus thagomizers.

My phone cuts through the silence. Kat says, "Jay wanted to talk to you."

I sigh. "How much did you hear?"

"Everything. It's okay, we all hit rough patches." She stops her music. "Still you're doing great."

Jay interrupts her in the playful way he does everything. "Bro!" A bunch of people shush him. "Sorry. Bro!" he whispers. "You are awesome! You helped someone read minds! You found someone who dances and creates tornadoes. Your brothers control water and insects! That was not you being an animal. It was the you, you! I can't wait to see what wildlife you'll bring to us!"

I hide the smile he's bringing me, and the rose-colored cheeks he provokes. "I brought so much danger to your lives." I take a seat on the curb. My lack of words is a struggle. I like them, that's why they should be away from me and all my troubles.

"So? Life's so much more fun! You got this!" Jay's voice blows through the phone, creating a second wave of shushing. "Just believe in you like we do!"

I smile in response. I hate them 'cause they won't let me go that easily from their grasp. "Fine, but—"

"No butts!" Jay interrupts. He snorts at his own joke.

Kat takes over. "We'll be right here when you need it." She hangs up, mostly 'cause Jay couldn't be stealthy even in his sleep, I'd compare that to an animal, but animals don't like bringing attention to themselves.

I take a look at the sky, the mountains, and the park's trees. Even when the animals have vacated the area, they're expecting me to survive. I stand and take a deep breath. I repeat the words "I can do it" inside my head. As a reminder that if anyone here can do it, it's me. *I can break vehicles. I can fit through the rafters, and I can smell emotions. I can do whatever everyone else can.* I look at both sides of the street. Empty, as it should be. I lower the back part of my shorts. "Stegosaurus Tail."

The tail pulls me downward. My scales are desert orange, dull, not pretty like a sunset. The scutes are vibrant green, then turn red as the blood fills them. The thagomizers are ready to impale something. I'm forced to my knees and crawl beside the second car. My tail swings. It sinks into the buoyant tire. The vehicle deflates, with the copilot's seat way lower than the rest.

"I did it!" My smile is as wide as a hyena's. I aim at the third one. This time my thagomizers pierce the rubber and collide against metal. I pull my spikes out and the backseat gets closer to the ground. "I overdid that." My spikes are complete. *That's a relief.* I crawl beside to the first car and swing carefully to not break my tail. I prepare. One. Two. Three. My tail sinks into the rubber and gets ejected. The copilot's wheel deflates.

My tail shrinks and I pull my shorts up. As soon as I'm ready, I walk into the warehouse through the same door as the others. They stand right beside it. Kyra wags her tail after seeing me. Helena has one hand latched to the side of the door. Ardal just nods at me. He then turns and touches his ear.

The ringing cuts my ears. It suppresses the dogs' whines. My pupils darken. **The dogs!** "No. They got the dogs." I run, chasing the sound with Kyra behind me.

Wait! Ardal sends a message in my head.

I can't leave them suffering like that! It's my fault.

Theon stop!

I ignore it. The dogs need my help. I'm not letting anyone else get hurt. Kyra and I run past four aisles of crates and boxes. The fifth is wider than the rest. The only light comes from the skylight. Under the light, the three other canines lay shivering and crying. They're surrounded by three devices, which must be making the ringing sound. Whatever. I run toward them, passing boxes and containers. For one second, I ignore my instinct to stay back. *I can't let them get hurt or worse.*

I kneel beside the closest one. As I'm about to grab, it a wave of sound immobilizes me. I scream as my ears drown in noise. I cover them but it's not enough. The sound mixes chirping alarms, the low undertones of a rocket launch, the high decibels of concerts and the crass debilitating sounds of nails on a chalkboard. It feels like if the claws of an iguana scratched my eardrums.

Kyra comes to pick me up, but the sounds stop her. She falls beside me as they all cry and whine. Our inescapable jailer.

Sound. "Human ears!" The noise is too loud, I can hear all of it. My senses are never truly gone. My ears pulse. My body crumples to the cold cement floor. Its cold embrace doesn't give me comfort, only more pain. The sound continues beating on my ears. I scream as the sounds fuse together. There's no animal that can save me. None of the vertebrates are deaf. ***Ardal help me!***

We're coming.

The floor vibrates violently. Sound waves bounce of it. Meager pulses break the chaos inside our circle of pain. They are slow and methodical. That's not Ardal! ***Stay back! We aren't alone.*** My neck strains against the invisible force pushing me down. I see a man. A bald man with black eyes. He smirks as he looks at me.

The hair on my neck starts standing up. I remember this feeling and this man. He's unaffected by the unbearable onslaught. "So that's your ability." Agent Penumbra says in his nasal voice as he walks around the circle looking at the five unfortunate creatures. "Interesting." He touches his chin and continues to prowl. Armed men appear, creating a protective circle around us. Guns aimed at us and at the darkness.

I snarl back. ***Leave, we can't be saved.*** My face rests on the cold floor. It slowly warms as my breath and body heat transfers to it. I glance up, avoiding his black eyes. The sound overwhelms my right ear first. *Pop* My right ear is left in silence. It becomes a mountain spring. Fresh liquid flows out of my body painting my right hand red.

Helena wait! Ardal shouts in Helena's and my head.

Helena replies through our connection. ***We can't leave him like that.*** The floor vibrates with rhythmic footsteps. A hurricane of boxes and crates fly above me. A second gust lifts me into the air before gently laying me down. I turn to see Helena dancing rapidly. Her moves are sharp and slightly restrained. They're way too functional, and lack power. She's dancing fast, too fast. Gusts of wind push men down before they know who or what hit them.

Get up! Ardal speaks inside my mind. I can't see him, nor hear the words. I only see words being typed inside my brain. ***Helena, we need to leave!***

My other ear pops. The silence overtakes sound. My throbbing head is going to burst. The pain engulfs me.

I look back up. Penumbra walks toward Helena. His tenebrous smile is the same as when he tormented Thor. The same one he had after he did something to my brothers. Dreadful pressure envelops the compound. She looks at him for a second. Helena's dance stops. The swan is gone, in its place a roped crocodile. She covers her eyes and falls to her knees. Penumbra points at her. From the shadows, two men take her down. One puts handcuff on her. The flowing wind comes to a standstill. They drag her past me to the exit.

Her dad shakes his head to denounce her dreams. He points at a doctor's coat and at a piece of paper. The smell of medicine and anesthetic. These silent images are a modern film. Ardal and I are spectators. He turns toward me, his eyes watery. My eyes flaring red. He opens his mouth, but I can't hear him. I can't hear myself anymore, yet I know what I said to him. ***Cut the link. We'll save her.*** Ardal's *voice is no more.*

As one of the men carrying Helena steps beside the circle, my feeble arms work to reach him. Red cheetah tears drop from my ears. My words are inaudible. My thoughts scrambled can only think of a predator. I see red. I want blood. Only one predator will satisfy me, the rightful raptor that will terrorize them. ***Deinonychus!*** My claws are almost the size of my hand. Small feathers grow along my arms. I raise my arms even when my head says to stop. I swipe, shredding his pants, his skin and muscle.

He raises his leg and kicks side of my head. I lay on the floor, staring as Helena's captors slowly drag her away. One of them limping. Two others drag me away from the light. ***I can't give in. One more try. Diplodocus tail. White-bellied spider monkey tail bones.*** My tail whips the uninjured man, holding him tight. ***I won't let go unless you all kill me.***

Penumbra walks my way. His voided eyes stare at mine. I force mine shut. My head is like a bomb, or a Pachycephalosaurus after a fight. The constant throbbing distracts me. ***They need me.*** I can't move. Kyra's body is on the ground. Her breaths are steady, but for how long? More footsteps, four more men approach my location. Two of them point their weapons at Kyra. My transformations disappear I'm human. Helena and I are carried away.

The men stop suddenly. They drop me to the floor. Vibrations run toward the end of the warehouse. Too many to count. *Did they put fireworks inside my head?* A kid, a really short kid. Weapons aimed at him. He stands there shaking uncontrollably, holding a slingshot. Penumbra walks past me. He wears the same smirk. Another victim falls into the hunter's trap. He stares at the kid. The kid looks away.

Instead of sitting by Percy stands in front of his friend. His eyes unfaltering suns. They stare right back at Penumbra. Penumbra backs down, stepping closer to me. He points at the children. One smiling, the other on the verge of tears.

From a-far an ocean blue dazzling light flashes in the darkened warehouse. Iridescent blue wings big enough to belong to a Quetzalcoaltus levitate in the air. The short kid with the disproportionate wings holds a harp, instead of his slingshot. He strums it, but sound is just a memory for me. The skylight shines in ocean blue and a pillar covers the dogs and me. Helena glows in a celestial blue. Lastly, one pillar of light shines in the far back. My body unwillingly returns to normal. The candor and warmth of the light douses the throbbing. Dries the blood. Most importantly, it gives me back sound. The armed men are forced away from everyone.

"Kill them!" Penumbra orders as he disappears from the warehouse. He tries to grab Helena on his way out. The pillar of light acts as a wall. He glares at me with his black eyes. Nothing happens. The pillar of light burns away the shadows he casts.

Bullets fire. Each bullet bounces of the blessed light. The light lifts us into the air. The dogs float without control, spiraling and barking joyfully. Somehow, I end up standing, my feet centimeters above the gray concrete floor. Helena's tears flow once she sees me. Her jaw softens as we witness a miracle from an angel.

In front of the angel stands Percy. "Stop! If you vow down to me, I will let you live." His voice is distorted. An angry presence hides between each word. I'm mistaken, the voice isn't angry. It's excited, and happy. It walks a path of delight in destruction. My sight turns red, but the blue light keeps me calm and still. More gunshots. The bullets again collapse when they meet the light.

"I love a fight." Percy turns into a tall man. A bronze helmet covers his face. The man handles a spear and a shield. The shield fosters a nightmarish visage. The spear has peculiar flame. Red dyed in blacks. Golden plate armor covers his body. The red cape creates an illusion of greater than life itself. His red eyes call to my primal instincts.

Unleash me! My body changes. Inside the pillar I become a dinosaur with a face not even a mother would love. Majungasaurus. Red and green scales cover my body. My nose is the pug's snout of the dinosaur world. A small horn grows on the top of my head. I roar and the light lets me out. I gladly crunch one man's torso. The rest run away from me toward the man with the spear.

With flashing speed, he's up close to the men running away from the carnage. The spear impales one man that tried to book it to the exit. Percy moves beside me and launches the spear, piercing three hearts. He pulls out a sword. Two heads roll and the body in my mouth drops. His sword points at one of the men going to the back light. I walk there looking above the containers, keeping an eye on him. My nausea is gone. Only desire for conflict, desire to fight, kill and conquer is left. His armor and cape are dressed in blood. The remaining men in black run at him. His shield opens like a mouth. Flames as scary as Penumbra consume those who run from the fight. Leaving only burned bodies and dried blood on the floor. He throws down his shield.

One valiant and lucky man connects a hit on the helmet.

"Finally!" Percy takes off his helmet. The scarred face of tanned man is revealed. The grim smile craves more. The armored man returns the punch. A loud crack resonates in the room. Percy lounges toward the others, leaving that first challenger on the floor. He continues the onslaught, leaving corpses in his wake. The floor floods with red liquid. The man finishes his work by destroying one wall, showing the way to the sunlight.

I see the blue pillar above Ardal fading away. Above him an armed man ready to shoot when the lights go out. He hasn't noticed me. He thinks himself too smart. I approach from behind. The claws on my feet are ready, but they aren't the weapon just an accessory as I kick him to the ground and step on him. Crushing his little frame. Bones snap like crackers. He screams. I leave his body wrecked, but he's alive. Until the man with the spear grabs his sword and cuts his back. The screams stop.

This man created a graveyard, and I helped him. I liked it and wanted to do more. Something is wrong with me. He walks toward the entrance. A cocoon of black and red flames covers him and his blood thirsty smile. The flames disappear and leave Percy lying on the ground. Body inert. He burps. That kid is, without a doubt, a chimpanzee.

The shining angel wings fade, leaving a sky-blue glimmer in the air. The small child floats until he lands. His wings disappear, leaving no trace. The light vanishes. Kyra and the other dogs sit inside their dry space. The puddles of blood form a perfect circle around where the pillar of light stood. Everyone except me is clean. My face is red, my mouth drips blood. My shoes are stained, and my hands are colored.

Ardal stands. He glances at me, points down. I'm naked. My shorts shredded; my shirt torn. My leather boots and jacket still intact. I make a run for any piece of clothing that can cover me, avoiding the corpses. Even fossil hotbeds have fewer bodies than what I'm seeing here. My chest doesn't hurt, and my arm doesn't throb. I look at my arm. The thread is gone along with the cut. My chest is a different story. Three claw marks cross it. They will remain forever.

Ardal runs for Helena. They hug. Her figure breaking the part of swan. Too fragile. She keeps her eyes closed to the decimation caused by Percy and me. Ardal picks Helena up. He comes near me. "Can you help her to the car?"

I glance at his pale face. His wide pupils. "Take her. I can carry the kids," I say showing him my arm and chest.

He nods, leaving me for the car.

The dogs divide into groups, one follows Ardal, the other stays with me. Even if tactical I think I will adopt Kyra, the one following Ardal seems very fond of him. I'll mention it to him when we're safe.

The short kid sits beside me. The he holds a slingshot tightly. "Sorry." He hugs me while his tears flow.

I pat his head. "It's okay. Let's get your friend and leave." Kyra helps him up. I pick up his bloodied friend and make it out unscathed. "What's your name?"

"Cassiel." He takes my hand and follows along.

CHAPTER TWENTY-NINE: NORTHERN MIGRATION

June 10, 2013

I sit down at the cafe near the baggage drop off. The people flowing in and out of the airport build up my headache. This infinite migration of people would be enough to send my senses into override, but right now they're focused on those men watching us. Their stares are like wasp stings on my back. They aren't able to cloak the bitter smell of gunpowder or the clanking of metal with their every step. **This is the worst idea I've accepted to. And it's probably not my last.**

Roy, Daemon, and Percival sit on their own. Percival boasts about his superiority. Roy dismisses it and Daemon asleep beside them. He snores loudly, but with his coffee on the table, the manager won't try to wake him up. I look back at the line where Helena, Cassiel, Lucas, Ardal and Ardal's mother wait to be attended. A couple more minutes and they will be.

Perfect time to distract myself on the phone. I gloss over Lucy's group messages about the three new drawings. A girl surrounded by flames. One shining under the starry sky. The last one looking like some sort of chimera. She has bull horns, bat wings and a whip-like tail. I don't even bother messaging Kat; the end of her day isn't near enough. With her, DJ and Jay all scattered through the world, I have to keep tabs on the times and days. Jay happily sends me pictures of him in California and Kat of every new city she visits in Europe. DJ barely tells me if he's fine. I feel like I'm destroying his vacations in Japan.

I pick up Haruka's number and message her after reading her last response.

Haruka: I searched for their descriptions. I'm sure about what I found.

Theon: You know it sounds insane. Percival summoned gods. He was Ares?

Haruka: He got possessed, but yes. It can't be crazier than what you or what Cass do.

Theon: You're telling me he's an angel?

Haruka: His abilities have to be.

Theon: It's a headache. Magic exists, now I have to worry about that. And all the abilities that aren't related to nature. I can't figure it out.

Haruka: I won't go out. I'll try to help.

Haruka: Try to have some fun and enjoy your trip.

Theon: I will. I'll see you in three weeks.

I pocket phone and shift back to the couch. Ardal and company pass by. His mom is dressed casually, a complete one hundred and eighty from her usual elegance. Jeans, shoes, and a blouse that looks light as air. She stands near Lucas and Cass. The kids smile and play around her. She follows closely keeping an eye on both.

I look away. The words become easier if I don't look at any of them. "Thank you for allowing Lucas to go." My fingers pinch the jeans at the height of my knees.

"Make nothing of it." Her thin lips form a smile. "I'm just glad to finally meet you. Ardal can't stop talking about you." She adjusts her glasses, then looks at him purposely avoiding Helena as if she was forbidden territory.

I glance at him. When Ardal notices me looking, he turns away. I muster, "Surely nothing good."

"Ohh no sweety." She covers her mouth briefly. "He always mentions how smart you are, and how you worry so much about others. I'm glad Ardal found a friend like you." She blinks twice with the same color eyes he has. I guess that's where he got most of his looks and manners. She turns to Lucas and Cass as they play. "Anyway. We should head to the lounge and wait for our flight."

Cass stumbles. "But I want to play a little bit more."

She pulls her purse up her arm. "I know you do, but you wouldn't want to miss the flight and treats?"

The two kids jump up and down. "Treats!" They both run away from her.

Ardal's mom shakes her head while smiling. "Children." She walks after them. "Remember what your parents said." That makes them return to her side. She turns back to Helena. "We will wait for you outside the lounge." The three step up onto escalator and disappear from view.

Helena waves at them. She turns to me. "How safe are we?" She sits on the chair next to me. Ardal and her have been excreting the unsavory smell of fear.

I glance around. There are two cars outside, two men by the entrance, one next to the vending machines, three I can smell from the baggage drop off, and one sitting at the other side of the cafe watching us. I would estimate at least five more, but I just can't tell anymore. There are too many to follow. "For now, safe."

Daemon wakes up from his slumber and pulls a chair to our table. "For now?"

"Yes, for now. We're traveling, our guards are up. They'll wait until we feel safe. I'd assume the middle of our vacations." I toy with a napkin as I dispassionately say everything on my mind. "That's how hunters work. They wait for our weakest moments." I glance at the exterior door. "This applies to the ones traveling. If you are staying here, then they will try to get you as soon as we leave. Find the girls and you'll be fine." I fold the paper on the table, forming a triangle toward the guy staring at us.

Roy glances at the paper and nods. He already knew, and I'm not surprised. Ardal also nods, taking the hint to suppress anyone else's urge to shout.

I look at Helena. "Wednesday, Thursday, or Friday. That's when they'll make a move on you. Rely on Corinna, she can give you aid from afar."

She shivers in response. "But we don't want to fight."

Ardal shoots a look at me as I open my mouth.

I reply. "You don't have to."

Ardal shakes his head as if I was going to say something terrible. He takes her hand. They walk to the escalator and talk.

I keep playing with the napkin, ignoring my inner monologue. It's in vain. One way or another we'll have to fight. They are hunting us relentlessly until they catch us, or we die. It eliminates fleeing. When you're chased by felines, sure you can run away, they tire fast. Once canines begin the chase, there's no other option than to fight back. They won't tire. Helena can always fight indirectly if she chose to, but for some reason, she believes hurting them is wrong. Her winds could push them away send them flying in tornadoes, but she chooses to not use them. It's like telling a porcupine not to use their quills. They will die. I understand Lucas and Cass not wanting too, they're kids. They hope for the best, but Helena is a teen. She should know these people are a menace.

Roy pokes me. "Bruh, you are fucking pissed." He smirks beside me. "I'm living for it."

"I'm not." I don't move, just keep looking at her and Ardal.

"Bruh, why you staring?"

My voice growls. "I'm not." I watch the two lovebirds hug and say their goodbyes. Helena climbs the escalator and her hair trails behind her like she gained the wind's favor again.

Percy pulls his chair next to me. "You're so mad!" He sits on the table, blocking Ardal and Helena from sight.

"No." I push him aside. "I'm not. Leave it." My legs push me away from the table.

Daemon and Ardal take their seats. I look away. Roy smirks. Of course, he relishes my downfall.

Daemon takes a sip of his cooled coffee. He turns to Ardal. "So, what's our plan?"

Ardal shrugs. He looks past me. Gaze lost in the background. The rest of the group begrudgingly turns to me. Percy and Roy keep smirking as if they know something I don't. Perfect more people for Roy's lion pride, as if there weren't enough of them already. Daemon doesn't bother looking at me for an answer he expects Ardal to have them. I'm fine with that. I'm sticking around to ensure survival.

"Don't look at me. He's the elk of your herd." I point at Ardal.

"Theon," Ardal says with a lack of effort reminiscent to his attitude the last month.

I bite my tongue, preventing more venom like substances to spew from my mouth. I scratch my palms. This is over soon. I can worry about Kat, DJ, and Jay, and forget those in a group for at least some time. "You find the girls. If I'm right, you'll get more than just three." I stop scratching and try to end this conversation as soon as possible. "Before you all ask, I think people with abilities attract each other, or at least we awaken each other. Like how members of the same species find each other easily."

"We don't need them. All you need is me." Percival stands on the table which brings everyone's attention to us, specially the staff. Not as tired as a sloth, but close enough.

Roy keeps smirking. On his best behavior, he doesn't look up at Percy, but down to his seat. "Hell yeah. What fucking happened that day?" There's a moment of silence. "Oh, Yeah, fucking right. Percy can't remember how he almost killed everyone." He points at Percival's seat. Percival grumbles as he sits back down, and the eyes of the cafe patrons turn back to their own business.

I pick up my bag from the floor. "I'm leaving." I take three steps away from the table, and slightly turn back. "Good luck." They don't answer, not that I expected anything less. *I just want this to end, maybe being apart will help all of us. It'll certainly help me escape Ardal treating me like the burden I am. It was nicer before, but I didn't deserve that. As long as I give them what they want, they'll keep me around. That's the best I can hope for.*

That's not true. Ardal speaks inside my thoughts in a monotone voice. *If you only saw what they did. You make it so difficult to be around when your mind is always talking down on yourself. We all have stuff to worry about.*

You only put up with me 'cause of my knowledge. Sorry for being a burden to you. Once this is over, you won't have to see or hear from me ever again.

That's not what I want. I don't see you just as a teammate or a way to make it through. I thought what my mom said would help you notice. I can't save you and I can't force you to do things. Only you can. I'm trying to give you space so you can think.

I'm sorry for everything. I make things harder than necessary. I really try my best, but every time I take a step, it feels like I fail. And what about you? I can smell your fear. What do you need?

I can handle it.

I want to trust you, but it's been a month. You stink of fear. You say I need space. What I need is to know that you guys will be okay. I don't want others to be hurt because of me.

We can talk about it when you come back.

Okay. As I'm about to take another step, I take a breath. I can't leave like this. *I know I haven't been easy to be around and that I was abrasive when we met. I'm sorry about everything. I hope we can be friends.*

We have been for a while. Come back alive.

I will. Take care. I walk away from the cafe. Climb the escalators and go through the tedious process of flying to a different country. If it was up to me, I would fly there myself. It would take me days, maybe weeks, but it would be a fun trip. But I can't. Not with those men watching us. *Is there something so wrong with enjoying our abilities? Why wouldn't they want us to live our best lives?* Maybe Corinna will have some answers.

I wait for three hours, then the lady in the booth calls, "Passengers on flight four-seven-five-one-A to New York can now begin boarding at gate twenty-eight."

CHAPTER THIRTY: WILDEBEESTS

It's my first time abroad with my abilities. I never noticed that cities and their people had special scents. New York City smells like a landfill. Its people smell much better, a mixture of exasperation and junk food. According to Roy, I'll be in the afternoon news. He's a very encouraging member of society. And for once, I agree with him. If these men wanted to catch me, they would leave me stuck in New York City. I'm at a complete disadvantage here. There's plenty of animals, but way to many people for me to use my abilities.

One more flight and I'll be out of here. Corinna has to be at the gate our flights are leaving from. Focus. This place is too crowded, too many people, too many scents. Can everyone be quiet for one minute? I close my eyes and focus. My stomach rumbles and my focus shifts to that of my basic needs. I smell vanilla. Well, whatever it is, I'm buying it. With a vanilla milkshake in one hand, a burger, and fries in the other, I resume my migratory path to the gate. If I could do so without raising alarms, I'd eat my food tiger shark style, but alas, I can't. There are too many people, too many teens at the gate. And teens bring about one thing: phones with cameras. It's too much of a risk.

I slurp my milkshake. The vanilla won't help me find Corinna, but it makes it more doable. Around me, people act like a sardine school. They move perfectly without colliding. The movement of migrating people never stops. Except for me. I slurp again allowing the sugar to act as a barrier between the excruciating human pollution overwhelming my senses and me. I take another step. My shoulder bumps into someone else's.

"I'm so sorry. Are you okay?" This gray-haired guy with a scarf speaks with a slight Hispanic accent. He shows me the palms of his hands and steps back.

I look up to meet his gray eyes. "I wasn't looking were I was going. Sorry." I look at his clothing. No signs of stains. I sigh in relief. I'm not getting into trouble in the airport yet. I glance around for Corinna. ***Where is she? I can't even track her since I've never got the chance to had her scent.***

"I insist. I wasn't paying attention." He pauses for a second and fixes his peacock blue scarf, so both ends are exactly the same length. He checks his hat before looking at me again. "Are you Theon?" He scratches his eyebrow, mimicking my broken one.

I step back. He could be with Corinna, but given my circumstances, being wary of him. Animals don't die because they take the safe route, they die when they are pushed to a moment of desperation. I flex my legs, making sure the movement doesn't disturb my lunch. "Who are you?"

He raises his hands to his chest. "Ambrose. Corinna's brother."

"Corinna has an older brother?"

"Younger brother." He shakes his head. Wrinkles form on his forehead as he frowns. "She didn't tell you about me." His shoulders slump and relax. "Typical."

I shrug. "She does that often?" I still keep distance between us. The less attached and friendly they are to me, the easier it'll be for them to accept that the expectations Ardal and the others build are not happening.

He grabs the back of his head. "Yeah, more often than you think." He gives me a nervous smile. "Follow me." He walks by two aisles of seats before leading me into the gate.

I chase behind him, following the silver hair and unusual hat. We keep walking until we are almost in front of the bridge. Only the empty special blue seats remain. He turns to the blond girl talking to her phone. "Cory, you didn't tell Theon where you were."

She stares at her phone. "You're late." Her voice is monotonous. Her eyes stay on the device. She's worse than Roy. At least Roy looks at people when he regards them as inferior. She doesn't even do that. It's the same disregard a saltwater crocodile gives to everything when it's full.

I leave space between her seat and mine, and drop my bag. My food rest on my lap. I munch on fries before replying, "How was I supposed to find you?"

She grunts. "It's logical. We're taking the same flight." She musters a look at me and rolls her eyes. "You are also part wolf." Her feet point away from this conversation. She's infuriating.

I take a massive slurp of milkshake to calm my jittery nerves.

Ambrose stands in front of her. "Cory, you should be more considerate." He shakes his head.

"Why does it matter?" Her eyes stay immersed on the device.

"Ask your phone." He sits down between us and turns to me. "I'm sorry about my sister. She can be something else." He opens a notebook. It's filled with cartoons and drawings. He takes a pencil from his pocket and flips through the notebook until he arrives at a blank page. He turns to me. "Uhm" He touches his neck and stares at my fries, then goes back to a word filled page. Between each stroke of his pencil, I catch him glancing at me. He bites his thumb, then glances again. "Do you mind if I draw you?" His cheeks turn pink.

"I'm nothing impressive." I slurp from my milkshake. "I won't stop you."

"No, it's okay…" His voice lingers, a puppy begging indirectly.

Why would anyone draw me? I'm nothing of note. It's not like drawing a whale or butterfly landing on a flower. Those are spectacles of beauty and awe. I'm just me and even then, it feels like I'm not that much. I don't get what Ardal, Jay, Kat and now Ambrose see in me. "It's fine." I twiddle my thumbs. I avoid using my nails to scratch my palms.

He takes notes on the size and shape of my body. "Thanks, you won't regret it." I activate my snake muscles because they're strong enough to keep me in place.

Not long after finishing my meal, we board. Corinna takes a seat right beside the Wi-Fi. Ambrose swipes my luggage putting it with his. He sighs in defeat, sitting beside his sister. **What an odd pair. Who am I to talk?** Roy, Lucas, and I are different classes entirely. I look away from them, both distracted by their devices.

With the order of a wasp's nest, the rows are filled with people my age. Or around it. I head to the tail. The last seat opens right beside a velvet ant haired guy. He stares outside. On the other side, a guy and a girl sit together. He turns towards me and smiles. Swiftly move my gaze towards the front.

"Check you out. I know I'm a catch, but the blond one in the first row is great too." He grabs my hand and kisses it.

I pull my hand and face the aggressor. The guy winks at me.

"It's not like that." I wave my hands erratically.

"Ahhh, you lean to the other side. We could make it work. We can invite red hair too." He points at the innocent bystander beside me.

A hand flies across his head. If ravens were human, they would look like this girl. "Stop freaking people out!" She turns to me. "I'm sorry. Mercurio doesn't get boundaries sometimes." She smiles and raises her hand, her arm a rainbow of hair bands. "My name is Jess."

I hide my hands from the pair. This is too much and too weird. "Hi Jess, my name is Theon." I attempt to smile back, even if it's forced.

"He didn't mind, see?" Mercurio pokes at her, sending a wink my way.

My stomach turns. I look around to see if there are any other seats away from him, but the plane is filled. I'm stuck beside him. It freezes my body. This is wrong. I inch closer to the red head sitting beside me.

Anna's face turns red. "Mercurio!" she shouts at him.

"Okay, I'll stop." He turns to me, still smiling. He keeps his mood up, as if nothing happened. A badger roaming the forest.

"Uhm, hey, when did you get here." My neighbor says, oblivious to the recent events.

I turn to him. "A couple of minutes ago."

The eyes of a curious fox sparkle, and the crimson fur glimmers under the lights. At least he seems warmer and more genuine than Mercurio. I focus on him to prevent another event with the other two. They continue to argue, which sounds more lie scolding. She probably came to nanny him. I feel bad for her.

"You remind me of a video game character." He points at my broken brow. He tells about this game I've never played. I try not to think how many times people have commented about my eyebrow. How I look like a cartoon character or a comic book character. I divert my gaze to the front. Ambrose turns back a couple of times and waves at me. More people turn back to see Mercurio being pulled back into his seat as he begs for forgiveness, mercy, and someone to save him.

"Are you okay?" He pauses. "My friends say I get distracted too easily. Sorry, my name's Zach." He sits there grabbing his flaming hair. Awkwardly smiling at me.

"I'm Theon. I'm okay. I thought what you were saying was interesting." He never asked about my scar, and that alone deserves my attention.

CHAPTER THIRTY-ONE: BIRDS OF A FEATHER

Arriving to our destination alleviates the pressure of the city. The smell of oak and summer dew. There are little to no people walking around the airport. All the people from the plane take the same bus. The ride is peaceful, with the exception of Mercurio making awkward jokes and Jess to reprimanding him. They're like lions and hyenas, never a quiet moment around them.

Once we descend the bus, I can take it all in. The open green fields beckoning the animals to run around. The playful red squirrels run up and down the trees. Ravens and eagles shadow us from the skies, their dark silhouettes lost behind the pines where an owl sings her chorus. The light scent of pollen and skunk fizzles in the air. On the ground, raccoon, and porcupine tracks. I could get use to this, nature wherever I look. It's green and sunny, but cool. Clear skies. I need this.

I look at the human structures that balance nature. Some are old and made of brick, others are glass and metal. Other than the high schoolers, not many people walk around. College students and professors are a rare sight. Peaceful silence. I know it won't last, but I enjoy it while I can.

I'm the last one to head to our dorms. It gives me time to settle into the differences between here and Monterrey. It's a drastic change for my senses. The lower pollution makes it brighter. My ears and nose get a break as there aren't many city sounds. Since there's less stone and asphalt vibrations travel faster, and are more easily dispersed in the soil. The electroreception isn't pulling me everywhere.

My dorms are made of brick and stone. Outside, the animals relax. Inside, they bustle with human life. It reminds me of how prairie dogs manage their dens. Not a single moment passes without bumping into someone. Students run around carrying furniture and baggage. Others chatting in the hallways. I pick up my key. Two-oh-nine. I go down the hallway and up the stairs. The second floor is less chaotic. A few people with baggage or negotiating room trades. Further down the hall I find my room.

I pause at the door juggling keys, bags, and my schedule. I have ecology and game design as planned, but the third program stops me cold. I gulp so hard I almost choke. **Forget the room. Where is Corinna? I need to find her. She needs to fix this.** I force the schedule inside my pocket. My sweaty hands juggle my phone. I type erratically.

Theon: Why am I in the leadership program?

Corinna: Seemed logical since you're in charge of this whole operation.

Theon: I'm not the leader! I gathered the people. Ardal is the leader. Ask him.

Corinna: Ardal said you're the leader. He says that without you, the whole thing falls apart.

Theon: You! I hate both of you. Once I get back home, Ardal is going to listen to me.

Corinna: Spoken like a true leader.

I could complain to Ambrose, but that seems petty. She's too human, beyond reasoning with. I stomp, letting my anger flush out of my system. My keys shake in my hands as I stare at the door. **Please let me be alone.**

"Hot stuff!" **Not him!** Mercurio stands beside me. He leans on the wall beside my door. "How did I get the hottest neighbor in summer camp?"

The air stays inside my lungs for longer than it should be. I forget how to put the key inside the keyhole and leave this conversation. Mercurio is not the neighbor I would ever choose. Without Jess, there are no boundaries. "I'm not sure how the skunk is the hottest creature in the vicinity." I force the smile. If he notices, it bothers me, he will continue to tease me.

Before he gets a word in, someone saves me. Ambrose comes out the door behind Mercurio. "Pick up your stuff." He glances at me, then back at Mercurio. With one hand, he presses Mercurio's shoulder. "We're neighbors. That's great news. Is everything alright?" He kinda blushes when I stare at him. Everyone in this place acts like they've never seen a skunk.

I get a hold of my key. "A bit nervous." I stare at the door. The fur on the back of my neck stands up. My senses are trembling.

"With me around, you should be." Mercurio winks.

Ambrose pulls him away from me. Thank you, nature, for sending me a weaver bird the size of a giraffe. "Don't make me call Jess."

"Call her! She has no power over my charms." Mercurio smiles defiantly. He dares Ambrose to do it.

Ambrose picks up his phone. *Click* "Hey Jess, Mercurio wanted me to pass you a message."

Mercurio's tanned color shift to polar bear white. "I was kidding! Don't call her please!" Mercurio gets on his knees and begs Ambrose as they go inside their room. "Ambrose babe, have mercy on me."

Ambrose smiles at me before closing his door.

The key easily slides between my fingers. I inhale for a minute before I twist the key. One deep inhale more and I push. I close my eyes delaying the inevitable. My eyes open to the two beds filled with stuff. A guy sits on one of them and tinkers with his computer, going from one tool to the other.

I close the door behind me. "Hi Zach. Which one is your bed?" After a couple of minutes without response, I sigh and make my way to the opposite bed. The floor is clear for the most part, although his luggage and clothing do clutter part of the path. On the bed there's a bigger box, that I move to his desk. I glance at the ceiling and walls. Only his computer and the lights pull on my electroreception. No cameras. I relax a little. "Gorilla muscles." My arms grow thicker but still look human enough. With one arm, I gather his belongings. With the other, I juggle mine and order them on the bed, before giving up and putting everything under it and pretending it's organized. The only thing I organize is the smaller pack with emergency clothing for transformation issues. I throw myself on the bed and lay down.

I focus on my ears, listening for beeps and static, but the only noises coming from the building are other students running around and talking. Phones ring every once in a while. Zach's computer makes mechanical sounds, that I disregard. I take a moment and check my phone. It's around the time Kat gives an update and I rather be there, just in case.

Kat: Everything's okay here. How are you doing?

Theon: Alright, my roommate hasn't noticed I lifted the bed with one arm. Are the animals treating you nicely?

Kat: Yes! Thank you for letting me choose cats to watch over me. They're so cute!

Theon: It's the least I could do after ruining your vacations.

Kat: You didn't ruin them.

Jay: Bro! I get an escort of dogs and puppies! I love Cali so much!

Theon: Glad you like it.

Jay: Man, you made our trips so much better. I'll get you Zoo-veniers.

I glance away for a second before Lucy sends two pictures to the other group chat. The one with everyone. One picture has a boy with dirty blond hair running through a storm cloud. Lightning courses across the image. It illuminates his face and sports clothing. The second one of a younger kid with glasses. Most of his face indistinguishable because of the extreme red light his eyes emanate. Corinna is the first to reply as always.

Corinna: I'll find them soon enough.

Corinna: The girls we're looking for are Aurora Ruefern, Cleopatra Rosetta, and Astrid McEnzie.

Percy: Easy peasy.

Ardal: We're on it.

Theon: Corinna, who's your roommate?

Corinna: I don't know.

Ambrose pulls me into a private chat. I clear my head to see if I can hear Mercurio begging, although I'd rather not 'cause what if he is saying something nerve-racking.

Ambrose: Jess is her roommate.

Theon: Good luck Jess.

Ambrose: She'll be fine. Unless she likes to talk. You have a roommate.

Theon: Yes. Zach. It's been thirty minutes, and he hasn't noticed I walked in, cleaned the room, lifted the furniture and my luggage with one arm. I'll be fine if it stays like this. Don't think he'll notice me, which is all I need.

Ambrose: Great! Cory told me about your abilities. She asked me for help with the drawings.

Theon: Ohhh! Okay, that sounds good. Welcome to the team.

Ambrose: Thanks! Take your time to get used to it. Let's all have lunch together.

Theon: I like the idea. I'm not sure why your sister wanted me here, we could have met in any other place.

Ambrose: Don't ask me. She's difficult.

Theon: I'll see you at lunch. I'm going to relax for a bit.

I sink into the mattress and mute my phone for an hour all. Silence and peace. No one whose life depends on me doing anything. No peril or imminent death. No humans hunting me. I can just relax a little before everything gets destroyed in the wake of the hunt. Little by little my mind drifts, allowing me to release the stiffness restraining my body. I feel like a jellyfish or an octopus, free, to be however I want to be. And right now, I just want to be alone. The awkward kid who loves animals, who wants to be normal for just one day. Think of the possibilities. I stare at the white canvas ceiling. My senses temporarily retreating absorbing less information than usual.

Birds chirp in my windows. A skunk passes by the dorms. Mercurio and Ambrose talk on the other side of the wall. Their conversation is muffled. It's better that way. Zach is oblivious, entranced by his laptop. That complete and absolute dedication provides space he has unknowingly given me. To fade away and escape to my head. One long, deep sigh breaks the silence in the room.

"Ohh hey. You're the guy from the plane. Didn't see you there." Zach says from his bed. The mechanical sounds of his computer stop. He awkwardly rubs his temple with his thumb.

I pick up my phone, almost an hour. That's a record. "I'm Theon. You were busy. It's okay." I sit up, facing him and his sheep leaf slug eyes. Headphones hang from his neck. "I moved your stuff. Didn't know which bed you wanted."

He puts his laptop aside. "Zach." He waves.

I grin. "I know. We met on the plane." I stand and head to the small bathroom at the side of the room. I glance in the mirror. Eye bags. Messy hair. The usual.

"Right. Sorry." He pauses until I am out, half changing bed. He picks up one of his tools and loosens a screw. He places it on his nightstand.

I stare at his awkward laptop. It looks clunkier than most. Way heavier. I could hide a family of gerbils in it if it was hollow. The more I look at it, the more intrigued I am. The keyboard glows in a rainbow pattern. It has three fans. The screen looks vividly alive. "What were you working on?"

He gives me that unaware smile he gave me on the plane. "I got some new parts. I replaced the RAM, SSD, and the GPU." He keeps talking but the message is lost somewhere along the way. It doesn't help that he's speaking in a language I would never understand. If I was Corinna or DJ, I would be fine. He goes on and on. There is an earnestness to his smile. Something as simple as talking about what you like becomes contagious.

The best I can do is nod and smile. He doesn't care if I get it or not. He's enjoying himself and I can get lost in thought. We both win and finally someone isn't expecting me to have an answer. He doesn't seem to care about me in any way, only in what he is doing and that's all I need. That's everything I need. "And the SSD does what?" I ask, tilting my head.

He jumps onto his bed and pulls out a thin rectangle. "The SSD is a storage device." His face animates. He gushes over that small piece of metal and plastic. He takes a good look at me. "You got it?"

I shake my head once. "No."

"You could have stopped me." He puts the piece back on the bed. "I'll go slower."

I don't want you to stop. Keep drowning me in terms and concepts I don't understand. Keep silencing the nerve-racking voices that tell me we're all in danger. Keep going and don't stop! Cause for once in my life, I'm normal. I feel normal. "Your passion is contagious. I didn't want to stop you." It's a half truth, but no one ever blamed the mimic octopus for pretending to be something it's not. We do it to survive.

He slows. "That's weird. My friends always say keeping up with me is hard." His freckles are way lighter than Roy's. In a way, I like the accelerated passionate guy speaking about computers more than this one. I can see his gaze drifting away.

It points at the sky, then shifts toward me. "Your turn. Tell me stuff you like."

I grab the back of my neck. "Animals, nature and video games." It gives me an idea. I open my luggage. In the middle of a coffin of clothes, there are two jewels. Two controllers, one white, the other black. "Want to play some games with me?" I hold the dark one next to my heart. The white one closer to him. The dark beast and the passionate human.

Zach takes my controller. "Yes!" He opens his laptop. "We should use mine."

I place mine on my bed. "Let's wait until after lunch." **Will he accept if I invite him to lunch?** "Some friends and I are eating lunch together. Want to join?" I put my hand on my chest. If he says no, we'll be stuck as roommates. It'll be awkward.

He pauses for a bit. One second of tension before returning to the world. "Yes."

I celebrate the small victory. I made a friend, maybe. On my own terms, not depending on abilities or the internet. ***It was me! Maybe, just maybe, there's something of value hidden inside me. Maybe I'm not an animal to him, just a normal guy.*** I place my hand on the door. It vibrates. The weight of it leans toward the room. I pull the door open. Mercurio falls. His face stamps the wooden floors. Ambrose stands back, shaking his head. He waves at Zach, then at me.

I signal with my free hand to Zach. "Let's go."

"Wait." He puts on his basketball shoes, before jumping out of bed and chasing after Ambrose and me.

CHAPTER THIRTHY-TWO: SARDINES IN THE SEA

June 21, 2013

Zach and I have been roommates for almost two weeks. We've had our ups and downs. Mostly ups. The downs are him being distracted when I need help with the only technology class I'm taking. I didn't know game design had programming. I'd thought it was more planning and creating the concept more than programming. His silence manages to comfort me even when I'm distressing about the situations the others have gone through.

Lucas, Helena, and Cass found the boys Lucy draw in her vacations. They made a blizzard in Cancun. The tropics have never been colder with temperatures dropping to minus twenty degrees Celsius. It's not as impressive a feat as getting the catholic church to debate whether Cass is an angel. It's very strange, but most of the people agree he is. Kat says it should alleviate the pressure on his group. Attacking an angel would be scary and society won't like it. First time society works in our favor. I concoct an idea that I'll leave for later.

In Monterrey, Roy, Ardal, Percy, and Daemon found the Ruefern sisters. They are still missing to find Astrid and Cleopatra, but that has given them some space. A larger pack is stronger. Ardal hasn't mentioned anything, but the news said something about night becoming day for a couple of minutes during a new moon. I'll be up for a treat when I'm back.

Kat, DJ, Jay, Lucy, and Haruka are fine. It seems the hunters haven't figured out Kat or Lucy have abilities and that's fine. Kat and Jay have become celebrities in their locations. They're all over social media with cats and dogs. Kat has a million followers! Jay has ten million! They call every day to tell me about their adventures and they're living the blessed life of a well-treated pet.

My group is struggling to keep it together. I'm juggling four papers. Half of them aren't even mine. If I finish the guidelines for the game Zach can program the rest, which leaves visuals and story. I'm not sure why Jess is researching the DNA structure of a woolly mammoth, but I'm helping her. Mercurio needed something about the healing properties of fish scales, so I'm also doing that. And I have to write my own report about the preservation of the African elephants through a very specific method and organization. **What is this? I thought I was going to study animals; not what people do.** I click enter and save the document with the guidelines. "Zach. I sent you the stuff." He diligently types but doesn't respond. I wait for some signal of acknowledgment. The same way howler monkeys would talk to each other in the mornings, but I get nothing. "Zach!"

Everyone turns to me. He scratches his flaming hair. "Did I miss something?" He looks around, then meets my eyes.

"Instructions of the game are ready." I sigh. I glance at the clock, ten at night, and I'm not even halfway through. "Jess, I'm starting with yours." This document has numbers and statistics with terms that make no sense to me.

Mercurio winks from across the room. "But love I thought you would do mine before hers. We have a special connection." He starts to stand from his kneeling position.

Ambrose grunts before speaking. His red hat covering most of his hair. "Mercurio don't move. I'm not done yet." Ambrose returns to the drawings on his desk. There are easily fifty pages of drawings. Most of them colorless for now. He shakes his hand, giving it a well deserve break before drawing more.

Jess shoots them a glance from between the beds. Mercurio squirms back to his position. She juggles a couple of Mercurio's papers and a structural design for Ambrose of the Fibonacci sequence applied to the human body. My head spins as I think about what she's doing, and I'm glad to not be the one dealing with it.

Corinna speaks without looking away from Zach's desk and her laptop. "We need to finish our project tonight."

My dry tone has little to no life. "What about the game, Zach?" These were supposed to be vacations and I'm doing schoolwork.

"We already decided my project was a priority," Corinna says, contesting my patience.

"Why? The game is due on Monday. Your project isn't due till the end of next week." I put the laptop on my bed and rub my eyes. I shake my head before sipping from my water thermos.

"I fell behind because I found the two kids last week." She barely moves. A direct animal comparison would be unfair. Unless it's a water bear, those could never move and be fine.

I throw my hands in the air. "It took you one day." I turn toward the window as the rain collides against the glass. "And you didn't need to do that. We were fine without them." I lean against the wall. Lightning illuminates outside temporarily. Animals won't go out in this storm.

"You said they needed a trick to survive." She shrugs.

I pause. "You were spying on my conversation with Ardal?" Everyone except Zach is looking at us. Ambrose holds his head as if it were about to explode. Jess and Mercurio are calmer, but share glances.

Ambrose stands up. "Stop!" His cheeks are red. He and Corinna look at each other. He points at the phone without saying anything else, then takes a deep breath.

Zach looks up. "It's time for a break?" He looks lost among the six of us.

I dryly say, "No."

Ambrose signals me to stop. "I could use a break." He sits on his chair organizing the drawings by need, importance, and project. A few of the drawings are left scattered on the desk. None belong to his notebook, the one kept in his bag all week. It refuses to see daylight. It gives me impression of a little roo, not ready to jump out of the pouch just yet.

Mercurio stands. He winks in my direction, then he moves to Corinna's desk. He leans over, making sure she can see him. His elbow presses against the hard wood, and his presence tests Corinna's patience. She continues to type her project, but for some reason I doubt she's working on it.

He combs his hair flatten it with his right hand. "Why don't we take a break together, all night?"

She scowls. "What's the purpose of this one?" She points at Mercurio without bothering to glance his way. Her blue eyes glow refracting the screen.

"Ouch." Mercurio leaves her alone as he should have from the beginning. He passes the stretching Ambrose and Jess who is helping Zach get the food out for our break. "What's the deal with those kids?" He wraps his arm around my shoulders.

I sigh and copy Corinna the best I can. "I hate to admit it, but I agree with Corinna. Why is he here?" I sound tired and annoyed, not cold, and dispassionate like Corinna. I keep looking at the storm and how it makes everything so silent and calm, even when it's chaos. Even with the moon hiding behind the dark clouds, the world is clear as midday.

Ambrose walks closer to us. "I felt bad for keeping out of this."

Jess pulls Mercurio away from me. "I told you to leave him alone." She drags him to the other side of the room, closer to Corinna, who isn't bothered by the display. "What did you say about kids?"

Zach scruffs his hair. "Why is Mercurio here?" He adds, as if not listening to anything, then turns and smiles at me. Unlike Corinna and I. there are no traces of negativity, only curiosity and obliviousness. He puts his laptop away. Safeguarded from the cookie crumbles, vegetables, and other morsels we took from the cafeteria before it closed.

"We need to leave." Corinna closes her laptop. She picks up her bag, collecting three phones, the laptop, chargers, and a couple of other devices to put in it. She turns around and watches us. "Now." Her free hand rubs her throat. I've seen that before. She emanates this punchy smell, the closest smell I've experienced to it is fear.

Ambrose approaches her. He puts a hand on her hand. "What's going on?"

"They're here. I'm an idiot. I let my guard down." I pick up my spare clothing pack and phone. Everything else can be left here. Corinna and I move like ants in a colony. Efficiently taking what we need. "How much time do we have?" I focus on the sounds inside the building, a few snores here and there. What's out of place is the marching and the surprised voices of the other residents as their doors open.

"Ten minutes." She taps her clock and moves to pack a tablet.

Ambrose joins us. Papers and colors fly around the room. His masterful pieces are put in a binder before landing in his bag. The others look at us, grabbing bags to store our belongings.

Jess grabs my arm as I put another food-filled container I sneaked from the cafeteria for this exact moment in my bag. Her brown hair frames her face as her maroon eyes connect with me. "What's happening?"

Corinna steps up. "You need to leave." She points at Mercurio and Zach.

"Cory. They can't. They're our roommates." Ambrose fixes his hat. "They'll be questioned. We need to bring them." He picks up his scarf and ties it around his neck.

This is the last thing I want. Three more innocents stuck in our problems. The alternative is risking them anyway. I glance at Zach. I'm not sure what he sees. His eyebrows raised. I stand against the window, hoping this sliver of normalcy never ends.

Corinna approaches the front door. She pushes Mercurio away.

"We can't leave through the front door." I say. "They're at the first floor." I turn back to the storm. The only way out is through the small window. Big enough for humans, but too high for them to walk out normally. "We have to use the window." Lightning strikes ominously. I place my fingers under the edge and pull up. The window stays still. Stuck! Of course, it's stuck!

"It's the second floor."

Mercurio grins. "We could make the jump. A twisted ankle might be a great way to get a catch." He inches closer to Corinna. "That's why you have me here." Mercurio raises his eyebrows like heroes do in movies. Except this isn't heroic, it's desperate. I can smell his overflowing hormones.

I pull up my sleeves. "Lowland gorilla arms." My arms become as long as my untransformed body. The black fur and skin start at my shoulders. I ignore the sound behind me and force the window up. Even with this strength, it takes me longer than I wanted. Water and wind drift inside, swirling paperwork around the room.

Ambrose stands behind me and looks down at the darkness. He takes a step back to look at the others and at my arms. "We'll explain later. Pick up anything of importance and come with us." He looks out the window again. "It's far. The rain will be a problem."

My arms return to their normal, cream-colored skin. "Not that far." I hand him my bag. "Hold on to this." I take off my shirt and my pants and everything that might rip apart with this next transformation. Jess and Zach stare at my chest scars. Clean and extremely visible.

"We skipping the first date." Mercurio whistles as I climb out the window. "Mercurio likes it." He takes a bunch of books and notebooks with images of the human body and organs. He slides around the room, taking whatever, he needs, including part of the rations I stashed.

Lightning strikes again. Illuminating the half nature half, civilized world around me. Ambrose blushes, seeing me naked. The window frame rejects water, creating a slippery surface. I take a final look at the group as I hang out from the second floor.

I close my eyes and let my feline instincts take over. Wind and water buffet against my skin as I fall. The chilly weather contracts my muscles. My feet connect with the ground, and I instinctually roll back. I stand on the grass, only the light of my room reveals me.

I clasp my hands in front of my face. "African elephant." My body lumbers forward and back. The weight pulls me down. Gray, dry, thick skin covers me as I become more than myself. My ears flap. My nose manipulates the grass. And two massive tusks curve upward. I glance at the window. The four who haven't seen me do anything like this before stare, their jaws open. **Goodbye, normalcy.** I shake my neck and turn around slowly. My rear faces the building and I face the darkness. I take steps back until I feel a wall. I contain my need for words. One stray thought will announce my presence.

I expect Ambrose to be the first one to ride. Yet someone much lighter jumps onto my pachyderm back. She grabs up a bag, dragging herself to my neck. My trunk reaches back, she passes me the bag before sliding back to the others. I hang the bag on my tusks, waiting for them to move on. She repeats the process. This time, a second body stays on top. A waterfall concentrates on my middle back. That small waterfall circles around me as it moves closer to the base of my neck.

"Get me down," Corinna says, unamused. My trunk wraps around her waist. She's heavier than I expected. She slides from the side of my neck. Halfway down, she pinches the tip of my trunk. The shock sends an urge to trumpet. I stop myself from moving. Although she probably can't see my eyes in a new moon night, they are sending a warning. The light coming from the rooms helps me see her carrying two bags and an umbrella. She barely moves. One or two grass blades crunch under her weight.

Another individual jumps on my back. He slaps my rear. "When do I ride the other side?" Mercurio announces himself. I don't react. If I do, we'll be caught. Jess's slap throws Mercurio off my back. He falls on the shrubs surrounding the brick structure. With a grunt we both know he's okay.

Ambrose slides out the window. "Is he okay?" He carefully sits on my back, making his way to my neck.

"He's fine." Jess pats my head, giving me the needed signal. She slides back to pick up the last rider.

I do as she says. My trunk wraps around Ambrose's hips. I drag him to the side. Once again, my trunk stops around my tusks. He's lighter than Corinna, by a large margin. I try to lower him, but I'm scared of dropping him the wrong way. "You can put me down." He pats my elongated nose.

"This isn't right. We should stay," Zach says from the window.

Jess replies, "We need to leave. Look at him. He's an elephant." She rubs my back. "The scientific progress we could make!"

"I don't care. This is not what I thought camp was," Zach replies. His shadow covers part of the ground before me.

"Three minutes," Corinna says. Her voice covered by the lightning. My inability to talk impedes smooth operations. Mercurio and Ambrose wander, using my body as a guide to the front.

Ambrose holds onto my tusk, "Zach, it's different. And that's okay. You can do it."

Jess helps Zach out of the room. He slips but she keeps him on my back. Jess pats me. "Zach, close the window." I wrap my trunk around her. She pets my side with a kindness she often forgets near Mercurio. "Let me go." With that, she crunches the grass below and splashes in a puddle, on her way to the others.

Zach shuts the window. He carefully crawls up my body like a baby monkey. His hands shake. His legs loosen their grip on my back. When he reaches my shoulder, his left leg hangs lower than the other. I turn my neck trying to distinguish everything, but the lights mess with my blue and violet adapted night vision. His weight shifts to the left. His hands slip.

My body shifts back faster than ever. "Lion eyes." Night is as clear as day. Zach's midair. With the strength of the elephant, senses of a lion and reflexes of a pigeon, I throw myself under him. **He isn't getting hurt under my watch. I brought him to protect him, so if anything happens, I'll take every single blow. Their lives are worth the paint.** He lands in my arms.

He can't see me in this darkness. He can't see my smile. The fall wouldn't have killed him, but it just might have killed a piece of me if I didn't get to him. "I got you." I put him on the ground. There's a moment I stand in front of him, forgetting the mission. A sliver of normality gone, forever.

Mercurio puts his arm on me. "My hero." He poses dramatically. For once, Jess has abstained from slapping him. She sighs in an extremely disheartening way.

"One minute." There goes Corinna's time.

I take a step, passing her. They stand in a line. I'll lead them out of here. Who needs light? "Grab my tail."

"What tail?" Jess points at my lack of one.

I give my back to them. "Diplodocus tail." The whip-like tail stretches between them. Corinna does as instructed. Ambrose and Jess follow after. I turn to them again. "No lights. Just tell me where we're going." Mercurio grabs the tail tip. If Ardal was here he would hear my mind growl. **Mercurio!** He tugs my tail.

"Take us to the med school." Jess raises her voice. Her hair flattens as the rain drenches it. "We can do some stuff while hiding in there."

"There aren't any patrols there. Can you secure a route to the medical school in campus?" Corinna's phone flashes blue. "Straight ahead, through the woods, avoid the tennis court, then cross the bridge." Monotone, with no rhythm.

The six of us go into the wooded areas. In our window is the shadow of a man. He lights up the outside, but the only trace of us is four circular prints on the grass. I stood as an elephant for far too long. It will take them some time to figure out those puddles are footprints. He aims at the woods, but by then we're well hidden behind the trees. The winds and thunder roar violently. Eventually, the fifth hand takes hold of my tail closer to the middle. From time to time, their curiosity gets the best of them, poking the scales to prove they're real.

CHAPTER THIRTY-THREE: SOUTHERN NESTING GROUNDS

The medical research building is nothing impressive. From the outside, it looks newer than the dorms and some of the halls. Wind howls. The sky pours. And lightning strikes multiple times. The elements batter us and the doors. I raise my arms. "Black heron wings." My wings seem to fuse with the surrounding darkness. They halo above my head, forming an umbrella to cover the others. Corinna lets go of my tail and stands beside me. She opens her mouth and coughs. Coughs that are comparable to hippo grunts.

Ambrose pulls her back. "You need to rest."

"Can we walk in?" I turn to her.

She shakes her head, pulls out her phone and points at it.

Corinna: We don't haev ascsce.

Corinna: have access

Okay. Corinna making a mistake is like if crocodiles suddenly weren't prepared to do what they evolved to do. I glance at Ambrose. He shrugs. His index fingers chase each other in a horizontal centrifuge, where neither will catch the other. The storm worsens and as much as my room could be shelter, they'll be searching for us. "Jess, we have no access. We can't go in." Everyone lets go of my tail, so take the signal to retract it.

Once Jess stands beside me, she bites her nails. I give her a minute under the cold rain before she turns. "We need to get in. It's the best chance we have to know what you can do and how."

Corinna: We can't barek in. The amlars will tgriger if we don't use an ID-card.

Understanding our abilities would be a life-saving survival tactic, but if we trigger the alarm, they'll be rushing toward us. With four and a half transformations left, I can't do much to protect myself or anyone else. And animals right now are hiding I shouldn't bother them with something I can deal on my own. "We can't. Unless you can find a way to get in without triggering the alarm system."

Zach walks past us. He kneels in front of the card reader and tilts his head before touching the device. Nothing happens. "I can open it for us. Could you keep the water away?" He stares at me. I nod in response barely moving shielding him from the torrent. He lays his backpack beside him, and pulls out some screwdrivers and a small cable cutter. "I need some light."

"I can give you that." I pause. The angler fish's light should be more than enough. "Angler…"

"Do you have a limit?" Ambrose interrupts me.

"Seven. I've used two and a half." I stay still, my body the immovable shield that covers Zach from the storm.

Jess takes the cue. She leans near Zach and lights her phone's flashlight. The light shines over the gray metal. She glances back, keeping the light steady. "Save them. If what you said on our way here is true, we'll need them."

Zach leaves the cutter in his pocket. He dexterously removes the screws and the gray cover. I can't see what he's doing, but it involves wires, a screwdriver and cable cutters. "You know my favorite color?"

I nod. "Azure blue. You always chose it when we played. Why?"

"I forgot to ask yours." He fiddles with the four cables as if calculating all the options. "What's yours?" He loses himself in thought.

I'm sure he asked this before. There isn't a point to the question unless he needs time. Fine Zach, I'll indulge you even when I know our friendship can't work due to everything going on. "Tropical-leaf green." I close my eyes as lightning strikes and the people surrounding me generate electricity, pulling my sense everywhere. Of the four cables only two have a continuous flow of electricity. "Green and blue have a flow of electricity. Be careful."

He glances at me. I smile, though he can't see it. I'm a shadow and he basks under the sun. "I knew it was those two. Thank you, anyway." He taps the cables. "I don't want to destroy it. It doesn't feel right."

My phone beeps intensively. I can't answer it. It's probably Jay telling me about his day, though he never sends this much. Wings weren't made for object manipulation. The phone keeps going and going.

"Cory, he can't check it," Ambrose says. He shakes his head, glancing away with a pained expression. "She says if you don't destroy the panel, she will."

"But…" Zach mutters.

I guess his relationship with machines is like mine with animals. Injuring them or taking advantage of them is the worst thing I could do. We trade glances. Maybe I can copy from Ardal's survival strategy. "I know this is probably the worst you could do in your mind. If it was an animal, I wouldn't be able to do it either. But if you need me too, I can do it or I can find another way in." I'm ready to transform into a rat or a mouse and get inside.

Jess speaks up, "If it was alive, I wouldn't agree either."

"No. It's okay. I said I could." Zach turns back and cuts the green wire. He waits a second, putting his hands around his ears to amplify sounds. He leans to the electrical pathways and with cutter in hand he snips the blue one too. "Open the door. I think, the alarm is down."

Mercurio casually pushes the door open. We wait, but the darkness is silent, and it grows deeper inside the building. Mercurio steps inside and holds the door. He halfway bows, one of his arms extended inside. His tongues sticks out as he winks. Mercurio's large athletic frame makes it very awkward. Jess passes him and slaps the back of his head. He straightens up. Corinna and Ambrose follow.

I keep covering Zach, waiting for him to put everything away. He picks up the cover and starts screwing it in. The process is short, and I stick to my position. I can handle the rain hitting my naked body for a minute longer. Zach takes his bag and walks through the door. Once inside, my feathers turn to tanned skin. Phone lights are on, so I close the door behind us.

Mercurio leans into me. "Theon, my man. When are you coming with me to a beach party? With that scar, you're the perfect wingman." His fingers pass the jagged, rubbery surface.

My skin crawls. It feels like an army of ants walks on it. I push him away agitated. I stumble into the wall, but I don't say anything. My arms wrap around my chest, covering the discolored area, protecting it from interlopers. Corinna takes off, ignoring the scene. With the lights aiming at me, it's hard to see her face, but I imagine something a kin to Roy's disappointment would be her natural response.

Jess comes from the side and kicks Mercurio in the shin. He stumbles against the opposite wall. "What was that for?"

In her eyes is the rage and determination of a grizzly bear, but there's a glimmer of kindness and loneliness. "Jerk!" She turns away, running toward Corinna's triceratops coughs. "Wait for me!" Her light disappears once she reaches the second floor. Some of the water drops contain a melancholic smell. Those can't be rain.

Ambrose is the first to come near me. He nods, laying my soft bag beside me. He ignores my body and looks straight at my face. "Take your time. We'll wait upstairs." He turns away from the doors, aiming his flashlight at Mercurio. He tilts the light up, then aims at the stairs. Mercurio runs after him. He shrugs as if nothing ever happened.

Zach glances at me. He stays there waiting. It isn't my first time naked 'cause of my abilities, but it is awkward. I unload my bag. A couple a cookie filled containers fall and my clothing drops to the floor. It consists of a t-shirt, jeans, socks, tennis shoes and my underwear.

"Sorry." Zach turns around, not looking at me. "I wanted to ask something." He scratches his chin, and reeks of cortisol, which makes me anxious.

I pick up my underwear. I avoid turning toward Zach until at least that is covered. "What did you want to talk about?" I throw the question in the air, hoping for no response. The less he knows, the better. Maybe we could return to normal. A normal friendship, no abilities, no danger, no nothing.

"How did you get the scars?" He doesn't turn.

I knew this would happen. They're too noticeable and too big. I gulp. I could lie about it. I put on my jeans and shirt. If they saw me for who I was, they would run away. "Something happened and I lost control. I did it to myself."

"You must of had a good reason." He doesn't try to peek at me.

I stand and pick up the food containers. "I'm covered." I look out the glass door. "It was a fit of rage. They shot my little brother."

He takes a step to stand beside me. "I think you're like a hero from the movies or comics, or video games." His voice echoes down the hall, which makes it seem like there's a crowd saying it. He illuminates me with his flashlight. I can't see past it. My lion eyes have gone away. "You might struggle, but that's a hero's journey."

Why do you have to do this to me? I'm not a hero. I'm a wild, uncontrollable beast. I want darkness to swallow me whole or the storm to take over. I hold my chest. "I'm not a hero." I stare down at the shadow created by his light. I press my free hand on the cold glass. "I don't know what you see to make you think I'm a hero."

He nudges me with his elbow. He doesn't care. Or at least it seems that way. "You let me talk about what I want. Never complain that I get distracted. You sit with the animals on campus and give them food and company. I think a hero does that; he's nice to others." He's oblivious. The good kind. It makes me feel like I'm fine no matter what. "When I fell, you jumped to catch me." His feet sway him back and forth.

"If it wasn't for me, you would have been safe." I can't bear to watch him or the others. I feel like I'm being eaten alive. My scars face him. "Would a hero do that to himself? Would he kill?" As much as I enjoy Zach's company, he's safer without me in his life. *I don't deserve people like him.* My senses flicker. The sounds and smells dissipate for just one second.

His feet bounce with his movements. "You kill minions in video games." He gives me a smile and does his best to push himself near the glass to meet my eyes. "Sometimes we do things we don't like or agree too. It doesn't make you less of a hero. It makes the journey different."

I look away once more. ***Zach, you got to stop. You can't be around me I'm trouble. I don't want to drag others into my issues.*** I look down at my covered scars. It feels like only yesterday when I got them. "Yes, but that doesn't mean you have to be at risk."

He starts walking to the stairs. "See, you are a hero." He smiles in a way reminiscent of Kat. Warm. Smaller. His eyes wrinkle with it.

I look at his dark green eyes and try to reciprocate, but I can't. Even now, everyone helps me. I'm dead weight. I haven't done anything for animals or my friends. And Zach keeps helping me, when I haven't done for him. ***I wish I could feel like a hero. I'm not.*** "Hey, could you do me one favor. Don't treat me differently because of my abilities. I want us to be friends, not superhero teammates."

"We can be both." He turns back to me. "Where is everyone?" He just realized we're alone? It brings a smile to my face. That's the Zach I know. The one I'd rather be around. Distracted and not noticing everything. In a way, it helps me take the pressure off. With Jay and Kat, there are lingering thoughts and attention. But Zach doesn't mind and neither do I.

"I'll take us to them." I grab his wrist and follow the scent of unmeasured testosterone. Artic background. The frozen wasteland resembles a hospital, and yet it's different. Rows of doors and unlit lights. The scent goes up two floors. Then toward the center. Toward the only bulb that lights the way. The door swings open.

Jess prepares a chair and other machines. Ambrose sits, looking at multiple notebooks. With a pencil in hand, he dots a page and moves on. Mercurio prepares needles, glass tubes and some kind of straw. Finally, Corinna sits, it's the first time I've seen her without a machine. As per usual, she doesn't react much, but her groans permeate the area. I turn back at Zach, letting go of his hand. He doesn't notice.

Jess points at Corinna. "We need to take some samples and test you. What you can do could be the future." **When did she have the time?** I shouldn't be surprised that everyone around me is a weirdo, a troublemaker, Corinna, or a prick. She slides her student ID through the gap in the door and opens it. Revealing what looks like a closet with many small devices and screens. "Mercurio will test your blood." She points at me, moves around the room, and takes Zach's hand, then Corinna's. "We'll check the MRI to help Corinna."

"Do we have time for this? We should get ready for when they come." I block the door. The weird contraptions all over the room concern me. The syringes curdle my blood. One machine swirls tubes. Another looks like a box with a screen. A clear plastic container with other instruments inside. And a bunch of flasks. A computer connected to it shows speeds and a lack of results.

"Knowledge of oneself is the best way to prepare." A couple of Jess's wrist bands become hair bands. She wraps them forming a messy bun. "Do you know the details? Why can You transform? Why certain animals? Why is it different than Corinna's or Ambrose's abilities? Why Corinna's language jumbled? How can she even connect to machines in that way?" She keeps going through a list, barely mentioning Ambrose's ability. Most likely since only Corinna knows those details. "Blood samples and tests for you." She locks her sights on me.

"What do you have to lose?" Ambrose stands from his chair next to his sister. "I'll stay here and make sure things go well."

"You'll need some chains and cuffs." My tone is serious to the point that it sounds like a threat. "This could trigger as a survival mechanism."

Jess nods and leaves the room with Corinna and Zach. She guides them to the next floor, leading them to the tests she wants to do on Corinna.

"So, you like it rough." Mercurio approaches. He leans in, his mouth millimeters from my ear. "I promise it won't hurt." He pulls away and walks to the other side of the room. He wears blue gloves and a white lab coat. He turns toward me with his usual carefree smile, which I've learned to interpret as malevolent. With one finger, he hits the side of the needle. My stomach twists knowing what's to come. I sweat and contort. Blood rushes through my veins at quickly. The idea that he will do something to my body is repellent.

Ambrose takes me to the seat Mercurio has prepared. "Everything will be okay. Trust us." He covers his hair with his hat and helps himself to a pair of gloves. The blue latex gloves contrasting with his more carefully chosen attire. Ambrose stands near me with his usual concerned look. Mercurio just giggles. I close my eyes to forget the pain and anxiety building up inside. A cold liquid is gently rubbed on my inner arm. I take a deep breath. The unpleasant sensation of the parasitic worm going in puts a strain on my nerves. Vital liquid leaves me.

Once I open my eyes, everyone is back in the room. Jess and Mercurio tinker with machines that mess with red vials. Zach uses his laptop. He stares into the distance before returning to his duty. Corinna lays down with her bag beside her as Ambrose watches over her and me.

He walks to my chair flexing his legs to be at my height. "You're awake."

"How long was I out?" I scratch my black, oily hair.

He looks at his phone. "Two hours. We wanted to let you rest since you might be the one fighting."

"Right." I look around. The grogginess hasn't left. If anything, it's taking over me. "Anything new?"

He waves at Jess. She points with one finger upward. Ambrose yawns, then turns back to me. "She can explain it."

"Have you slept?"

"No."

I stand and gesture to the chair. "You should."

Ambrose sits and pulls the hat down, covering his eyes. He maintains his position and doesn't curl or slump. He seems as if he were staring down the hall.

Jess waves at me, inviting me to join her. Zach doesn't notice me as I head over. He stares at his laptop. Now that I look at it this one is lighter and more refined. Corinna's. He stares diligently at screen; the rest of the world is inconsequential. I wish, I was like him. Life would be simpler.

I lean on the table Mercurio and Jess work on. "Ambrose said you found stuff." For the first time I wince at my arm, and the two purple bruises inside my elbow.

Mercurio stands before me. "Not, bad for a first time."

"You missed the artery. Twice," Jess reprimands him. She has added four more hair bands to the bun. "Yes. Corinna's brain had areas that were completely deactivated for the moment. Specifically in the temporal lobe. That's why she couldn't write well." She sighs then puts a single drop of blood on a slide, sandwiches it and sticks in under the microscope. After a moment, her mouth twists. "Your blood acts different. It binds, but it doesn't."

"What does that mean?"

She stands in front of me, holding my hands. "It means you have human DNA, but you also don't." If she thought this would affect me, well she's right, but not for the reasons she thinks. Animal DNA brings a smile to my face. It's the human DNA that makes me feel conflicted.

CHAPTER THIRTY-FOUR: THE DEPTHS OF CAMOUFLAGE

June 22, 2013

In her excitement Jess has woken everyone and now paces before us. "This is the discovery of the century! Theon, your immune system should be attacking your cells when they change, but it doesn't. Your blood could be the key to regeneration, to cure auto-immune diseases and make more effective transplants." Jess turns to Ambrose. "We need to run tests on you. The implications and betterment of society could be in your system."

"Jess, slow down." Ambrose yawns. He stretches himself over the chair like a cat. He rubs his eyes as he wakes from his short nap. He yawns again, causing a chain reaction among us.

Jess unbinds her hair, letting it cascade down to her shoulders again. "But all the good we can do for the world! It could save lives."

I understand the feeling, but what about me? *What does that mean for me? Will I be locked away so my blood can be harvested? How is that different from what the men hunting me want?* "I get it, but what about me?"

She paces around the table awaiting the other results. "Without the rest it's hard to tell." He touches her earlobes, pinning them between her fingers. "But your blood is in a constant state of flux. I only have theories, but maybe your DNA changes constantly between all the species. That's how your body is able to transmute into something else. It also seems to barely affect functions. You keep the same capacity in every form, or at least it seems like that from the elephant."

I find myself a seat next to Zach. I sink into the chair. "That makes sense. I'm still me when I'm another animal." I pause and look at the door. The hunters will have to come here eventually. "How do we make sure they leave us alone for now?"

Ambrose pulls a notebook and pencils from his bag. He starts drawing. "I can hide us." He raises his notebook. It's a wall. Compared to my portrait, it's nothing. He made me look like I deserve attention. That I'm slightly worth it. He's the DaVinci of modern times. He's the human version of the weaver bird.

I pull out my phone. "What if they come back?" I hold the phone with both hands. This way, my nails avoid my palms. "Will we have to repeat all this? Hiding? Being hunted? How many more people will be targeted cause they are around us?"

Jess takes a seat in front of Zach and me. Her brown hair flows past her shoulders. "Explain." She pulls a chair for Mercurio next to her. Mercurio takes the seat facing me. He has the same mischievous smile as before.

"Since I discovered my abilities, I've been hunted." I look around, making sure they're following me. "Not only me. People related to me. Other people with abilities. I'm not sure for what reason. To enslave us, kill us, capture us, or study us. I only know they don't want people discovering that everyone can do this." My head lowers approaching the table. "I don't want anyone else I care about to get hurt." My palms lay flat on the black surface.

Jess puts her hands on top of mine. "It sounds like what I said. I'm sorry. I don't want that. I want to make things better for everyone."

"We can make things better together. Imagine all the discoveries we can make. All the changes to science, and the people we can help!" She takes my hand. "Your abilities can change the world." She forces her attitude to be cheerful and joyful, but I can smell the sadness and pain in her. "Mercurio is helping. He can treat you if you get injured. he knows first aid and the basics of medicine."

Mercurio stands, "I can do more than that." He blows a kiss our way. I hide my face. He flinches as Jess prepares another punch. "No, please." This buff guy being scared of a girl is something I've never experienced. It's akin to the myth of elephants and mice, but elephants aren't scared of mice. They're more like a honey badger and a leopard.

"How can we say no to a superhero team? And to a friend in need?" Zach closes his laptop. He packs up and slides it into his bag. "They're at the entrance."

We run for our belongings. Jess wakes Corinna. Mercurio hides the machines. I pick up bags and collect them at the door. Zach slowly follows me with his own set of bags.

Ambrose keeps drawing as fast as he can. With Corinna waking up, Jess returns to me. "What do they know about your powers?"

"I think they believe I control animals with minor transformation." I scratch my head. How much have I shown them? For all they know, I'm a bleeding heart, who saves animals and a monster who murders people.

"Cory, can you make the cameras see us transforming into swallows?" She puts air quotes on the us transforming.

She looks up. "Yes. I could." She coughs again. "What's the point of it?" She opens her laptop preemptively. I guess Jess is the real deal, or she knows more than I'll ever get to know about Corinna.

"Woah!" Ambrose stands up. He forgoes his drawing. "That's too risky."

Corinna dismissed him. "Why do you want that?"

I see where this is going. It's like the stripes of zebras. We don't fight, we pretend, misinform and camouflage. "You want to disorient them. We use your ability to misguide them and their lack of knowledge about mine to do make sure they don't suspect it. That's our way out if we camouflage with Ambrose's ability." A smile creeps up my face. ***Why didn't I think of this before? It's so obvious. Animals do it, why not me?***

"More than that. Information is queen when trying to win." Jess smiles.

Corinna clears her throat and looks at her open laptop. "In two hours could you show the cameras Theon and all of us transforming into swallows, flying…" She raises her eyebrow.

"Northwest. Canada in the summer is where a lot of birds would go," I say.

"Northwest." She coughs. A fumble of letters without order or meaning follow her clear, specific sentences.

Ambrose opens his notebook. "It's ready. Cory won't be able to talk for a while. Her brain gets messed up after using her ability too much." He picks up his materials, joining us at the door. "We just need a place to put it."

"What if we play seven minutes in paradise?" Mercurio moves his eyebrows up and down. We sit in silence, waiting for Jess to slap him. **How would seven minutes in paradise work? We are four guys and two girls. Are we rotating them? Unless Mercurio is the one rotating with all of us.** I shiver. I don't need that. I don't think I could survive him.

Jess put all her stuff including my blood inside her pack. "You're a genius! The supply closet!" A smile creeps up her face.

Mercurio is dazzled by the lack of punches. Ambrose and Corinna follow her example, packing away her stuff. Ambrose has the organizational skills of a Vogelkop bowerbird. His pencils and colors are carefully placed in different boxes. He adds a post-it note to the page he needs, then closes the book. Once done, he joins us, passing me my bag, which is only missing my phone.

I take out the brownies. "Maybe I can squeeze in one more transformation, just in case." I munch on them. Licking the edges of my container as to take advantage of every single ounce of energy I can get.

Corinna makes signs with her hands. She points at herself. Then she thumbs up beside her head. Finally she pretends to have to claws on her chest. She lowers them at the same time. She crosses her arms and taps her foot, waiting for an answer. Mercurio shrugs. Ambrose shakes his head and turns away from his sister pretending not to know her.

I've never been good at charades. I back away. "Did you get it Zach?"

He hums. "Sign language. I can't read it. It's different for the USA version."

"Let's follow her." I grab him by the wrist.

He tilts his head. "The first word was 'I'." *Did he even listen to me?* "Right, sorry thought I could finally help the team." His lips curve downward.

My adrenaline is kicking and I'm dragging him behind, he keeps up with me as we leave the room with our bags. "You've done more than you think." *Keeping me sane for two weeks is more than helping. For once I feel normal, like I belong. The others expect too much from me, but you expected nothing and treat me as who I am. A guy.*

Corinna holds her hands like fake guns, pointing at the door. She slowly moves towards the target, then points back to herself.

Zach turns and smiles. "She said follow me." He proceeds to do the movement and point at her with his version of the gestures.

Corinna takes Ambrose's hand. She drags him into the complex. Jess and Mercurio follow.

"See." I smile at Zach, and he smiles back. "You did more than you thought." I lead the way following Mercurio's scent. He smells too strongly, musky even.

"I did." Zach smells like a bird's first successful flight. His smile is small but radiant.

I lose track of the others. With eyes closed, I focus on my ears and nose. Boot steps echo from the floors below. Sheepish voices come from the same direction. The storm has picked up pace. Water bombs collide against the structure. Winds howl in a fit of rage. Thunder and lightning strike near grounds.

Squeaky footsteps go down the stairs. We follow. "Where are we going? Is this like a metal gear game, 'cause—"

I place one finger over my lips and that's all that he needs to understand. The trail of squeaks and cookie smell ends on the second floor. Four figures stand in the middle of the hallway. Honestly, I have no idea what they're doing. I'm going to call it the forum of the lemmings. "What's going on?" I poke my head between them.

Jess replies first, "We found it." They stand in front of white door leading to a small room. She opens it, revealing orderly stacks of shelves and racks filled with boxes, gadgets, and more boxes. She steps in, taking Mercurio with her.

We follow her. The shiny neon labels invite us to explore. Ambrose holds his notebook close to his chest. In the corner of the closet a space between shelves large enough to fit us.

"How much time do you need?" I ask just in case we missed something.

"A minute," Ambrose says, using his pencil as a ruler. He glances at Jess then continues to draw. Jess stays still. Thunder and lightning crack. "Could you give me some light?" Corinna complies shining her flashlight that could easily blind anyone.

"If you need it. I'll distract them. I can buy us time." I take one last deep breath before stepping back.

My arms stop midair. "No." Zach holds my arm. I try to step away. He presses tighter, leeching me to him.

I sigh. "It's a precaution. I can act as lookout and if you aren't ready, I'll do my stuff." I exhale. "Could you let me go?" I step forward but am yanked back. Losing my balance, I crash to the floor. "What was that for?"

Zach still holds my arm. He looks down on me, scowling for the first time since I've met him. "You don't get do overs or extra lives." He sighs and his face softens. "I'm not letting you go." One of his feet presses my free arm. It doesn't hurt or anything. In fact, I could get out of it without my animal shapes.

"Fine. Could you get off me?" I tilt my head, pointing at my pressed arm.

He steps off, and helps me up.

Mercurio slides between us. "I knew you liked it rough."

"I wasn't going to fight him." I slip off their grip.

Mercurio leans into me, "'Cause you would win?" Again, he wiggles his eyebrows. I wished Jess wasn't busy with Ambrose to help me. Zach steps back.

I push Mercurio away. He's like a horsefly looking for blood. "'Cause he would." That turns their heads. "I wouldn't use my abilities for that. How would that make me any different from a bully? Without abilities, I'm a normal guy."

Mercurio slips away. "It's getting hot in here." He winks, pretending to stop following our movements. His eyes tell a different story, stalking us. A useless display, if you ask me. A snow leopard waiting for the moment the mountain goat slows. I keep the door closed, listening for the hunters.

"Ready," Ambrose whispers.

"Form a line. Zach, me, Theon, Ambrose, Cory and Mercurio." Jess leads us to the back wall. She places each one of us in order.

Ambrose crosses his fingers, "I hope you're ready." He opens the notebook. The drawing crawls out, covering us in deeper darkness. My hands explore forward. The wall is real. The wall, the paint, everything feels like the one behind me. ***That's amazing. We're getting out of this. We're saved!*** The only difference is that it smells like colors. Not a complaint, but it could compromise our location. Howling wind rushes through the main corridor. Three pairs of wet footsteps come in. Thunder crackles.

A man steps closer to our closet. "We're in the building, ma'am. Starting the search for the six missing students."

"Understood. I expect news," she replies, colder than Corinna. Not emotionless, more like a bullet piercing the mark.

"You heard her. Find the kids. Dead or alive." The other footsteps slowly walk forward.

Everyone sweats, filling the room with my onions, Ambrose's fresh graffiti, Corinna's new gear scent, Mercurio's wet muskrat odor, Jess's fairly normal smell and Zach's cinnamon and dark chocolate smell.

Nervous thoughts flood my brain as the footsteps get closer. "Everyone. Can you promise something?" My voice lowers.

"It depends," Jess replies.

"If things go wrong. Say, I took you hostage. That way, they won't do anything to anyone else." At the end of that sentence, I bite my tongue. Holding any emotions in.

"No. Don't make us do that." Zach breaths heavily. He tries to reach for me, but I scoot toward Ambrose.

"Cory says yes, but I won't let you either." Ambrose pats my shoulder.

"I will, because my plan won't fail." Jess takes my hands. We squeeze the life out of each other. Ambrose and I take each other's hands. We stand in silence, waiting for the inevitable. Short, rapid breaths take over my body. My heart and mind race with malignant thoughts. Drips of sweat fall from my armpits. The eternal darkness obstructs whatever hope I have.

Polished metal creaks. The darkness is a little less intimidating. The hunter's footsteps reach the supply closet. The door is opened, and lights bounce off the drawn wall. A few rays penetrate it, letting us see each other. Jess's face copies the Saharan sand viper. Rigid, afraid, and bitter. Her hands betray the calm, encouraging words she rallied earlier. On the opposite end of the spectrum is Zach, head down. Ambrose shows his teeth. Like Jess he's more of reptile than person right now. His lack of energy and warmth reminds me of a leatherback sea turtle.

The boots get closer; the light is brighter. "You heard what happened in Monterrey?" A voice on the other side of the fake wall asks.

We hold our breaths. The makeshift wall groans. Its insides won't bend.

"Yeah. Third-degree burns. Some have gone crazy they said they saw a dragon." The gruff voice is further away.

"A dragon? I believe it. Last time they saw an angel, everyone except Agent Penumbra died." His body weight shifts the wall's balance. Water? We're dry. I push my feet against the wall, but a piece of it is missing. Water! The men are soaked from the storm.

I let go of Ambrose. I touch the wall. It's cracking. He looks at me. Nervously nodding. Hold his pieces. I copy him using my arms and legs. The others copy us strengthening the wall from our end as one of the hunters puts some weight to it and soaks his side.

"This wall is weird." The man pushes against the wall and small holes appear where the rainwater makes contact. Light collides against us. We do our best to move out of them. To remain like the larvae an aye-aye would hunt. He keeps pushing. The wall fades a bit more. Black lines cross the white surface. It takes effort to not grumble. A piece falls on my arm. It bounces of silently. The other guy gets closer, he presses against it too. The two bulldozers trying to take down our nesting tree.

"Stop messing around!" A woman's voice commands from the hallway. It has a hunter's tone. Same one from the radio.

"Yes, ma'am," they reply. Moving out and closing the door.

The wall crumbles silently on top of us. It's eerily unnatural. The pieces are weightless. The only reason the fall gravity. Even a feather weighs more than them.

The wall flies away. Ambrose's book catches it on a page. Corinna stays in her corner. She sits beside her brother and hugs him. Ambrose stares at his notebook. A drop of water collides against the page. He silently sobs. I think from fear. We were so close to dying. His hands shake uncontrollably.

Mercurio looks unaffected, and I don't enjoy that. He sends a kiss flying toward me. I step back and bump into the original wall. Jess hugs me, then hugs everyone, everyone except Mercurio. She ends by the door, out to see if we'll be safe for the rest of the night. Mercurio stands with her. The whisper, but my attention is driven to Zach, who sits in the corner.

"Zach." I sit beside him. "I shouldn't have asked what I did. I just didn't want you to be in trouble." I look at the floor. Now he will see me as what I am. A selfish, horrible monster. One that doesn't think about the other people in his life.

"I got scared when the wall began to fade." He scoots closer to me. "I don't think I would have let you do it on your own." He mumbles something before continuing. "You're a hero 'cause you want to protect us. But you don't have to do it on your own."

I embrace my knees and stare at the floor. I guess I just need to say it, "My life is finally worth something because I can save others." I could keep my thoughts hidden because Ardal isn't here, but I shouldn't. My senses fade away for the night. I curl protecting myself from the others.

Zach stays near me. "You are worth it, always." I can tell he smiles. He leans on me. His odor flickers cinnamon and chocolate. If there is any certainty in this situation, it's him and his honesty. He doesn't know my past, only my present. He has no reason to pity me. It's comforting.

I raise my head. "I'm glad you think so. You're great too. I couldn't ask for a better roommate and friend." Those dark green eyes call me. Even in the darkness, I can see the verdant glow. The smooth flattened fiery fur starting to dry. I poke his fluffy stomach.

He giggles and pushes my hand away. "Stop."

Jess turns to us, interrupting Mercurio's monologue about how sorry he is. He doesn't smell remorseful. She places one finger over her lips and shushes us.

He pokes me back but hits my scar. My nervous system has long abandoned the area. I give him a slight smile. "Fennec fox ears." My ears move individually, one rotating to follow the echoes from the hallway, the other facing forward, then to the side hearing both of the other two conversations in this room. Zach carefully pinches my ears. His fingers thread on my fur. The ticklish sentiment runs down my nerves. I can't control it. I laugh. "Stop. My ears get ticklish with the fur." I take his hand and pull it away.

He yawns. It invites me to yawn too. With the power of my senses, I do my best to keep watch. The two of us snooze off leaning on one another. When we wake in the morning, I feel better. My powers are not gone, and neither is him. We don't act strange. We're tired. We did what friends do, leaning on the other.

CHAPTER THIRTY-FIVE: LOVEBIRD AND THE SHY FOX

August 2, 2013

Light gives way to the purple darkness of dusk. Ardal's family was kind enough to allow us to have the meeting in their mountain cottage an hour from the city. Risky move if we're tracked, but they assured us everything will be covered. The cooks and maids left us with enough food, and we shouldn't need anything else. The sliver cutlery shines against the white and gold plates. The dining table holds five kinds of meats, two salads, soup, and snacks. That's not even taking into account the five different kinds of juice, three sodas, water, and alcohol in the fridge. Ice cream and cake, brownies, and cookies. It's a banquet, not a frenzy.

Lucas, Helena, and Cassiel bask under the last rays of the sun before heading inside and taking their seats. Roy has been at the table since we arrived, placing himself at the head. It has caused the ire of Percy. Little does he know that Roy relishes that attitude as much as he enjoys singling out Daemon. Daemon has isolated himself from the groups. He's an island in the middle of the marbled bar. I take my seat on the porch. Many like the day, but I enjoy the coolness of the night. I don't fear it since I can see clearly.

Ardal hangs up the phone and walks my way. "We should take a seat." He points inside. It's far away enough that they can't listen to us, but close enough to see what's going on.

I lean back, staring at the sunset, and push the box I'm saving for later further behind me. I admire the view, nature everywhere, save from a couple of houses here and there. You can see it all, the forest turning into city and the city becoming a semi-desert on the other extreme. This is nice. A small amount of relief before tonight's chaos. Given that the group has chosen me to give the news and strategy, I have to in there soon, but here in the open, I feel more like myself. "I'll go when everyone is here." I scratch my palms at the thought of it.

"Everything will work out." Ardal leans on the handrail on the other side of the walkway.

My jumpy legs creak the wood. "So, when are you telling me?" I shoot him a glance. *He better remember what he said to me before I left for camp. I know he purposely avoided me in July, but it's August and he has to talk to me about what's been going on. There isn't any point in coming together if he can't say that.*

I remember. He glances back. Ardal picks up the box and puts it by the door. "Theon and I will be right back. We need to talk."

"Okay." Helena waves at us.

Ardal closes the door and nudges me to follow. He takes the path around the house to the back. His face turns from a confident smile to a hippo's grimace.

I follow, keeping track of his pheromones. Yet again, fear. My stomach swirls. I hate the smell, and I hate more what will come. I bite my lips before saying anything.

He strides as if showing me around, but I think he's stalling. Once we're far away from the others, under an oak, he slumps against it. He's thinner. I know soccer season was over, but wow this is too much. The purple eyebags hang from his face. Micro-vibrations pump from his arms. He tries to cover them but ends up pressing tightly his chest.

I watch him for a couple of minutes before tapping my feet. "I can't read minds, but I can smell the fear." Wind gushes. The leaves flutter between us. "Have you talked to anyone about it?"

He throws his arms down. "No. It's not the time." His voice shies away from his confidence and strength. *What happened to the wolf, the lovebird?*

It has to be my fault. I should have talked to him sooner! "When will it be the time?" I cross my arms. If he's acting like me. Then I'll take the inverse role. *I can be a wolf for once. I can do something for him. I can be useful and valuable.* He stays silent, avoiding me.

"Tomorrow." He shifts under the shadow of the tree. "Today is hard enough for you." No half smiles and no mind reading.

Did he lose his ability to be intrusive?

"No. I can hear you." He stares at the house, more or less to where the dining room is.

Now that I think about it, Helena's movements haven't been fluid. Long gone is that dancing swan. She now behaves like the rigid monitor lizard.

"I can handle it." He doesn't answer. He watches me carefully to know my next thought. I sigh. "The way to ruin it is by not talking. I doubt things will go smoothly." I glance at the distant city breaking the verdant greens. "Jess's research, Corinna's inventions, Kat's ideas are fine. My plan will make them hate me." I resist the urge to scratch my palms. My claws have been acting up since I decided on this course of action. I reach out, but midway there my arms drop. I can't.

His green eyes absorb the orange tones of the fleeting sun. "You don't need more pressure. You struggle too much. If I say anything, I'll fail you as a teammate." He tries to give me the captain's pose. Back straight, chin up. The light hits at the right angle, almost signaling him as a chosen one. That true role model of a species.

It falls flat. I'm the reason he feels like this. That he can't share stuff. ***I'm the worst. I'm not even the bare minimum of a pack member. I don't deserve people like them. It sucks. I don't want to be the kid I was before. I want to be worth their time and space.*** At the very least, I can try. "Then that means I'm failing you as a teammate. But most importantly, as a friend." He lights up a bit. His lips curve upward just one inch. "I was a horrible person to you before, and you treated me nicely. Much better than most people. So please let me return the favor. Let me be someone worth being your friend." I shrink. This is wrong, I'm begging. I'm actually begging. The thought slithers inside me, *what if I'm just a parasite?*

You aren't. Ardal's voice resonates in my brain. His smile is forceful. "After that, I have to tell you. Well, I can show you." We both appear in a black, empty space. We float midair. He's right in front of me. He looks how I remember him. Buff, alive, sure, and wearing his sports jacket. Strange, he looks so tall. *I'm about to show you memories. Helena's and mine.* His mouth never moves.

I look down and my brown paws float in the air. Orange fur covers the rest of my body. I'm a European red fox.

Don't worry, this is our minds. This is how you see yourself. An animal is like you, but with the way you talk about yourself, I never thought of a fox. He smooths my bristled fur patting my head and back.

The first image is of Helena sitting at the table. In front of her a man and a woman. They look serious, barely looking at her. As Helena moves, our vision moves. Whatever she does and sees it's from her eyes. Whatever we are seeing is not normal, not like the memory we saw of me. This feels more personal, but distant at the same time.

Helena raises papers to the table. "A dancing company wants to hire me. I want to dance."

Her dad barely looks at her. Her mom touches her hand. "Sweety that's an amazing hobby, but what about your grades and medical school?" She raises her mug and takes a sip.

"Mom. I want to dance. That's my dream. I don't like medicine or seeing injuries." She places the papers to the side.

Her dad looks serious, cold, and scary. He looks at her like my dad looks at me, as a disappointment and a waste of space. "You are to study medicine and have a successful career as a doctor. We can't have you running around in dresses and slippers while starving. Think of your future for once. All the people you will help as a surgeon."

Helena's arms shake. "I can help people through my dancing. Give them hopes and dreams. Help them smile when they're sad. And I'm happy dancing. I feel like I can fly." Her hand reaches toward the light bulb covering it at the right angle so that it hits her like a spotlight or the first rays of dawn.

Her dad slams the table. She hesitates. Her mother shakes her head disapprovingly.

Her dad looks at her directly. It feels like he is admonishing my very animal soul. "No! In this house none of my children will be unsuccessful. You'll go to medical school. You'll graduate and get a good career. It's final."

Helena stands and runs through the house. She passes trophies and awards. She runs upstairs to her room crying. Sobbing. It feels like she got stabbed in the heart. I know it isn't her emotions. Ardal can't do that. Her room is white. There's no music and no color. White over white over gray. Lab coats hang from the walls. Piles of books about medicine. No posters. Nothing other than the sound of nature and herself. She walks toward the window and tries to open it. Metal bars fall on the outside. She looks back and the wooden door has become a metal hatch. The walls write their own lists and orders.

Helena must be a doctor.

Helena must save people.

Helena do this and that. And at the end of the list, my name ordering one last thing. Helena, you must fight. The scene goes black. The sobs die down.

I'm trembling in Ardal's arms. *I'm horrible. I did this to her. I'm a monster and tonight she will confirm it. I'm doing to her what people do to me. I can't go through with this. I can't do this.* The words float around us in a peculiar green color.

Ardal shakes his head. *You didn't know.* He keeps me in his arms, not letting me go.

You tried to warn me. I didn't listen.

You had things on your mind.

And she did too.

Theon. This is why I didn't want to tell you. You'd do this. I can't show you the rest. He puts me down on the… ground? Whatever where we stand is. It's confusing.

I tilt my small canine head. *The rest? You have to.*

No, look at you. You're blaming yourself. He points at me. The height difference makes it look like he is scolding a puppy.

I'm at fault. I have to fix things. Show me the rest.

Fine.

This scene is darker. Someone sits. A dim light showers them in luminescence. His eyes move, revealing the precarious situation. Hands bound to the chair by leather straps. His chest struggling against bindings. No one else is in the picture, at least not visibly Only darkness. In front of him a movie plays. First, the movies show Daemon alone. Crowds move away from him; they frown signaling him he should go away.

Another image plays, Helena longingly looking outside a window. It's not barred, but it feels that way. She turns around to a room with a man cut open inside it. She stops and sighs. A stark difference from when she helped me. Her face is dull and apathetic. She puts her gloves on and starts picking at him with her medical instruments.

We jump to another scene. This one has Ardal's parents wearing rags, not the beautiful clothing I've seen them in. At their feet, a grave reading: *Ardal the Third. He could have been so much more.* His parents cry. His mother collapsing on his dad. They cry and the echoes follow us to the next place.

A soccer field. His team loses the match. His friends aimlessly look at the air. Ardal isn't there. The referee marks the end of the game. From the speaker, "The Bears once again score no goals."

I'm not sure why, but this next moment feels like the last one. Lucas cries on the ground as the water floods the area. Roy curses at the air. A black swarm forms above to attack. And a T-Rex falls to the ground. His scales drips blood. The dinosaur becomes me. Blood covers the ground, and my chest struggles to rise. My body fails to move and the color of my skin drains. The scene fades to black, but I know I just saw my death.

You were living with that for months. And you didn't tell me.

Yes. It was for your own good.

And your own good? That isn't right.

I know. How was I supposed to tell you, Theon? I'm scared you'll die, and I can't help you.

You just did. I smile as much as a fox can smile. *What are you afraid of?*

Failing the people, I love.

So Daemon ends alone. I die. Your team losing. Your parents being poor and seeing their child disappear. Helena being trapped.

Your brothers dying right after they saw you die.

You can't blame yourself for that. We made the choices that took us there.

But if I can nudge it a different way.

I rub my fur against his jeans. Red strands attach to it, leaving a nice contrast between orange and blue. *You can't force us to change. Did you force me to like you and be a friend?*

No.

I face him. Once I'm right in front of him, I sit down. My tail sways from side to side. One would think he domesticated a fox. *Then?*

I can only help and intervene when I don't push it. He takes a seat with his legs crossed. Now that he is closer to my height, he looks less displeased.

Will your parents losing money be your fault?

He looks up at the expanse. *No, they're too smart for that.* He smiles. I'm not sure what he's seeing.

Will your team lose if you miss one match? I take a step closer to him.

Maybe.

My left front paw taps the ground. *But the world didn't end. They will adapt and survive for next time.*

Right.

I stand proudly. Pointing with my nose at the distance behind him. *Focus on what is within your control. At least that's what animals do.*

He picks me up. *I hope you're seeing what I see right now.* He gets my snout close to his head. Our noses rub against each other.

My body jiggles. My mouth appears to be laughing, and I would if I could. It tickles. **What?**

Why you should be the leader.

I recoil at the thought. ***I don't see that. I'm just helping my friend.***

Same here.

He brings us back to the real world. To the topaz skies disappearing to umbral purple. I step back, giving him the space, he needs after showing me the horrific scenes he's been reliving. Although Helena's must be her own if she saw Penumbra directly. I divert my gaze. "How come I was a fox there but in my head I wasn't."

"I call that a mindscape. Our minds make spaces. It's not in mine or yours. But it let us see ourselves like we think we are. Your memory was a memory, so you saw yourself as you. But in your mindscape, you are a fox and I'm…"

"A wolf." I smile. "Or a lovebird."

"Yes." He steps forward and hugs me. "Thank you for helping me."

"Thank you for being my friend." I bite my lips. ***I will make this right. I will make things right for all of them.*** We sit there for a while. He has tired eyes. His force smile sends less electricity. His body sends way less electricity. After some minutes, we go back to the front porch. I say nothing because it's my fault he's that way. And yet I keep those thoughts hidden, 'cause he would have been right. I can't deal with those thoughts, 'cause I fear them more than he thinks. I should carry the whole responsibility for this situation, and that's what I'm going to do. But that voice in my head keeps getting louder. It says, ***wait until he figures you out. Wait until he gets to know how terrible you are. He will leave you like they all do. Because you aren't worth the pain and suffering.***

CHAPTER THIRTY-SIX: CRIMSON MACAWS

I follow Ardal back to the porch. Jay's golden oriole car shimmers in the last of the sun's rays. Ardal looks at the car, then at me. He nods, staying by the door.

"I can greet them if you need more time." I sit on the wooden steps of the porch. My back faces the house, and in a sense cuts Ardal's responsibilities short.

He takes a step back. "I'll take you up on that." He walks away.

Once the car parks beside Ardal's crimson convertible, Jay runs at me. "Bro!" He tackles me. "I missed the shell out of you!" We stumble to the grass beside the porch. Jay has his lively labrador smile. He's centimeters away from me. His long eyelashes, his smile, his dark skin, even his casual jeans and tees are so familiar. I can't believe it's been almost three months since I've seen him.

I smile back. "I missed you too. Can you get off me?" I gently push him to the side. He stands and helps me to my feet. I playfully punch his shoulder and he does too. "It's good to see you." I say as I look at the others.

Jay rushes past me. "We'll talk later." He runs to the table smiling and jumping around greeting everyone and making new friends. He then rushes to the kitchen shouting, "Ardal! Bro! You gotta show me those new tricks!"

Ardal laughs weakly. "Who told you about them?"

"Erasing memories and causing pain. Here I thought you were just a better phone." Their voices die down as everyone in the dining room rises to surround Jay and ask about his Californian trip.

DJ passes me and waves his hand. As per usual, part of his hair covers his face. His cap almost fuses with his smooth black hair. He stands at the door, glancing at the others. "Where's the box?"

I turn, pointing beside the door. "Beside the door." The box has exchanged hands four times before it got here. Corinna designed the devices inside with Ambrose. Zach built them. DJ programed them. I delivered them to the party. They all agreed I should keep them until the time came. I guess the time is now.

"Thanks." He takes the box to the table in the living room. "I want to check them once more." He walks to the sofa before I can even nod. His hands deftly juggle the small square metal devices. He hunches over as he probes them with his tools.

Haruka and Lucy pass me, barely giving me a wave.

Maybe I should have asked Ardal to take over, but then his problems would get bigger. No matter what I do, I'll choose horribly.

My head sinks between my knees. My thumbs dig into my palms, uncovering the skin, driving the pointed ends closer to my own blood. I need to fix stuff with Helena, Ardal, my friends, Daemon and who knows who else. My legs tremble uncontrollably. Darkness has risen drowning me with it. *At least like this, no one will see my palms or anything else. I can be useful and worth to keep around. They won't think I'm dead weight.* I rake my hands through my hair. The black mass imitates the American porcupine's quills, all aiming at different angles. Someone puts their hand on my back. *Someone knows. It's just a matter of time before they all catch on and kick me away.*

"Theon, are you okay?"

Kat sits down next to me. I nod. "Yes, sorry for bothering you."

She sighs. "Can you tell me what's around us?" She rubs her fingers against my back. Pressing them at some points. I slow down.

"There's grass. Wood. Chatter. The cooling winds." I take a breath and rise a bit. "The city's night skyline. The pool's breeze. The swaying branches under the gusts. Food and drinks. Three German shepherds. A box with weird technology. A lot of people." I put my left hand over my heart. "Flickering fireflies. The rattling of snakes. A stalking cougar. Birds ruffle their feathers in the trees' canopies."

"That's a pretty picture." She leans to me and puts her hands on my right arm. "Want to talk about why you're feeling down?"

I shake my head, but my mouth betrays me. "I messed up."

"That's okay. We all do." Her voice harmonizes with the wind. "Why do you think you messed up?"

My free hand touches the porch's boards. It grounds me but reminds me that I'm different. I'm not a human, I'm an animal. My DNA is animal. "People aren't going to like what I'm going to say." I exhale with force and the grunt of a hippo.

"Not everyone is going to be happy about it. That's fine." She presses my arm. "I can't help you if you don't talk to us. I can only say that I believe in you. I know you're trying to make things better. So, believe in yourself." She flexes her legs, about to stand. "I'll give you some time. If you need, we can start a bit later." She walks inside.

I can tell she smiles, and everyone smiles back at her. Everyone likes her. Kat would never be left behind or abandoned. *That has to be the reason people hate me. I'm not likable. I'm not like them. I don't know what Ardal and Kat mean by believing in me.* It sounds like the final song a cicada sings before dying. Loud but futile. Death is but a meeting away from us. And I'm the one singing the tune of our demise.

CHAPTER THIRTY-SEVEN: PACK OR HERD

If I were to step inside, the mood would change. Daemon would stop talking to DJ. Cass wouldn't get piggyback rides from Jay. Ardal would become serious. Lucas and Helena would go silent. Their joyful moments would end, and I would be the cause of it. Only part of the moon shines tonight. It looks like it wants to run away and leave me in darkness.

Even if the moon left me, I wouldn't be alone; animals in the mountain have set a perimeter. The puma is constantly watching me. The raccoons and mice are inside the rafters. Deer and boar prance around the area. A mother bear rests nearby with her cubs. Owls have taken to the trees with the bats. Three German shepherds guard the house. And right under the porch, a snake slithers in its den. Against my requests not to endanger themselves, animals have taken the job of looking after me. They shouldn't give up on their survival for me. The group is more valuable than the individual.

As darkness creeps one more car arrives. The headlights block my view of the vehicle. It must be the people I haven't met yet. The lights turn off, revealing six individuals walking toward the porch. Shoes clop as they walk over the stone path. Five girls and one guy. The girl in the lead walks as if she owns the place. She walks like a panther.

I stand quickly. I can't let anyone see me like this, or they'll know the truth.

She comes into the light of the house. Her high heel boots bring her to my step. She's dressed immaculately in tight light jeans, an olive blouse and a jacket that doesn't reach past her ribs. Her hair goes from brown to a golden yellow at the bottom. She looks up and down with her brown eyes. They roll as she takes one last look. "Looks like my work is cut out for me."

I smile nervously at the display of jewels and accessories. I clasp my hands behind my back. "I'm Theon. Is there something wrong?"

"Aurora." She flicks her hair back and points at my shorts. "Disastrous. I know it's hot but have some decency. Shorts are not flattering. Not with those long, hairy legs." She fixes her jacket and her purse to be perfectly poised. "The colors are fine, I guess. But you could do so much better. And getting clothing a size bigger doesn't make you look good."

I step back, looking at my apparently very hairy legs. "Shorts allow me to transform without getting tangled. And the size allows me to get out of it before ripping it apart." I stutter as I speak, doubting every word. She's like the girls in school. She'll judge me and decide of who I am before learning anything about me.

Her ring finger taps her lips. "I underestimated you. We can work out details on how to get you from fashion disaster to superstar, if I like what you propose." She taps her heels and takes another step.

The others follow her, and if she's like the girls from school, then she likes the attention. "If you like to be in the spotlight, I think you'll like my plan."

She walks to the door, then turns back and smiles, "I'm interested, but I'll leave the surprise for later. Give your big announcement some flair." Her face straightens into that judgmental look girls used to give me. "And don't disappoint." She walks inside shining as bright as the north star. It makes everyone turn her way.

Following her is a girl in a pink dress. She stops beside me, pulls a fist of something from her purse, then extends her hand. Silver glitter forms a mound on her palm. She giggles playfully and blows. Part of the mound becomes dust sticking to my clothes. My green tee-shirt sparkles like the scales of a green mamba. I dust my shirt, only making the effect even harder to miss.

The girl behind her pulls her away. She sighs. "Sorry about Madilyn." She continues without looking back. "I'm Celeste." Celeste drags Madilyn inside through the luminescent room Aurora has made.

I'm paralyzed. Next is a girl in fine clothing with different colored eyes. One is sapphire, the other emerald. She can't be older than ten and yet she has the same poise as the cranes. She half bows, "I'm Cleopatra Rosetta. My friends call me Cleo. A pleasure to meet you."

"Hi Cleopatra." I stare. She's dresses for a formal party. "It's nice to meet you." **Am I the only one not dressed formally?** "Make yourself comfortable." I signal to the door.

She giggles, covering her mouth. "I think I will." Once she enters the house, takes off her heels and puts some slippers. She takes off the dress to reveal a blouse and jeans. She gracefully waves at everyone, attracting attention.

Finally, the last two come. A girl with a mane shakes my hand vigorously. So much for the remainder of my sloth-like energy. Her shirt has an image of a megaphone and the words, *Rise up! Make them listen!* She almost pulls my arm out of my socket. "Astrid. Big fan of your cause. Equality and protection for all. Your statement as the T-Rex spoke to me. We have to tear things down if we want change."

I smile nervously. **What is she talking about? That was an accident. There was no purpose. Are people interpreting that as a statement?** I scratch my palms. Sweat trickles down my neck. Talk about impending disappointment. She'll be more disappointed than the first time I tried to fly. "Right." I look at the guy. He looks like a predator looking at someone invading his territory. "Nice to meet you both."

"That is Zamir." She leans closer to my ear. "He doesn't get it. You started this change in the world. He'll realize you're good." She steps back, pulling Zamir into her arms.

He glares at me. Doesn't say a word and drags his feet inside.

I follow and close the door. The vibrations in the kitchen overwhelm my sense of touch. The enclosed space makes a difference usually vibrations dissipate, but here they build each other up. I won't need this sense. DJ and Daemon look at me, reluctantly nodding at the realization that it's about to start. DJ thumbs up the equipment, signaling the equipment is ready. Daemon takes a while longer to join us.

The dining room settles as everyone takes their places. I'm at the head, opposite Roy, with Kat, Jay and Ardal nearest me. *At least these three can take over when I mess things up.*

You won't. You'll do great. Ardal speaks in my mind.

DJ hands me my phone. "It's ready."

"Thank you." I start a call with Zach. My screen turns blue. The image is almost tangible, making it look like Zach is sitting in front of me. A bunch of people gasp as he takes space on the table. I stand my phone beside me, adjusting the image to not block anyone else. Kat, DJ, Ardal, Percy, Jay, and Roy call Jess, Ambrose, Corinna and Mercurio, and two other kids. "Now we're all present."

"This is impressive," Ardal says, staring at the spectral figures. It's easy to look through them, but they look so real.

I reach out to touch Zach. The image fizzles. My hand goes through it.

Corinna crosses her arms. "With more time and resources, I could have made them better."

"Cory, take the compliment." Ambrose fixes his hat. He waves at everyone, smiling kindly at the new faces.

Aurora smiles in response and nods approving at the new people and strong introduction.

"The people who hunt us are getting bolder, and we have some ideas about how to stop them." My palms face downward hiding the pink tissue. I signal at Corinna, Jess, and Kat to take the lead. I bite my lips with sharp fangs. My stomach squirms as if octopi wiggled inside me.

Kat gives me a thumbs up through Zach. She opens her mouth, but words don't come out. It still feels like she's encouraging me.

Jess phases through the table, half her body above it. She looks perfectly normal. "Before we do that. I'm Jess. With the help of Cory and Kat." —she points at the two other speakers— "we think we found some clues about your abilities." She points at me.

Everyone waiting for Jess to continue. Ardal, Kat and DJ lean in closer to Anna's hologram. Jay does the same. Roy, Percy, and Aurora lean back, too cool to be invested right now. The rest go silent. Whatever they want to say will wait for Jess to be finished.

Jess nods in recognition to the attention. She turns to me. "Could you show them your ability?" She smiles kindly. "So, everyone can understand your case."

"Sure." I scratch my hair. Nothing big or rigid. The last thing I want is to scare them or destroy Ardal's home. Something adorable and small should do. Not too frail as to be injured easily. I glance at Ardal, remembering the creature I saw in the mindscape. "Red fox." My body shrinks. Orange fur covers my limbs. My snout and ears elongate. The clothing drops to the ground. My head pops above the table.

"Aww." Madilyn tilts her head. "He's so cute."

One of my ears folds to the front. Zach playfully tries to touch it. His hand goes right through me. We look at each other for a second before Kat intervenes. She pets the back of my head and rubs my folded ear. I make a noise that sounds like bird chirps mixed with a purr.

Celeste grabs Madilyn, keeping her on the seat. "Focus." She turns to Cleo, stopping her from joining in the petting.

I hide back under the table, transforming back into my simple Homo sapiens form, the one filled with scars and a dulled heart. The process takes less than a minute. Putting my clothes back on takes longer.

Jess talks. Part of her body phases through the table. The blue light bounces on the glossy surfaces. She steps in front of her seat. "I did a couple tests on Theon. His DNA had five recognizable species DNA during the analysis; one of them being a woolly mammoth. As you know it's extinct. I believe his DNA can mutate to any species that has lived."

I zip my khaki shorts. "Only vertebrates." My head and neck slide through the t-shirt's orifice. "I tried invertebrates, but I think that belongs more to Roy."

"Fuck yeah. They know who to follow."

Her holographic hands reach for a small book. "Noted." There's silence until she places her book behind her. "Mercurio and I are interested in doing tests on all of you. We're extremely interested in Percy, Cass, Madilyn, Lucy, Ardal, Corinna and Ambrose. That's not to say the others aren't interesting but your abilities contrast with Theon's the most."

I'm come out from under the table and take my seat. Jess signals to Mercurio.

Kat interrupts by raising her hand. "Sorry for the question, but what kinds of tests?" She looks cheery and optimistic as she glances around the room. Reading everyone and feeling them. **Why isn't she the one in charge?** Her voice travels through the room. Clicks, taps and tension in people's bodies releases.

Jess nods. "Non-intrusive. MRIs, Blood sample, body scans, among a few others. We want to understand how your bodies are affected by the abilities. Or if they are affected." As she confirms what Kat knew, the room relaxes more naturally.

Mercurio fixes his hair and turns to the group. "I can get us set up for private consultations in a hospital in Mexico City." He winks at Jay.

If he knew Jay like the rest of us do, he wouldn't even try. Jay continues to smile absently.

Cleo clinks her teaspoon against a glass. She waits for silence before speaking. Percy and a holographic boy snickering becomes the only discussion anyone hears. Once they realize what's going on, they smirk as if nothing ever happened. A pale imitation of Roy. They aren't even close to a lion; they would be lucky to be considered badgers.

Cleo taps her lips with a napkin cleaning off them vanilla frosting from her cupcake. "Should I arrange a trip to Mexico City for all of us?"

I sigh, considering the circumstances, it isn't possible. Our recent trips should make it clear that we can't travel in groups and some of us can't travel at all. "They attacked us last time we traveled. They'll only get more aggressive, and we don't know to what end." If they followed me three flights away from home, they're capable of sabotaging the plane and kill us. From what Ambrose told me, they followed the trail Corinna left through Canada up to Alaska, where they gave up.

Mercurio giggles. "We'll start with Amby and Cory." He blows a kiss to both of them.

Corinna fiddles with her phone, while Ambrose looks my way and shrugs. Jess pulls her hair into a bun and ties it up. This causes Aurora to shake her head disapprovingly.

"You're all cool with those wannabe doctors probing on you? Taking your blood! Using us as lab rats?" Zamir crosses his arms. The room nods.

Roy puts his black boots on the table. "Killing the mood." He rolls his eyes.

Celeste waves her glass. Her black eyes focus on the water swirling inside. "They have the tools and knowledge. We need to know what's happening to us." Her words end, and the flow of water does too. Her glass stands on the table beside the Spanish ham sandwiches she brought from the kitchen.

Zamir growls. It doesn't have the necessity for survival animals have, only a bitter complain lingering in the air. He stares at me. He knows as well as I do that, I'm the reason this is happening. Even Daemon seems bothered by how he stares. Daemon's cowardliness has faded. He whispers to Roy. Roy in turn whispers to Percy and texts to someone else.

Kat waves at everyone. "Hey!" Her red hair acts as a beacon. If Zach was in his normal colors, he would compete with her. He still has my attention, but I better be ready for Kat. She might need my help with the explanation. Kat smiles, causing a wave of smiles back at her, even Zamir. Cass waves from under the table, which causes Lucas to go under. Kat says, "I know some of you are curious about why you got your abilities when you did. I think I have an answer."

"Really?" Zamir asks. The words are harmless, but the tone is defiant and aggressive. His muscles send more electricity than I'm used to. They contract and pull at my sense distracting my other sensory receptors. I'm forced to devolve my electroreception for now. Without the push and pull of electricity, I can get a clearer view of everyone.

Aurora dismisses the boy. "Sit down, peanut gallery." She waves at Kat. "Listen to her. I love the hair, by the way; we should have a sleep over and do make-up and hairstyles." The girls nod. Even Helena joins in. I didn't know how unbalanced the group was before this. It was always a boys' night, or Helena and Kat with all the guys.

"Thank you! I would love too." Kat spins in her seat, showing off her hair. "Can we talk about it later?"

"Yes. We'll finish this, and then we can spill the tea." She takes a sip from her teacup. *I'm so confused.*

Kat does what she does best, smiles, and spreads her joy. "I believe it's caused by a specific psycho-emotional state unique to each of you. Thank you, Theon, Helena, and Lucas, for letting me talk about you."

I wave awkwardly. Helena does the same. From time to time hear Lucas and Cass giggle. Or see them running to the kitchen for brownies and cupcakes.

"Lucas loses his abilities when he lies. Helena, when she feels trapped. Theon, when he fails." Kat says bluntly, causing me whiplash.

Failure? No, it's not failure. Every time I lost my powers there's been a natural reaction in my body. I feel inadequate, unworthy, doubtful. Failure could be confused with my own reservations that often happen at the same time. I guess it all comes down to that moment when I first got them at that horrid party. The moment I thought I did deserve some semblance of happiness and friendship. "It's not failure…"

Now everyone's eyes are on me. I can see Helena relaxing. Lucas peeks from under the table, smiling as he usually does. Tapping his fingers to a slow melody Kat taught him.

"I lose them when I doubt."

Kat made us tell her about every time we lost them. The day we got them, what we did that day. She was very thorough. It was uncomfortable. I felt exposed and safe. It was a strange combination. I don't think even Ardal reading my mind would make me feel two opposites at the same time. She reaches out to me, her hand softly patting mine. Her eyes sparkle as bright as fireflies in the night.

I take a deep breath. "Maybe we can summarize the trigger with one word."

Haruka stands up. "Like a word of Power. This is going on my blog!" She pulls out a notebook. The page she chooses has my name and a brief description of what I've done and can do. It even has a graph with stats and random quotes.

"Sure." I shrug. Lucas is easy. I tap the table. "Honesty." I glance at Helena and think of her memories and Ardal's fear of the future she may end up with. Of that hopelessness. Her room and house becoming a cage. "Freedom." I touch my palms. So far, the words have positive connotations. Mine should too. If doubt takes away, then the opposite will give it to me. "Confidence." I point at myself.

"What's mine?" Daemon raises his hand. He looks like a statue, rigid, but extremely proper for his standards. His fingers are covered in black sooth.

I scratch the back of my head, scrambling all my hairs in each other way. "Animals didn't want to tell me because it would affect how I acted. I think they believed that each person should figure it out on their own. Helena, Lucas, and I did. I think Ardal and Roy have an idea about theirs too. I'm sorry, I can't help with that, but at least you know where to start looking."

Daemon nods. He isn't angry or sad. He looks guilty, and to a certain degree disappointed. He smells as if he was in the rain for hours, trapped in a cave filled with guano and then dragged through the streets. Nothing unexpected. Whatever he's dealing with; he has to come to terms with it. Just like I'm trying and struggling to do.

"Why are you the leader then?" Zamir raises his voice. His short hair style does him no favors in looking approachable. He still glares at me. **Have I done something to him?** He looks like a tiger whose territory I invaded. Even more than that, it might be purposeless. *I've done nothing to him, it's the first time I meet him.*

Percy breaks the mixture of whispers and silence I left in the room. "I should be the leader. I'm better than him, never lost my powers." He stands on the chair. A kid in the hologram challenges Percy. The two of them start boasting, which causes a chain reaction of who's the leader and why.

"You both fucking suck." Roy doesn't demand anything else. He calls upon his followers to acknowledge their own failings. After all, a pride has to cull the weak.

Both Aurora and Astrid snap their fingers. "Facts."

The discussion becomes a matter of who's the best leader. Roy's end of the table becomes untamed chaos and disorder. They shout and bargain. They brag and tease each other like a troop of chimpanzees. The noise rises. It echoes inside the room with nowhere to go. I grab the sides of my head. Ardal does the same.

I think Ardal can hear me. **You said my mind was loud. Focus on it.** My wolf hearing fades, leaving only human.

Thanks.

I nod as the sounds become normal. Nothing saturating all the channels. If someone comes my response will be delayed. I can work around that. Smell and sight are still available, although sight is meaningless without windows looking at the right angles.

"I rather have Theon as leader than any of you. He knows what we're dealing with better than the rest." Ardal nods back at me. **Focus on what I'm saying.**

Kat raises her hand. "Same here. He's trying his best to get this to work."

"Work?" Zamir stands up. "Look at us! We're freaks. Monsters! How will this work?" Zamir wears all black. Strange my UV sight detects nothing. As if no UV light bounces off him. The infrared works fine, I can see the red and white. UV should still work. Small areas should glow in blue or purple. It makes me raise my broken eyebrow.

This is diverting the plans too much. I can't deal with feral humans like this. I know Lucy and Cass don't like their abilities, but they aren't aggressive about it, which makes it easier to keep going. In a sense, I ignored what they really wanted. I shouldn't have. I close my palms into fists and take a deep breath. "The animals have told me our abilities are natural. Everyone is capable of them." I scratch the back of my head as the conversation shifts.

Cass and Lucas pop out from under the table next to Helena. Their faces light up. Helena whispers to calm them. Ardal stares at me. Twenty people has to be putting a toll on his abilities.

Zamir slams the table. "Impossible! This isn't natural!" He breaths heavily and glares at me. I didn't deserve that, yet. I begin to sink under the table.

Cass does too, with Lucas close behind. Roy's collective raises their eyebrow. They don't say anything. Roy looks at me, giving me the lead. Daring me to lose control in front of this herd that I never asked for. This role that was never meant to be mine, and most importantly, this responsibility that is better off with the likes of Ardal or Kat who understand the others.

I rise up a bit. "Tortoises, elephants, and the older species have confirmed that it's natural. We are the norm. It might not seem or feel like it, but our abilities are normal."

DJ looks amazed, but more relax than when he first saw me. He takes his cap off and smiles at Kat.

"Can we trust them?" Celeste expresses much more emotions than Corinna. That isn't saying much, but she isn't reptilian. She clasps her hands like an adult. Any voice that tries to speak above her or me is interrupted by her dead stare.

I shiver. "Yes…" I phrase the words in my mind. "Some of these species have lived for more than a hundred years." I pause. They might not trust me or the animals maybe, I should give more. "Animals gain nothing from lying to me." I straighten. That's the truth. Animals wouldn't try to hurt me or deceive me. Animals are positive presence in my life.

Celeste nods. "I was worried about that. Thank you." She looks at Aurora and Madilyn. Serious and calm, but extremely relaxed.

Ardal sends a psychic message. *It's time. Are you ready?*

No. I glance around, they await for my response. "It's time you hear my plan."

CHAPTER THIRTY-EIGHT: HUMAN IN WILDERNESS

Streams of sweat spring from my body. The plan. The legendary plan I have created. I take a deep breath, pulling in every scent I can: sweet sugars, savory meats, alluring fruits. A flowery perfume becomes a pungent reminder of the people around. Most of that can be traced to Madilyn. Aurora, Cleo, and Roy are more subtle in their choices. There are different pheromones. Fear, rage, sadness, guilt, nervousness, anxiety, stress, and a couple of joyful ones. Jay and Kat have to be the happy ones. The rest are closer to the aftermath of a Christmas island red crabs' migration. And gunpowder, I can't believe that smell never stops following me. *Gunpowder? Ardal!*

Ardal replies in my head. *I heard. What's the plan?*

I panic and call for the two people that can help us. *Get Roy and Kat.*

Why them? Ardal asks, he stays silent, pretending everything is fine.

They know people.

Roy asks through the link. He judges me with one look. *What did you screw up this time?*

Is everything okay? Kat chimes in a mild manner.

I do the only strategy from the animal world that might work. Diversion. ***No. Someone has gunpowder. Can you talk to Corinna and figure things out while I distract them with the plan?***

I bet it was fucking Zamir. He's lame. Roy complains. His gaze has shifted to Zamir.

I'll talk to Corinna. Kat offers.

Ardal gives me a quick nod before going silent. ***I'll go inside of a couple of minds. Will talk to you if I find anything.***

Great! More issues. This will be worse than anticipated. I have to adapt and plan. Do my part. They have things under control. What's that phrase again? Right, we should do like superheroes and be public. No that sounds awful. Animals that are famous and on display, dolphins? Whales? A baby panda rolling down the hill. "I've been thinking about it and for me, there is only one answer to dealing with these hunters. It won't be fast, but we have to show ourselves to the world." I bite my lip. One of my canines has become a full fang.

The air thickens. No one expected this of me, or at all. Lucy and Helena make space between them and me. Lucas and Cass hide back under the table. Roy shrugs. The rest are awestruck. Their mouths gapping Roy's flies could swarm inside if he so desired. Daemon looks stoic, his scent is sheer terror waiting to be unveiled. Zamir still hates me. Jay and Astrid are bouncing in their seats.

Helena is the first to speak, "But…" She covers her face.

"Yes. Let them know who we are and then *bam*! They won't know what hit them." Percy's golden eyes shine with the magnificence of a golden eagle, and yet they are stuck to a kid that acts like a marmoset.

"No. We do it like in video games. We keep our identities covered." I explain.

Zach's hologram leans into my ear. "See heroes. You are one."

The whole room listens. It alleviates none of the tension.

"What's the point?" Corinna looks away at what I assume is another screen. Ambrose pinches the bridge of his nose. He walks away from his phone and back in the same manner as Jess did earlier.

Aurora smiles at me. "A display." She stands up, pushing her chair back. Her hands rise to the level of her face. "Love the idea. We need to work on execution." She points at me, then turns at everyone else. "None of you scream memorable for the right reasons. I know your situation, but fashion disaster in the waiting." She turns to Helena. "Pretty, but lacking strength." Then points at Lucy. "Overalls. Who are you, my mother?" Her next target is Zamir. "Forgettable." She goes after Roy. "Needs work." And last, she points at Astrid. "Too much statement, not enough fashion forward." When she flicks her wrist, the light reflects in just the right way off her golden bracelet to make it look like a star. "We need to work on all of you. If we're making a statement you have to be un-for-gett-able."

"What's wrong with my shirt?" Astrid shouts.

Aurora rolls her eyes and slowly takes her place. Her hair perfectly aligning to her intent. "The statement is wonderful, but how much more impact would it do if your looks also made a statement?"

Ambrose interrupts, "I get it."

"A connoisseur of the aesthetics. You're close enough eight out of ten." Aurora looks at everyone, evaluating what needs to be done. "Maddy, be a darling and take over hairstyling. No sparkles." Her voice is condescending. It reflects a sense of superiority, but her expression is warm.

"Aww. Okey dokey. They'll be so pretty." She throws her hands upward, pretending to throw something in the air. Nothing falls on our plates or food. I know she would have thrown sparkles if Aurora wasn't here.

Ambrose scratches his cheek. "I meant the purpose. Fame and recognition."

Roy puts his feet on the table. "We'll be motherfucking rich and powerful!" Roy's smile is unnerving.

Celeste sighs. "No. If they target us and a hero disappears people will get suspicious."

I nod. "In a sense, we're using the display and recognition as protection. Our alter-egos as camouflage. It will last for a while until we can figure out how to not be targeted."

DJ raises his hand. "There's an eighty-five percent chance this works without issues. The other fifteen are dubious. The important stat is the hundred percent chance of becoming a beacon to others with abilities. The more people know." He twists his cap backward.

"The more will be able to join us and help." Kat completes his sentence.

DJ takes her hand. "Exactly." They share a glance. "Your plan is not only giving us protection, but setting the stage for the other phases. Defense. Recruitment. Offense. I can't say it'll be a success, but from what I'm looking at it'll be promising. I'll have my computer run simulations later in the week."

Jay jumps out of his seat. "More superheroes."

"More villains." Zamir keeps his arms crossed, glaring at Jay and at me. Okay, Jay doesn't deserve any hate.

Animals in nature will unite if there is harm for all. Ants, bees, different schools of fish and herds in the savanna. I stare back at him. "Does it matter? Our priority is living through this, and it will be theirs too. So long as we're all hunted, we have the same enemy. Even naturally opposed forces join together for survival. It works in nature, and it'll work here."

"You compare us to animals?" Zamir snickers. His hands hide deep inside his pockets. "We're human, we're different."

My blood boils. My limbs shiver at the coldness of what the others might think. Compared to animals, they might not take it well.

"Humans are part of the animal kingdom. We are technically animals," Jess says dismissing his comment. She keeps her notebook in hand.

Helena waves in my direction. "Will we need to fight?" She has been avoiding looking at me for the past twenty minutes and addressing me doesn't change that.

"No and yes. While we are 'heroes'"—I do quotation marks in the air—"no. We could rescue people from an accident. Protect a forest. Stop a natural disaster. After that, we'll have to. Our lives are on the line."

"Oh." She looks down, passing her fingers through her hair. They damage its usual weightlessness.

A few others don't receive the news well either. DJ looks stoic, but he trades glances with me and Kat. The giggles under the table stop.

I close my fists, preventing my nails from digging into the skin. "Sorry, I don't think any other way helps us."

"We could give ourselves in." I don't even have to look at Zamir, to know it's him.

"I'm not risking our lives on that bet!" I stand, hands pressed against the table. My nostrils flare. Even DJ came to accept that we couldn't take such chances.

Ardal shows me his palm, signaling me to stop. I do. Ardal stares blankly at Zamir. His green eyes don't feel any different, but there is something about them. "I read their minds. Their plans were to kill Theon, no questions asked. Capture and torture Helena for information. Indoctrinate Cass and Percy to work for them. I don't know what they would do to the rest of us."

The room is dead silent. The stench of fear emanates from everyone except Roy, Percy, and me. Okay, that was a lie, I'm afraid for a different reason. Not the gunpowder. I've been shot at multiple times, and I can only feel pity for the people using those weapons. They're cold and distant and can only kill through an impersonal device. It's a way to forget you committed an atrocity. The reality is they're too scared to be responsible for what they've done. It's unbecoming of a creature of nature. That's why we carry the weight of it all. It's survival, but it doesn't mean we should get used to it.

"I know you are afraid, and I am too, but we can do this. Together." Kat's voice reassures everyone in a way that I never could. Her voice carries over, and her determined tone calms them.

Still, I soon return to anxious thoughts of demise and death. "Percy, Cass, Helena, Corinna, Ambrose, and I are the priority targets. We need to get our personas out there fast." I glance at Corinna, then Zach. When I see him, my stomach feels like it's being strangled by an anaconda. If he only knew me, he wouldn't think of me as a hero. A hero doesn't do these kinds of things, doesn't plan to prevent disasters just to get fame and glory. "Jess and Corinna could you set us up?"

They both nod.

We got the person. Ardal speaks into my mind. He barely moves, just sips from his soda and glances at me.

It's fucking Zamir! Roy looks unimpressed. That is hardly new. He's had that look since the reunion started. *Fucker has a gun.*

How did you know? Ardal replies inside our minds.

He's fucking lame.

You don't have to be mean about it. Kat's voice without the lightness of the birds and the cheeriness of the macaws is not hers, just another voice in the crowd.

It's the truth.

How do we handle it? I stumble on my thoughts mixed with the voices talking in my head.

"Zamir. Why the fuck did you bring a gun in here?" Roy doesn't move. He doesn't even look at Zamir or anyone but me. He smirks. Roy is ready for chaos and disorder. The room is paralyzed.

Zamir crosses his arms. His muscles tense. His disturbing glare focused on me.

Bingo! Ardal shouts inside my head. ***Sorry.***

I tilt my head and sniff the air. Everyone turns to me. The scent of food and fear has been circulating the house all evening, but the gunpowder smell has stayed in one place. Either Percy, Cass or Zamir brought it. As much of a cretin as Percy is, he wouldn't do something that dumb. And Cass cries when he sees people getting hurt, so it's not him. "So, it was you who brought one." I point at Zamir.

"Now you're accusing me?" He arcs his black brow. "I don't agree with you, and you accuse me of bringing a gun? Who'll be next? Helena, Arvo, Celeste?" This causes the herd to look around suspiciously.

DJ takes off his cap. "I never said I didn't agree with Theon."

Everyone turns to Zamir. Those near him inch away.

Corinna's blue light moves up. She coughs twice before being able to speak clearly. "Why is your identity hidden behind government level firewalls?"

Zamir stands pushing away his chair. One of his hands inside his pocket, the other on his side. "Everyone's is," he barks.

Ardal pushes his chair back. "I learned something about fear. It makes your thoughts easier to read. You protected the memory of the gun so hard, but when Roy mentioned it, I could see your memory of packing it."

Percy and Helena push themselves away from Zamir.

"Ugh. What's the point of pretending?" The hand in his pocket remains still. Just like that the house suffers a blackout. The phones and our friends from away fizzle. A couple figures move in the dark.

Roy starts proclaiming a decree, "Spiders…"

"Jaguar." I choose my animal and my body starts transforming.

"Everyone…" Kat does her best to de-escalate the situation.

Maddy chants, "Sunshine…"

Lights come back on. I'm frozen. My paws support my weight on the table. My tail static in the air. Fur covers me, but I can't move. Everyone is a statue. DJ blocks Kat, her mouth open and her words incomplete. Maddy is in the middle of a spin, her mouth also open. Roy's condescending look aimed at Zamir, the order incomplete and his army unavailable. Ardal reaches for Helena. She, on the other hand, looks as if about to shield Jay. Percy looks pissed, so normal. Aurora and Celeste look unimpressed. Cleo grew translucent wings and is the size of a hummingbird. Daemon is nowhere to be seen. And Astrid's hands hold flames.

"I can't have you four using your abilities. You are too dangerous." He points the gun at Roy, then Maddy, followed by Kat and me. "Madilyn don't do anything." He points the gun back at her.

How does he know about Kat? We kept it a secret. I can still move my eyeballs and blink. That's something I can work with that.

DJ is the first to reply. ***I don't know. We didn't say a thing to anyone.***

"It's too bad I can't get the ones away, but capturing you is good enough." He pulls out a phone from his pocket.

I can't move! Helena diverts our attention to the real problem.

I think, ***Me neither.***

He fucking interrupted me, Roy complains.

My chant, Maddy adds.

All the voices lack emotion, but their fear and anger saturate the air. We need Corinna or someone who wasn't caught in this frozen moment.

Fucking genius think of something! Roy demands.

We're going to die! Haruka speaks.

No, we won't. I can't let them think like that. ***Ardal a mindscape.***

On it.

Everything goes dark. Black is the only color in the mindscape. Ardal still looks like himself. I'm the red fox. Everyone else appears. Roy wears a crown, Maddy a princess dress, and Daemon orange prison garb. Helena has shackles on her ankles. Celeste appears to be in her forties, but Cass looks like a baby. Someone skulks in the shadows and there is a giant foot behind Roy. DJ is dressed like a DJ. Lucas's outfit divided in half vertically. One half basketball outfit, the other a blue suit and tie. Astrid has a mob of Astrids behind her. Haruka sits behind a computer and Lucy is inside a house completely separated from everyone. Cleo, Aurora and kat look like before.

I'll never get used to this. I forget that my thoughts are shared. *Focus. What do we know about him?*

His power paralyzes people. Haruka shrugs. Her whole body is covered by books.

Celeste stands without moving or giving an expression. *It works with objects too. I can't make the table bigger.*

Can anyone move? Helena's shackles drag over the ground. They sound as if they're scratching rocks and minerals.

I can. Daemon looks at the ground.

Cass and I too. Lucas bounces from one foot to the other. His outfit completes itself when one foot isn't touching the ground. He switches between the basketball gear and the blue suit.

Daemon… Kat stops short.

I know. I'll stop him, Daemon says.

Wait, I say before he can leave the mindscape. *Let's think of it more… Why can you move, and we can't?*

Baby Cass rolls around crying. Daemon picks him up and puts him to sleep on his shoulder. Daemon absently looks past me. *We're under the table.*

Is anyone else capable of moving? Even if it's just your fingers. I look around.

The figure skulking in the shadows is the first to speak. *I can move my tongue.* Jay's voice. That's not normal. He's cold, absent, a shadow of the person I see every day. Another friend I failed.

Hurry up! I can't hold this for long. Ardal closes his eyes.

Right. I nod.

I can move my toes, the Astrids say in synchrony.

He threatened Maddy. Why? What's your power? I pace, restraining my urge to claw myself.

I can do magic. She twirls and as she does sparkles fly out, then disappear into the air. *But not if I don't complete my spell.*

Then why threaten you? Wouldn't it make more sense to point the gun at Percy? His power is the most dangerous. My thoughts scramble.

The giant foot stomps. *I'm that awesome.*

No fucking way. Roy falls asleep on his throne.

My head is spinning. *Maybe the threat wasn't for Maddy. If they threatened Lucas, they wouldn't do it for fear for of him. It would be from…*

Fear of you. Several people complete the sentence remembering what happened when Lucas got shot.

Aurora. He fears you. I point at her.

So basic. How dull. Aurora flicks her hair. *Seriously, grow a spine.*

What's your power? I ask.

I can shine. Honestly, none of you would be able to handle it.

I put the pieces together. *You made night to day. If he fears the light, his power might be manageable. He can paralyze things when they create a shadow. Daemon, you won't be able to help, neither will Lucas.*

Slow down. DJ takes off his headphones. *Explain.*

Shadow Paralysis Majojutsu. Haruka raises her hand.

I scratch my ear with my paw. *Sure. His ability is shadow paralysis. In order to paralyze an individual or an object, they must create a shadow. That's why Astrid can move her toes and Jay his tongue. And why the only unaffected people are under the table? He has two plausible weaknesses intense light and complete darkness. In theory a psychic infiltration is possible too.* I look at Ardal. He shakes his head, struggling to keep us here.

Cleo raises her hand. **Excuse me, but Aurora said we couldn't handle it.**

Aurora's ability might be the best one, but not the only one. I think he doesn't fear Percy 'cause he has to speak, or shift like us. It's up to Cass.

I can't keep the mindscape.

We're back in the dining room. Still frozen. Zamir's phone is halfway up. The world feels so slow. I close my eyes. **Cass, we need you to do something. Light the room up.**

But my slingshot. He starts sobbing.

We'll die if you don't. My muscles tense. Frustration builds as my body is unable to reply to my wishes.

He's just a kid, Helena intervenes.

Cass, please. We need you, Daemon calmly says.

He's our only shot. I can't let anyone die, not because of my oversights. I'm panicking.

You never met Zamir before. Ardal raises his voice.

I should have. We can't use half our abilities. If Aurora uses hers, he might shoot someone. Percy can't do his stuff. That leaves your mind reading and Cass. I'm not letting anyone take a bullet, it's not right.

Fine. I'll erase his memories of us. Ardal sighs in my head.

Helena talks over the panicking voices. ***Ardal, you don't have to do this.***

I have to. I can't let Cass do it.

Do it! I shout.

Fuck it!

Theon, don't! DJ and Kat denounce our decision.

Lucas is busy consoling Cass, but mumbles, ***That's wrong.***

Celeste has the last word before the link breaks. ***We don't have another choice.***

In the time it takes a peacock mantis shrimp to pincer, it's over. My body aches. Muscles rigid. Bones stiff. I launch myself onto the table, transforming into a feline. I stand on the table as a full-grown Jaguar, but I'm late. Astrid has the gun pointed at Zamir.

She takes the rounds out of the gun, then puts it on the table. She looks my way. "Sorry we put you in a tough spot. I can't help with the superhero plan, first I gotta help Zamir." She points at Zamir.

"Where the hell you're taking him?" Roy stands up on his chair. "He tried to kill us!"

"I've known him for a while. I think I can help him. If he forgot you, he might tell me what he wanted to do." She drags him out. Zamir looks tiny compared to her.

My body turns human again and surveys the disaster. Helena holds an unconscious Ardal. Cass sobs under the table. Lucas and Daemon don't come out. Kat and DJ help Jay out of the room. Most of them barely look at me. I pick up my clothes and go outside. I put whatever isn't completely ruined. Mainly the shorts. Outside, the city shines just as much as the stars. Then there's me, struggling. *I failed. It is my fault.*

"Bunch of losers! If you were as good as me, you'd be fine." Percy walks away, making a as he leaves the vicinity. He disappears into the night.

Cleo's next. She stands beside me. "Excuse me. I apologize, but I must decline the offer for now. I'm not ready for a burden that big."

"I understand." All my wind is gone. This is a disaster.

She bows and makes her way out with telephone in hand. The darkness consumes her.

Aurora looks me up and down. "Our offer stands. We'll get you from fashion disaster to model." She hands me a handkerchief. "We want to see what you're capable of before going through with the whole thing."

"But Aurora, I want to help." Maddy chases her.

Aurora turns to her. "No. We can't put blind faith. Let him show everyone that he's a star too."

I nod at her, sinking deeper into my thoughts. The night is ruined. I should have never done this in the first place.

The night gets darker and darker. Ardal regains consciousness and takes Helena and Daemon home. Cass's parents pick him up, slingshot in hands. After a while Jay drives the others home, assuring me he'll talk to me tomorrow. Kat waves at us. Her usual smile gone, but she keeps her warmth.

My phone beeps as Lucas and Roy keep their distance from me.

Jess: Sorry the night got ruined. What happened?

Corinna: I need to make the phone EMP proof.

Ambrose: I won't join. Erasing someone's memories isn't right.

Mercurio: That means more Theon for moi.

My brothers join me on the porch as we wait for Ardal to give us a ride home. Roy laughs as he reads a text. "Man, the lightning boy is an idiot. I told him I was a better hero than him and he stayed." This doesn't make me feel better, and he notices it. Roy glares at the distance. **This is about the party. I'll hear about it tomorrow and next week, and every week until it happens again.**

"I don't know what I want. Erasing someone's memories doesn't hurt, does it?" Lucas looks in the direction Cass went.

I hunch over. "I don't know." My phone beeps.

Zach: Are you okay?

Theon: I think so. What do you think?

Zach: I don't know. They made a chat without you and started talking about what happened. Did you have to do that?

Theon: They didn't leave me a choice. Aurora made it sound like her ability could hurt all of us. And Cass was the only one with an ability that could help, but he didn't want to. So Ardal did it, even though I would have rather done it myself so people wouldn't dislike him.

He doesn't reply for minutes. Ardal comes back to take us home. He barely speaks or uses his ability on the way back. My phone beeps away.

Zach: I know you had your reasons.

Zach But.... Erasing someone's memories. That's a lot.

Theon: Zach it's okay if you hate me. I get it. I'm a horrible person.

Zach: What? No, I didn't mean that. It's a lot to process.

Theon: Okay.

Zach: Okay. What are you going to do?

Theon: The plan. On my own.

Zach: Don't do it alone.

Theon: I can't risk anyone else.

Zach: What about you?

Theon: After tonight, I don't know any more.

Theon: So where do we stand?

Zach: I don't know.

CHAPTER THIRTY-NINE: BREED

August 5, 2013

Ardal's car harbors exotic species for him. Species I have decided not to look back at. Having Jay and Kat here is unique. Roy forcing us to take him with us is as rare as a vaquita in the wild. Lucas didn't come 'cause he needs space. Everyone else hates me to some degree. Aurora and her sisters are busy designing some outfits. I haven't shown my face to them, dreading their expressions when they see me for measurements.

I glance at my phone. Zach and I haven't talked. Sometimes we get distracted and forget to talk, but by that last message imprinted in my screen, I can only feel dread. *What if he only wanted me around as long as I was a hero? I wouldn't doubt it. I'm not a good person. Much less a good animal. I'm empty and voided of anything that made me special. I doubt people want me with or without powers.*

I put my phone back in my pocket. My hands too, safeguarding them from prying eyes. The leather gloves don't slide as smoothly as I would have liked. I must wear them; they're the only thing preventing more damage. I face the streets. The air is stale, despite the car being a convertible. The wind roars, but when it gets to us, it stops. Silent and heavy.

"Hey Fucktard! Tell them you lost your abilities!" Roy kicks my seat.

Ardal glances at me, black sunglasses covering his emerald eyes. "Is that true?"

I know he's reading my mind. Why lie about it when he already knows? I nod, "Yes. They're gone." I squeeze my fists. For once I don't have to dig through my palm's skin. I let the rush of pain drown my anguish. The noise inside my head leaves when the pain triggers.

"Bro, you can't do the thing!" Jay leans on my seat. His face too close for comfort.

Why is he here with his goofy smile? Why am I here? There's no point to this. I'm not worth their time. I sigh. "I'll be fine." I try to distract them with something different. "What about the others?"

Kat pulls Jay away. She sits between him and Roy. Her reflection follows my movement. "Roy, Ardal, Lucas, Corinna, Aurora and her sisters are the only ones with abilities." She respects my space. Or maybe the seat belt does a better job than an octopus's grip to keep her away.

Great, another thing that's my fault! I look at the woods and the dried-up shrubbery. The landscape that once meant something. Today is a reminder of how alone I am. Never fitting. Never wanted. Never worth the trouble. The waterfall overshadows the landscape. It seems Ardal and Jay want me here whenever they think I need help. It's a compulsion to show that things aren't fine. That we need to work on out survival strategy. "Why are we here?"

The car slows, and Ardal parks at the edge of the clearing. "We need to talk. You aren't fine."

"I am fine." The words are quills in my mouth, ready to launch at anyone who threatens me.

"Don't fucking lie to our faces!" Roy breaks nature's silence. "Shit ain't fine." He raises his voice in fervent rage and frustration. He gets off the car, tapping his feet like Lucas.

I get off the car too. My voice quivers. "What do you want Roy? I'm powerless! Friday was a disaster. Almost everyone hates me! Why are you four wasting your time on me? I don't get how anyone is believing I can do this. If I mess up, everyone dies, or another Zamir happens." I punch the car door.

"Hey, easy," Ardal says, looking at his car then at me. He stares longer than I'd like.

"The car's a sensible lady." Jay jumps to what was my seat.

Ardal pulls him back. "He gets it." He turns off the vehicle. "What's that?" He takes off his glasses and stares at my hands.

I hide them slowly. **There's no point in denying it. He will read my mind. He's always in my mind.** "Why do you care?" I walk deeper into the woods. "You were in the chat. Why not join everyone else?" I keep going. The forest isn't that welcoming anymore. It's dark and lonely. The animals have fled, all because of me.

"You knew about that?" Ardal gets out of the car.

I lean on the first tree near the forest. "Zach told me before he stopped speaking to me." My hair dusts off the bark. Brown pieces get stuck to my left side. A few pieces scratch my ear. "He dislikes me."

"Zach was one of the few to leave." Ardal approaches slowly. "He said it felt wrong to speak about you behind your back."

Roy's voice is that of a commanding dictator and not a copy of my emotional instability. "Those fucking cowards! I called them on their shit. Aurora left when I did." I can tell he smirks. That's how Roy is.

"DJ and I left after Roy. If they had issues, they should have told you. DJ agreed and left. He said even if you two disagreed, he knew it was unfair to put all the blame on you." Kat waits a minute before continuing. "He's giving you space, but I don't think that's right either."

Jay runs past the others and stands beside me. He shakes my body as he smiles, like he always does. "There was a chat? No one invited me." Well, that's new. Jay, the popular guy, wasn't invited to a group chat.

Kat giggles. "You didn't say anything bad about Theon."

"Never." He jumps in front of me.

Ardal takes a couple more steps. "I stayed cause Corinna asked me to monitor them. They asked me to guide them. I won't agree to guide them. We put too much pressure on you. When I asked them what they would do in the same situation, they were silent. They haven't spoken since."

My hands sink deeper inside my pockets. "They would be better off with you in the lead." I look at the ground. Behind me, sandy soil changes to pebbles and moss. Roots and the ground flora hide the paths under their entangled growth.

"Maybe, but you know the abilities better than anyone." Ardal takes another step.

I sigh. "Not exactly. Zamir seemed to understand Kat's."

"He was with the bad guys. They know more than us." Ardal stops moving. This is a hunt, a different kind, but a hunt, nonetheless.

Kat is the furthest away. She doesn't come closer. "We need you to calm down. Let us help you." Usually, her words become air. Just like air, unnoticeable. An invisible force the body assimilates without thought. But this time, her words tangle themselves on my limbs. They try to pierce my skin and force their way in. "Calm down," she said, but the words crawl upon my ears. They try to drag me under like a crocodile does to its prey.

This must have been how Zamir knew about her power. It's sweet and kind when you're willing, but now it's drowning me. "I can't let you do that. People get injured around me. I'm not worth the effort. Everyone is better off without me around."

Ardal is still moving closer. His footsteps squelching in the wet soil "That's it!" Ardal grabs me by the shoulders and throws me to the ground.

I keep my hands in my pockets as I fall. There's no way I'll let them see it. I don't need that. And they for sure don't need it either. If I fall and hit my head, it would be taking a weight off their shoulders. I close my eyes. Let gravity and the ground do their work. Without me, none of them are in danger. My clothes become a net Jay catches me in.

Jay smiles at me. Effortless as Jay always is. "I got you." He slowly lowers me to the ground.

The canopy me from covers the sun. Leaves oscillate in the strong winds that herald the impending month of rain. There's nothing for me here. Even the earth is hard. It repels and despises me.

Ardal puts his weight on my legs. His hands press my knees. "Jay. His hands."

Jay turns. His head goes back and forth between Ardal and I. I recoil. Try to squirm away, but it's futile. Ardal doesn't budge. He stares at me. He has that look. The disappointed one, with bags under his eyes. The one everyone gives me. I grip the cloth in my pockets and my body tenses up. I want to imitate the opossum, the armadillo, even the porcupine. Except it can't. *I'm not that anymore. I'm not an animal. The thing that hurts the most is that I'm a simple human, and I have nothing left.*

"Sorry." Jay grimaces. He slowly pulls my hands out of my pockets. He easily gets my limbs to move against my will.

His face is pained. He sighs heavily, as if losing part of himself. There's no puppy smile. Instead, he has a long frown like a bulldog or a basset hound. He takes my leather gloves off. Pulling them slowly, careful not to injure me.

I don't react. I stare at the darkness of the forest. At the depths of something different.

The leather gloves fall right beside me. Jay let's go of my hands, stares at the bloody bandages. "I can't do this."

Kat steps into view, right behind Ardal. "What's going on…"

Jay walks into the forest. "This can't be happening." His body shakes. His steps stumble through the undergrowth.

"Jay wait." Kat walks past me. Before she follows Jay, she turns to Roy and motions at the car. "Get the first aid kit." She trails Jay, pleading for him to slow down. To talk to her. Her words seem to work as they settle into a steady stride.

"The fuck did he do?"

Ardal ignores Roy. He looks at my bandaged hands, crawls to my side. Ardal unwraps the bandages hardened with blood. I can't help but wince.

Ardal turns to Roy. "Get me some water too."

"Fucking shit! I'm no servant!"

Ardal tries my other hand. The bandage comes off cleanly. No pulling on my skin. No re-opening the injuries. He stares at the uneven crevasses. The torn skin trying to mend itself. The solid crimson that was once a liquid brewing from me.

Roy gets us the tools of someone else's trade. He drops them beside Ardal. "That's fucked. So, fucking, fucked. You might fucking need stitches. Dipshit." He picks up the water and slowly pours it on the still bandaged hand. It's fresh and cool, but painful and rough. My lungs want to scream, but I shouldn't. **What's the point?**

Ardal starts cleaning my other hand. He never looks at me. "Why didn't you say anything?" He presses a little too hard and a trickle of blood pumps out of my hand. If I had my animal senses I would know if he was grinding his teeth. If his stench was one of anger. Seeing I won't reply, he changes the question. "Does it hurt?"

I shake my head. "Less than everything else." My voice could belong to a corpse.

Ardal's grip softens. "We're friends. You should have told me. I could have helped you."

"Like I helped you?" The question sounds more like an attack.

He wraps a clean bandage around my hand, covering the worst of it. "You might not believe it, but yes. You helped me. You don't see it, but you did. I have a friend who got me to understand. Who helped me when I was down? He helped people I care about. And yet he does his best to hurt everyone who cares about him."

"It's for the best."

He shakes his head. "Don't give me that. I can read your mind. I know you think we see you as dead weight. Have you ever considered it's all in your head and we like you? Not your abilities, not for taking the lead or your intellect, but for who you are?" Ardal waits until the bandages from my other hand are wet enough. "I've seen your memories. They don't look like reality."

Everyone will judge me. Everyone will think I'm sick or weak. That I'm broken. "What do you mean?"

He slowly unwraps the wet bandage. "You think you're broken. I only see someone pleading for help. Who, despite his best efforts can't handle, his burden alone." He cleans the hand. This one is in worse shape than the other. It's a crisscross of destruction, blood, and wounds. A wasteland where skin can't repopulate. "Needing help is natural. We all need someone. I needed someone to show me that the world isn't perfect and that my way won't always work. That if I focus my efforts on what others need and want, I can help. I know you think you're worthless, but you aren't." He finishes wrapping my hand. Hiding it from the world. They don't deserve to see such violent displays against oneself. ***You're doing it again. We all have our issues. There's nothing to be ashamed.*** Ardal sends a telepathic message.

"Idiots. Useless people don't save others all the fucking time. Useless people aren't motherfucking geniuses. Useless people are cowards. They run away when shit gets tough. And you haven't done that." Roy throws my gloves at me. "Use your brain for once. How many people wouldn't be amazing without you? How many would be dead?" He rolls his eyes. "You are the densest son of a bitch that ever lived." He glares at me.

"But…"

He slaps my face. "Don't start." He stands and turns away. His black hair curls, covering his ears. It's not long, nor it consume much space, yet he inspires the fear of a lion and the command of the honey badger. "There's only one person in this world who matters. If you want to prove you are worth it, do us a fucking favor and prove it to yourself." He walks away.

Ardal gives Roy a fast-passing smile. "He's right." Ardal extends his hand. "We trust you. You don't have to prove anything to us." He glances to where Roy had stood. Ardal is the wolf I've always wanted to be. Maybe it's just for the best that I don't think about it. **He leads and cares. He stays behind, offering guidance and protection and, for some reason, he thanks me for that, but I know he did it all on his own.**

You're missing the point.

Maybe I am. They could have easily given up on me after seeing my hands. After Ardal heard of my attempted suicide. Or after things went south the first time. Yet they stay here, with me. This dysfunctional and functional pack, made of people who would never be considered part of the same clan. I lay on the ground with the gloves on my chest. A proud lion, that never falters. The compassionate crimson macaw, who always lends herself to talk. The joyful Labrador, cheering from the back. A reliable lovebird, taking the moments to help. *And lastly me, the shy fox.*

Cunning, Ardal corrects.

Cunning red fox. I give in to his input.

Better. For the first time today, he agrees with me.

I raise my hand. Ardal takes me by my forearms. He pulls me up with ease. I want to bite my lips and hide my face. *I still would like to run away, but that would be abandoning them.* I can't do that to the pack. Not because I'm sure about the future or about myself, but because if they think I can help them, then I should.

Stop that thought.

"Can you not live in my head?" I put the gloves on. They strangle my bandages, constricting the movement of my hands. It's fine, nothing I can't handle.

He turns to the car and walks that way, joining Roy. *Until you can catch yourself, not a chance.* He turns back, smiling warmly.

"Fine." It sounds more forceful that I wanted. "I'm sorry for breaking my promise."

Roy shoves a box at Ardal. "It wasn't that fucking hard. Apology accepted." He picks up another, considers it for a second. "Forget it." He walks away from the car, closer to the waterfall. "Actually, fuck it. Carry this for me." A swarm of flies surround Roy and carry his box. The black cloud follows him as he settles near the trees, he places his hammock.

Kat pops out of the shrubbery. "Hey, we're back." She waves at the two of us. Her red hair contrasting with the ever verdant green. She thinks she can pretend to have walked all the way around, but there are leaves and twigs in her hair that give away her true location. While Roy and Ardal slapped sense into me, she and Jay hid in the bush. I wish I could understand why.

Jay follows her. He's quiet and serious. He tries to give his usual carefree smile, but it isn't working.

"I'm sorry Jay. I didn't mean to worry you." I look away and stop myself before Ardal intervenes inside my brains.

Jay dashes to me. He takes me by my stomach and squeezes the life out of me. "I'm so glad you're back, Wildlife."

I struggle to breathe. My lungs can't expand. How can Jay deconstruct my ability to speak while he builds up his ability to smile with me? "What?"

He puts me on the ground. "Your hero name. Wildlife, 'cause you're allowing us to live a real wild life."

Ardal says, "Jay, help me with these boxes." He winks at me as he nods to the rest of the packages.

Jay runs to Ardal. The two of them carry boxes to Roy's location, and unpack. The silverware and containers Ardal brought are a surprise.

Kat pokes my shoulder. "He was really worried."

"I know. I didn't have to smell it, but now I can." I glance at the forest. Green and brown decorates her hair. "I know you were in the bushes."

"Was it okay?" She pulls me toward the group.

We take a step before I stop. "No. We all saw what happened." I sigh. The saliva in my throat prevents me from speaking. "Asking for help is hard. I didn't want to lose more people." I bite my lip. My nails resist the urge to scratch. The savage urge that would destroy me.

"I know. You aren't losing us." She pulls me to the others.

Ardal sets up a long plastic table. Jay unfolds chairs. Kat lends a hand as she places a green tablecloth. She moves swiftly between the guys to help finish up. Roy on his side has spiders building another spider silk hammock. A bunch of flies and ants move around following his orders, creating a pathway from the table to him.

I pick up my phone. There's one last person I have to talk to.

Theon: Hey Zac. Are we still friends?

Zach: When did we stop?

Theon: Just worried because of Friday. You said I don't know.

Zach: Ohhh right! I forgot to call you yesterday and tell you I left that chat. It's not fair.

Theon: Ardal told me about it. Thank you.

Zach: For what?

Theon: For being my friend.

Zach: Thank you too!

"Group hug!" Jay tackles me. Soon after, they all join. Roy gives me a pat on the back and nods an inch. ***We're one pack. I get it. I can be worth it, as long as I see myself that way. Am I a pack leader? No. I just want to be me, the guy who loves animals, who protects his friends, who lives his life by his rules.*** We sit at the table covered in food that Ardal brought. A chorus of animal voices joins the celebration. They celebrate the return of their friend. For today, I came back to life.

CHAPTER FORTY: PEACOCK'S DISPLAY

August 6, 2013

  I stand under the harsh noon sun. Sweat trickles down my skin, my hair is drenched as if it has been underwater. Kyra wags her tail beside me. Kyra needed a walk. I left Thor behind, so I didn't have to carry him. My fingers press the doorbell. I want to press it again, but I control myself. I tap my foot as a way to relieve the desire to pressing the button multiple times without rest. My hands find shelter inside my pockets. They're covered by gloves, but the bandages are still visible to anyone paying attention. I turn back to the street; it looks the same as mine. A couple of pigeons stand guard in the nearby trees. until they fly after the old lady leaving breadcrumbs.

  What do I say when I see them? Friday was a disaster. I pace. Kyra sits still. She barks, and it's the only thing I can understand. Barks. I'm still struggling to understand animals. My senses are back. Every few seconds I check the street. ***Are they following me? Does Zamir remember?*** If that's even his name. My head is spinning, and my stomach follows. I hold my fingers in place. I can't show weakness.

  The door opens and Aurora comes out fashionably late. Her hair style is the same, not much has changed since last time I saw her. Except her home clothing is less flashy, baggy pants and a loose blouse. "Ugh, I'll be back." She closes the door in my face. After what seems to be thirty minutes of silence and barking, she comes back. This time she wears perfectly tailored jeans, a blouse that doesn't cover her belly button, a vest-like jacket, and her accessories. "Come in." She opens the door, and guides me to a room.

On my way there, I notice a lot of pictures of her mom and dad. They look so happy. I try not to distract myself on them. She opens the door. It's one of those rooms filled with mirrors and a small platform, like those in a mall dressing room. She looks at her own clothing, and looks at me. Her face is disgusted.

"After today, you aren't allowed to be tasteless." She puts on glasses. Catches me looking. "I'm gorgeous, I know. I need the glasses." She waves the rounded, black framed glasses. "Contacts aren't as comfortable." She puts them back on her face.

I turn to the mirror. **Am I that badly dressed?** There's nothing wrong with my clothes, it's just an average t-shirt, jeans, and boots combination. Maybe it's my hair or the hairless line cutting my left eyebrow in half. Maybe I should wear hats to cover my lack of hair style and shadow my scar. Could it be that I'm slim? Maybe it's that. *Ahhhhhhh!* I want to shout. I sway uncomfortably. My hands never leaving the safety of my pockets.

A giggle comes from the door. "You are funny." Fully in pink, Madilyn comes in. No sparkles this time, but she wears neon pink over purplish pink, with reddish pink and pink pink as complements. I move my eyes away from her every couple of seconds before I strain them. She takes a seat inside the room, holding what seems to be a baton. Her smile is everlasting. She fixes her tiara. "Could you be a fox? That was super cute."

"He's disappointing. He acts your age while being older." Celeste stands by the door, playing with a yo-yo. Her stare is colder than Aurora's. I want to hide my face. I distract myself with her yo-yo. She's doing tricks basics like walk the dog and around the world. Her yo-yo moves are a part of her. An appendix of sorts, like the lights of an angler fish dangling in front of her.

"She's really good, but she never goes to competitions," Madilyn playfully comments. Her head tilts, her tongue shows more pink, and she closes one eye. Wow, now she poses, to try to take the spotlight.

Celeste shrugs. She shakes her head. "It's a childish thing. I do it to improve my motor coordination."

"Being childish is fine. Sometimes you have to let go and have some fun," I say. I like having fun even if people call me immature.

She turns back. Her yo-yo moves faster and more erratically. With sharp, fast steps, she leaves the room. I look down. **Who am I to talk? Look at me, I never have fun. I have to act like an adult all the time.**

"Don't take it personally. She's been like that for a while." Aurora glances at my hands. She has a measuring tape in hers.

I take my injured hands out. They heal at a sluggish pace.

She looks at me up and down, stares at the gloves. "Are you gonna fess up?" Aurora wraps the measuring tape around me. "Jess said you had special requirements." She waves at Maddy. "Waist size eighty-three centimeters"

Maddy goes to a drawer, pulls out a notebook and writes what Aurora dictates.

"I have to wear animal materials. They can shift with me." I rub my sleepless eyes, trying to stay awake and in balance. Kyra lays down beside Maddy. She gets pets and ear scratches. She melts into the floor. Her eyes, for once, confuse me. At one point they look reptilian green. "Fess up about what?"

"Your hands, silly." Madilyn steps next to me with the notebook.

Aurora sighs. "Leather, wool, cashmere, Angora rabbit and mohair." She kneels, wrapping the measuring tape on my leg multiple times, dictating measurements for Maddy. "Eighty-five centimeters." She looks at my boots, bites her lips. "You aren't completely hopeless. The boots stay. Match it with something."

"Does a leather jacket work?" I extend my arms as she pokes them up. She nods. With her approval, I can respond, "An accident."

"If you say so." She points her hand to my collar bone. She's almost dramatic, but never feels too over the top. Paradise bird might not be the best comparison. Leafy sea dragon fits her a bit better. Ornamented, elegant and unique. "Do you have a hero name? We got to make the outfit match you."

My face softens. Maybe, Friday was a complete disaster, but today is not. Maybe we can still do this. "Wildlife." I look away. "Jay chose it. I like it," I almost whisper.

Maddy speaks up, "It's lovely." She flattens her pink onesie and tilts her head before writing the name.

Aurora takes a minute to respond. "Simple. Catchy. Almost perfect. We can work with that." She measures my shoulders. From behind, she the measuring tape surrounds my neck. "Anything I should know."

I hold my chest. "I have massive scars on my chest. I don't want anyone to see them."

"Light colors don't suit you anyway." She turns toward Maddy and claps twice. "Be a darling and show my designs in the mirror?" Aurora steps off the small platform and takes the notebook. She slowly goes through the details, writing down what her sister missed.

Maddy stands beside me. "What spell should I cast?" She twirls around, sparkles fly. "Ah. This will be perfect." She poses beside me, pointing at the mirror, "Mirror mirror on the wall. This guy is a bit too tall." She boinks my head with her baton, does a perfect spin switching sides. The baton touches the mirror. "Show us the creature he will become." She takes a step away. "Wildlife of them all." She waves the baton and poses for one last time, imitating a ballerina.

The mirror turns pink and purple. The borders turn gold and ornate. In the center, me. Fists resting on my waist. The leather jacket moves with mirror-me. The brown leather gives way to brown fibers on its edge, and the back forms half a hood. My dark green t-shirt assimilates the colors a guinea turaco. A decal slashes three black claws on my chest. The pants fit to my legs. The brown boots break the blue contours of the pants. Finally, my eyebrow scar hides under a raccoon mask. My hair is a bit longer, wilder, like a spiky hedgehog. I step forward, reach out for him. ***That isn't me. How could it ever be me?*** "Is that me?"

"Yeppy!" Maddy jumps to my side. She stands on the tips of her toes as she skips.

Just like how Lucy drew me. He looks more impressive. My eyes get watery. I never cared for how I looked, but this version of me looks unattainable. The spell described me. How can it not be me? Tears flow from my eyes. I'm dazzled. I give in to a smile. "I love it."

"As you should." Aurora winks. She walks beside me, checking every detail. She looks at my hair. "One thing." She scribbles something down, but I can't take my eyes away from the mirror. "Clothing doesn't make anything. It's how you wear it. If you look good, you'll feel good." She pauses. "You need to own it. Work it." She snaps her fingers thrice in a triangle motion.

I look at my palms. "You knew."

"A girl has her sources."

Madilyn waves her wand. "Kat and Ardal told us. It's okay, things happen." The mirror returns to showing the three of us in our current attire.

I turn my back to the enthralling display and stare into space. "Can I ask something?" My voice goes quiet.

"Sure…" Aurora rolls her eyes and walks away.

I hide my hands in my pockets. Gravity pushes me a small degree down. Kyra joins me, rubbing her fur against my knees. "You can do these amazing things. Why stay and help me?" I sluggishly turn back to them.

Maddy skips next to Kyra, scratching her ears. She flutters around, spinning the baton. She does a flip in the air, landing on her feet. "We believe in you. We have faith and hope."

Aurora crosses her arms. "You got them here." Her hand spirals in the air, implying something I should get. "We'll fashion you. It's up to you to shine as bright as the stars." She hugs the sparkling acrobat. The mirror reflects that. "If you do well, we can help you."

I want that so badly. To get us out of this mess. I'm not sure if I can do it. Monkey in a desert. Bird in the abyssopelagic zone. Fish in the stratosphere. Those would describe me right now. "I'll try my best."

Aurora flicks her hair. "You know what they say. New look, new you." She leads me outside. Kyra on Maddy's side. The four of us stand in the door.

Aurora waves. "We'll be watching."

Maddy hops by the door. "T-H-E-O-N." She poses as those letters, then jumps leaning toward Aurora. Her hand making her ear look larger. "What does that spell?"

"Theon," Aurora cheers with her.

"Go Theon!" She jumps. "We'll cheer on you!" They wave at me. Kyra and I turn the corner and disappear back home.

I keep thinking about how I'm going to execute the plan in ten days. How will I save hostages on my own? A hero. ***What a joke. I'm a kid trying to survive. I just want to be me.***

CHAPTER FORTY-ONE: THE HUMAN'S DEN

August 16, 2013

    I crawl through the crack under the door. My small black cylindrical figure allows me to slip in without a hitch. The cold, shadowy hallway is the opposite of outside. It resembles a cave, scarce life, and engulfing darkness. The only difference is the natural light streaming in from the windows. I'm not alone here. Rats crawl in the ventilation system. Pigeons scout the skies. And on the tenth floor a group of hostages I have to rescue, and their captors. I have no clear instructions on what to do with the captors, but my abilities don't give me many openings. I have to be perfect, and as much as DJ dislikes the idea, they have to die. Roy argued their death would make the hostages cheer for me. He hasn't failed on reading people, so I will kill them.

    The lobby is massive and well lit. There was chaos at some point. Vases and plants tipped over; the chairs tumbled around. One table was used as an ineffective barricade. I walk through papers and trash. Around pebbles, soil, and a puddle. I know they were in a hurry, but knocking the water dispenser over is wasteful and purposeless. I move past it all, past the elevators Corinna told me to avoid.

    I turn left. Marble stairs lead up away from the safety of the ground floor. After this floor, I'll be limited to what forms I can use. I stand in front of the giant steps. They become smaller as my body becomes normal. My human façade is covered in leathers and mohair wool. The materials feel like part of me, an extension of my skin. The green t-shirt has black claw marks on it. My boots and socks are still fused with my body. My feet are covered in scales and invisible hairs that stick to any surface. Walking is a challenge, but it's better than wasting a transformation, seeing as I only have six left. The gecko feet have been with me since I became able to transform again, five days ago. The raccoon mask. That is newer, but it doesn't feel like it took any energy from me. It hides my scar and my facial features.

Finally got you. How are things going? Ardal reconnects the psychic link with me.

As planned. There's no one nearby. Are the cameras off? I take my first step up the stairs.

She said so.

Good. I sigh. *Ten floors up.*

I know, but it was our only option. The rooftop was harder to get in from. He replies. *Are you sure about all of this?*

As sure as I'll ever be. I rush the first flight. The faster I get there, the sooner this will be over.

Fucking finally. He might break the stairs with that massive pair. Roy joins the conversation.

Just be careful and take it easy. It's ten floors up, Kat chimes in.

Wildlife! Wildlife! Let's go bro! Jay shouts inside my head.

Give them a show to remember and a hero they'll never forget, Aurora says in her own encouraging way.

I smile. This is what I've always wanted, people around me no matter what. I can do it because they believe. On the seventh floor I slow down pace. Oxygen fills my lungs, and my body readies itself. Every breath deep and silent. My steps are calculated, as if walking on cotton. Not even the sticky hairs on my feet make a sound. The windows are black on this level. The shadows in the building grow the higher I get. I don't know how, but Corinna covered this building in darkness where I need it.

I steady my heart. This isn't like that time in school. Here, I'm predator. I make the rules and I will take anyone down. On the eighth floor, my steps are light and partial. The stone is cold. Corinna allowed the AC units to remain on. The heat would have killed a bunch of people otherwise. It would have made sneaking in harder. Sweat can be smelled even by humans. I get the added bonus of the AC unit concealing any sound I make, which isn't much right now.

Ninth floor is more or less the same, though the air is thick in scents. The AC's recycled air isn't enough to quell the stench. The nauseous smell of fear. The provocative smell of anger. Somber tears release a slow, lethargic scent. My body repels all attempts to fall into that attitude. And of course, the last scent makes me want to run at them. It fills me with jittery energy. Gunpowder, the scent that chases me. Naturally, where there are animals, there are hunters. This is a hunt I can make my own.

I stop in my tracks and close my eyes. One hand touches the stairs. Vibrations won't travel as neatly here as with soil or water, but I can get an estimate. There's constant trembling and shaking, has to be the hostages. They are the strongest vibrations. It's safe to assume ten to twenty people are there. The other signals are way too mild. I can hear the echoes of voices, arguing about time and places and cash. Theres three of them. One is tapping their feet rapidly. The more subtle and quiet vibrations come from movement. The intervals are erratic and easily mistaken as nothing. They come in pairs, four pairs. **Seven hostage takers?**

How bad is it? Ardal asks. It grounds me in the moment.

It stinks. I'm on the last flight of stairs.

Good luck! Jay and Kat say one last time before they can't talk to me anymore.

Thanks. I'll talk to you soon. I glance at the dark stairs. There's a little bit of light piercing the dark hall, but not enough to worry about. Not yet. I should begin. I inhale, regulating my heartbeat matching it to who I will become. A perfect hunter extinct due to unforeseeable circumstances. As Aurora said, make them never forget you. As my breath leaves my mouth, I whisper, "Smilodon populator." With golden fur like a lion, stripes like a tiger and fangs that don't fit inside my jaws, I have a form that will scare them.

Every step I take is cushioned. Silenced. Even in darkness, I should care about my next move. My ears shift on their own. They catch different sounds. People sob as if they expect to die. Multiple footsteps slowly walk in patterns. Left, then right, or circling around. One of them taps their foot fast. I should figure out if that one is friend or foe. If it's a foe, it's one less issue I have to care about, already on edge makes them likely to run.

I reach the last few steps. Two lights crisscross in my direction. My body lowers upon the floor, avoiding detection for the moment. I lie in wait, observing the assailants who block my path. My first two victims. They hold long guns and have holstered knives. No one said things were going to be easy. If it was, there wouldn't be a show. I have to lure one of them here. I do the thing I'm not supposed to do. Growl.

"Who's there?" his voice trembles. Just by pitch, I know he is thin and small.

On of the lights moves. "Check it." That one is bigger, maybe even stronger. Their voice bolsters confidence. If he was the one moving to the stairs, I would easily win. Take out the stronger members and the weak ones run.

"No. You heard it?" The higher pitch voice shakes. The metal on his belt clinks.

I growl again, and he whimpers.

"It's probably a trick to scare us." He takes a strong first step my way. "They wouldn't release a lion." His light moves up and down as he walks toward me.

My tail swings left and right. It knows as well as I do; the hunt is on. My hind legs tense. Strength gathers in my back quarters to take him down without a struggle. My claws extend. Only one set of steps makes it to the stairwell. Powerful, prey. My heart reverberates as the drums of the hunt beat with us. My brain is mine, but there is a part of me that's influenced by the animal I am. And the Smilodon wanted to hunt wants a challenge. Hope this fits.

The candid light shines above me. He's looking for a human. The man takes the last step I need him to take. He's at the edge of falling into my fangs. My eyes refract the light. Shinning in their own right. He catches the glimmer, he starts to take aim, but it's too late. I'm on top of him. My jaws clutch his throat. My claws clasp his clothing protecting him from the worst. From the hallway, the lighter voice screams and cries as my target and I roll down the stairs. I never let go. By the time we're on the ninth floor, he doesn't move. Blood continues to pump. Covering the white marble in red.

"Open up! There's a tiger!" The smaller guy is crying by the door on the upper floor.

Woah! That's insulting. I don't look like a tiger. Did he miss the part where I don't have orange fur? What about my fangs? I knew people weren't knowledgeable, but that's borderline dumb. I was planning to spare him, but if he can't even tell the tale properly, there's no point. I move up the staircase. My claws hide inside my paws. My body stays near the stained floors. I'm ready to sprint and jump on him. I gain line of sight.

The door slams out. He's pushed away. I guess he has to wait, until I deal with the more capable individuals. DJ is going to disapprove of my actions, but it's better than what most will think. It's survival, not a matter of pleasure or morality. We do what we must to live in the long run.

"Where's Chris?"

"A tiger killed him! I saw him get dragged downstairs," the panicked guy chokes on his words.

The masked man slaps him. "Idiot! Stay here or help, but don't get in my way." He walks my way. This guy aims his gun and his flashlight downward. Part of the corridor is illuminated.

I stick to the darkness, running to the left. I slowly move up careful of making any sudden moves. People get skittish when they think something moved in the dark, a natural evolutionary reflex. One that makes this harder. His flashlight shines on the crimson trail. Spatters of blood smear every couple of steps. He traces them. A few steps down, he stops. The light shines on one detailed print. My paw in blood.

It's now or never. I jump him. The flashlight flies away. We become visible for the guy at the door who screams even more. Our large shadows us play out the gruesome scene. My fangs pierce his neck. He falls down, crashing into the wall. His gun slips from his grasp. The black machine of death stays still on the staircase. The man's breaths are heavy and desperate, but his body doesn't move. I release him from my maws. Blood springs from the wound. I grip his shoulder and drag him up.

The man doesn't fight probably because of the lack of oxygen and blood loss. I keep dragging him.

The guy next to the door is gone. I glance up at the fork in the hallways. The bathroom signs are to the right. Alright, I drag the body with me. Slowly but surely, I make it to the toilets. They are pristine and clean. I can only imagine an icy white color in darkness. I keep dragging the body to the end of the bathroom. The blood trail looks murky and black. His body sits against the wall.

I move under the sinks, barely fitting under the metal pipes. I position myself closer to the entrance. Surely one of them will chase after their friend. One of them will come to see what did this. At this point, the tiger story will seem believable enough.

I lay patiently waiting for the moment to strike. Seconds become minutes. The door slowly swings open. Light shines over the trail of blood. The corpse at the end of the room. The white spaces with no paw prints. The human walks in. Just the same as the others, weapon, light armor, and nothing more. He turns frantically. His sixth sense must be going haywire. He knows he's being watched. The darkness must be feeding his paranoia. He steps closer to the body. Once he's right in front of it, he crouches.

He releases the trigger. Uses his free hand to check the body. First, he shakes it. No response. He puts his fingers on the corpse's neck. I crawl out from under the sinks, and I silently step toward my prey. He hasn't moved, just keeps checking the body. As if they had any sense of camaraderie. Another step. My claws extend. My weight gathers on my back legs. I leap on his back. He shouts, but my fangs sink onto the back of his neck, and he goes quiet. His vital functions work, but he doesn't move. I keep severing chunks of him, making sure he doesn't stand or do anything I might regret.

The door swings briefly. I turn to see one armed guy. The light hits me, and he screams as he runs away. His voice echoes down the hallways. I walk away from the mess I created. My body shifts, getting taller up to mirror height. My face covered in grime. My hands darkened with blood.

Are you finished? Ardal speaks into my mind as soon as I'm human. **Corinna is complaining that you're in the bathroom.**

I open the faucet. My hands dip in the cold torrent of water. **I am. You guys said I have to look presentable.** I press the soap dispenser. Usually I wouldn't do this, but the hostages are normal people. Blood will scare them, and maybe scar them. My hands and arms feel smoother. The water and faucet look darker.

Oh my god, he's learning! You go girl! Aurora cheers me on.

I'm not a girl, but thanks. My hands form a cup. When enough water gathers inside it, I clean my face, sinking it into the water. The water becomes murkier. I repeat the process until the only liquid on my face is water. I form the cup again and sip it. My tongue juggles the water inside my mouth. It scrubs my teeth. I spit the water out, and hope for the best. That's as blood free as I'll get. ***Could you tell Corinna to turn on the elevators? I need her to bait them into looking away from the door. After that I only ask that she keep them open without the elevator waiting for people.***

Right.

I dawdle in the bathroom checking if there's any other preparation I could take, but there isn't. My only human form is this one. I'm not equipped to fight them head on. Bullets would kill me, especially with the bigger forms out of the question. Anything heavier than buffalos would bring the floor down. Even hippos and rhinos are a stretch.

She says she can, but that will only leave her with the ability to mess with the cameras if things go wrong.

I'm fine with that. Wait until I'm right outside the door. Then we start. I jump over the trail of blood, and open the door. The darkness is still unreal. Unfortunately, the next part won't be as easy. Corinna said the room the hostages are in couldn't be obscured completely and that makes me vulnerable. I shouldn't use more transformations than needed. I open the door slowly, making sure my movement are undetected. I chirp once. The sound bounces back to me. Clear.

I walk back to the crossroads and turn right. Straight down the hall. I can't miss the bigger doors of the conference room. I step to the side and use my gecko limbs to go up the wall. I crawl onto the ceiling as an extra precaution. I position myself next to the door and wait for my signal.

From inside, high-pitched chimes ring every couple of seconds. They're barely audible because of the sobbing hostages. One man demands, "Someone's at the elevator. Cover it." Some scuffled footsteps move away from the door.

I press my hand against the squeaking wooden door and slowly crawl through. One arm sticks to the door, preventing it from moving. The other reaches for the ceiling to make my silent approach. My arm glue to the cold ceiling. With one push from my legs, I leave the door behind. I look down. The man turns to the swinging door, then scouts the room. He shrugs and goes back to the elevator, marking the eighth floor.

I look at the hostages. A kid stares directly at me. I put my index finger on my lips. The kid nods and glances down at the others.

It will only hinder me if they notice me or if the hostages move. My nocturnal vision is useless in this partially sunlit room. The hostages are huddled next to the window, across the room. I can focus on them later. What matters are the three hostage takers. Two of them are in front of the two elevator doors. The last one stands closer to me that I like.

I crawl left, away from the elevator shafts. I take three steps closer to the windows and five further from the elevators. I use a free hand to trace a path toward the shafts. It's going to be close, not ideal, but I'm somewhat behind all of them. I know of only one animal with the capability of tackling all of them at the same time. Elevators mark ninth floor. Now or never.

My toes release from the ceiling. Then my fingers. On my way to the floor I say, "Moose." My hooves clop against the carpeted floor, as the elevator chimes. I lower my head. My antlers cover the necessary space. The hostages gasp at my transformation. Good grief. Can't they be silent and let me do my thing without dying. The hostage takers turn around.

I charge. I catch the one closest to the door. The other two take aim. I keep running at them. The elevator doors open, but none of the react. Their attention is on the male moose charging them. The guns feel like they move in slow motion. My antlers pick up the second one and then the third one. I stop a meter away from the shafts as I shake my head. The three of them fall. Their screams echo even after the hard thuds collide with the ground floor. The doors close and the assailants are done.

I shift back into my human form. There's no point being a moose when everything is over. My raccoon mask covers my face, and I'm still wearing Aurora's designed clothes. I turn to the still shivering hostages. A couple of them stare, which is uncomfortable. "Are you okay? It's time get you out of here." I put my fists on my hips, 'cause Zach said it was a good idea, that it made me look like a hero. Judging by the looks, it doesn't.

CHAPTER FORTY-TWO: CALL ME WILDLIFE

"Who are you? What do you want?" A man stands, blocking my way to the hostages. His cheek is bruised, and his lips cut. He crosses his arms, clearly not impressed by the pose. Zach's going to be disappointed, but I'm not doing that pose again.

I return to my usual slightly slouched position. "I'm Wildlife. I'm here to rescue you." I stand still. Any movement might scare them.

"You were just a deer," He says. I appreciate the interest, but it's not the time. I just want to be done with this. Save the people, execute the plan guarantee some peace for myself.

I raise a finger. They flinch. I lower it. They return to panicked states. "I was a moose, there's a difference." ***Why am I arguing with a human who doesn't bother to get species right?*** "We can talk about the moose, or we can get you to safety." I offer my hand. Maybe Roy was right, I shouldn't care so much about people not knowing animals.

He's reluctant. "You're right. Let's get out of here." He signals the hostages to stand. None of them look to battered. If anything, it's weird how little harm came to them. Even the abductors were fairly simple to take down. None of them shot more than once. ***It doesn't make sense. Fear should have made them more trigger happy.***

I won't complain. I sigh. This is fine. I can get used to things going smoothly for once. "No one is badly injured?"

"No. Already checked them. Minor injuries at worst. They never shot their weapons." He helps a little girl with flowers in her hair, up. "Did you deal with all ten of them?"

Strange, not using their weapons. A building like this should have a guard. Even if they offer little to no resistance, why not pull the trigger? ***What was their purpose? I don't remember hearing anything about negotiations.*** "Ten? There were only seven pairs of footsteps." I pause, thinking back, but my senses are accurate. I shouldn't have missed anyone. "Sorry. You said ten?" My eyes go wide. "We have to leave. Now." ***Ardal! Something isn't right. Link the others.***

The people look startled. I can't scare them anymore. Adults help kids stand. I head to the door. The elevators won't be functional. I turn to the man who has been talking to me. "Can you describe them?"

We're here, Ardal replies.

The fuck happened! Roy shouts.

Why were they taking hostages in an office building? Why are there kids here? They never tried to shoot anyone. Shouldn't there have been guards in the lobby? How could my senses miss three perpetrators? This can't be happening. I feel sweat gathering above my fur.

Ardal says, **There were no events planned here. You're right. Get out. Now!**

The man from the hostage group nods. "A big burly man, a creepy bald one with a large nose and one that looked like an astronaut."

Fuck! We messed up! Roy shows a degree of care.

Jay wait! Kat shouts. I can only imagine what they're doing. Preparing to leave the car to help me, to save me. That's not an option anymore.

Jay is frantic. **We gotta help him! Bro, we're coming.**

No! Stay there. Ardal. I want you out of my mind. For the first time in my life, I take a survival tactic from Roy. I have to be a commanding lion if we're going to make it out alive.

Ardal and Jay both try to talk me out of it. Especially when Ardal knows how delicate his ability can be around Penumbra. **We can't leave you alone.**

I can't risk you all. Trust me. Please.

He's right. Aurora calms them down. **We can only do one thing. Let him blow our minds. Become a star.**

After all, bio-luminescence shines brightest in the deepest of pressures. I picture her nodding. If anyone understands what's at stake, it's Aurora. My life for the group. Live or die, I will give them the chance they need.

Fine.

Sweet silence. I can focus. I've got a minute or two before things go south. I tell the man, "Hug the walls and stay close to the window area." My hair rises. The air is charged with electricity. If I stand in the center, these people will be fine. I embrace for impact.

The people follow I order. They keep to the concrete walls. There's too much fear, too much sweat. That's how I missed it. If they didn't move, I couldn't sense them. The helicopter, the sirens, the pheromones, the marching abductors. It was all a distraction. I shouldn't have breezed through.

The rodents in the vents squeak, "We're here to help."

I squeak back, "It's fine. Only come out if I really need it." They squeak back without saying words. I really need to learn how to communicate better.

I feel the vibrations of someone down the hall tapping their foot. They're waiting for me to make my move, which means I can take another minute to get ready. Penumbra and the other guy I can deal with. Berserker is the problem. I glance at my hands, then look back at the window. This better work. The hostages are a problem. I'll make do with three transformations or six partial. I gulp. A surge of electricity rises. A really big one.

I take two steps forward. I can handle it. Famous last words for anyone without the strength of a Giganotosaurus. Much like the doors, screams explode within the room. Berserk pushes me across the room until I crash against the glass. It cracks. I step forward. The cracks expand. A mosaic about to break. I shrink to center myself as the door flies out the building, shattering the window.

My right arm burns. I can't move it. It feels off, like it's not connected to me. I take another step. Trickles of blood on my back destroy Aurora's work. She's going to be angry. One more step. Shards shred my flesh. A glass storm covers use for a brief second.

Blood flows from every part of my body. I stagger and look up at the three hunters. Berserker, who overpowers me. Penumbra, who wants to break my mind as a sadistic game of tic-tac-toe. And the masked one, the astronaut, wants to rob me of hope. He's in full body armor, so I guess he fears me. I can't beat them, not like this. Not in their own game. If I play their version of survival, then I'll die. I'll have to defend out of the box.

I shiver at Penumbra's nasal voice saying, "We didn't think you'd fall for this, Theon." Of course, they think Wildlife is me. I gotta play this better than them. They know my voice. Time to give it a twist. I need blue whale's vocal cords.

A trickle of blood flows down my scalp, and traverses the opening on my brow. "You must have me mistaken." My voice is deeper and distorted. The O's and U's are elongated, but I'll pay that prize. "I'm Wildlife. I won't let you harm these people." The sun's rays illuminate me and my side of the room. Silence. This is bad.

Berserker's eyes are red flares. He looks at my bloody self, and they glow even brighter. "You got guts. Looking forward to spilling them." He laughs. It's a resounding bell, so loud the hostages step closer to the window.

I stand tall. I won't let them take me without a fight. "Then I have nothing to worry about." I wince as my arm sways with the wind.

The astronaut points at me. "You? Bleeding and with a bad arm? Don't make us laugh." He copies the pose I did earlier. A naturally vain human. The hostages are looking at me, wondering if I can save them. I don't need a pose to be the hero they need. "We have an offer. If you come with us, we won't kill you."

Penumbra raises his hand. "The offer is for you, Wildlife. We could use someone with your unique skills. Why stay and be killed with all those people? They won't like you. They'll abandon you or turn on you when they get the chance. Do yourself a favor. Leave them." He extends his hand to me.

I could leave of my own will. I glance behind me. A flying snake could do the trick or even a draco. People have done nothing for me. They hurt me a lot, more than anyone deserves. More than anyone should have to endure. My legs tremble. I can leave. Forget about all of this, become an animal forever. I could be free. It would mean abandoning my friends and the people who are still by my side. My friends showed me there is hope and kindness, that my life is worth. I'm not going to waste it running away from being who I want to be. I can be both animal and human. They aren't mutually exclusive.

Turning my back on my friends and these people trapped in a situation they never asked for would be unfair. They're innocent. Survival demands I leave, but for the sake of my pack, I have to stay. I'll stay for everyone who needs me. I'll be the one who protects those without a voice. "People do hurt others. And sometimes they do it because they want to. I can't be certain about the people here, but I don't get to decide, they do. Their lives and their choices will be theirs, just as mine are mine to make. I choose to be myself, my way. The pain is worth it in the long run."

Penumbra shakes his head. "Disappointing. We hoped you were reasonable enough."

I know what's next before it happens. With all these people around and at this height my options are limited. I take a deep breath. "Diplodocus tail. Ankylosaurus tail club. Stegosaurus scutes." A long whip like tail stretches out the window. The end is bulky, pulling me back. Bony plates grow on my back. The scutes on my tail turn red. Gravity pulls the fifteen-meter tail, smashing it against the windows one floor down. "Climb down." I glance at the adult who I'd spoken to before. "Can I trust you to get them to safety while I deal with stuff here?"

"Yes. Let me give you a fighting chance." He approaches and grabs my dislocated arm.

Fangs pierce my lips. A red spring is created under my breath. I force my good fist to close.

"This will hurt." In one quick move, he puts it back in place.

There's a click. The scream stays in my throat, a pained roar rumbles through Monterrey.

I can feel my arm, but I don't dare to move it. "Why?"

He let's go. "'Cause you are a hero. I'll get everyone out." He pats my back.

"Right." It's weird to hear a stranger use that word in reference to me. I'm a guy doing the right thing. I could have left, but then I wouldn't be better any than Juan or Maria, or everyone else. "Get them moving. And don't listen to a word they say." I point at the three hunters.

"You heard Wildlife. Use his tail. Use the plates to climb down." He stands near the base of my tail. Encouraging others to climb down.

The first ones are heavy, but once I find my footing, my tail is stable. The shards of glass embed themselves in the soles of my feet. Blood refracts from the glass shards marking the beginning of the end, for one of us. I can stand up for those who can't, the way animals stood up for me.

CHAPTER FORTY-THREE: THE FIRST HERO

The three bodies holding on to my stegosaur scutes pull on me. At this rate, we'll all die. I need a way to fight back without moving. How am I going to do that? They only need one bullet to end me or if they learned their lesson last time, the right sound. Both are terrifying, but I fear sound more than the weapon. A bullet could stagger me, but even with an injury, I can hold on and fight. Sound is the worst-case scenario.

I smile nervously. My eyes never look straight ahead. If Penumbra's abilities work as I think they do, looking at him is a mistake. I shrug, trying to imitate Roy and Ardal's natural confidence. "So, what's your goal here. Surely either one of you could have killed us." I need time to think. Venom is one of my defense options, but I doubt Berserker would care about that. My best option is running away, but I can't. I glance back to check on the hostages' progress. Less than half of them are free.

"You, of course." Penumbra smiles, his sunglasses cover his eyes. "And your colleagues." My body jerks as a heavier hostage makes its way down my tail. Penumbra pulls out a walkie-talkie. "Our leader hoped to meet you. He sees potential what you have done and can do for our cause." He toys with the communication device, clicks the button, and aims the speaker toward me.

A weight lifts from my tail before a new one goes down. Fifteen to go. I keep my center of gravity low, preventing the hostages from pulling me out the window. "You have a terrible grasp of how to talk to people. And that's coming from an animal like myself." I swipe some of the blood coursing down my face with my good arm. "Kidnapping, attacking, and threatening people aren't clear signs that you want to talk."

"That's on my team," a voice says through the device. Corinna won't be able to track it. We really weren't prepared for this. "You're right. I send my apologies for the distress we've caused you."

I smile weakly, holding my arm in place. "I can't say I accept that, seeing as I'm bleeding."

The voice again. "We had to make sure you didn't escape like the last times."

I shrug. "This is the first time I've met your team. It seems you've known me for longer." Keep the conversation flowing. That's what Ardal said I should do if I needed to buy time. Kat mentioned appealing to their emotions. Everyone has them so if I can make them hesitate, I'm already ahead. "Not a good first impression. But you aren't talking to me to apologize." Everything has a purpose. It'll buy me more time.

The scurrying in the vents grows louder to my sensitive ears. Don't react. They're building up. Okay, I have two strategies I need to play simultaneously. Berserker is still the problem here. He'll beat me in any battle. I don't think even my electric eel abilities could stop him. Flying seems the best way to survive. Now, how do I get Penumbra close to me? I don't need to bite or inject. I can shoot my venom; I need his sunglasses off.

"Right. Clever. You have survived six months on your own. I'm offering you a proposal." He pauses.

It gives me a chance to look back at the thirteen people behind me. They move fast once adrenaline kicks in. So long as they are careful climbing down. There are no safety nets and no ways of looking after them if they fall.

The device continues, "You can join us, or you can renounce to your abilities. The decision is yours."

"I like it better when they fight back." Berserker cracks his knuckles.

My left leg wants to move backward. I fight against the instinct. Instincts have never failed me, but today I have to listen to my frontal lobe. I'm not a scared impala blindly running from a lioness. I'm like the crow. I have to think tactically. Rely on my brains. I gulp. "I guessed you wanted that." I glance back and the hostages are hesitating to move. Some are even gravitating toward our assailants. "But that isn't the whole story. If I join you, none of these people would survive. And if I don't, I'll also be a casualty. My options are let them die, or die with them. Not the best options."

"Yes, but you could also erase their memories about this day," the voice says.

The implications are terrifying. Ardal's nightmares about Helena and Daemon would come true, same with Roy. I doubt he'll allow anyone to tell him what to do. What would happen to Jay and Zach if these people figure things out? The pack's survival is at stake. I won't let them down, but I also have to keep these hostages safe. If they live, Penumbra's group will be under more scrutiny. I take a deep breath. "Before I answer, I have a question. Why is it important to keep what we can do hidden?"

The person on the radio chuckles. "For the safety of the masses. Too many people would abuse their abilities."

The astronaut is unreadable. His helmet makes it harder to guess what he thinks, and his thick clothing captures the odors in a textile prison. Penumbra arcs his brows. His mouth makes an upside-down smile. Berserker smirks. He awaits his chance, knowing it's coming. Knowing as well as I that he could destroy me. Swat me like a fly. Last time my ribs almost cracked; this time, I think he'll shatter them.

I glance back. Eleven hostages remain. I hold firm. "Might be, but if everyone has access to them, we could make advancements in technology, science, the arts, and help protect the planet." I shift my weight constantly to avoid the glass shards sinking deeper into my feet.

"They would kill and murder. They would steal and try to conquer." The voice from the radio sounds displeased with my answer.

I don't think I'll be able to delay much longer. "I'm here. I haven't done anything like that." I turn back. Ten. Can they climb down faster? At this rate, at least half of us will die.

He chuckles again. "What about the acclaimed Insect Thief? Or Monterrey's Monster, wouldn't that be you? Aren't you the one who scared game hunters in the mountains?"

I knew this could only come to bite me back. How can I twist it back? There has to be an animal that can help. My mind wanders to Aurora and Zach. They aren't animals. Zach said I was a hero, 'cause I did the right things. And he's right, stopping hunting is right. But Aurora flashes the pretty of a colors poison dart frog. To us it's pretty, but to other creatures it's a warning sign. We distorted the view, so what's one more? "Protecting flora and fauna is right. There's no action from other people to help, so I'll do it."

"So harassing and disturbing hunters is right? Just for a bunch of animals and plants." The three of them look at me, awaiting an answer that will unleash a storm.

I bite my lip. Slow my pulse. I won't let them anger me. I won't let them insult nature like it's worthless. The vents keep rumbling to the sound of claws and squeaks. My fangs let go of my lip. "Someone has to stand up for nature. Since those with the means won't." I point at their group. "Our world needs heroes. I'll be one, if I must."

"But you can't deny the Insect Thief's actions."

Eight hostages remain. "As far as I know they haven't hurt anyone. Only stolen. I can't speak for them though. So, I won't give an opinion." He's hell bent on Roy's actions, which means I have to make them less than something else. Make them minuscule. Roy has never hurt people while stealing, in fact he only hurt people in self-defense. Most of the damage was done by the rest of us, and in self-defense. It's like corralling a diamondback rattlesnake and expecting it to lie down and die. No, it fights back to survive. The rattle was the warning, and we gave it. They forced our hand to bite. This isn't our fault. Then it occurs to me. "But your group does exactly what you want to prevent." I take a deep breath and clench my fists. I soak in the rays of sunlight feeding heat into my cold body. Being part reptilian makes a difference here. "You want to keep us under control while your lackeys do all the things you claim to want to prevent. They kill the innocent. They torment the weak. They hunt those who seek to live their lives and do good. The destroy property and harm those who don't want to be involved." My voice rises. I feel the animal DNA pushing through, giving me life to sustain my claim. "So, tell me, how are you not the ones in the wrong?"

"It's different."

I shake my head, taking the opportunity to see the seven people left behind me. "No, it's not. That's an excuse all bullies use. It's all different if you do it, not if I do it." I grin. I know Corinna, Mercurio and Jess will laugh about this. Undeniable logic. "You're way worse than a petty thief who never hurt anyone. You willingly destroyed lives. Ended them. If you think your actions are different, then you've already became what I knew you always were. A sad human, looking to overpower those who want to rise." My nostrils flare.

"It's for the sake of the world. Can't you see our actions are justified?"

I tilt my head. "No. It's not justified. Even in nature creatures don't seek to destroy others. They seek to evolve, and maintain balance. Right now, I see a human drunk on power, afraid of others, trampling over lives and dreams. "Five people left. They aren't siamangs, but they are getting there. "Behind me, there's a city that believes it's justified living out of harmony with nature. A culture that believes it's justified imposing ridiculous gender norms on people and rejecting those people if they refuse to comply." I can feel my body wanting to shift and tear them apart. I have to remain calm and collected. I have to be still like the Nile crocodiles, and wait for the moment. "The only thing that is ever justified is change for the betterment of the world. And what you are doing doesn't change anything." One more glimpse back. Three.

"We are protecting everyone."

I sigh. They're beyond reason. I understand now why Kat and Jay act the way they do. Sometimes you have to let others realize the fault in their thoughts. I get it. "You're protecting yourself." I calculate the distance between me and the enemies. "Sticking to the same rules and standards as before requires nothing." I think about the people backing me up and the animals around me. "But changing, that requires bravery even when you're trembling in fear. Change hurts, but not as much as standing still. So come what may, I'm done fleeing. No matter what happens, I won't be broken, and I will stand tall against whatever the world may throw at me. Whether it's you people"—I point at them. My body steady and stoic. I feel like an aurochs.—"or a group of bullies. I'm Wildlife. Defender of the voiceless, protector of the weak, and hero of the animal kingdom!"

Only the leader of the hostages remains.

He holds from my scutes, nods, and gives a thumbs up. "Good luck. I believe in you."

I smile. For once, I believe it, and most importantly, I believe in myself. I will survive. I will live.

An order comes from the radio. "I see. Do with him as you see fit."

CHAPTER FORTY-FOUR: UNLIKELY SURVIVOR

Cool air mingles with the hot gusts coming from outside. The scent of fear is strong, but coming from an unexpected direction, as if the source was right in front of me. Strange. I tried the axolotl regeneration, but it was in vain. My arm is still sore, and I know a fight is coming. I think about my encounters with Penumbra, Berserker, and the astronaut. What have I learned?

Three monsters stand before me. No matter how much Ardal would say I'm a smart, cunning person, even he would falter if he saw this. This is a nightmare. I'm not equipped to fight them head on. Tugs on my tail still prevent me from moving. The shards of glass puncture my feet. If they were smart, they would send Berserker against me, and I would lose. He's easily the size of a gorilla. Guy is massive and his red hair is outshined by his glowing bloody eyes. I have to avoid that outcome. My chances against him are null. Escape is my only survival option. Unless I can isolate him from attacking. If I somehow lure in the other two, maybe he'll hold back, wait to attack on his own.

I've seen Penumbra twice before. He enjoys tormenting others. I shake his creepy smile from my head. They way he relishes making people fear is horrendous. He toys with his food but doesn't eat it. The only time he lost his footing was when

Roy and Lucas actively intervened. Mostly Roy managed to irritate him, but that wouldn't be enough to unbalance him here.

I wish Ardal could listen to my thoughts right now. He would know what to do. Penumbra's abilities will be tricky to counter. For all I know, I have to fight blind since even animals are affected by his power. That's not an option. There has to be a weak point maybe not in the power, but in him. There has to be a better way to learn about him than blindly guessing.

Everyone's ability says something about them. Lucas and I love what our abilities do, but I loved animals before I got my abilities. Roy and Aurora's abilities reflect their personalities; a king and a shining star. Their abilities are about who they are now, in the present. What about Corinna and Ardal? Their abilities simplify something they wished they could do, something they wanted in the future.

Where does that leave Penumbra? Past, present, or future? The fear pheromones are my only clue. They could come from only two individuals, him, and the astronaut. The astronaut isn't fearless, but he isn't fearful. If anything, he's defiant like Berserker. He enjoys the challenge. Penumbra is afraid. His power reflects his personality then, and his desire to make people more afraid than him. I let a smile slip onto my face.

"What are you smiling at?" The astronaut guy says, putting his hands on his holster.

I glance at him. "Nothing." I shrug and my body lightens. It knows.

I'm not sure what the astronaut's power is, but it doesn't matter. I just need every rodent in position. They can take them out.

"I was thinking on how sad it is for you three to gang up on me. I get it animals do it in the wild, but I didn't think big guy was the kind to stoop to that level." I cross my fingers, hope this next line works. "He seems capable of taking things down on his own. I guess he's here to babysit the bald one."

The astronaut laughs.

"Call me Berserker." He nods approvingly. There's hope. He turns to Penumbra and punches him in the shoulder. "Penumbra is pretty weak. Someone has to save his ass." The glow from Berserker's eyes shines brighter. The sense of pressure is gone. I don't feel like someone is stalking me for my pelt. I try to maintain my calm. If they don't see me getting anxious or fearful, I can manage.

Penumbra's face changes and his forehead creases. He turns to his allies as he speaks and points at me. "Take him down. It's an order."

The astronaut shrugs. "You aren't my boss." He points his gun at me, nonetheless.

I stagger. I should have expected that. He doesn't play around. I have enough shape changes to handle a bullet, so long he doesn't hit my head or heart. The astronaut might not be affected by my words, but he was never the intended target. I take a second to listen to the world. Winds whisper. Crowds gasp and shout from the distant ground floor. Glass cracks under the weight of the ex-hostages. In the vents, the grating sound of claws clicking against metal and the squeaks communicate a path forward. They're almost above the astronaut. "Why would you boss around your babysitter? I though the more capable one got to be in charge. At least that's how it works in nature."

Berserker smiles at me. It seems genuine, but after what Zamir did, I'm not sure. "Nah., I want to take him on my own."

Penumbra takes off his sunglasses, uncovering the black voids he has for eyes. "I'm surrounded by idiots. Don't you see he's afraid of you?" He stares right at Berserker's glowing eyes, but nothing happens. Berserker looks amused at the attempt.

My ears perk up. I can't keep neutral. I have to smile. Some people would fear me because of the way my teeth look Some would call me a villain for clearly having darker intentions. "I'm not sure about that. Fear is contagious after all, and you stink of it." I take a whiff. His fear smells like a crippling, stagnated tear. The smell is similar to my fear. Mine used to smell like burning plants, the smoke beckoning me to run away.

He turns and aims his gaze at me. "What do you know about fear?"

I close my eyes and shrug. "That you are pathetic. Inflicting on others what you can't tolerate yourself. You're afraid, but feel better by making others feel the same. I guess you're afraid of me, or maybe Berserker, since he seems unaffected by your abilities."

"I'll show you who's afraid," Penumbra says. His footsteps draw close. He walks in a manner that imitates Roy's swagger, but Penumbra is a pale imitation.

"You?" Time to try one last trick. I've always used words to transform. This time I need to do so without them, after all, words are the manifestation of thoughts. If I focus, I might be able to do this without alerting them of my plans. I close my eyes for one second. **Spitting cobra fangs and venom glands. White rhinoceros eyes.** My teeth become fragile and light. They extend backward. Two long fangs are ready to move at will. The world looks blurry. Penumbra will be blurry until he is four meters away from me. After that, I'll just have to close my eyes and shoot. Nothing moves withing my scope. I stare at the point he was.

He grunts. "Why is it not working?"

"Maybe I have short range vision, or maybe your power is pretty bad." I focus on the blurry figures in the back. "I'm leaning toward the latter."

Penumbra comes into sight. The figure is there, but the details are blurry at best. I need to keep that way. His mouth and eyes are specs on his face. It looks like a bad movie or computer game. Things merge and distort. He's too close for me to speak, he'd notice my fangs now. Sound echoes in the empty room. He takes a couple more steps. Not sure how close he is. Maybe one more step. I pretending that my tail still carries more weight than it should. Penumbra becomes clear. His blackened sockets stare at me.

I open my mouth. My fangs extend, pointing toward him. Yellow liquid sprays upward as I move my head back. I only need one drop in his eyes and he'll be out. Liquid splashes over his face. He raises his arms to eye level too late. The yellow liquid rolls down his face pretending to be his tears.

Penumbra steps back and screams. His hands covering his eyes. I take my chance. My eyes return to normal. My fangs become teeth. Penumbra is stumbling around. He's helpless. I could tell him an easy solution, but if he can't see, he can't make us afraid. Penumbra collides with the wall opposite the elevator shafts. He uses it to guide his path.

Berserker smiles. He leans against the wall beside the door and waits for his moment. He has to know I stand no chance against him. Meanwhile, the astronaut aims his gun at me. I can't tell what's going on in his mind. My legs are flexed. My arms ready to shift. My throat holds the call to war.

The astronaut shoots. I don't move. I have to continue with this charade, for my plan to work. If my enemies think I'm incapable of moving, I'll catch them off guard. My leg feels like it's been punched. I fall to my knee. Blood pours from the hole in my pants. Aurora isn't going to be happy. I crawl closer to the window. Glass presses against my gloves. Fortunately, the leather and bandages prevent small shards from reaching my skin.

The astronaut takes his mask off. He isn't much different from me. Black hair, dark eyes, and more or less my age. His ears are pierced, bunch of earrings hang from each side. He takes aim again. "I'm Diego. This is payback for last time."

I squeak, which makes him smile. The vents tremble as thousands of rodents fall from the ceiling. Pour from the shafts and walls. A black and brown flood consumes the room. They ignore Berserker. Their survival instinct keeps them clear. The rats and mice swarm Diego, biting and scratching. They tear him apart. Soon enough it's a ball of rodents with him at the center trying to escape as they drag him to the floor.

I stand. My left leg holds most of my weight. Blood trickles all the way down to my feet. It's just me and Berserker now. I can handle him. I can fly and he can't. Alright. I don't move. The precipice is just three steps away; I can get there as a bird. My body lurches. My energy levels are dangerously low, but I know I have one more transformation. I grit my teeth against the pain. Berserker can't see me weak, or I'll be done.

Berserker's eyes are scarlet red, just like a red-eyed tree frog. His neck cracks to each side. He loosens his shoulders. "Finally, you and me." He smiles. The moment he looks at the blood trickling down my leg, his eyes become like two suns. The tension in his body is on a different level. My electroreception feels like he's the center of gravity. His smile keeps growing under the crimson glow. "Make it fun."

I look up at him. "I'm not here for your entertainment." My heart pumps faster, draining me of my vital liquid, and worse, of my energy reserve. "If anything, I'll disappoint." There is one thing I need him to do. "Let's get this over with. I'm here. Come and get me."

His reply is a simple one. He charges at me. He's faster than I thought he'd be. Maybe faster than a horse. What mess did I get into this time? It doesn't help that he's way taller. His steps make the floor tremble and crush the glass into fine sand. I quiver in response. My body fails to respond. I trip and fall to the ground. My tail pulls me to the edge. I look at the floor. Pain locks my leg; I won't be able to glide.

At his speed, he won't be able to stop. I hold on to the window's edge ignoring the glass shards cutting into me, but this is my last chance. Whatever survival instinct left kicks in. The world plays out slowly as shards of glass fall with me. My tail recoils back. The blue sky and the searing sun watch as I let the winds decide my fate.

Berserker shadows part of my view, jumping after me. He's a desperate creature looking for food. Berserker falls faster than my droplets of blood and they stain his already red face as he flies toward me with his unquenchable thirst for my demise.

He might hear my words, but I hope the wind and city sounds are louder than me. My arms cross over my chest. Here it goes, with half a transformation to spare. "Rock dove." I spiral downwards, becoming a gray meteor of feathers. The ninth and eighth floors pass me fast. Berserker reaches out for me.

I lean away from the building; in a fall that will prove someone's death. Berserker swipes at the air, creating a gust that pushes me further away. He does it again, trying to reach me.

His fingers bluntly strike my rectrices. A few flutter upwards. He will catch me soon. I extend my wings and the wind pushes against them. I allow it to take me up.

Berserker swings his arms and legs. If I'm built to avoid peregrine falcons, I can avoid a man losing control in the air. He swings his left arm, creating more gusts of wind. My wings push down against it. He tries to swat me out of the air, but that's like trying to force a shark to stop swimming by pushing water in its direction. He tries to kick me, but I weave between his legs and then I'm above him.

He keeps falling as people scream. I keep flying and dripping blood. I fly far away toward the city, but not far enough. My body in its weakened state, staggers in the air. Any current pushes me where it will. I lose altitude. My wings feel heavy, though they're as hollow as a cave. My feathers slow my descend. Flashes of the red car I'm flying toward come and go as I get closer.

Buildings get higher. The ground closer not by will, but by the nature of my skills. Just as I'm about to hit the ground, I change form. The worst thing I can do is stay as a dove. There would be no way for anyone else to help me. The soles of my shoes hit the asphalt. My body gives in, rolling to the ground a meter away from the car, where I collapse on the burning asphalt.

Theon!

CHAPTER FORTY-FIVE: CLEVER FOX

August 19, 2013

It's early in the morning, earlier than I usually get up. We're getting a classroom on the first floor because stairs are hard for me now. The sun is peeking over the mountains and the sky is purple and blue. After seeing the bandages and the wobble in my walk, the administrative staff decided I not only needed to be on the first floor, but in the closest building to the student drop off.

I glance at my phone while the secretary prepares her desk, insisting she help me to the classroom. Every news outlet shows images of me. Some of the hostages too pictures while I wasn't paying attention. Corinna leaked a couple from the building's security system. The news calls it a lucky shot that they saw the way I transformed, but I know it was planned. I shrug it off. I never wanted the attention. I was fine being merely another creature of the world, but this is what I need to survive, so I'll endure it.

The secretary takes my uninjured arm and walks me to class. Even with her help, my pace is slow. My right leg begs me to stop, and my left arm is unusable for a while. If it was up to me, I would have a red kangaroo tail to support me, but I can't; Wildlife is a hero and a wanted man.

The secretary is watching me struggling to walk.

I smile at her. "I'm okay. The cuts are irritating with all the bandages."

"You could take classes from home." She slows her stride and halfway turns, an invitation to go home.

I shake my head. "My doctor said I would be fine." He didn't, but I don't want to go home. Lucas and my parents have made it awkward. Lucas barely talks to me. I'm fine with that, but my parents have been scolding me for getting injured on a mysterious hiking trip I decided to take. Mostly they're mad I went hiking with friends and they didn't want me to. Roy has been mediating, and by that, I mean, he said it was his idea. My parents got quiet when Roy took responsibility because he sent their complaints to the curb.

"Are you sure? We can accommodate it."

I take another step forward. "No, thank you. I'm fine as it is." I turn away. Ducks trail behind me, then pretend to turn toward the green areas. Squirrels playfully chatter in the trees. Doves and magpies watch over me from the rooftops. It'll all change once I step inside.

The secretary is kind enough to leave my bag on the seat next to the door. She waits for me to sit before speaking again. "If you need anything, the faculty has been told to assist you."

"Thank you." I wave at her with my good arm, and I take a deep breath. She smells like perfume and lavender, but underneath it there's a warm smell. It moves around, but lacks the energy of anxiety. Concern? There truly are good people in the world. It's time I accept I'm as much a part of this species as everyone else, though I'm also part of every species with a vertebra. I can be part of both worlds; some people like me for who I am, and animals stick with me, even come to my aid every chance they get. I might fit in both worlds completely, but that doesn't mean I don't have my pack filled with people and animals alike.

I slowly take out my materials for the class with my one functional arm. Flying did a number on my dislocated shoulder. I'll need months to recover completely according to the doctor. Even with the axolotl cells working, it'll be about the same time to heal, but it'll ensure I don't become permanently prone to repeating the injury. Pens, notebook, liquid paper, and the good old trusty brownies. If Minos could come close to me I'd have a feast for the both of us, but it's impossible. Kyra, Thor, and the tortoises made it clear they'll keep their distance because of how it could be interpreted. So, I have to endure being a lone wolf for a little longer. **What's a couple of weeks compared to years of loneliness?**

I can't even slump in my chair without feeling pain. I take out the bottle of black tea I made myself and try to relax. I wait alone for a couple of minutes, hoping Jay and Kat arrive early. With them around, I feel I could do anything and everything. Most importantly, I could survive the awkwardness of Lucy, Haruka and DJ being in the same classroom as me. I won't get my hopes up. Jay's puppy attitude will delay him until the bell rings and Kat is usually late.

The door swings open. *Please be Kat. For once, let her be the first to come in so I have help dealing with people asking about my non-existent hiking trip.* I'm not sure how I'll handle that without her. I turn back to the door carefully so I don't stretch my neck too much and see a person I thought I wouldn't see again. "Juan?"

His darker skin and black wavy hair contrast with his crystal blue eyes. We look at each other without saying a word. "Sorry, I didn't know you were in this class. I won't bother you." He closes the door. His shoulders droop.

I have a bitter taste in my mouth. I can't help but stare, not because of what everyone says about him, but because I've been an idiot. He was just a kid like me. No one is perfect. I know I'm not. Even animals and plants have things they aren't good at. I lick my lips to try to get rid of the vile flavor in my mouth. I shift uncomfortably on the chair, turning away from him and his path to the other side of the room. The pit in my stomach rises to my esophagus.

I know Kat and Ardal would say I should talk to him, that things will be fine. Honestly, after ten months I doubt it. I was rude to him. Roy would slap me in the back of the head because I'm being a coward. I bite my lip before the words in my head are able to form. "Hey…" I silently debate if talking to him is the right choice. Anyone I interact with immediately gets dragged into my issues. "How are you liking this school?"

Juan turns around. He searches for another person, even looks for my phone. He points at himself. "Better than the last one. I thought you didn't want anything to do with me." He places his laptop on the desk, then searches for something inside his bag.

"Sorry, I wasn't thinking straight."

He shakes his head. "You know I meant the things I said." He acts cold, but his tone lowers. In the same way a sunny day can become a dreadful minute through the bellow of a jaguar on the prowl. It makes sense. I acted like an irritated Euplocephalus.

I sigh. "I know. I thought pushing you away was the only way to ensure people didn't harass you. I also meant the forgiveness thing. You didn't do anything to me." I bite my brownie.

He stops rummaging through his bag. "And I didn't help you either." He turns around clearing the wavy hair off his face. "You still thought of me, and the consequences more than I did. I wanted to do fix things."

I glance at the door. Someone taps their feet outside, but waits for the two of us to finish our conversation. "Somethings can't be fixed. We just have to move past them. I was so bitter about how they all treated me that I forgot to see that other people could be kind. That was a mistake." My ears twitch at the sound of a second pair of shoes stalling outside. The girls do their best to keep it low, but it's in vain. Lucy and Haruka should know better than to whisper.

"You've changed." He smiles.

I feel more or less the same, happier maybe. In a sense, more complete than I was before. I look down at the sling and the bandaged leg. "Well, I'm covered in bandages."

More people gather outside. There are three, maybe four people. The scents mix up too much to tell.

He shrugs. "Not what I meant." He pauses to give me a minute, then asks, "What happened?"

"Hiking accident. I tripped and fell off a cliff."

"You what?" DJ forces the door open. He looks at me, at the sling and the stiff leg. He glances at my bandages and careful movements. DJ takes two steps and ends up beside me. "Why didn't you stay home?"

"Doctor said I was fine. Dislocated shoulder, a couple of cuts, and an almost broken leg. Nothing serious." I bite my cheeks, honestly, I would rather be home, but not being here would be more suspicious than attending class in this condition.

"Right." He keeps walking to the front seats with his laptop. He also pulls out his phone, looks back at me, then points at it.

DJ: *Are you sure about this?*

Theon: *It's my only survival strategy. I thought you didn't care.*

DJ: *I don't agree with your methods. No matter what happened, you did the right things. There's some hope for you.*

Theon: You know there isn't, but what about hope for the rest?

DJ: 100% chance if they all work together.

Theon: How's it looking now?

DJ: 25%

Theon: Would you reconsider joining?

DJ: I don't know if I can be useful. I'll think about it.

I look up at him. I might have cleared the smog with Juan, but my problems just multiply. I can respect his decision. There's no point in forcing him to evolve into what I need. I have to stay let him evolve into what he wants.

Lucy and Haruka wait until I turn to the front of the class. As much as they try, I can hear everything they do. I can smell their nervousness. The vacillation in their steps, hesitating to come into sight. Not much I can do other than pretend to be alright. I sink into my thoughts, pretending to not notice them. They take their seats far away, imitating Juan.

Kat and Jay get to class and take the seats near me. They both smile and team up with me for all the lesson.

As class ends, I mutter, "Are you ready for the weekend?"

CHAPTER FORTY-SIX: UNTAMED

August 30, 2013

SWARM has overshadowed the news of Wildlife. I smile. Finally, my face is out of the media. Roy has taken over. He sparked a debate over whether doing something good makes him less of a criminal after stealing for the past year, or if it doesn't matter. Whatever the results, I believe that doesn't matter. No creature can be defined through one lens. One can't blame a lion for looking down on everyone in his territory when he'll also protect the territory and everyone in it. The only downside is that Roy is acting more entitled than before. He's been insufferable to everyone outside our small group. It's not that he likes them, but there's a degree of camaraderie or respect. The glint in his eyes looks more alive than before, although something tells me he isn't even close to done.

Kat pokes at my unharmed shoulder. "What are you smiling at?" She leans in, tiptoeing to try to see my phone's screen.

I lower my hand and show her some of the statements Roy made. "Interviews aren't free. For more details call my agent." "My business hours are nine to two. Don't fucking bother after those times." "You can shove your complaints up your ass." I shake my head as we wait under the tree by the school entrance. "He really did hog the spotlight." I stare at the pictures of him not sure how Aurora made him look so powerful.

The sleeveless hoodie and the crown portray him being in control. No one questions him. The golden necklace with the octopus design is great.

"You hate the attention." She tugs my arm.

I tilt my head, on the lookout for Ardal and his car, not because I want this moment to end, if anything, I dread what's next. Tonight, will be brutal. If we make one wrong move, everything will be over. "It's not that. I'm just nervous…" I let the words linger longer than I should.

"Chill! Bee happy." Jay buzzes. He shakes me as he takes my backpack and pokes at my stomach. I appreciate the attempt at levity, but I do need a moment.

Kat puts her hands on Jay's, calming him. "Be careful. He's still healing."

I giggle. "Don't worry about it. It's only my shoulder. Everything else has basically healed." I swallow the pain that surges from my leg and shoulder. There's no point in them knowing I'm not there yet. Specially since I have to help tonight. I abstain from scratching any part of my body. With my abilities back I don't want to risk my claws accidentally incapacitating me or sending the wrong message. I'm especially wary of Kat or Ardal realizing if I did so. I return to my phone to message someone who was owed a message earlier.

Theon: I can't hang around today. Ardal and Aurora have their debut. I have to be there.

Zach: Hmmmm. You still have the sling.

Theon: I'll be fine. I just have to distract anyone from interfering with them. Roy will be there.

Zach: Okay.

Theon: What if we hang tomorrow? We can still play some games and talk.

Zach: You have boys' night.

Theon: You remembered that?

Zach: I got an agenda. He sends a picture of it. Green with video game character decals.

Theon: Nice. Why did you get one?

Zach: 'Cause I wanted to pay more attention. It helps me to take notes.

Theon: Hey, don't worry about guys night. You're part of us. It isn't fair to leave you out because you aren't in the same city.

Zach: I wasn't invited.

Theon: Now you are.

Zach: I don't know.

Theon: Come on! It'll be fun!

Zach: Let me think about it.

Theon: Sure. I'll talk to you after we do the super heroing thing.

Zach: Good Luck.

I stuff my phone inside my pocket. My friends are still engaged in their own bubble of talking to everyone and spreading joy and happiness as if it were medicine. All the students and teachers leave with grins and laughter. I can't say I blame them. It's difficult to be in anything other than in a good mood around these two, even for me.

Ardal's red convertible parks right in front of us. He takes his sunglasses off. His smirk exudes confidence and warmth. He knows things will go well. We're sure Corinna's idea, and my plan will work to perfection. "Get in." He lowers the sonorous sounds of his music to accommodate my sensitive hearing.

"Shotgun." Jay goes to the back and drops the bags in the trunk. In the meantime, Kat takes her seat behind the pilot. I waddle to sit behind the copilot. Jay secures the trunk and then jumps in front of me.

"Ready?" Ardal asks, but before we can respond, we're driving away from school. The students look at us. Some have snake jaws. Everyone will be talking about us next Monday. I don't want that. At least Kat and Jay will be able to take the heat of it. Most of it will be directed at how they know Ardal. When in fact Ardal and I are closer than most would assume. A tightly knit pack made out of a labrador, a crimson macaw, a red fox, a lovebird, a lion, an African elephant, a kookaburra, a bird of paradise, and a saltwater crocodile.

"Yes?"

He fixes the rear-view mirror, so both Kat and I are reflected in. Even with the sunglasses, I know he's looking at me. "Did your injuries heal?" One of his eyebrow's arcs.

I stare at the city as we take the same route, we always take to his mountain home. It has become our base of operations. "I'm fine."

His sunglasses lower, revealing his emerald eyes. "I don't have to read minds to know you lie." He sighs. "Just take care. Mercurio and Jess warned you about the regeneration."

I put weight on my good arm while looking at the slower cars that blur to my different senses. "I know. I'll be careful." Regeneration isn't a foolproof solution. If my arm isn't attached properly, it will regenerate deformed or unusable. Worst-case scenario, we'll have to cut it off. It might take years to fully grow back. I'd rather not lack an arm for longer than I already have.

"Promise." He pushes his sunglasses back up.

I roll my eyes. "I promise." I hum to the melody the stereo plays. Ardal has prepared music that resonates with me. It reminds me of Lucas. "I've been thinking about something DJ said."

"Bro, DJ talked to you? Dope!" Jay raises his arms above us, feeling the wind. If it wasn't for Ardal, he would be standing up in the convertible. Letting go.

Kat smiles in my direction. "What did he say?" She lets her hair go. It resembles a fiery trail, a fox tail or a chestnut horse mane flowing in the wind.

I scoot closer to the middle so everyone can hear. "That we need everyone in order to have a chance. I want everyone back, but not because of that. I want to help them. It's the least I can do after some of them got dragged into this because of me." I put my right hand on the copilot's headrest to leverage myself closer to the front.

"I think that's a great idea." Kat chimes in. Now she's right beside me, between Ardal and Jay.

Ardal breaks a laugh. "You've changed. I'm proud of you."

"Thank you." I blush, mostly because those are words, I thought I would never hear. *I'm worth something.*

Ardal glances at me. "You were always worth it." He must have seen me make a face, or he just knows me well enough to know my inner thoughts. I don't complain 'cause he's right.

"Bro! We have to call everyone. Dibs on Ambrose!"

I put my hand on his shoulder. "I appreciate the help, but we have to take it slow. Help those who need it more." I drift back to what Ardal's fears showed. Daemon and Helena are urgent. They need us right now. They don't need *us* though, they need Lucas. Lucas is just a kid, but I think Roy and I can handle that. "We start with Lucas. He wasn't opposed to being a hero."

Kat tilts her head and puts her hands over her heart. "Aww. I miss him."

"Mini-Theon!"

Ardal agrees. "It's settled."

I turn to Kat. "I know this is asking a lot, but could you help me with talking to DJ?"

"Sure."

"Bro! I'm calling Haruka! She has been writing about us. If I tell her, she'll come back." He pulls out his phone and dials her number. *What has she written about us? About me.* Checking will make it worse.

"Ardal. Do you have a codename?" I distract myself from whatever Jay and Haruka are devising. Their machinations irk me and raise the fur along my body.

"No."

Jay puts the phone down. "Lovebird." He looks at me. "Theon gave me the idea. He said lovebirds make bonds for life, just like your telepathic connections." His long eyelashes can never hide his excitement.

Ardal smiles. "Would you see me as a lovebird?" His reflection looks my way.

Before I thought of him as a wolf, but his leadership and teamwork are an extension of his nature. "Yes. Loyal, caring and always there. You are the human lovebird."

"I'll take it." He continues to drive to our destination.

We fall quiet with only the music and the call to Haruka's only interrupted from time to time by Jay's laughter. Roy, Aurora and her sisters should on their way too. I hope the world is ready for Aurora's and Lovebird's debut. It will be a night to remember. I look at the urban jungle surrounded by nature that doesn't seem so gray or dull anymore. There's something in it worth protecting. Who would have known that both inside and outside of the verdant crown were people who would make me part of their pack.

I am an animal, a teen, a human, Wildlife, but above all, I am Theon Untamed.

I'm the world's first hero. I'll do whatever it takes to guarantee my friends' survival.

Theon Untamed's Diary - Year One

Acknowledgments

I'd like to acknowledge all of the wonderful people who helped me get to this place and their contributions that got Chronicles of Heroes to where it is right now and in the future.

First of all are the amazing writers from my writing group Lauren Domagas, Chiara Head, and Wendy Diliberti, for helping me improve my writing to a point where I feel comfortable about sharing my stories with the world.

To Genevieve Clovis, my incredible copy-editor.

To Maximiliano Vera, he designed the cover of the book. His incredible artistic vision made it possible to have a book cover that I would never have been able to dream of.

To my brothers, Adrian, and Andrés, and to my friend, Sabrina. At every step of the way they made it possible that I was thinking about the design, the cover, the back-cover among other things. Trust me when I say that nothing would look or feel like it does without their sound advice and amazing eye for detail.